Floating City

Born and raised in New York City, Eric Lustbader graduated from Columbia University in 1969. Lustbader has had a number of fascinating careers. In addition to having written numerous bestselling novels, including *Black Heart*, *The Ninja* and *Angel Eyes*, he introduced Elton John to the American music scene. He spent fifteen years in the music industry in various capacities, including working for both Elektra and CBS Records. He is a former writer for *Cash Box* magazine where he wrote lead stories on new rock acts. In that capacity, he was the first person in the United States to predict the success of Jimi Hendrix, David Bowie and Santana, among many others.

Lustbader has taught in the All-Day Neighborhood School Division of the NYC Public School System and has also taught preschoolers in special Early Childhood programmes.

Eric Lustbader, who travels worldwide in researching his novels, lives in Southampton, New York, with his wife Victoria Lustbader, who works for the Nature Conservancy.

ERIC LUSTBADER

FLOATING CITY

A Nicholas Linnear Novel

HarperCollins*Publishers*

HarperCollins*Publishers*
77–85 Fulham Palace Road,
Hammersmith, London W6 8JB

Special overseas edition 1995
3 5 7 9 8 6 4 2

First published in Great Britain by
HarperCollins*Publishers* 1994

ISBN 0 00 647598 1

Set in Linotron Meridien by
Rowland Phototypesetting Ltd
Bury St Edmunds, Suffolk

Printed in Great Britain by
HarperCollinsManufacturing Glasgow

Acknowledgments

First and foremost, to Jeffrey Arbitol, for invaluable assistance in the creation and handling of 114m and all matters nuclear.

To my own Washington and Southeast Asian Information Central: Sichan Siv and Martha Pattillo Siv.

On matters pertaining to Saigon and Vietnam: Sesto Vecchi.

To Katy, for her company and for her perfect present, *The Ink Dark Moon*.

To Nick Sayers, for his assistance in the details of the London section.

To Tomomi-san.

Nicholas Linnear's air transportation is scheduled exclusively by Bob Kunikoff, Valerie Wilson Travel, NYC.

for my beloved Victoria:
my tireless advocate; my best friend –
without her I would no doubt float away

The hunting lanterns
on Mount Ogura have gone,
the deer are calling for their mates. . . .
How easily I might sleep,
if only I didn't share their fears.

Ono no Komachi

It's all very well in practice,
but it will never work in theory.

French management principle

The Jungle Line

*In nature a repulsive caterpillar
turns into a lovely butterfly.
But with human beings
a lovely butterfly turns into a
repulsive caterpillar.*

Anton Chekhov

Shan Plateau, Burma

AUTUMN 1983

It was said that they called him Wild Boy because he had seen every Tarzan film, knew every Tarzan's name from Elmo Lincoln onward. He had his favorites, of course, but he claimed to love them all.

They – that is, the mountain tribes of the Shan – had no reason to disbelieve him, since Tarzan films were the rage in the foothill towns below that were lucky enough to have a projector, and able to rent films flown in from Bangkok.

Truth to tell, the Shan who knew Rock – which is to say all of them who were involved in the growing, harvesting, refining, selling, and shipping of the tears of the poppy – called him Wild Boy because they had seen him screw together his custom-made rocket launcher, slap it over his right shoulder and blow his enemies into kingdom come.

Over the years, one opium warlord after the other had tried to kill Rock, but Wild Boy had been, in his own words, 'born and raised on rock 'n' roll and war'. He was a veteran of Vietnam, at the war's height, in charge of recruiting CIDGs, Civilian Irregular Defense Groups, from the Wa, the Lu, the Lisu, all the mountain tribes of Burma, and from the Mekong Delta-born Cambodians, to fight the Viet Cong.

He was one of those rare, blood-soaked demons who found that he could not do without the proximity of death. He loved everything about it: the smell of it, the

13

cessation of hearts and spirits it caused, the noise of it or the stealth required to achieve it. But he loved, most of all, the contentment it brought him, the softening of the hard edges of his mind that, like diamond blades, sought to chop his reality into incomprehensible pieces.

He was not one of the casualties of the war, who returned home with their heads filled with ARVNs and helicopters and a tide of burst bodies and running blood so high they could never climb out the Pit. The Pit was Asia, and they had been in it up to their eyeballs.

So had Rock, but the difference was he reveled in it. Because he emerged from the war, for the first time in his life, with a purpose. And that purpose had led him here, to the Shan Plateau, the metaphorical apex of the Golden Triangle, that area where China, Burma and Thailand came together, where the altitude, the weather and the soil were ideal for the growing of poppies.

Rock not only accepted the attempts on his life, he welcomed them. He rightly saw in them not merely a macho test of his skills, but a path to his acceptance up here in the rarefied air of the Shan Plateau. And he knew these people well enough to understand that without acceptance, he would be forever adrift, a kind of jungle wraith, no better than a beggar really, making his living going from warlord to warlord, selling his own particular brand of death. Besides, in their eyes, he was a Western barbarian.

Without accepting him, the Shan would never trust him. And without their trust, Rock knew, he would never get rich. Rock wanted very badly to be rich. It was the only thing that mattered to him, save the manufacture, subtle or swift, of death.

In the end, he defeated everything they sent at him, defying General Quan's public threat that 'your agony will live forever'.

14

It was General Quan, opium warlord of the Shan Plateau, who had over the past five years systematically murdered his rival warlords – all Chinese – and who now had a monopoly on the richest and most productive poppy fields in the world. As a Vietnamese, General Diep Nim Quan was better supplied – officially, cheerfully from Saigon – than his rivals, who were obliged to barter inferior arms from itinerant Soviet black marketeers.

A goddamn Vietnamese, Rock had thought, *that's who I've got to deal with here. Who said the war was over?*

Rock was on his way down the mountainside. He had been waiting for the money that had been promised him, but had never come. Now he was on his way to Rangoon to telex his partner. He had to know how long the delay was going to be.

He stumbled across Mai, who was lying along a path with a wooden cart overturned on her leg. It was the animal pulling the cart, however, whose leg was broken.

Even Rock, with his acute sense of paranoia, had to admit that Mai was irresistible, with her golden, glowing skin, her long, lithe legs, her huge eyes and her firm, hard-nippled breasts.

Rock had righted the cart and seen to Mai, then shot the animal to put it out of its misery. He had expertly skinned it, quartered its flesh, scraped down the bones.

Wild Boy had become like every Asian; he never let anything go to waste. In fact, it was safe to say that he thought of himself as Asian. He might once have been American, but now nationality had ceased to mean anything to him. Every so often he would finger the metal dog tags that still hung around his neck, as if, like jade to the Chinese, they were a powerful talisman. But he never looked at them. He was Rock, the Wild Boy, a state, a country, a law unto himself.

15

He loaded everything – the meat, the skin, the bones (for soup), the girl – into the cart. When he lifted her up, her long nails gently scratched his skin. The sapphire in the lobe of her left ear sparked in the sunlight.

Rock pulled the loaded cart himself seven miles to his temporary camp. Though he had been on the plateau for three years, he did not yet have a permanent home; that luxury would only come in time, a perquisite of acceptance and trust. For the present, however, he needed to make it difficult for the assassins to find him; it was part of the game, yet another demonstration of his skill.

Mai told him that she came from a farming village high in the mountains, 'at the top of the world', as she put it. By which she meant amid the poppy fields.

He could see that look in her eyes. He recognized it because he had seen it so many times before throughout Southeast Asia, and because he was so attuned to the Asian mind. It was his size. He was six foot two. In the States that was medium tall; here in Asia it was gigantic. Rock laughed to himself. He could see right into her mind. She was wondering if all of him was that big. Soon she would find out.

While she tended to the deep purple bruise on her leg, Rock made dinner, a stew utilizing the fresh meat he had brought back. When the pot was simmering, he set about scraping the inside of the hide to prepare it for tanning. While he worked, he wondered about her long nails, something one would never see on a farm girl. His sixth sense – what the Japanese, under whom he had studied hand-to-hand combat, called *haragei*, the divine energy – began to flood his mind with the clarity of insight.

When he looked up, he saw Mai standing naked just outside the flap of his tent. He stared at her, thinking, *This one is special*. His hands and forearms were covered

16

with blood. He could feel himself getting hard. It had been some time since he had been with a woman, but, seeing Mai, he knew that it wouldn't have mattered if he had had sex an hour ago – he would still be hard.

He dropped his enormous Marine combat knife onto the red underside of the skin and stood up. He saw Mai's gaze lower from his face to the place between his legs. He stood out a country mile. Then she turned and went inside the tent. Rock followed her, bent over slightly from the fierceness of his erection.

Inside, she was kneeling in the dimness. She beckoned him on, then held her cupped palms in front of her breasts. Rock unbuckled his belt, and she did the rest. She held him tenderly in both hands.

Her head bent, the cascade of her lustrous hair fanned his naked thighs, the flutter of a nightbird's wing. She touched him first with the tip of her tongue, then laved him with the flat of it. At length, she used her lips.

She engulfed him and, as he watched with slitted eyes her cheeks hollow, Rock had that flash of insight that the Shan call the Ruby. He knew by her skill and her expertise who she must be. He knew where she had come from, and who had sent her. He knew what he must do.

She sucked slavishly at him. One hand gently squeezed his scrotum, the other snaked between his thighs to probe his other opening.

Rock bent over and, encircling Mai's tiny waist, slowly inverted her until her breasts pressed against his lower belly, her thighs resting on his shoulders. He felt as vibration her moan as he plunged his face into her humid mound.

She tasted of mango and spice. He tongued her while her loins tensed expectantly, then all through the spasms caused by her contracting muscles. And again.

She sucked all the harder, moaning for him to come.

17

Rock put her on the floor of the tent and entered her. It was not easy. He was very big, and she was small. But, gradually, she accustomed her engorged flesh to his.

Rock began to stroke long and hard, feeling her thrusting up on him with what seemed genuine desire. Even as his eyes began to glaze, he was in touch with *haragei*, connected with the treachery and deceit spun like a web around him.

He was about to come, and he let her know it, grunting and thrusting even harder. Felt her lifting her right hand from his shoulder where it had been gripping him with sweaty abandon. Saw, out of the corner of his eye, a bright gleam, like a darning needle, the metal jacket fitted over one long nail, its tip dark and lustrous with poison.

He grabbed for her hand, but he misjudged her quickness, or his willpower was not quite strong enough, and he began to ejaculate into her. He lost his hold on her wrist, saw the nail, curved like a scorpion's tail, blurring in toward the side of his neck and his carotid, knew he'd be dead within seconds.

Devoid of conscious thought, afloat in the void of *haragei*, he smashed his elbow into her face, feeling with some satisfaction the crack of bone, feeling the heat of her inner tissue, the smell of her blood like a rose bursting open.

Then he had her right wrist and, taking hold of her forefinger, plunged the poisoned nail into her solar plexus.

The next morning, he made the steep, grueling ascent into General Quan's territory. It had rained during the night, and the day was hot, unusual at this high elevation. Rock was sweating by the time he sighted the first of General Quan's patrols.

He put down his bundles, set himself against the bole

of a tree, and ate a bit of dried fish in the cool shade. He took some water from his canteen. When he was finished, he set about making a fire, hanging up his stewpot. He poured the contents of one of his bundles into the pot.

By that time, General Quan's patrol had spotted the smoke from his fire. They were coming, AK-47s at the ready. There were five of them, he saw. Perfect. He began to whistle the Doors' 'Light My Fire'.

Wild Boy got out his rocket launcher, fitted the pieces together. When the patrol was in range, he loaded, fired, and took three of them out in a brilliant blaze.

'Get me General Quan!' he yelled in their peculiar dialect. 'Tell him Wild Boy wants to see him.'

The remaining two soldiers scrambled away, and Rock settled down to wait. An hour later, they were back with someone of some rank. The two Shan kept their distance.

'Who are you,' the commander said, 'to demand General Quan leave his compound?'

It was a matter of face, Rock knew. In Asia, it was always a matter of face. The man who forgot that, or thought he could circumvent it, would never survive in this part of the world.

'I am Wild Boy,' Rock said, hefting his rocket launcher. 'I demand nothing. I requested an audience with General Quan. I am a courteous man. To demand is to act the barbarian.'

The commander, who had heard of Wild Boy, was nevertheless impressed by this speech. He grunted. 'The general may grant you an audience if some concessions are made. For instance, recompense must be made for the three men you killed.'

'An unfortunate mistake. I was merely attempting to defend myself.'

'General Quan will not accept this explanation. There are now three families who will go hungry.'

'I will pay so that they will not go hungry,' Rock said, knowing the drill.

'Do you have gifts for General Quan?'

'Certainly. Only a barbarian or a witless man would come empty-handed to an audience with the emperor of the Shan.'

Thus mollified, the commander waved Rock upward. Rock packed his gear with great care. He made a show of breaking down his rocket launcher, stowing it away, to further allay whatever fears the commander might still harbor.

The commander led the way, the two soldiers flanking Rock on either side. He had no fear of them at all. He was now under the benevolent protection of General Quan. If the patrol was attacked at this moment, the men were bound to safeguard him even at the expense of their own lives.

General Quan's compound was bristling with armed men when the patrol arrived. It seemed as if every available man had been ordered to be in attendance at Rock's arrival. This rather primitive display of territorial superiority impressed Rock. It meant that he was being taken seriously. That boded well for the interview.

General Quan had been dispatched to the Shan five years ago to begin to funnel the fabulously rich vein of illegal commerce to be had here in the direction of his terribly impoverished country. He knew he had more to fear from the Chinese opium warlord then in control of the Shan Plateau than he did from the pitiful attempts by the ragtag Burmese Army to clean up an area essentially impossible to police.

He was not to be seen when the commander ushered Rock into the main building. Rock was left alone, with not even a young girl to serve him tea. This was quite deliberate on the general's part, since it further displayed his superior position.

An hour later, a young woman did enter. She was quite beautiful. She averted her gaze from Rock's and knelt before a blackened hole in the floor across which was an iron post and, gathering dry twigs into a cone, started a fire. Carefully, she placed three hardwood logs across the flames. Then she rose and left.

Another half-hour passed, during which time Rock heard nothing but the dogs barking outside, and orders being shouted by someone.

General Quan arrived in a flourish. He wore tanned leather breeches, and a rough muslin shirt over which he sported a goatskin American military flight jacket with a patch of the Fourteenth Air Force on the right sleeve. Unlike the other Shan warlords Rock had met, he wore no jewelry save a necklace of rubies and sapphires, the largesse of the Burmese lowlands. He was attended by two Shan bodyguards armed with machine pistols.

The young woman re-entered with an iron kettle and a pair of earthenware cups on a lacquer tray. She hung the kettle on the iron post over the fire. Tea was served, hot, thick and sweet, in the Thai tradition. It was quite bracing. Rock hadn't had decent tea in six months, and he took his time, savoring it.

At length, he said, 'I have agreed to make recompense for the disagreeable incident this morning. Of course I was at fault, and I wish to make amends to the families of those unfortunately dead.'

General Quan considered this. His commander had already reported as much to him, of course, but he was gratified to see that this Wild Boy had decent manners, after all. Not that his civilized comportment would stop General Quan from having this foreign devil killed. He

21

had become far too dangerous to be allowed to remain in the Shan States.

General Quan could see the greed in the foreign devil's eyes as easily as he could feel the slime on a slug. Wild Boy wanted a piece of the tears of the poppy — what else would bring a foreign devil all the way up here, an interdicted area as far as the Burmese government was concerned?

Huh, his wa *is not so strong as the stories tell*, General Quan thought as he eyed the giant from over the rim of his teacup. *Now that I have him here, I will humiliate him for the loss of face he has caused me among my men. Then I will bury him up to his thick neck and let the ants and the sun take care of him.*

The only possible cloud on his horizon was Mai. Where was she? And why had she not killed this foreign devil, as she had been ordered to do? Perhaps, the general mused, she had not yet devised a clever way of meeting him. Then, unbidden, the thought arose, as black and ugly as dung, that something had befallen Mai. Perhaps she had been hurt in the jungle or again kidnapped by one of General Quan's many enemies. His scrotum contracted painfully at the thought. What would he do without his precious Mai? She was his talisman; everything good that had happened to him had occurred while she was with him.

General Quan smiled at Rock. 'More tea, perhaps?'

Rock nodded. 'Thank you for your hospitality,' he said, bowing. 'I am unworthy of such munificence.' As he watched the beautiful young woman pour, he wondered whether this one might be Mai's sister. For as sure as he was sitting here now, Rock knew that Mai belonged to General Quan.

From his longtime contacts among the Wa, the Lu and the Lisu, he had heard the jungle rumors about Mai's prowess in effecting, as the Chinese termed it, the clouds and the rain, eliciting spectacular orgasms from her lover. But he had treated them as just that, rumors that picked up embellishments from each mouth that passed them on. Until Mai had taken him between her lips. Then he knew – the Ruby had told him with a certainty impossible to ignore.

When they had finished their second cup of tea, Rock said, 'In addition to the recompense for the grieving families, I have brought the general a special present.' He began to unpack his stewpot and sacks. General Quan's men reacted by lowering the muzzles of their machine pistols.

'Food!' Rock cried, laughing, as he ladled the stew into the pot, hung it over the fire. 'Food fit for the gods themselves!'

The general watched the proceedings with a jaundiced eye. 'I have been paid in rubies, sapphires, jade and gold. But never with a meal.' He was not displeased, however. Good food was one of his passions, as Rock had heard from his contacts.

Wild Boy ladled out the stew, placing it before General Quan who, leaning over the steaming bowl, inhaled deeply. 'It smells delicious.'

He signaled to one of his bodyguards, who slung his machine pistol across his back, picked up the bowl and, dipping two fingers into the stew, ate several mouthfuls. General Quan watched him expectantly.

At length, the bodyguard belched, gave a curt nod, and handed the bowl back to his leader. General Quan made no apologies for this seeming lack of manners and Rock did not ask for one.

General Quan took up a pair of golden chopsticks encrusted with rubies and sapphires, settled the bowl in the palm of his hand and, holding it just under his chin, commenced to shovel the food into his mouth. He was like a mammoth machine; even Wild Boy was impressed by this engine of consumption. The general paused only once, and that was to gasp, 'It tastes even more delicious than it smells.'

'You are most kind.' Rock bowed again. He held out his hand. 'Please. Allow me to refill the general's bowl.' He stirred the bottom of the pot with his ladle, then loaded up the bowl General Quan handed back.

While he watched the general continue his shoveling act, Rock said, 'I had heard that the general enjoys his women fully as much as he does his food.' He turned his head in the young woman's direction. 'Now I know the truth to those stories.'

The general's small eyes were almost closed with the pleasure of gorging himself on Rock's magnificent stew.

'I have also heard,' Rock said, 'that the jewel among the general's women is one named Mai. Is she here, General? Might I see her?'

'Uh.' There was only a momentary lapse in the shoveling act.

'No? Oh, what a pity.' Rock smiled. 'Well, I'm not surprised, I suppose. Such a rare treasure is not so easily on display, even for favored guests?'

'Uh.'

Rock shrugged. 'But, then, who knows, perhaps Mai is not so far away from us at this moment.'

General Quan was almost finished with his second bowl of stew. His face was glistening with a combination of sweat and grease. He glared at Rock. 'What nonsense are you speaking?'

'Have you reached the bottom yet? Of the bowl, that is?'

General Quan probed through the remnants of the thick sauce. 'One more piece of delicious meat.' He picked it up with the tips of his chopsticks, was about to pop it in his mouth when something caught his eye.

24

He held the piece of meat out so that he could see it better. He shook off the excess gravy.

What he saw was the unmistakable glint of a magnificent Burmese sapphire, and he thought, *Ah, the foreign devil is very clever – here is my real gift.*

But then his eyes opened wide and everything he had just eaten came spewing out, along with a long, low wail.

The sapphire was embedded in a whole, human ear. His beloved Mai's ear.

BOOK I: Legends of Evil

*You will always find
some Eskimos willing to instruct
the Congolese on how to cope
with heat waves.*

Stanislaw Lem

ONE

Saigon/Tokyo

Nicholas Linnear was waiting for his man. While he did so, he drank a warm beer and observed the cockroach as large as his thumb survey the filthy room as if it were the shogun in feudal Japan. He was in a third-floor front room of the Anh Dan Hotel, a thoroughly unpleasant establishment that nevertheless suited his purposes. The sickly light thrown by one disheartened forty-watt bulb exposed the cracks, noxious stains, and peeling and discolored paint. It worked when electricity was provided (which wasn't all that often) if one touched two ends of the exposed live wires together at the point on the wall where a plate and switch should have been. The smells of raw sewage and stale sex pervaded the entire hotel, and outside the appalling clamor from Nguyen Trai Street was an incessant and disreputable companion at all hours of the day and night. This was Saigon after all and, worse, Cholon where, sooner or later, all the dregs of the city ended up.

Nicholas turned to look at Jisaku Shindo, the Japanese private detective hired by his partner Tanzan Nangi to unravel the mystery surrounding the murder of Vincent Tinh, the former director of the Saigon branch of Sato International, the giant *keiretsu* – conglomerate – Nangi and Linnear co-owned.

'Do you think he'll come?'

'The friend of a friend said he would.' Shindo's clipped speech cut through the humid atmosphere.

Nicholas mentally reviewed the activities of Vincent Tinh. Tinh, it seemed, had had a private agenda. He had used his job at Sato International as a mask to conceal his nefarious business, stealing and selling the proprietary technology of Sato's ultra-secret Chi Project. Under Nicholas's guidance, the Chi Project was creating a revolutionary generation of computers that was a quantum leap beyond anything currently on the market or elsewhere in development. Based on neural-network technology, the first-generation Chi computer processed data in the same way the human brain did.

Like most criminals – even those of the genius class – Tinh had been undone by his greed. Cobbling what he could purloin of the Chi technology with elements of the new American Hive computer (also based on a type of neural-net chip), he created here in Saigon a bastardized hybrid that he began to sell on the vast and immensely lucrative Southeast Asian gray market.

Because of Tinh, Sato-Tomkin – the American arm of Sato International – and Nicholas in particular had been accused by the Americans of theft, illegal manufacture and espionage leading to treason. Nicholas, who had hired Tinh in the first place, had a compelling personal as well as a professional stake in finding out how much damage Tinh had done before his demise.

Even more alarming, now that Nicholas was here and had listened to Shindo's perspective on the situation, he had come to the conclusion that Tinh wasn't the only key to the severe blow given to Sato International's business and reputation.

For instance, who had constructed the Chi-Hive hybrid? Certainly Tinh had lacked the requisite knowledge and expertise in advanced computer design even to attempt such an audacious leap of faith. Indeed, merging two parallel but undoubtedly different precepts

30

of cybernetics was a feat beyond an overwhelming majority of technicians. Sure, there were a million cyber-tekkies out there who could burrow their way into an existing system, but it would take a theoretician of remarkable talent and insight to do this job.

Whom had Vincent Tinh found for such a difficult task?

And then there was the question of Tinh's curious death.

According to Chief Inspector Hang Van Kiet of the Saigon police, Vincent Tinh had been killed accidentally while trespassing on property he did not own. The said property was a vast creaking warehouse in the northern district that stored barrels of sulfuric acid, salt, gasoline, bicarbonate of soda, and potassium permanganate. In other words, it was a drug factory. Nicholas knew that Van Kiet was lying.

Last week Shindo had interviewed the chief inspector. Van Kiet, a wily-faced, slender Vietnamese with the yellow eyes and teeth of a back-alley predator, had doggedly kept to his story that Tinh's death had been accidental. When Shindo had pressed him, he retaliated by intimating that because Tinh had trespassed it was far better to leave the matter where it lay, in a closed file.

Shindo had wisely not revealed that a friend of a friend had smuggled him a copy of the autopsy report, which showed that while Tinh had, indeed, been burned in a vat of sulfuric acid, the coroner had also extracted twenty-five heavy-caliber machine-gun bullets from his flesh. This was information, Shindo had decided, that Van Kiet was better off not knowing he possessed.

Shindo had sized up the chief inspector quickly – this was a necessity in his business – and reported that he suspected Van Kiet knew far more about Tinh's demise than he was willing to share. Shindo made it

31

abundantly clear to the chief inspector that he was willing to barter US dollars for information.

Van Kiet's face had closed as tightly as a vise and he had abruptly terminated the interview, an odd and downright discourteous reaction for a Vietnamese. This was very bad news, indeed. It meant that the chief inspector had been impolite out of a sharply honed instinct for survival.

Law and order had no meaning in present Saigon – at least none that would make sense to any civilized human being. This was a city – indeed, a country – so inured to the dogs of war that its society had been reshaped by the utter lawlessness that was one of war's major byproducts. A ferocious form of negotiated anarchy ruled here. As a result, the police had less power than the army, which, in turn, had less power than the dark, mercenary forces that swirled at the periphery of society – hidden yet subtly defining it. These were men who, as children, had been bred and nurtured by the frenzied chaos of a centuries-old war waged variously against the Chams, Cambodians, French, Chinese, Russians and Americans.

It had been a war that, like a great serpent shedding its glittering scales, periodically transformed itself until, at the end, it had become some perniciously mutated form of psychedelic happening: an absurd agglomeration of dropped napalm, mind-altering drugs, massed ordnance, high-decibel rock 'n' roll, a cornucopia of destructive hardware, a release from poverty, mass confusion, a concentrated discharge of hatred, an eerie, macho game of chicken. In short, it had been the ultimate clash of high-visibility mass murder and animistic death concealed by night.

Every official in Vietnam was on the take; it was simply a way of life. But Van Kiet had demurred. Why? Fear was the only emotion strong enough to overcome avarice. There was, then, the ominous threat of corrupt power in very high places, pulling strings that made even the chief inspector of the Saigon police jump. That had put the investigation on a whole new and dangerous plane, which was why Nicholas was here now, and why Shindo resented him.

Shindo continued to smoke and did not look at Nicholas. He was slim, of average height, with the closed, set face of an old man. It was a face quickly forgotten, even if seen at length; it had no distinguishing feature. This was a distinct asset in his line of business; others in his profession had to work at being invisible. He wore a white shirt, gray polyester slacks, and a dark patternless tie as narrow as a knife.

Nicholas, languidly drinking his beer, watched the cockroach, which was surely more at home in this third-world tomb than he would ever be. Dark light spun off its pale carapace, deforming it. He looked upon the insect benevolently, as a kind of compatriot from whom he could better learn to survive in this steaming jungle of a city. His visits to Saigon had been infrequent, unlike Shindo, who came here often. Shindo had many Vietnamese friends, acquaintances and contacts.

From an adjacent room Nicholas heard the heavy rhythmic thuds of bodies on a bed, the animal grunts, the liquid sucking sounds of fierce coupling.

Shindo removed a gun from a holster at the base of his spine. It was an army .45 of American manufacture, nine years old, maybe more, and must have cost a small fortune, but he was right not to trust his life to any of the cheaper Soviet- or Chinese-manufactured handguns for sale in the back alleys of Cholon.

'I have bought a gun for you,' Shindo said unkindly. 'Do you know how to fire one?'

'I do. But I never use firearms.'

Shindo grunted, ground the butt of his cigarette

33

beneath his heel, lit another. 'This is Saigon. It's not like Japan, it's not safe at all. Even a baby in diapers can have a gun.' He was clearly disgusted. 'What will you do when one is aimed at you?'

Nicholas was a ninja, but he was also *tanjian*, a hereditary member of a syncretic psychic discipline far older than any martial art. The essence of Tau-tau was *kokoro*, the membrane of all life. Just as in the physical world the excitation of the atom was the basis for all movement — not only human, but light, heat and percussion — so, too, did the excitation of *kokoro* give rise to psychic energy. Thought into action was at the core of the *tanjian*'s training.

Akshara and Kshira, the Way of Light and the Path of Darkness, formed the two primary teachings of Tau-tau. Nicholas had been trained in Akshara, but all the while Kansatsu, his *sensei*, was embedding within him certain principles of the dark side. Some believed that it was possible for one highly disciplined mind to contain both Akshara and Kshira, but invariably, over the centuries, the dark side proved too powerful, overwhelming those adepts who sought to embrace it, corrupting them without their being aware of it, and so it was rarely taught.

However, as he delved deeper into Akshara, Nicholas began to understand the lure of Kshira, because it became clear to him that the Way of Light was somehow incomplete. This was how he had formed his theory that in the beginning of time Tau-tau was fully integrated, the light and dark hemispheres one far more powerful discipline. Somewhere during the centuries, the ability to harness Kshira had been lost.

For uncounted centuries the goal of *tanjian* adepts was to form Shuken, the Dominion. Shuken was the whole, the perfect integration of Akshara and Kshira. Without Shuken, which was the one key, adepts who attempted to study both paths of Tau-tau were invariably destroyed by the dark side. Thus had Kansatsu met his fate, overwhelmed by the potent evil of Kshira.

Was this, too, the fate Kansatsu had envisioned for Nicholas? Surely there was a time bomb ticking inside Nicholas's head, readying itself to destroy him. That was why he was desperately trying to discover the secret of Shuken.

But Shuken had proved a highly elusive state. It was achieved only through *koryoku*, the Illuminating Power. Nicholas had been told that Mikio Okami possessed *koryoku*, which had been a crucial factor in his rise to power, his dominion over all other Yakuza *oyabun*. Because of this, Nicholas had a personal stake in finding Okami alive and in good health: he wanted to extract from him the secret of *koryoku* and, through it, Shuken.

'Put the gun away. You have other things to concern you,' Nicholas said, his thoughts returning to Shindo's resentment of him.

Shindo, firing up another cigarette from the butt of the last, seemed as distant as a statue of Buddha. The weapon disappeared as if it had never existed, but it was clear from his movements that he had a certain facility with guns.

'Did you have friends in the war?' Nicholas asked, trying to connect with the PI. Shindo regarded him for a moment through a haze of curling smoke. He lounged against the greasy wall like a pimp in a brothel. 'I knew people . . . on both sides.' He took a drag of his cigarette, blew smoke in a furious hiss. 'I suppose that surprises you.'

'Not really. In your business – '

'Now you have real reason to distrust me.'

So that was it. Shindo felt Nicholas's arrival on his turf was an expression of his employers' lack of faith in him.

'If that was the case,' Nicholas said, 'I would have terminated your contract immediately.'

Shindo's shoulder came off the wall, as if he might evince some interest now. 'What do you know of the war, anyway?'

Nicholas considered a moment. 'So much has been written about how traumatized Americans were by the war, but it seems to me there was something else far more sinister at work, something most people either did not want to talk about or did not get. Kids from all over – from the inner-city ghettos and dying small towns – were given unlimited use of deadly weapons. They were trained to use submachine guns, hand-held rocket launchers, flame throwers, and were told killing was more than okay; it was expected of them. I think for some of those men the war became an intoxication almost beyond imagining, a better high than pot or heroin; it was a mind-altering experience. But how could it be any different? These kids were thrown into a reality beyond law and endowed with the power of life and death.'

Shindo was watching him now through eyes slitted by smoke and emotion. 'Yes,' he said after a time. 'It was just like that.'

The couple next door had finished their sweaty exertions, and Nicholas could hear drifting in through the open window a few bars of a singer lamenting in Vietnamese-tinged French something about a soul alone and in torment. The sentiment, exaggerated by a voice filled with perverse sexual pathos, seemed perfect for Saigon.

There was a peculiar note in Shindo's voice, and Nicholas wanted to identify it. 'The war was very personal for you.'

Shindo walked across the room. 'I had a lover. Once, he was a soldier. A grunt who served here.'

'And survived.'

'In a manner of speaking.' Shindo watched the glowing end of his cigarette. The song, building to a crescendo, cascaded through the room in a ghostly swirl. 'In the end, he didn't want to live anymore. He couldn't. The demons the war had embedded in him were eating him alive.'

It was odd, Nicholas thought, how one could tell a perfect stranger what was otherwise unthinkable. 'What happened?'

'What needed to happen.' Shindo seemed carved out of the humid night, as if he belonged here rather than in Tokyo. 'I'll tell you what's funny. The people who were here, who were fighting the war — and now I mean both sides because, in the end, there was no difference, really — they *needed* the war. Insanity had become the norm for them, their reality, and they were sunk so far in it they couldn't get out. They dreamed of the war — it drew them like a flame, fed their worst instincts, buried their humanity beneath a foul bed of killing lust — and they never wanted it to end.' His eyes lifted from the tiny ember to Nicholas's face. 'What happened was this: I killed him in the manner he asked me to.'

The contralto, nearly finished, was abruptly drowned out as another couple threw themselves into sexual convulsions, louder this time, so that Nicholas had the impression that the man was taking the woman quite violently up against their common wall. If they weren't careful, they'd be electrocuted by the live wires as had a man and his whore earlier that day, or so the leering proprietor had informed them. Sex and death, never far apart, were almost indistinguishable in Saigon, Nicholas thought.

The cockroach was unperturbed, unlike Nicholas. But then it hadn't understood Shindo's story. The floor was vibrating to the ancient ritual, and Nicholas was sure he could smell female musk. He moved across the room, away from the disturbance, away also from the open window, which could announce his presence in this native area as surely as if he'd been centered in a gilt frame.

'He'll be here soon, if he's coming at all,' Nicholas said. 'Time for you to leave.'

'I still think it's a mistake for you to see this man alone. We know nothing about him.'

'I'm the one who knows the ins and outs of the neural-net chip. If he's suspicious and quizzes you, we'll be dead.'

'We can both —'

'No. He told me it had to be one-on-one. If I were him, I'd turn tail the moment I saw the two of us.'

From his new vantage point Nicholas could see a wedge of the teeming street. *Cyclos*, three-wheeled cab-bikes, whizzed by alongside old Soviet-built trucks belching clouds of noxious diesel smoke. Flocks of cyclists squeezed by on either side of the larger vehicles, and every so often a so-called marriage taxi rumbled by, old American gas-guzzlers from the fifties or sixties, finned like a spaceship, wide as a boat. Packs of ragged street urchins played dangerous games of pickpocket with businessmen seeking to open low-overhead, high-volume manufacturing in newly booming Saigon by day and an unbridled sexual smorgasbord in Cholon by night. Soldiers in their khaki uniforms rubbed shoulders with saffron-robed Buddhist monks, scantily dressed prostitutes, and a legion of amputees and the deformed. There were always the maimed in Vietnam, young adults scarred by the war and children deformed by its aftermath, dioxin-based chemical defoliants such as Agent Orange.

As they had repeatedly for months, Nicholas's thoughts

returned to Mikio Okami. Okami was the Kaisho – the head of all the Yakuza clan heads, the *oyabun*. He had been a close friend of Nicholas's father, Colonel Denis Linnear, during the American occupation of Japan in the late 1940s. Nicholas had promised his father to help Okami if the Kaisho should ever need it.

That time had come. Okami had had a stormy relationship with the members of his inner council for some time. It appeared that Okami's final break with them had occurred over his alliance with Dominic Goldoni. The inner council had been part of a scheme that Okami had set in motion. Known as the Godaishu – Five Continents – the group implementing the scheme had been woven from carefully chosen elements within the Yakuza, Japanese government, Mafia and US government to create what could only be described as an international criminal conglomerate, skimming off staggering sums of money from arms as well as from legitimate businesses. As profits multiplied, the inner council began to agitate to move into other, darker areas of business, such as drug trafficking.

Okami and Goldoni both rebelled and had clandestinely formulated their own plan. Their alliance was betrayed; Goldoni was brutally murdered, and Okami, in his headquarters in Venice, had asked for Nicholas's help. In Venice, Nicholas had met one of Dominic Goldoni's sisters, Celeste, who was also pledged to help the Kaisho. In the end, Okami had been forced into hiding, one step ahead of his death. Now, while Nicholas was in Vietnam, his longtime friend, ex-NYPD homicide detective lieutenant Lew Croaker, was in New York shadowing Goldoni's other sister, Margarite, in hopes of following Okami's Nishiki network back to Okami himself. Sooner or later, Margarite, who had inherited the mantle of power from her brother, would make contact with the network, since it was the Nishiki that provided the dirt on both influential politicians and captains of industry that had made the Goldoni family pre-eminent in power in America's underworld.

Nicholas felt compassion for his friend. It could not be easy for him to maintain his distance from the woman he so obviously loved and, at the same time, discreetly spy on her every movement. Nicholas could only guess at the turbulent emotions such actions would bring up. Nevertheless, he and Croaker had determined it had to be done.

It was Nicholas's belief that Okami had gone deep to ground. And Okami, it seemed, was leaving clues to direct Nicholas and Croaker toward Avalon Ltd and the Nishiki network. Why? At first Nicholas believed it was because Tinh had been a supplier of the company. But now he realized Okami was telling them that Tinh was just a small piece of the puzzle. Again, Nicholas found himself wondering who Tinh's business partners had been.

Tinh's body had been picked up by a man posing as his brother. In fact, Tinh had no family, and it was subsequently discovered that the man who had claimed him was Yakuza. Could this man have been a member of one of the families of the Kaisho's inner council?

Curiously, he gave as his business Avalon Ltd, a mysterious international arms-trading conglomerate. Embedded within its closely guarded computer system, Nicholas had found reference to something known as Torch 315. The assumption that he and Lew Croaker had made was that Torch was some sort of new weapon and that 315 might be a date – March 15. While they had no direct evidence for this, the fact that Okami had directed them to Avalon Ltd gave the assumption a good deal of weight.

Nicholas knew that Okami wanted him to track down and eliminate those responsible for trying to assassinate him. Did the way lead here to Saigon where a Yakuza posing as Vincent Tinh's brother and an employee of Avalon Ltd picked up the corpse of the murdered man? Why give the firm's name – and particularly *that* firm? Was Nicholas again being subtly manipulated by the Kaisho? This was another compelling reason for him to come to Saigon himself.

Nicholas could not surrender the suspicion that Okami, in directing him toward Avalon Ltd, was also directing him toward Torch 315. It was a vital piece of the puzzle the Kaisho meant him to solve.

Nicholas saw a figure heading across Nguyen Trai Street in a direct line for the entrance of the Anh Dan Hotel. He put down his beer bottle, automatically glancing at his watch as he turned away from the window.

Midnight.

'There's no more time for argument. Get out of here, Shindo. Now.'

His man was here.

Naohiro Ushiba, striking a familiar pose, faced the massed lights, cameras and questions that had become a fixture at his ministry ever since the scandals of 1992 had ripped apart the tightly bound weave of Japan's political, economic and bureaucratic infrastructure.

Ushiba was Daijin, chief minister of the Ministry of International Trade and Industry, Japan's single most powerful economic-political entity. It had been MITI that had fueled and directed Japan's postwar economic miracle through its policy of high-speed growth. MITI had targeted which industries it deemed would benefit Japan the most, using rebates, discounts and tax incentives to make it beneficial for the large *keiretsu* – conglomerates – to switch into these industries. With new scandals unfolding almost every week – the latest being

41

the agonizing reformation of political power lines – the political, business and financial infrastructure of Japan was coming apart at the seams.

The world had changed considerably in the thirty-nine years since the Liberal Democratic Party was formed. Then, it had stood for the future of Japan; the only alternatives were the Communists and Socialists. A succession of LDP prime ministers had joined with the Daijins of MITI to build Japan into the economic colossus of the present. But the LDP had grown fat and corrupt beneath the burden of almost four decades of unchallenged power, and now, in the most recent elections, they had been brought to their knees. Perhaps, Ushiba thought, it was time.

Now the inevitable had happened: it was MITI's turn to be racked with extreme pressure and public scrutiny. Two of its senior ministers had been indicted in a computer-software kickback scheme that involved several manufacturers who had been granted an excess of dispensations from the ministry.

Ushiba, who was determined to hold the moral center in the firestorm of scandal and controversy, had dismissed the offending ministers with alacrity. Even the predatory press had been impressed with the speed and thoroughness of his internal investigation. However, damage had been done, and a cloud still hung over MITI, as evidenced by frequent newspaper editorials and magazine pieces.

As a result, every question today seemed to be excruciatingly difficult. 'How can you explain away MITI's involvement in the artificial real-estate boom of the 1980s that has now turned into a disaster for our economy and our banks in particular?' asked one reporter.

'The idea behind the upward prices of Japanese real estate was sound and was researched thoroughly before

42

being put forward,' Ushiba said smoothly. 'In the eighties, the yen was so strong that our economy was being crippled by spending overseas. Raising real-estate prices at home was an excellent way to regain investment in Japan.'

'Daijin, what can you tell us of the stories we've heard lately of Yakuza involvement in our economic politics?' another reporter asked. 'Specifically, what about Akira Chosa, who seems to be moving into the power vacuum left by the disappearance of Mikio Okami.'

Ushiba cleared his throat. His lean, muscular body was surmounted by a head whose beautiful features might be termed effeminate. Unlike Western cultures, the Japanese had a history of such men being heroes. *Bishonen*, they were called, exquisite young men who existed under the aegis of an older individual.

'As you gentlemen of the press know, Akira Chosa is *oyabun* of the Kokorogurushii. This clan name is ironic and quite typical of the pathetic mentality of Yakuza. *Kokorogurushii* means "painful". The word *Yakuza* is made up of the numbers in a losing hand at gambling; there is, always, within the Yakuza an undercurrent of a kind of self-flagellation, a sense of having to pay a penalty for living a life outside the law.'

Ushiba looked around the room, his dark eyes liquid in the TV lights. 'Having said that, let me also state that the Yakuza have been more active of late. In fact, we have uncovered a systematic pattern of ethically questionable business relationships between individuals within the Yakuza and certain major equity and financial firms. Chosa is, indeed, exerting some muscle, but I can assure you that MITI and the Tokyo prosecutor's office are working together to see that these extralegal connections are ended once and for all.' Ushiba leaned forward a fraction to emphasize his next words. 'Chosa is just one of the *oyabun* whose business is like a poison

43

in the blood of Japan. It must be expunged as rapidly as possible.'

'Can you tell us what exactly is being done, Daijin?' a third reporter queried. 'The Japanese economy is in bad enough shape without Yakuza clans draining it still further.'

'I agree completely,' Ushiba said. 'I assure you that we at MITI are on a crusade to curb all illegal activities of any nature. We must, at all costs, restore public confidence in our way of life. I needn't remind you that over the decades MITI has been the staunch watchdog in our country's phenomenal but often difficult and painful economic growth. MITI never once flinched from its duties. Now we see our mandate as expanding. You can count on MITI to protect the interests of the people of Japan.' He went on to give them an impressive list of statistics his ministry heads had compiled on areas of corruption that had been cleaned up or were currently under investigation, answered several more questions, then turned the press conference over to a dark-faced man of impressive countenance, Tanaka Gin, the most renowned member of the terrifying Tokyo prosecutors with whom Ushiba had been liaising for months.

Back in his office, Ushiba ran a hand through his hair and found it wet. With distaste, he went into his private washroom, swallowed a pill. He pushed a towel over his hair, then splashed cold water on his face.

Though he had initiated these press conferences he found them to be an increasing burden. However, he was locked into them. He had become like a poster boy or a talento. His brainchild had given him a kind of instant celebrity, and since this devolved onto MITI, it was deemed beneficial for the beleaguered bureaucracy as a whole.

His intercom was buzzing when he returned to the

office. His secretary announced that Yukio Haji wished to see him. Ushiba glanced at his jam-packed schedule book. He did not see Haji's name listed, but since Haji was one of the young ministers whom Ushiba was training, he bade his secretary send the man in.

Haji, in a somber mood, entered, sitting in a steel-frame chair that Ushiba indicated. Haji was an earnest young man who had come to MITI with the highest possible grades, honors and recommendations. Ushiba had been determined from the outset to make something special of him.

'Daijin, I know how busy you are, but there is a serious matter that cannot wait.'

Ushiba sat back, lit a cigarette while he studied the young man's unlined face. Here was a product of the new Japan, under pressure to perform at full capacity at every level of his education, examined, probed, pushed at every level after graduation. Being accepted at MITI was his reward, but Ushiba made certain he knew that was not the end of it. Haji might be a product of post-modern life, but Ushiba was seeing to it that he was possessed of *kanryodo*, the spirit of the samurai-bureaucrat. A code of honor, as strict as the ancient samurai's Bushido, operated here, and recruits either accepted it as gospel or they were transferred to another, lesser ministry.

'What is the problem?' Ushiba said.

'I went to my checking account to pay my rent this month and found that I had insufficient funds.' Haji drew forth a folded sheet of paper. 'Please accept my resignation. I am leaving ministry service. It is clear that I have worked hard but learned little.'

Ushiba took the proffered resignation but did not open it. Instead, he opened his lighter, put the flame to the corner of the paper. When the last ash had crumbled from his fingers, he said, 'How much do you owe?'

45

When Haji told him, he wrote out a check, which he handed over to his astonished protégé. 'Read the *Hagakure*, the *Book of the Samurai*. Your ignorance of its wisdom is your true transgression.' He did not ask what Haji had spent his money on because he did not care. All that mattered was that *kanryodo* be adhered to, that misconduct within the class remain undetected by those outside. 'Youthful indiscretion is understandable, even to be expected. I do not intend to lose one of my best recruits because of it. I am your superior and so responsible for you. Take the check and we will say no more of it. The matter is settled.'

The Vietnamese was not much of a man. Nicholas was disappointed by the appearance of the slightly built individual in the doorway to his hotel room. The cockroach was gone, scuttling for its lair the moment the rap fell upon the closed door. Nicholas had stood aside while he opened the door left-handed.

The man limned by the buzzing fluorescent of the hallway was slender, slim-hipped. His face was partly in a shadow cast by his American-style fedora. He was dressed in a finely tailored business suit that nevertheless had about it the unmistakable lines of a made-to-measure job. His tie and shirt were woven of Thai silk, and he smelled faintly of a floral cologne that made Nicholas's nose itch. The whole had a vaguely affected look that he did not care for, but the man was careful to keep Nicholas's right hand in view, and this was impressive because in this instance it would have been Nicholas's primary weapon.

The man stepped into the room, said, 'You are Goto?' That was the pseudonym Nicholas had given the friend of Shindo's friend who had agreed to help them.

'Right.'

46

The man looked around the room with curiosity rather than suspicion. 'Ready to go?'

'I don't know your name.'

He shrugged. 'Call me Trang. One name's as good as another, isn't it, *Chu* Goto?' Trang smiled, revealing white, even teeth behind pouty lips.

Nicholas grabbed his jacket and they went out. He didn't bother to lock the door behind him; he had paid for the room in advance and he wasn't coming back.

'You always pick such, ah, luxurious accommodations?' Trang's voice had a husky, midrange tone, as if he were a heavy smoker and drinker, which, Nicholas thought, could be all too true.

A bevy of half-naked women were lounging in the entryway to the hotel. They were as over-made-up as rock groupies and just as young, Nicholas thought. What a life. They made sucking sounds with their lips and grabbed at their breasts as the two men pushed past them. They smelled of cheap perfume and of sex.

Trang had long, quick strides and Nicholas had to push himself in order to keep up with the Vietnamese as he darted amid the late-night throngs that swarmed along Liem Van Chau Boulevard. Choking exhaust from the traffic combined with clouds of smoke from street stalls at which meats and vegetables roasted over charcoal fires.

What Nicholas had told the skittish friend of Shindo's friend was that he had obtained a prototype of a second-generation neural-net chip. What he needed was a theoretical-language technician who could decipher the new technology and build a workable machine around it – fast. And whoever it was, Nicholas had cautioned, had better know how to keep his mouth shut. The idea had been that whoever had put together Tinh's computer with a first-generation neural-net chip would jump at the chance to get his hands on a second-generation chip, because upon learning of the illegal computer Nangi had moved to shut it out of the East Asian gray market.

The promise of a second-generation chip was like being offered a billion dollars tax-free – the possibilities were unlimited for constructing a cybernetic machine so advanced it would blow all competition out of the water.

Seventy-two hours later, the friend of a friend had phoned him to give him the particulars of the meeting. Nicholas had agreed to the date and time – the next day at midnight – but had changed the venue to the Anh Dan Hotel in Cholon, where Shindo was familiar with the layout, including entrances, exits and cover, as well as the general surroundings. That was sensible, as well as prudent. It was essential, Nicholas had long ago discovered, to catalogue what he called 'the smell' of a site for any rendezvous – a mosaic of sight, sound, smell, taste and feel. Because to know when a site didn't smell right you had to be familiar with all the pieces that fit together to make the whole.

Nicholas understood the pressure under which Shindo had been operating. It was imperative in paranoid Vietnam to make any inquiries under cover of maximum security. Unstable political factions still vied for power with a fractured military, mountain insurgents and ethnic vigilantes, so all foreigners were automatically suspect. But beyond that, neither Shindo nor Nicholas knew the identity or the strength of the enemy. Vincent Tinh and those in his operation may have been involved with drug smugglers, black-market munitions specialists, power-crazed Chinese mountain warlords, Yakuza – the list was endless. Still, there was one ubiquitous truth: all of these factions were exceedingly dangerous and all had spies in and around Saigon. Outnumbered and outgunned, Nicholas knew he had to step carefully lest the weight of his unknown enemy come down on him and Shindo all at once.

'Trang,' he said now, taking a chance, 'how long did you work for Vincent Tinh?'

'Vincent Tinh?' Trang was brought up short, a stone in the stream of traffic eddying around them.

'Yes.' Nicholas searched Trang's face looking for duplicity, but finding something else, something he couldn't put his finger on.

A deafening roar filled the street as a covey of motor-bikes swept past, the echoes of their exhaust thrumming off the shopfronts. A blast of rock 'n' roll sped like a manic race driver, Mick Jagger wailing about war.

'You worked for him, didn't you?' Nicholas said.

Trang swung his head so that his eyes went blank in the streetlights. 'If I had, I'd be dead now.'

By which answer Nicholas knew he had hit a raw nerve. Even if Trang hadn't worked for him, he knew some of what had happened to Tinh and why. That made him instantly valuable to Nicholas.

He reached out. 'Just a minute, Trang —'

But Trang pulled away, darting ever faster through the swelling throng, and Nicholas found himself sprint-ing after the Vietnamese. What the hell was he up to?

Trang was hurrying southeast, toward the Kinh Ben Nghe Canal that acted more or less as the southern boundary of central Cholon. A pair of monks in saffron robes, their faces serene and observant, turned their heads as he pushed by. A gaggle of kids tried to grab at him, their outstretched arms like a forest of sea anemones. A streetwalker eyed him from behind out-landish false lashes. She looked like a Carnaby Street tart circa 1969. It appeared as if all of Saigon were caught in a weird psychedelic time warp, desperately trying to reconjure its heyday, which was, perversely, during the height of the war.

Nicholas had nearly caught up to Trang when he thought he saw Shindo moving toward him at the periphery of the crowd. Then the image was gone, and he hurried after Trang, who slipped through the throng as easily as an eel through a coral reef. Nicholas's anxiety increased as he recalled Shindo's warning about this place. This was his turf, not Nicholas's.

He slipped past a cluster of people, sprinted across a brief clear section of street and made a lunge for Trang. Someone was heading toward the Vietnamese from the opposite direction. Nicholas was reaching out to protect Trang when he heard a sharp report.

At almost the same instant, the head of the man beside Trang blew outward like a cracked melon. A hail of blood, tissue and shattered bone erupted, and Nicholas found himself prone on the ground. The smells of incense and death mingled in his nostrils. A shocked silence gripped the narrow street, followed by the first wail of a human voice, picked up and echoed by others.

Nicholas, on his knees, sank into Akshara, spiraling downward toward *kokoro*, the heart of all things. He chose one of the ages-old rhythms of Tau-tau, beating upon the membrane of *kokoro*, creating the psychic resonance that transformed thought into deed. Light flashed, then dimmed, colors bled one into another as time warped outward and away. Thus armed, he opened his *tanjian* eye, expanding his psyche outward. The man was dead. Automatically, his psyche searched for another *tanjian* presence, but found none. And then, his attention returning to the corpse, he saw the dark tie, narrow as a knife. It was no longer patternless. A Jackson Pollock-like spray of blood was spiderwebbed across it.

Oh, Christ, he thought. *It's Shindo*.

He reached out, but Trang was suddenly crouched beside him. 'No! There's no time!' he shouted in

Nicholas's ear, and hauled him to his feet. Trang made an abrupt turn to the left, disappearing into darkness. Nicholas, with one quick glance back at Shindo's sprawled body, followed him.

What happened was this: I killed him in the manner he asked me to, Shindo had said about his lover. But now Nicholas realized that he had been talking about himself as well. He couldn't stay away from Vietnam. The war had caught him up in its malignant thrall, and in the end he died as he had wanted to, in-country, from an enemy bullet.

Together, Nicholas and Trang hurtled down one narrow back alley after another in such rapid succession that Nicholas lost all sense of direction. He supposed that was the point: if he was confused, so would be anyone trying to pursue them. He wanted to ask Trang a dozen questions, chief among which was, had that shot been meant for him?

At last, they broke out onto Tran Van Kieu Street. Ahead of them, the dark waters of the Kinh Ben Nghe Canal gleamed in the lights from the city. They raced toward the bridge upon which Con Gluoc Street spanned the canal. Beneath it was utter blackness.

Trang slipped beneath the bridge. Nicholas hesitated for a moment, looking back over his shoulder. He did not care for the darkness. He did not know Trang, could not for certain trust him. What if this was a setup?

What good were these doubts? he asked himself. If Trang was for real, he needed him. Shindo was dead and Trang was now his only lead in the investigation. All he knew for sure was he'd never find out standing still.

He ducked his head, slipping into the blackness. He was immediately up to his knees in filth. The stench was overpowering. But now, as his eyes adjusted, he saw a dim outline of a small boat tied up against the stone pilings. Trang was moving in the darkness, and Nicholas heard a rustling of cloth. Then Trang clambered into the boat, untied it and pushed off while Nicholas leapt aboard. The craft rocked dangerously, and Nicholas was obliged to stand spread-legged in the center in order to bring it back to stability.

By that time they had emerged from beneath the bridge. Nicholas scanned the shoreline, looking for anyone with an inordinate degree of interest in them, but the exercise was fruitless. Too many faces, too little light, and the inconstant rocking motion of their passage, defeated him. He opened his *tanjian* eye, searching for a malign presence, but the welter of people provided too much interference. Mind reading was not among the advantages of the *tanjian*. Adepts could, by a clever combination of psychic insight, observation and intuition, come to an approximation of it, but it was not true mind reading and had to be treated with a great degree of caution.

It occurred to Nicholas that they were too vulnerable out on the water, and he turned his attention to Trang in order to tell him this.

Trang had disappeared. In fact, Nicholas saw with a jolt, he had never existed. The slim figure running the noisy outboard motor was without the fedora and suit, and now Nicholas recognized that it was feminine in every way. This was the oddity he had instinctively registered earlier but could not quite pull into the light of consciousness.

'Shit,' he said, sitting down heavily, 'who the hell are you?'

'My name is Bay,' the young woman said. He could now see her for what she was: a beautiful Vietnamese with clear skin, large, luminous eyes and long, cascading hair. The hat, then, had been an essential part of the disguise, not an affectation. He had to admire her; there was no trace of the portrait she had so skillfully painted of Trang.

'What happened to Trang?'

She smiled with pouty, sensual lips as she steered around an oncoming boat, giving it a wide berth. 'Let's make it simple and say Trang was killed back there on the street.'

'No. A man who worked for me was murdered, and you simply left him −'

Her head turned toward him and her black eyes bored into his. 'That man could have been you. You'd do well to remember that. Did you see what was left of his skull? What you seek is both illegal and very dangerous, *Chu* Goto. Whose responsibility is the man's death, mine or yours?'

Nicholas opened his mouth to reply, but his tongue seemed to have trouble working. She had startled him not only with what she said but with the force she had used.

'Men changing into women, a murder in the street, running from an unknown and unseen enemy. What's going on here?'

'This is your journey, *Chu* Goto. You asked for it.'

Nicholas said nothing, digesting all that had happened from the moment this disguised woman had appeared at his hotel-room door. What rankled him the most was that he hadn't immediately seen through her mask. His pride had been pricked and, what was worse, she appeared to understand this. What exactly did she know about him? He had assumed that here in Saigon he wouldn't be recognized.

'You must trust me,' Bay said in an urgent tone. She maneuvered the boat into a darkened, deserted slip on the opposite shore. Nicholas estimated that they were just over three miles southwest of where they had boarded the boat. 'I'm going to take you to the man you want to see.'

'The theoretical-language technician?'

Bay nodded her head. 'The Russian Jew, yes. Abramanov.'

TWO

Tokyo/Saigon

Akira Chosa, *oyabun* of the Kokorogurushii family, drank in the dense, resonating knell of the shrine bell. The bell, made of a composite of bronze and copper, was the height of three men. It had been cast more than two hundred and fifty years ago at the same shrine foundry that had turned out some of the finest samurai armor and *katana* Japan had ever seen.

At dawn, dusk and midnight the bell was rung by a trio of Shinto priests propelling a thick beaten-bronze post, hanging horizontally by the side of the bell. Its hemispherical head was wrapped in a square of specially woven indigo cloth that was replaced each year on the last day of winter in a ceremony that took the better part of an entire day.

Chosa, a devout Shintoist, had attended this ceremony every year since he had attained manhood, and more than once he had knelt, shaven head bowed, in the midst of these priests, praying to the gods of the shrine's sacred camphor-wood trees from which it was built, the piercing white snow that lay atop its eaves, and the crepuscular moon that illuminated them all, with blood on his hands, the remnants of affairs of business or of honor.

This was before he had been elevated to the rank of *oyabun*, but the blood marked, like the rungs on a ladder, his ascent through the ranks of the Kokorogurushii.

Chosa could not fail to hear the beating of the great

shrine bell and be moved. Like art, this symbol of his inner beliefs affected him far more deeply than did his dealings with humans which, in his opinion, were insignificant and ephemeral. In the end, Chosa fervently believed, only the cosmic symbols survived in the mind, the heart, the spirit, the places of eternal wandering.

As the sound swelled, enveloping him, he wept. He licked his lips, tasting in his saliva this deep tolling as if it possessed the bitter tang of hardened steel. It did not seem to matter to him that, twenty floors up, he could not see the shrine, hidden as successfully as a mushroom in a forest of cryptomeria. Hearing the beating of the bell was what was important.

He listened, tears streaming down his cheeks, even after the beating had ceased, straining for each echo as it rose up the night-black canyon of steel and glass, dying away in the tungsten- and antimony-tinged air high above Tokyo.

When at last the final reverberation had played itself out in the confines of the room, he turned from the window, which he had thrown open just before midnight. As he did so, the octopus on his back and sides rippled its eight arms. This elaborate *irizumi*, the traditional, highly charged tattoo of the Yakuza, spread over his torso and upper arms. The octopus was a great brown creature, eyes full of violent sorrow. It was garlanded with *sakura* – cherry blossoms – as if it had emerged from a hillside in Nara, rather than from the depths of the ocean. Four of the octopus's arms were engaged in a struggle with a fierce, bearded warrior wielding a battle ax; the remaining four arms erotically embraced a magnificent semi-nude woman. The dual nature of the octopus was rampant in Japanese legend; its sexual potency was believed to be unparalleled. And why not? With eight arms, it must surely be a better lover than a man.

The octopus in motion, Chosa faced the Plexiglas case placed against one otherwise bare wall. In it resided a life-size wax replica of Marilyn Monroe in the one pose from *The Seven Year Itch* that had passed from mere fame into genuine legend. Legs spread, hands splayed between her legs, a startled moue on her face, this Marilyn mannequin wore the same dress the real one had worn when stopping on a subway grate while hot air billowed it up around her sensational thighs. Chosa had paid through the nose for it. In his replica, a small motor blew the air upward, the dress eternally waving like the flag at the grave of the Unknown Soldier.

'What is it you see in her?'

The unmistakable voice turned him slowly around until he was looking into the exquisite face of Naohiro Ushiba, Daijin of MITI. Ushiba gazed with obvious distaste at the image of Marilyn. 'Everything about her is so ... exaggerated, as gross as an American cross-dresser.' He made a parody of the moue Marilyn used to seduce the world, making Chosa laugh.

The sound irritated Ushiba further. 'It's like a corruption of the soul, this image.'

Chosa shrugged. 'Whose soul? And what is your definition of corruption?'

Ushiba glowered at Chosa. 'I fear the dark night of the American psyche is imprinting itself on you. You know my definition of corruption: American work ethic, American hedonism, American shortsightedness, American elitism.'

Chosa smiled. 'So dour, Naohiro. So different from your ebullient act in front of the press.' Chosa gestured at the cityscape outside the windows. 'Look out there. We are the land of the empty symbol.' He pointed to the Marilyn replica. 'Now that you have a degree of celebrity you should be more sympathetic. This is just

57

another symbol – and quite a fascinating one. Who better than we to understand it?'

Chosa was an impressive man. His wide face and chunky body appeared attached without the need for a neck, the beach-ball head smashed cruelly down between massive shoulders.

The *irizumi* made him seem larger, more commanding than he might otherwise be. The force of the tattooing, the hyperimaginative covering of his flesh in colored inks, served the same purpose as a mask might on someone with less personality. Ushiba, who knew him better than anyone else, was of the belief that its facade allowed Chosa the freedom to employ chimerical personality shifts without the leash of conscience or remorse, as if the creatures crawling over him might be responsible for this behavior and not Chosa himself.

'You make me sick,' Ushiba said, but his glance briefly touched the spot on Chosa's flesh where beast and woman joined most intimately. 'These bastard Americans . . .' He seemed to strangle on bitter emotion.

'It's the Americans we're in bed with who make you sick,' Chosa said, moving into the kitchen to prepare tea.

'That we need them at all is galling.' Ushiba lit a cigarette as he followed Chosa. 'I wonder that you don't feel it.'

'Oh, I *do* feel it.' Chosa put water on to boil, taking cups from a cabinet, measuring out tea. 'But, unlike you, I've learned to live with it.'

This suite, part of a triplex Chosa owned in the building, was reserved only for him and his occasional guests. Bodyguards and servants lived in the rooms below. He was one public figure who cherished his privacy. Midnight might seem an odd time to meet with the chief minister of MITI but, after all, Chosa was Yakuza, and such direct links between the underworld and the bureaucracy required absolute security. That the Daijin Ushiba was an adviser to the former Kaisho's three-member inner council was a secret no one involved wanted known. Since Tomoo Kozo's death late last year, the inner council consisted of Chosa, Tetsuo Akinaga and Tachi Shidare, a young man elevated to Kozo's position of *oyabun* of the Yamauchi clan. With the exception of Shidare, who was as yet too young, these men – along with Ushiba – were reigning members of the Godaishu who had become discontented with Mikio Okami's power as Kaisho. After months of bitter debate, they had agreed to oust him, but, somehow, someone unknown had transformed that decision into a death sentence for Okami.

'It's humiliating.'

'No.' Chosa turned on the Daijin abruptly. 'It's humiliating being privy to your weakness.' He poured tea into two cups, and they sat at the kitchen table, staring into one another's face.

'Yes.' Ushiba blew out a cloud of smoke. 'My doctor tells me my ulcer is worse. The Americans are making it bleed; don't you think I have reason enough to despise them?'

Chosa handed Ushiba the tea. As he did so, he gave him a skeptical look. 'Oh, yes. But you delimited the Americans. Just like you helped us delimit the Kaisho.'

'Murdering Mikio Okami. Is that what you term *delimiting*?'

Chosa raised his eyebrows. 'Okami is dead? Do you know something I do not, Naohiro?'

'Well, no, of course not.' Ushiba made a grimace of pain, wrapped his fine fingers tightly around the earthenware cup. 'I was merely assuming his demise.'

'With Okami that would be a mistake.' Chosa drained his cup, ran his fingertip around the bottom, picking up the limp tea leaves. He deliberately ignored the Daijin's pain; to do otherwise would make Naohiro lose face.

'But surely if Okami were alive, we would have heard some word of him by now.'

Chosa sucked his fingertip into his mouth, chewed meditatively on the bitter leaves. 'True, I have heard no word of Okami. But his would-be assassin is now dead, so firsthand verification is impossible.' He smiled, putting his hand over Ushiba's. 'Don't worry about the Kaisho. His power has been destroyed. It is as my grandfather said, "Count as friends only those who have the ability to destroy you."' Chosa cherished these moments because they were the only time when he could confront Ushiba honestly.

'If you truly thought Mikio Okami was alive, you would do something about it,' Ushiba continued, as he tapped ash off the end of his cigarette. '*He* was your problem.'

'Yes. The Kaisho.' Chosa's face was thoughtful. 'A latter-day shogun. What a disaster he was for us! So much power concentrated in one man. Disgraceful!'

'Disgraceful only because he managed to put himself beyond the scope of even your power. I, myself, could admire him for that.'

'Pah!' Chosa appeared disgusted. 'With all your spies don't tell me you didn't know I was the one who ordered his death.'

Ushiba's beautiful face turned hard. 'Your habit of making fun of me will be the death of you one day. I assure you I knew nothing of that plot.'

Now Chosa could not contain his mirth. 'Of course the Americans have put a hole in your stomach. You've been busting a gut trying to understand their humor.'

' And you' – Ushiba scowled – 'have picked up too much from them.'

'Well, if so, I've lost nothing in the process, so I wish you'd quit worrying about it. Bad for your stomach.'

'So's this tea.' Ushiba pushed the cup away from him. He got up, went quickly to the bathroom, leaving Chosa alone with his thoughts.

It was true, Chosa thought mournfully, the Americans would be the death of Naohiro. That would be a sad day, for he, Chosa, would lose his edge with the other *oyabun*, his shining path to the ministries of Japan. Well, it was a difficult decision, but he knew he must plan for that day. Naohiro was not getting better, despite the best efforts of his physicians. He should have been in hospital months ago for a week of intravenous drug therapy and utter calm, but Naohiro would not – or possibly could not – agree to it.

Naohiro possessed *kan*, a word adapted from the Chinese that referred to the home of a ruling mandarin. In modern Japanese it was the definition of power for the bureaucrat, and was the basis for the word *kanryodo*, the way of the samurai-bureaucrat.

Naohiro was a true samurai-bureaucrat. His work at MITI meant everything to him. The one sure way to kill him quickly, Chosa mused, would be to take him away from his work. The physicians knew that so they had not insisted.

Chosa revered Ushiba; he might even in his own way love him. But Chosa was, first and foremost, a pragmatist. In the world of violence and treachery that he inhabited, there was little room for compassion or sentiment except as acceptable symbols at specified and infrequent intervals.

Ushiba returned to the kitchen, white-faced and silent. He lit another cigarette, stood silently smoking for some time.

Knowing he had offended the Daijin, Chosa now sought to win back the ground he had lost. He went to the refrigerator, brought back a carton of milk from which he filled Ushiba's teacup. 'Cheer up, my friend. At least, you don't have to worry about Tomoo Kozo anymore.'

Ushiba gave a disgusted grunt. 'Crazy *oyabun*! He tried to destroy Nicholas Linnear and wound up being killed by his prey.'

'Look on the bright side. The Kaisho's inner council is better off without him.'

Ushiba shrugged as he sat down. 'That may well be true, now that you and Tetsuo Akinaga have agreed on Tachi Shidare's accession to *oyabun* of the Yamauchi clan. You two will have more control than you did when Kozo was the Yamauchi *oyabun*.'

Ushiba scowled as he looked down into the milk. 'But you had best make certain Linnear never discovers that it was Kozo's man tailing his wife when she had the fatal accident. Considering how he feels about Yakuza in general, he'd come after all of us, not just the Yamauchi. The police we can control through the politicians whom we own, but Linnear is the one man who can destroy us.'

Chosa grunted. 'We've made certain that Linnear will never learn the true nature of the incident. The truck driver knows nothing more than he gave to the police in his statement. There was no mention of the white Toyota. Even Tanzan Nangi has no idea that Kozo was having Linnear's wife followed. Why would he? Kozo was crazy, we all knew it. What did Kozo have to gain by having her followed?'

'That's simple. Once Kozo learned of the link between Okami and Linnear, he put Linnear's wife under surveillance in hopes of finding her husband.'

'Who was this man she went to meet, who she spent the night with in a Tokyo hotel?'

'He was her lover, an advertising executive.' Ushiba

continued to stare into his milk, smoke curling around his face. 'They were both innocent.'

'Yes, but we didn't know that then. All Kozo knew was that the man was an American who, upon arriving in Japan, had gone straight to Tanzan Nangi. Kozo, already wary of our American partners in the Godaishu, became suspicious.'

'Paranoid, you mean,' Ushiba said in contempt.

'There is always a whiff of paranoia to suspicion, isn't there?' Chosa was thoughtful for a moment. 'In any event, Kozo had Linnear's wife followed. She must have spotted the white Toyota following her and panicked.'

'So the death of Linnear's wife was accidental.'

'Not at all,' Chosa said thoughtfully. 'If you think about it, it's Linnear's fault. The life he chose to live murdered her. She was always looking over her shoulder, jumping at shadows.'

The Daijin laughed harshly. 'You've put an interesting spin on nasty events.'

'Nicholas Linnear. As you have said, he's very dangerous, highly skilled. There isn't an *oyabun* alive who isn't terrified of him.'

'Except you, eh?' Ushiba said archly.

'*Especially* me.' Chosa poured himself more tea, tried to ignore Ushiba's milky cup. 'I have a more realistic respect than most for Linnear's hatred of the Yakuza.'

'Don't let's bring a sense of personal vengeance into a situation that is already fraught with enough difficulty.'

'Is that what you think?' Chosa eyed Ushiba. 'I'm going after Linnear for a very good reason. Somehow, Okami learned of my plot to have him eliminated, and he responded in an altogether extraordinary manner – he enlisted the aid of Nicholas Linnear.'

Ushiba shook his head. 'But how was that possible? Linnear despises all Yakuza.'

'Of that I have no doubt. But, inside, Linnear is

Japanese, just as his father, Colonel Linnear, was. There is a family debt owed to Okami and Linnear is obligated to fulfill it. *Giri*. He became Okami's protector. *That* is why I have no faith in the assumption that the Kaisho is dead. And that is why I put it to you that Linnear must be destroyed.'

'Whatever arguments you put to me, I must forbid you to act against Linnear.'

Chosa looked at him archly. '*You* forbid *me*?'

'Listen to me, I am the voice of reason. Kozo tried it and he's dead. But I know you. You think you're better than Kozo. You think you can outsmart Linnear.'

'I *know* it. He is a man, after all, not a machine or a god. And he is vulnerable just like any man.'

'You will jeopardize the entire Godaishu because you want to prove your erection is bigger than his.'

'Spoken like a true woman.'

Ushiba stubbed out his butt, got up and went over to the kitchen window so he could drink his humiliating milk in privacy. Having to ignore Chosa's cruel wit was bad enough. He did not want to think about Nicholas Linnear or the pitched battle Chosa was precipitating. Instead, he peered through the glass. All he could see was a thicket of steel, tinted glass and ferroconcrete. It was quite a sight, a testament to how successful his policies had been, how far and how fast Japan had grown. *Too fast*, he thought now. *Like a child who has learned to run before he can walk, Japan now stumbles in its prodigious efforts to outproduce the West.*

Ushiba turned back to the *oyabun*. 'Linnear is *not* like other men.'

Chosa was very relaxed now; this worried Ushiba, who turned back to the window. He knew what that studied calm portended: imminent action.

'Rubbish. I happen to know the origin of Linnear's intense hatred for the Yakuza. I intend to make it

64

his Achilles heel. Men who hate deeply are careless men.'

Ushiba felt the knife twisting in his stomach, saw his grimace reflected grotesquely back at him. With a convulsive gesture, he brought the cup to his lips, drained it. The milk would not be enough, he knew. Just as the regulations he was putting into effect would not be enough to stem the tsunami of the economic slide.

The present was bitter indeed for him. The bureaucracy had failed in its promise to protect Japan's central banks, three-quarters of whose assets were in equities and real estate. With the Nikkei at less than sixty percent of its value of just a few short years ago and property values at ten cents on the dollar, the banks' assets were perilously low.

The present invidious cycle that had developed was proving resistant to Ushiba's best efforts to break it. The economic malaise had caused a flood of corporate bankruptcies, putting even more pressure on the banks' monetary reserves. This, in turn, had made investors so fearful they were continuing to sell equities at an unprecedented rate, despite the government's assurances as to Japan's overall economic health.

The trouble is, Ushiba thought sourly, *after all the scandals of corporate and bureaucratic kickbacks and illegal payments, the man in the street believes we deserve everything we've brought on ourselves – and he's justified in that opinion.*

He turned around, abruptly disgusted with these self-pitying musings. What was he so worried about anyway? They had the Godaishu. Whatever disasters were lurking short-term for Japan, they would not affect the Godaishu. The men who comprised the Godaishu, global in design, generating assets from all over the world, were insulated against any short-term setback, even the involvement of Nicholas Linnear. If Chosa said he had a way of neutralizing Linnear, Ushiba had no choice but to believe him. Anyway, he *wanted* to believe him.

He also wanted more milk, but he would not ask his friend. What good would it do anyway? he asked himself bitterly. Everyone, Chosa included, thought his pain stemmed from a bleeding ulcer. Good. He had fooled them all. How quickly they would be rid of him if they knew he had stomach cancer.

Inoperable. That is what he had told his physicians when they had described the aftermath of cutting him open: an invalid who could not even digest food on his own, riddled with bags, tubes and hoses like some subhuman beast. No, no. That humiliation was not for him. Better the silence of the grave.

'One thing I know for certain,' Chosa said, 'is that the Godaishu has a better chance of reaching its goal now that Mikio Okami is gone.'

Ushiba was pensive. 'Okami lost faith in what he had set in motion. Why? I ask myself this question over and over. Okami always was a patriot. He understood that purges needed to be implemented in order to stem the moral decay that had rotted Japan ever since the Americans forced us to adopt a constitution they wrote for us.'

'What does it matter? Okami is history,' Chosa said with finality. 'Whatever he thought no longer matters. We have our future laid out in front of us. It is our karma, my friend, and we are so close I can taste victory.'

Ushiba, wishing he possessed the *oyabun*'s surety of the future, said, 'Be that as it may, we still have problems that must be solved. The Americans, first and foremost, must be dealt with. Already their dominance in fiber optics and telecommunications is threatening our future. The twenty-first century will be dominated by those companies that can transmit data most quickly and efficiently.'

'Another reason to fear Linnear,' Chosa said. 'His company, Sato-Tomkin Industries, holds multiple patents on proprietary telecommunications technology that for now we can only dream about. Sato-Tomkin is currently in mainland China, India and Malaysia laying miles of fiber-optic cables that will one day transform those countries into true competitors of ours.'

'Once again, I warn you. Linnear is ninja and he is exceedingly clever,' Ushiba said. 'I have attempted to intimidate him with no success. He quietly brings to bear a force greater than the one leveled at him.'

'It's not your job to worry about Linnear.'

'No, but it's my duty to protect the Godaishu. Going after Linnear presents an unconscionable risk to us all. To involve him in our affairs now –'

'He is Okami's protector,' Chosa snapped. 'He's already involved.'

They were on a bus ride to nowhere. Or so it seemed to Nicholas as he sat beside Bay. The old crate that would have passed for a bus twenty years ago bounced along a potholed tarmac road. The interior stank of animals and urine; at every jounce the dozen or so caged chickens let out a chorus of raucous squawks that made the yellow bird jump in anxiety. The yellow bird was in a tiny bamboo cage beside the driver's head, wired from the ceiling of the bus. Nicholas had heard it said that Vietnam was the one country where people took birds for walks and ate the dogs for dinner. Shindo had cautioned him never to ask what kind of meat he was being served.

Perhaps this four-wheeled deathtrap was being used as a truck to transport these chickens to market, for there were no other human passengers and none were waiting for it along the dark, pitted road. How Bay even knew of its existence was beyond him, but it had been waiting for them three blocks from the spot where she had tied up the boat. Twenty minutes later, they were out of Saigon proper, heading southwest.

'Where are we going?' he had asked Bay.

'The Iron Triangle.' By which, he surmised, she must mean Cu Chi. This region had become infamous thirty years ago for its miles-long network of multi-level tunnels that allowed the Viet Cong to control the area just sixty-five miles from Saigon. The Vietnamese had begun the tunnels during the 1940s in their war against the French. The hard-packed red earth of the area made it ideal for digging and, decades later, the network had undergone extensive expansion and renovation until it stretched all the way to the Cambodian border.

Nicholas said, 'Bay, I want some answers now. What was your relationship with Vincent Tinh?'

Bay stared out the window. Her hair, bound in a long, thick tail, wound over her shoulders. She seemed a strong, motivated woman — no wonder her pose as a man had proven so successful. She had the kind of face that, though entirely feminine, would need minimal makeup to turn her into a convincing male persona. This almost androgynous nature made her all the more intriguing, especially because she carried it so unselfconsciously.

'He never employed me, though he tried,' she said at last. Her head was still turned slightly away from him, but he could see her in ghostly reflection in the dark window. 'He tried to make it with me as well. But I knew his reputation, knew that if I said yes to any one of his proposals, I would be sucked wholesale into his world.' Her fingers fidgeted in her lap. 'That I couldn't afford. I'm an independent operator — a kind of go-between, sometimes even a mediator between ... factions.'

'By "factions" I assume you mean drug warlords, arms merchants, terrorists and the like.'

Bay said nothing for a long time. The bus rattled on, the chickens squawked, and the yellow bird hopped from perch to perch as if stung by jolts of electricity.

'Whatever you may think of me, *Chu* Goto, I have worked very hard to gain an enviable position. I am beholden to no one, yet many people of influence owe me favors. I wonder if you understand the importance of this? Perhaps not. My country is different from all others. It takes time, patience and acceptance to understand the nature of Vietnam. I promise that judging us by your standards can only end in disaster for you.'

For someone else, perhaps, it would have been easy to dismiss the words of a woman. But for Nicholas, time, patience and acceptance were three virtues of paramount importance. Also, he had learned the necessity of 'seeping in', of absorbing by immersion the strange, the bizarre and the frightening. Vietnam was a terrifying culture to the outsider, and terror had a habit of placing its hand across one's eyes at precisely the wrong time. Bay was right: it would be a disaster for him to judge her as he might a Japanese or an American.

'I appreciate your insight, Bay,' he said carefully. 'Can you tell me anything about Tinh's death?'

'It was no accident, but I imagine you already know that.'

'Yes.'

'Do you also know that he was murdered in the Chinese manner?'

'Chinese? I don't think I understand.'

'Once upon a time, the Chinese warlords of the Shan mountains eliminated their enemies in the manner in which Vincent Tinh was killed. They shot them, then left them to be found in the acid that helps refine the tears of the poppy into opium. It served as warning to others who would try to betray them.'

'You mean they don't do it anymore?'

Bay ducked her head so that her hair swung across one shoulder. 'In a manner of speaking. They no longer exist. They have been supplanted by one man who now virtually controls the poppy trade.'

'Really? I have never heard of such a man.'

'I'm not surprised.' Bay's eyes watched his with neither fear nor judgment. 'To speak his name is to court instant death.'

'All right. I accept that. But is this man responsible for Tinh's murder?'

Bay's eyes, dark as coffee, held his. 'I will tell you a story about this place where we are headed. It is called Cu Chi. You have heard of it?'

'Yes, I have.'

'During the war, the Twenty-fifth Division of the US Army established a major base of operations in Cu Chi in order to deal with the VC menace so close to South Vietnam's capital. No one knew how the VC were able to maneuver at will so deep inside enemy territory. Months of grunts being found murdered in their tents every morning finally led to the discovery of the tunnels beneath the base camp, but at a horrific cost in human life. By sheer chance, the Twenty-fifth Division had made camp directly atop the tunnels.'

Nicholas thought about this for some time. 'Was Tinh operating too close to the man who now controls the poppy trade?'

'The poppy trade is not all he controls.'

No wonder Chief Inspector Van Kiet had refused Shindo's bribe, Nicholas thought. He was scared shitless. 'Bay, do you know this man's name?'

'*Chu* Goto, or whatever your real name is, I told you

70

that I was an independent operator. That does not mean I cannot precipitate enemies should I become foolish.'

They were interrupted by a guttural noise from the bus driver. Bay quickly went forward and Nicholas heard them speak briefly. Even from that distance he could discern the note of urgency in their voices.

When Bay returned, her face was pale. 'We're in trouble. There is a police roadblock ahead. I believe they are looking for us.'

'Why? We've done nothing.'

Bay jerked her head. 'Nothing except leave the scene of a murder, show up unescorted in a highly restricted area, conspire to trade in contraband materials, and those are just three of the legitimate charges that could be leveled at us.'

'Yes, but –'

'Thirty years in prison without a trial or hope of parole. It's a lifetime. And your government, *Chu* Goto, has no formal diplomatic relations with Vietnam. If you are caught, you have absolutely no recourse.'

She was leading him toward the rear of the bus, where the driver had opened the accordion door.

'And that's not even counting the obvious – that the police are on the take from people far more powerful than we are. If they catch us, we'll be lucky if we aren't executed on the spot.'

Her last words were cut off by the wind as she jumped into the night. Nicholas leapt after her without hesitation.

For a moment, Chief Minister Ushiba was blind with the pain. Then his vision cleared and he was able to see the simple wooden edifice of Yasukuni.

The hoarse shouts of patriots in years past still echoed through the smoggy afternoon, oblivious of the modern din of passing traffic.

The Yasukuni Shinto shrine, near the moat surrounding the Imperial Palace in the heart of Tokyo, had become a memorial for Japan's war dead, and to the bravery of kamikaze deaths, one of the war machine's most notorious sacrifices to a victory in the Pacific that had been doomed by superior will and radiation.

Ushiba resisted putting the flat of his hand against his gut, swallowed a pill instead. Now he took three a day instead of one, and he struggled to keep his mind sharp in the face of the potent painkiller. Where would it lead? He suspected that he was already an addict, unable to face each day without the mask of calm the narcotic provided, damping his suffering to tolerable levels.

He lit a cigarette, drew the smoke deep into his lungs. As he moved toward the shrine, he willed his legs into their normal stride, thinking as he did of the history of Yasukuni, how in the latter half of the 1930s it had become the focal point for the government-propagated right-wing demonstrations used to whip up the population into a militaristic frenzy.

Recently, a high court decided that ministers were forbidden to worship at the shrine in an official capacity because it violated the postwar constitution insisting upon a distinct separation between religion and the state. But, of course, that was an American-written constitution, and many ministers chose to ignore the court decision.

A few snowy-haired old men were at the shrine, soldiers no doubt, dreaming of the war and their part in it, remembering compatriots who were no longer with them. Ushiba ground his cigarette beneath his heel, then stood beside them. He rang the bell to wake the *kami* of the shrine, then clapped his hands twice, bowing his head in prayer.

He dropped some money between the red wooden

slats of the collection box, then he went to the nearby building. It appeared closed for repairs because signs were up and uniformed workmen were scuttling all around it. On closer inspection, however, it was clear that these were no workmen.

One of them, the largest of the lot, glowered at Ushiba before recognizing him. Then he bowed deferentially, took up some tools, and stepped aside.

Ushiba went into the building, which was a museum commemorating the kamikaze dead. Tattered flags, banners and hurried poems written in the blood of the heroes of the war adorned the walls, all of them carefully annotated.

And Ushiba, overcome with emotion, recalled a haiku:

> The wind brings enough
> of fallen leaves
> To make a fire

One man was in the museum, tall, almost gangly, so thin his wrist bones were knobs. He turned when he heard Ushiba, and a slow smile spread across his face. This was Tetsuo Akinaga, *oyabun* of the Shikei clan, and the third member of the Kaisho's inner council, which included Akira Chosa and Tachi Shidare, Tomoo Kozo's successor. Not coincidentally, these were also the *oyabun* who had helped build the Godaishu with Mikio Okami. Since the Kaisho's ousting, Ushiba's role, it seemed, had expanded from adviser to full-fledged council member.

'A fitting place for us to meet, eh, Daijin?'

'Indeed.'

Akinaga had the right to call him by name, but the *oyabun* seemed to feel more comfortable using titles rather than names. Ushiba privately believed it helped

73

Akinaga delineate in his mind the tangled webs of power that came together whenever the members of the Godaishu met.

He had steel-gray hair that he kept unfashionably long, pulled back in the style of the old samurai. His flat cheeks and stubby, flat nose made his deep-set eyes even more startling. Like Chosa, he was in his late fifties, but he seemed older. Age and, Ushiba suspected, the compromises of power had turned the corners of his mouth down so that he appeared perpetually disapproving of whatever came to pass. He was a man who had seen the turn of the knife blade from foe to friend, and therefore knew there was no substantive difference between the two.

'The quality of the silence here is extraordinary,' Akinaga said. 'Like the hush that comes over the countryside just at sunset.' He laughed. 'I fear I am becoming quite poetical in my old age.'

Ushiba, feeling the fire in his belly, understood. He knew that whatever solace was left him now came from the often startlingly juxtaposed imagery of his beloved haiku. And, of course, from what the Godaishu was about to execute.

The two men walked beneath the banners of the fallen heroes, feeling the weight and obligation of that most ambivalent of Japanese concepts, the nobility of failure.

'I have a great deal of respect for you, Daijin.' Akinaga nodded his head. 'Six months ago you informed me that you would be able to reverse the stock market slide. That was good news for me because many of the banks I control are heavily invested in Nikkei stocks. But the truth is I did not believe you. Government manipulation is one thing, but what you have done since then is nothing short of a miracle. In that time, the Nikkei has risen five thousand points. My banks' books are in some semblance of restoration; there is order out of chaos.'

'It has not been easy, I admit,' Ushiba said, 'and there is a great deal of peril in the government's pouring so much of its pension-plan money into stocks in order to increase share demand and raise prices. We've directed a number of rumors to run the price up on several large issues that were particularly sick. Also, we've had a lot of pressure for blocking all the new equity offerings for the past six months. Of course, we needed to do all this; the fewer shares floating, the bigger the demand must be.'

'And it's worked to perfection.'

'But once again it's artificial, like the real-estate boom we created. Our manipulations may have a serious downside none of us can see at the moment.'

Akinaga smiled. 'History is on your side, Daijin. I have faith that the market will not buckle. I'm convinced that we have seen the lows and are now firmly on our way out of our recession.'

Brought together by their profound appreciation of the past, the two men were reluctant to begin their painful business. They lived simultaneously in the past and in the future. For them, the present was insubstantial, existing solely as a bridge from one reality to the other.

'The question I have raised in council and will continue to do,' Akinaga said at length, 'is whether we can trust this other Mafia *oyabun*. The American mob is in serious decline. The sense of honor and tradition that made their bosses accessible to us has been seriously undermined by those willing to turn state's evidence because of revenge, frustration or because they are soft.'

Ushiba nodded. 'We must deal with Caesare Leonforte now. He's a hothead; he does not possess the cool, calculating mind of the brilliant don Dominic Goldoni. But, as we see it, that is to our advantage. We tried but could not control Goldoni – neither, it seems, could the representatives of the American government with whom he was supposedly working.'

Akinaga appeared unimpressed. 'What troubles me is not merely Leonforte but the number of unreliable and therefore dangerous individuals with whom we are obliged to deal in order to make the Godaishu work. The Mafia, the elements within the American government, even our longtime connection in Vietnam – these *iteki* make me nervous because we don't fully understand them in the way that Okami did.'

Akinaga shook his head. 'Even worse for us, Chosa doesn't see the terrible risks we are taking to attain our goal. His eyes are closed to the possibility of destruction – the horrible holocaust that might result from an error in judgment among people who are essentially alien to one another.'

Akinaga's face darkened and the interior was abruptly filled with menace. 'My worst fears have been realized. Chosa has become too close to the Americans. These *iteki* have no idea of our goals – their sole concern is money, the tons of it the Godaishu is reaping on every continent. They are mercenaries without honor or ideology. Even a momentary lapse could cause them to turn on us like rabid dogs.'

'And yet consider what we have just gone through,' Ushiba said. 'The unthinkable almost happened when Okami and Goldoni betrayed us. But you have seen for yourself the safeguards we have put in place. Goldoni is dead and Okami has disappeared. There is no need for concern. We are on course toward our glorious destiny.'

'Of course they were neutralized,' Akinaga said sharply. 'I saw to it. Okami was far too dangerous. He possessed *koryoku* – the Illuminating Power.'

Ushiba, stunned that first Chosa and now Akinaga were taking credit for the plot to murder the Kaisho, managed to restore his equilibrium in time to say, '*Koryoku*, I've never heard of it.'

'I'm hardly surprised.' Akinaga put his hands behind his back, giving him the aspect of a professor. 'I only learned of it by accident, overhearing Okami speak of it one day long ago. I did some subsequent research. It is a kind of deep meditation, and yet it must be much more – how shall I say it, a kind of second sight which allows the practitioner to achieve a synthesis of motive, intent and intuition that creates its own opportunity. In one as clever and as ambitious as Okami it became a strategic edge. I'm convinced *koryoku* is what allowed Okami to operate with the Mafia don Goldoni for so long without our knowing.'

'This *koryoku* would explain much of Okami's power and influence. After all, he's over ninety now.'

Akinaga screwed up his eyes. 'But what were he and Goldoni up to? We've put our best agents into the field in order to find the answer, with no success.'

At last Ushiba found himself on familiar ground; this had been a most disconcerting meeting so far. Akinaga had been busy condemning Chosa, and he, Ushiba, had found no sound rebuttal. 'Perhaps they have been looking in the wrong places.'

Akinaga was brought up short. He was not a man who tolerated failure. 'What precisely do you mean, Daijin?'

'I have learned that Okami discovered your plot to assassinate him. In response, he sought the aid of Nicholas Linnear.'

Akinaga's hand cut the air in a gesture of disgust. 'Nonsense. Linnear's antipathy toward Yakuza is beyond debate. Where on earth did you hear this fairy tale?'

'From Akira Chosa. And before you reject the theory outright, I urge you to consider – it could very well be

77

true. The history of Japan teaches us that the espousal of enmity is the best cover for friendship, *neh*?' The living truth of that statement was, for Ushiba, a guiding example of how the past inflected the present.

'Perhaps,' Akinaga said, clearly unconvinced, 'but the enmity Chosa harbors toward Linnear is well documented. It is clearly to his benefit to put forward this theory. That way, even if he is wrong, he will have his revenge on Linnear.'

Ushiba, seeing in the days since the Kaisho disappeared disunity beginning among the members of the inner council, struggled to continue his role of peacemaker. 'While no one, least of all Chosa, will deny his hatred of Linnear, I have brought your charge to him myself and he has denied it outright. Besides, if Linnear's enmity toward the Yakuza were genuine, what was he doing last month in Venice, where Okami has his headquarters?'

As Ushiba had foreseen, this revelation brought Akinaga to silence. 'All right,' he said at last. 'I'll accept this judgment for now. But I warn you, Ushiba, I do not stand idly by and allow Chosa his personal revenge. Linnear needs to be dealt with, on that I agree, because he alone has it within his means to destroy the Godaishu.

'But I have no illusions about Linnear. I am aware of his strengths. My father knew Colonel Linnear in the terrible years after our defeat. More than once the two of them called upon each other in difficult circumstances. I, myself, recall the Colonel with a great deal of affection. I remember his funeral well. It was the first and only time I saw my father shed a tear. No one else saw. He wore dark glasses and it was only because I stood at his side that I was aware of the depth of his feeling.'

Akinaga, gazing at the bloody banners of the kamikaze hanging over their heads, gave a little smile. 'But I know that the son is not the father. The Colonel understood the expediency of elasticizing the codes of American law, but I question whether Nicholas Linnear would be able to do the same. His is a rigid code of honor. If he had been a seventeenth-century samurai I believe that he would refuse to hire ninja to circumvent the laws of Bushido. He would have perished in the political imperatives of infighting.'

'Still, I would urge extreme caution with Linnear,' Ushiba said. 'There are stories that he is even more powerful than we believe. Stirring up a Demon Spider from slumber is not usually the best strategy. At this crucial time when the Godaishu is in its final phase of consolidating its power it would be better to do nothing to arouse his suspicions.'

'Perhaps. But when I hear arguments such as yours, Daijin, I am reminded of the hero Yoshitoshi, who set out to destroy the great Demon Spider that had slain nine thousand and ninety heroic men. When he found the hideous monster, it was sick and in pain because of the many wounds it had suffered at the hands of these heroes. It was incapable of defending its nest where its young lay sleeping.' His eyes, now seeming even more sunken into his face, were sad. 'The truth isn't always as we perceive it or wish it to be, Daijin.'

Ushiba nodded, thinking of Chosa's promise that he had found Linnear's Achilles heel. 'Yes. I suppose even Demon Spiders can be destroyed.' He gazed upward at the bloody banners of the kamikaze and thought again of the Demon Spider and his brood. Akinaga had meant the myth to be illustrative of Nicholas Linnear, but Ushiba suspected that it could equally exemplify his father, Colonel Linnear. Nicholas Linnear had within him the true nature of the legendary Japanese hero, a moral center holding fast in the face of overwhelming odds.

'You don't sound convinced.'

Ushiba drew his shoulders up, trying to warm himself. He would have loved a heavier coat, but he was determined not to show signs of weakness among these jackals. To do so would surely undermine his complex position of counselor with them. 'Akinaga-san, I spend half my days with the *iteki* Americans so I can say with an authority you lack that I cannot respect them. Unlike Chosa, I see their culture as a corruptive influence on Japan. But Nicholas Linnear is no *iteki*. In fact, I am convinced that he is not like other men. Chosa does not understand this.'

'Huh, Chosa.' Akinaga made a face as if being offered spoiled fish. 'I think he aspires to ascend to the Kaisho's throne even while he so artfully argues that the very idea of Kaisho is unacceptable since it puts too much power in the hands of one individual. I don't approve of his rashness, but I can certainly understand it. Imagine the stature of the man who destroys Nicholas Linnear. I see this excuse to destroy Linnear as another attempt on Chosa's part to gain influence over the rest of us.'

So Akinaga did not see the danger in involving Nicholas Linnear either. Like Chosa, he was too wrapped up in the personal maneuvering for power among the remaining *oyabun* of the inner council to consider the long-term ramifications of another abortive attempt on Linnear's life. Ushiba was abruptly weary of the constant infighting between these *oyabun*. How he missed the Kaisho, who, whatever his faults, had kept them united and equal. Since Mikio Okami's disappearance, it seemed every issue was viewed in terms of how it would impact the individual members of the council. Still Ushiba was surprised that he missed Okami, someone who, just months ago, he had wanted out of office.

'I swore an oath, as we all did. My duty to the Godaishu comes first.' Ushiba's hands, jammed deep in the pockets of his overcoat, were clenched into fists. 'The Godaishu is of paramount importance to me because I have seen that it can accomplish what our government never will – mastery over international trading in everything from computer chips to arms dealing, petrochemicals to drug traffic.'

Ushiba grunted. 'The time of the Godaishu is here at last. Our economy is in a shambles. Profits across the board are down, and many major *keiretsu* have given in to the unthinkable: downsizing operations by laying off employees and abandoning factories. Most troubling, the extent of the damage to our banking structure is still unknown. How many more will fail before we have seen the end of the disaster? And the crafty Americans are determined to see a strong yen. They claim it helps their trade deficit with us, but I know the real reason: they know that a strong yen cripples our recovery because it erodes our sales in all overseas markets. The Americans have us down and mean to keep us there for as long as they can.'

'Ah, but all of this havoc plays right into the hands of the Godaishu,' Akinaga said. 'The chaos of financial disaster is the perfect environment for us to flourish and expand, don't you agree?'

Ushiba nodded. 'Yes, I do. But this is all the more reason for the council to strive to work toward the one goal of the Godaishu: total global economic domination.'

The night sky was red and purple, as if it had undergone a savage beating. In a moment, Nicholas understood that this weird illumination came from the convoy of vehicles that straddled the last section of road toward Cu Chi. He cupped his hands around his eyes, saw to his horror not merely police cars but army mobile troop carriers.

'They've called out all the dogs,' he said softly.

'That's right,' Bay said. 'You must have some very powerful enemies, *Chu* Goto.'

'Perhaps we both do.'

Bay gave him a hard look. 'I pay a great deal of money each year to make certain I don't.' She turned away, slid back down the hillock against which they had flung themselves.

They were perhaps three hundred yards from the road. Already Nicholas could see the bus they had been on stopped at the checkpoint. The driver, hands on his head, was being questioned by an officer while a squad of soldiers swarmed over the vehicle like ants over a cube of sugar.

'There are too many of them,' Bay said as if to herself. 'We'll never make it overland to Cu Chi.'

'Let's get back to Saigon, then.'

'Impossible. It's already past three in the morning. It will be light before we can get there on foot and we'd be without cover. Besides, I have a feeling we'd run right into another checkpoint long before then.'

'Shouldn't we at least try?'

Bay shrugged, and they headed over the hillock, back toward Saigon. But within a hundred yards, she pushed him to the damp earth, pointing ahead of them where the headlights of jeeps and trucks lit up the horizon.

'You see, I was right,' she whispered. 'They're waiting for us. We are in the middle of a gigantic trap with the jaws slowly closing on us. We have only one way to go.'

They turned, heading back to Cu Chi, but by the time they reached the hillock, the situation had already changed. At *kokoro*, the heart of Tau-tau, Nicholas had allowed his senses free reign to quest outward through the darkness, and immediately he had encountered a host of malign presences on the move. He crouched beside Bay. 'They're coming this way,' he said.

Bay scrambled up to the crest of the hillock. 'How can you tell? I can't see anything.'

Nicholas, closing down his *tanjian* eye, said, 'Now you must trust me, Bay. There are at least a dozen soldiers coming this way. Maybe the driver betrayed us.'

'No, he wouldn't. He –' She broke off, closed her fingers around his wrist. 'Come on,' she whispered as if they could already be overheard. 'This way!'

Crouched over, she led him down off the right side of the hillock. Then she headed obliquely away from Cu Chi and the tightening net of Vietnamese soldiers. The land rose slightly, and Nicholas could smell the standing water of rice paddies. They ran like this for perhaps half a mile. Then, abruptly, Bay led them to her left. A moment later, the ground began to slope downward and, at some point, she changed direction again, heading more or less directly toward Cu Chi.

Nicholas could hear the sound of water. He heard Bay's whispered warning, 'Careful now!' and the ground, mucky with sand and bits of stone, gave way. Buried roots and rotting branches clawed at them, tearing their clothes and abrading their skin.

'Isn't there a better way to go?' he asked.

Bay hooked a thumb. 'Above us, the ground is packed hard and makes for easy travel. The only problem is, there's a minefield that runs for three hundred yards. Even the locals don't go near it.'

They continued scrambling down the treacherous bank and eventually found themselves heading along a riverbank. Their pace slowed as they searched for firmer footing in the morass close to the river. The musky scents of tropical foliage and decay lay heavy on the air, and the thick drone and chirrup of insects filled the night.

At a bend in the river, where a fallen tree reached out into the water, Bay held up her hand. She crouched down, staring fixedly at the tree for some time.

'Are you ready for a swim?' She slipped into the water.

She waited for him at the head of the fallen tree. The water was not so deep, but the current was surprisingly powerful. Movement along the dark, gleaming hulk caught his attention. A long adder slithered toward them, but Bay appeared unconcerned. She gave him a sardonic smile.

'If you lose your balance, turn on your back,' she advised him. 'You'd be astonished at how quickly you can drown.'

She let go of the tree and they began to make their laborious way upriver. It was impossible to swim against the current, which meant they had to half-walk along the silty, quicksand-like river bottom while the water rushed at them in an unending torrent. Nicholas guessed they had gone perhaps half a mile when Bay turned and pushed him against the smooth face of a rock.

'Wait here,' she said in his ear.

'What's going on?'

'The VC built many trap doors into the Cu Chi tunnels. A number of them came out into this river. The problem is nowadays they're never used or even explored, and the VC had a nasty habit of booby-trapping these exits.'

Nicholas watched her as she drifted away from him. For a moment she stood steady near the bank, then she ducked below the surface of the rippling water. Nicholas could feel the tension come into his frame, and he went into meditative breathing. He opened his *tanjian* eye and immediately sensed Bay moving toward the near riverbank. He was also aware of the trap door, and knew that the downed tree half a mile back had been some kind of marker. The projection of his psyche could find no evidence of a booby trap, but that meant nothing. His powers were normally blind to non-sentient things. Though he could sense a path in utter darkness, the essential nature of man-made energy was still beyond his current powers.

He could feel the stealthy encroachment of death and, so near to it, his thoughts strayed to Justine, his wife, who had died some months ago in a fiery car wreck. He would never quite get over the fact they had been estranged when she died. And, even now, he could not say whether there would have been a reconciliation. Too much damage had been done, too many wounds had been inflicted that, though healed on the surface, ran deeper into flesh and bone where they remained, hidden and all the more painful for that.

Celeste, the beautiful woman he had met and fallen in love with while trying to protect Mikio Okami, had returned to Venice. After the disaster with Justine he would not have asked her to stay in Japan against her will. Where had he been at the moment Justine's car had burst into flames? Entwined with Celeste or . . . The horror was that he would never know.

Bay had been down a long time. But Nicholas, whose own skill at breath control was formidable, was not particularly concerned. His *tanjian* eye would have picked up any sign of distress in her.

When she breached the surface of the river, she shook water out of her eyes, turned to him and said, 'The way is clear. Let's go.'

He held on to her ankle as they swam beneath the water. Dimly, he saw her push aside a small door, slither through. He went in after her, felt her push back past him, close the door.

There was barely enough room for the two of them. He was very much aware of being pushed against her body, their heat warming the water. Her fingers grabbed onto an iron ring at the far end of the underwater chamber and, a moment later, another door opened and they were moving upward, out of the water into air, musty and humid, but breathable nonetheless.

'Inside,' Bay said. A small beam of light came on, and Nicholas saw that she had produced a mini-flashlight. Obviously she had been prepared for this when she had come to his hotel room.

The beam of light swept across the narrow width of the passage, illuminating for an instant what appeared to be an odd-looking skull. Then Bay played the beam very slowly in a series of vertical passes. Nicholas estimated that the passage could not be more than two feet wide by three feet high. The light stopped on a shining thread not unlike a spider's web silk.

'There it is,' she whispered. 'Just below knee height.'

The booby trap.

'There might be another as backup,' Nicholas said.

Bay glanced at him, nodded her head. She ran her fingertips along first one side of the tunnel, then the other. The beam of light focused on a protrusion.

'Frag grenade,' Bay said. 'If the trip wire didn't get you, the shrapnel in this explosive device would have taken out your legs.'

. Bay showed him how to avoid contact with any of the buried triggers, and they clambered over the trip wire, keeping to the center of the passage.

Bay paused. Her beam illuminated the partial skeleton of a large dog, long ago stripped of all flesh by the small scavengers of the Cu Chi tunnels. Nicholas recognized the skull as the one he had glimpsed before.

86

'An Alsatian,' she told him as she stepped past the pile of bones. 'The Americans used the dogs to ferret out the tunnel entrances. Didn't work, though. The VC used pepper and uniforms from dead grunts to throw the dogs off. They also started washing with American soap, a smell familiar and friendly to the dogs.' She kept the light on the skeleton until Nicholas was past it. 'Poor beasts. They couldn't smell the booby traps the VC laid, and so many of them died or were maimed their handlers eventually refused to send them down here.'

She led him steeply upward, along a rough staircase of packed, clay-like earth and rotting timbers. There was a sickly-sweet smell that deepened as they rose. At one point, Bay paused, turned back to him, said softly, 'This is not a pleasant place, which was why it was chosen. The current authorities have only a limited knowledge of this warren. It's widely believed that American B-52 carpet bombing effectively destroyed the majority of the tunnel network, but that's not true. Lower-level tunnels were protected by this hard-packed earth and by limestone.'

They emerged onto what Nicholas assumed was one of these lower levels. It was like a city in one of the inner rings of hell. Everywhere Bay swung her small beam of light it struck human remains, not littered about as if after a firefight, but in all the myriad poses of everyday human existence.

This was the true horror of what he saw, not the bones of the enemy, but the remains of a banal day where people squatted speaking together in intimate groups, or lay napping in mean berths, crouched cooking a meal, or leaned, exhausted, against an earthen wall.

And with his *tanjian* eye open he was aware of not just what Bay illuminated with her mini-flash, but of all the skeletons packed into the darkness of this vast necropolis. He became dizzy with the welter of images, as if these soldiers, so long dead, still possessed weight and energy, instead of merely history.

'We're safe now,' Bay said, moving ahead through the tunnels. 'Neither the police nor the army would come down here even if they suspected where we were.'

'Why not?'

'Because they know this is a labyrinth in which we could survive for months without them ever finding a trace of us. Besides, it's too dangerous, even for them. As you've seen, these unexplored tunnels are still riddled with booby traps. Live ordnance, as well.'

'What about tear gas? They could flood the tunnels —'

'It wouldn't cross their minds. They know this place is riddled with trap doors and baffles to keep gas from spreading through the system.'

Nicholas shook his head. 'All in all, I'd rather be back at the lice-ridden Anh Dan Hotel.'

Bay smiled. 'Speaking of which . . .' She turned the flash on him and, bending down, began to peel leeches from his ankles, elbows, the back of his neck. 'You would have become aware of these in a couple of moments.' She nodded. 'You'd better strip.' He did as she asked, his gaze locked on her dark, luminous eyes. She inspected him with all the studied professionalism of a physician.

'You have a beautiful body, an athlete's body. The muscles are long and lean like a swimmer's, perhaps.' She had a bemused expression. 'This is not the body of a shady businessman or someone engaged in corporate espionage. So now I have seen beneath your mask, *Chu* Goto. I know what you really are.'

She reached out, lifted a leech from the inside of his

thigh. The hairs at the base of his neck stirred when he felt her fingertips there.

When she finished, she stood up. 'You are not shy about your body so I know you won't object to seeing mine.'

She peeled off her soaking clothes and handed him the flash. She was younger than he had thought, perhaps just twenty. Her body was beautifully formed, but it was not unblemished. Scars crisscrossed her lower back and the tops of her buttocks.

Nicholas peeled a leech from the base of her spine, then gently pressed a fingertip along one of the scars. 'What happened here?'

'Do you really want to know?' Bay had her back to him, and her voice was partially swallowed up by the pulsing darkness of the tunnels.

'Not if it's difficult for you.'

'I was thinking about you.' She took a breath, let it out slowly. When he made no reply, she went on. 'Someone turned . . . What word would I use?'

'Violent?'

'Ardent.'

Nicholas thought this over for some time. 'Then it was done . . . deliberately?'

'Yes.'

'By a lover?'

Bay swiveled around so that her eyes locked on his. 'Are you judging me again, *Chu* Goto?'

'I hope not.'

'Really?' Her head moved a little, the beam of light streaming past one eye, firing it, leaving the planes of her face in shadow.

'You made a convincing man,' Nicholas said. 'I can only admire you for that.'

That smile came again with its sardonic edge. There was nothing world-weary about her, nevertheless there was sometimes in her expressions the sense that she had been exposed to too much of life too soon. Her eyes had the look of someone who has gazed for too long into the fiery heart of a blast furnace.

'If the worst comes to the worst,' she said, crushing the leeches one by one beneath her heel, 'we can eat these.'

Nicholas did not want to think about the leeches. 'Did you agree to allow your lover to maim you?'

'It will sound strange if I say yes; and yet the answer is much more complex.' She turned her head into the darkness, as if hearing a distant sound. At length, Nicholas realized that she was listening to the past. 'It was the pain, you see. The physical . . . evidence. The scars really have nothing to do with it.'

'What did the pain do?'

'It made us real.'

In the deathly silence he could hear the last of the river water dripping off them, running into the red clay earth, past the bones of the dead, beneath the clawed feet of the rodents that scampered along the tunnels.

She chilled him, this young woman, not so long out of her teens, because she had needed such a terrible extreme in order to feel and to remember.

He felt sorry for her, but keen instinct warned him that any portent of this emotion in him would only enrage her. She did not want his pity, would, in fact, see it only as an enemy that required extinction.

They dried their clothes on an odd stove-like contraption called a Dien Bien Phu kitchen, where decades before the VC had cooked their food. A complex network of flues vented the smoke far away from the area. Kindling and wood were plentiful and, thankfully, Bay's metal lighter had not been damaged by immersion in water.

Naked, they squatted in the darkness, feeling the

spirits of the dead, restless and inchoate. Nicholas, all too aware of her breasts as they rose and fell, said, 'Why did you bring me here?'

'This is a kind of halfway point.'

He waited for her to continue, but when she remained silent, he said, 'Between where and where?'

'Saigon and . . .' She smiled to take some of the rebuff out of her shrug. 'It doesn't matter. Abramanov agreed to meet you here and nowhere else. He feels safe here.'

'This Abramanov is the man who worked for Vincent Tinh, who built the illegal computer around the stolen neural-net chip?'

Bay rolled the burning wood with a charred stick. 'Abramanov is the only one within five thousand miles who could have.'

Nicholas kept his eyes on her. 'Are you being deliberately evasive? *Was* Abramanov the one?'

'Yes.' She said it very quietly and with a tone that led him to think he had taken a pair of hot tongs to her.

'Bay, what is it?'

She shook her head. 'Don't ask me, please.'

'Why not?'

Her eyes closed for a moment, and he thought he saw the edge of a tear slide down her cheek before she turned away. 'Because I want to tell you, and I know if I do, you won't believe me.'

'Try me.'

The back of her hand went briefly to her face, and he knew he had been right about the tear. She turned back to him, gave him that sardonic smile. 'No. You don't trust me as it is. My mother once said to me that the biggest mistake one could make in life was to tell someone what he doesn't want to hear.'

'I'll listen to anything you tell me.'

'Um, I'm thirsty.' He watched her walk into the darkness. She returned a moment later with an American

91

Army helmet filled with water. She placed this atop the stove, let the water boil for some time.

While they waited, she said, 'Your friend Vincent Tinh came here often.'

'He was no friend of mine, but I think you already knew that.'

'I think that you did not know him.' She glanced at the helmet. 'It was here that he met with Abramanov . . . and the others he dealt with. He liked it here. He was comfortable in this darkness, this murk. He once confessed to me that to be surrounded by so much death made him feel close to life; it excited him.'

Nicholas was alerted by the word 'confessed'. The world inside Cu Chi began to change, as a mask slipped away, revealing a truth beneath.

'It was difficult to know what made him go on,' Bay continued. 'He never knew his parents or where he was born. He grew up on the streets of Saigon and almost died twice, once when he was very young at the hands of a local gangster, the other from American fire during the war. Truthfully, I don't know who he hated more.'

She rose and, wrapping her hands in her dry clothes, took the helmet off the fire. 'He was very good at that, hating. He ingested it like you and I eat food.' By this time all the exotic and unpleasant microbes teeming in the water had been killed.

'Did Tinh take you down here?' Because this is what she was telling him in her roundabout way, that she and Vincent Tinh had been lovers. Tinh would never have 'confessed' anything of his background or of his feelings to a business associate, and he had not been the type to have friends to confide in. But it was a universal truth that there were times when confession was the only thing that could heal the soul, and for Tinh, the choices were limited. Whom could he confess to but someone who shared his bed?

'Yes, often.' Bay dipped her finger experimentally in the water. 'He enjoyed making love here.'

'Did you?'

'Sex with him was . . . ecstatic. The place was unimportant.'

'Even so . . . potent a place as this?'

Bay lifted the helmet, handed it to him to drink. 'It was important to make him happy.'

Nicholas drank the water, then passed the helmet to her. All the taste had been boiled out of it, but it was delicious nonetheless. He watched her carefully while she sipped. Questions swirled in his mind, but they all led down one path and, with this woman, he was becoming convinced he needed to search for the unfamiliar in order to understand her.

'How did doing that make you happy?'

Bay passed her fingers through her thick hair. 'It was like the pain, you see. His reactions were real. When he was happy, *truly* happy – not drunk-happy or stoned-happy – he was a different person. I knew beyond a shadow of a doubt that I affected him. I could feel the excitement bubbling through his skin. That was important because at every other moment of his life he wore a kind of mask that he had fashioned from his past – fear, rage, poverty, the utter *aloneness* of his existence were the materials he used. But I was able to get beneath the mask.'

Nicholas sat back on his haunches, deep in thought. He could see how having such power would be of profound significance to Bay – a woman in a society that had little respect for females; a woman in a city where most people of her age and sex were selling their bodies on the street, increasingly prone to syphilis, hepatitis, AIDS and an early, unnoticed death.

Abruptly, he shivered. It occurred to him that the drama that had been playing out between Bay and Tinh was now in some fashion being repeated. For it was clear that upon Tinh's death she had donned Tinh's remarkable mask, and that he was now finding the human being behind it.

'Bay, how long have you been on your own?' he said at last.

'It's enough now.' She bit her lip. 'Let me alone.'

Nicholas went to his clothes. They were dry, and he put them on. 'When do you expect Abramanov?'

She glanced at her watch. 'To tell you the truth, he should have been here by now.' She grabbed her clothes. 'I think we'd better find out what happened to him.' She pointed. 'There's a contact spot about a quarter of a mile this way. If Abramanov couldn't make the rendezvous for any reason, a note will have been left there.'

The inner world of the Viet Cong grudgingly exposed itself to Bay's light as they made their way down the cramped tunnel. Nicholas could see that they were heading directly toward a section that had caved in and he wondered where she was leading him.

Just before the rubble began, she stopped and, crouching down, pulled on a metal ring. A trap door opened and she levered herself down. Nicholas followed.

They were now on the level below the cave-in; the way was clear. He began to have more respect for the engineers who designed and constructed this ingenious labyrinth.

They moved on. The remains of Viet Cong were always with them; they were traveling through a city of the dead seemingly without end. At length, they arrived at the contact point. There was no one there. Bay got down on her knees, felt beneath a broken-down series of berths.

'There is nothing here.' For the first time, Nicholas detected a note of alarm in her voice. Up until this moment she had been almost unnaturally calm in the face of harrowing circumstances. She looked up at him. Was that a trace of fear in her dark eyes? 'Abramanov should have been here. I don't know what has happened.'

'Maybe all the activity on the highway deterred him.'

But she shook her head. 'He would have entered the tunnels from miles away. The soldiers wouldn't have mattered.'

'Then either I've been double-crossed or we've both been.' He pulled her up by her elbow. 'It's time to get some answers.'

At that moment, they heard a sound.

'Someone's coming!' Bay whispered. She extinguished her flash. 'Quick, this way!'

They slithered backward into a pile of loose dirt, rubble and bones. The stench was as indescribable as it was unpleasant. Nicholas, lying close beside Bay, was aware of the extreme tension gathering in her frame. It was then a dull metallic gleam caught his attention and, shifting slightly, he saw the knife in her left hand. It was a Marine ka-bar, a large-bladed, wicked weapon, capable of cleaving through both sinew and bone.

She was staring fixedly and, following her gaze, he saw what she saw: the figure moving stealthily down the tunnel. Even in the darkness, even with it hunched over, he could tell that it was a soldier. So she had been wrong: they weren't afraid to come down here.

A flash of her rage, like being spat at, bloomed in his mind. He felt her intent in the split second before she moved. He could have stopped her, but to what purpose? He was coming to know her, and he knew she would only fight him and, in doing so, give their position away. He let her go, then launched himself

95

after her because his *tanjian* eye had picked up something that she could not as yet see.

She was like a cat, silent and small, and the Vietnamese soldier was not aware of her until the blade of the ka-bar was buried in his bowels. She ripped the knife upward with tremendous strength, and her victim screamed, the blood spurting out of him like a river.

He pitched sideways, against the wall of the tunnel, and that was when Bay saw the ugly muzzle of the submachine gun leveled point-blank at her. Her only weapon was still hilt-deep in flesh, and her eyes opened wide in astonishment and fear.

Then Nicholas was barreling into the second soldier. A string of explosions rocketed down the tunnels as the submachine gun went off. Nicholas drove his fist into the soldier's solar plexus, momentarily paralyzing him. The heel of his hand smashed into the man's larynx, crushing it. The soldier went down and stayed down. A soft gurgle of blood and saliva came from him. Then silence.

'What the hell is going on?' Nicholas snarled. 'You told me –'

'I know what I said.' Bay flicked on her flashlight. She began to hurry down the tunnel. 'Something's gone terribly wrong. This place has turned into a death trap. We've got to get out of here now.'

Every few feet she reached up with her bloody ka-bar and tapped the ceiling of the tunnel. The fourth time, she stopped, pushed aside a pair of false wooden beams. A trap door dropped open and she levered herself up through the hole. Nicholas followed, looked around. Bay was already several yards down the tunnel.

He heard her curse softly in Vietnamese.

Coming up beside her, he saw that a fairly new cave-in had blocked the way. They went back up the tunnel. Several hundred yards from where they had emerged, she discovered another trap door and up they went onto the next level.

The air was thin here, more musty than down below, leading Nicholas to believe that even Bay and her contacts hadn't explored this section of the labyrinth.

They made no sound as they went. Consequently, the noise from behind came to them clearly, chillingly. Bay put on an extra burst of speed.

Nicholas turned back, opened his *tanjian* eye in order to locate the source of the noise. That was when he heard Bay give a little cry. Immediately, he ran toward her.

Her mini-flash was on the floor of the tunnel, giving an eerie half-light to the scene. She lay stretched on the floor, a tapered cylinder beneath her legs.

'Don't come any closer!' she cried. 'Don't move! For the love of God, don't –'

There was a soft *thwop!* and an intense whitish-green light burned into his retinas. Heat like a raging sun blasted him.

'Ah, Buddha,' she moaned. 'Buddha, no.'

He thought at first that she had broken a leg, but she sprang back, almost colliding with him. She was staring with a mixture of horror and panic at a large patch on her left thigh that appeared to be burning.

Sensing Nicholas, she turned her head, thrusting the ka-bar into his hand.

'Quick!' She was breathless with fear. 'Cut it out!'

'What?'

'I stumbled over this unexploded artillery shell. It's filled with white phosphorus, what the Americans called Willy Peter. I've gotten it on me. If you don't cut it out, it'll eat right through my leg!'

He had heard the horror stories about phosphorus burns, air itself causing an incendiary explosion, and he knew she was right.

97

'Put your arms around my neck and hold on!'

He placed the edge of the blade obliquely against her burning skin, bore down hard on the hilt. Bay gasped, and tears rolled freely down her cheeks. She grabbed him, held on tight.

An eerie keening burst through her clenched teeth.

He sliced into her, using deft, efficient strokes to scoop out the phosphorus and the burning flesh. Bay's eyes rolled back in her head and she collapsed against him. All in all, he thought that was the best thing for her now. He used the blade tip to flick the gobbet of blackened flesh into the pyre of the leaking Willy Peter. The heat was almost unbearable.

He wished they were back by the Dien Bien Phu kitchen so he could cauterize the wound. Using strips of his shirt, he fashioned a tourniquet, then wrapped the raw wound as best he could.

Where had she been headed? Without Bay to help him he was lost within this labyrinth of the dead. He could sit here with her and wait for the soldiers to find them and execute them, or he could retrace the path they had taken from the moment they had entered the tunnels from beneath the river.

It took him almost two hours to make it back to the point where the skeleton of the Alsatian lay just in front of the shining booby-trap wire. For most of that time he had carried Bay across his shoulder, aware that she was going into shock even before her flesh became chill and her muscles contracted spasmodically. He wished he could do something immediate for her, but he was helping her the only way he could, by getting her out of there as quickly as possible.

Once, when they got near the area of the Dien Bien Phu kitchen, he had considered wrapping her in its warmth, but his *tanjian* eye, questing through the darkness, encountered the presence of more soldiers, so he carefully skirted the area, acutely aware of the need for both speed and caution.

He set her down near the Alsatian, as close to the wire as he dared. There was almost no color in her face, and she had not regained consciousness. Extending his psyche, he probed inside her. Her loss of blood had been considerable, the shock of the impromptu surgery was massive, and he knew that sepsis would set in unless the wound was thoroughly cleansed and she got significant doses of a powerful antibiotic within twenty-four hours. By concentration, he was able to reduce the level of pathogenic microorganisms reproducing at the wound site, but he could not heal her.

He turned toward the wire, went carefully over it. Then he reached back, lifted her up and across. He froze. Out of the corner of his eye he could see her elbow resting against the outcropped pin of the frag grenade buried in the wall. Very slowly, he moved her back away from him. Her elbow came off the pin.

Nothing happened.

Repositioning her, he lifted her across the wire and set her down beside him.

He lowered himself through the trap door, feeling the chill river water come up to the level of his waist. Then he maneuvered her through. In her state, he did not know how long she could survive underwater. He knew he had to be very fast; there was no margin for error. He hadn't gotten this far just to drown her during the last stage of their escape.

In the water he ceded control to his *tanjian* eye, trusting it to guide him unerringly through the two trap doors and out into the river itself. Bay was like a dead weight, dragging him down, entangling him in line and wire, fragments of rotten wood and decades of silt raised up from the riverbed by the powerful kick of his legs.

But at last he could feel the strong pull of the current

and knew he was in the open river. He got her head above water, striking out for the far riverbank. She was racked by a paroxysm of coughing as soon as he dragged her up the slope out of the water, and he was gratified to see no blood in what she spit up. Perhaps the cold had revived her. She began to moan as the pain cut through the temporary wall her endorphins had built. Opening his *tanjian* eye, Nicholas stimulated the area that produced these natural pain-suppressors.

'My God,' she whispered in a voice drugged by pain and shock, 'what's happened to me?'

'White phosphorus. I got it all out of you.'

She closed her eyes, turned her head away from him, her chest heaving still from her exertions.

While they had been buried alive in the tunnels of Cu Chi, dawn had come. The sky was pink and pale green. Birds called and an entire new set of insects droned and chittered in the underbrush. On the morning breeze came the strong scent of eucalyptus from the groves planted after the American defoliation of the area during the war.

He touched her on the shoulder. 'I know you're exhausted, but there's no time to rest. I've got to get you to a doctor.'

'No need to bother yourself,' a deep voice said from above them on the riverbank. 'I'm in charge of you both now.'

Nicholas looked up to see the figure standing over him, a pistol in his right hand. At the moment it was pointed at the ground beside him. Though there were perhaps a dozen soldiers around him this man was dressed in the uniform of the Saigon police. He was a slender Vietnamese, not very imposing if one was in the habit of judging people by their size. But he had a wily face and yellow eyes and teeth. Shindo had summed him up quite correctly: a back-alley predator.

Chief Inspector Hang Van Kiet.

'Stand up, both of you!' Van Kiet commanded.

'I'm a citizen of — '

'I said stand up!' The pistol was now leveled at him.

Nicholas rose, dragging Bay with him. She moaned, shivering, and he said, 'For God's sake, she's badly hurt. I had to cut burning phosphorus out of her leg. If you don't get her to a hospital soon, she'll die.'

'Is that so?' Van Kiet took a step down the bank, stared into Bay's white, pinched face. He touched the muzzle of the pistol to the bloody bandage wrapped around her wound and she cried out, nearly fainting. Then a curious smile wreathed his mouth, and his eyes snapped to Nicholas. 'Whether you live or die will depend on me now, is that clear?'

Nicholas said nothing, but then he didn't think Van Kiet had wanted an answer.

'You and this woman have been found in a proscribed area. What were you doing in the tunnels?'

'Sightseeing.'

Nicholas's *tanjian* eye felt the pistol coming up an instant before it did, but there was nothing at all in Van Kiet's mind as he squeezed the trigger.

The explosion rang out, echoing across the riverbank as Bay was blown out of Nicholas's arms, blood spurting from her chest.

My God, he's actually shot her!

Nicholas scrambled after her, knelt beside her where she lay, half in the water. As he turned her gently over, he heard Van Kiet's steely voice.

'D'you think this is a joke, man? You're guilty of espionage against the sovereign Republic of Vietnam and I know it.'

She was still breathing, but blood was bubbling everywhere. Van Kiet hadn't shot randomly; he'd meant to kill her.

'*Chu* Goto –'

It was a whisper, barely louder than the wind among the reeds of the river.

'I must –'

He bent over, putting his ear close to her lips. He could feel the struggle going on inside her: her heart laboring, her lungs filling up with fluid. He had brought her to this end, and he was horrified.

'– tell you –'

'Get him away from her!' Van Kiet ordered from behind Nicholas.

'Must know –'

The soldiers were coming, advancing down the muddy bank.

'– know about the Floating City –'

Gun muzzles at his back.

'Get up, man!' Van Kiet shouted.

'Yes, tunnels are . . . halfway point between Saigon and the Floating City.'

Van Kiet pulled him roughly away from the dying Bay. His ferret's face was dark with blood and rage. 'Fucker, murder and espionage are capital offenses. You're dead meat!'

THREE

Connecticut/New York City/Saigon

'Uncle Lew!'

The tall, lithe teenager flung herself into his arms.

'I didn't think I'd ever see you again,' Francine said, squeezing him as tightly as she could.

'I promised I'd come back, didn't I?'

Francie nodded, putting her head against his chest.

Lew Croaker's current assignment was so painful that he preferred not to think about it. Consequently, it was all he thought about. He was not by nature a perverse person, but everything had changed for him when he had met and fallen in love with Margarite Goldoni DeCamillo. Croaker had been investigating the murder of Margarite's brother, Dominic Goldoni, the most powerful and influential Mafia don in the eastern half of the United States, when, much to his surprise and consternation, he had fallen in love with Margarite. Francine was her daughter.

Francine drew him into the country-style living room. She was staying with a friend of Margarite's for a while. Francie had been bulimic, ill with the realization that her parents despised one another, that her father, Tony DeCamillo, had systematically abused her mother. Last year, Croaker had helped Francie face her bulimia and, so, had forged a close bond with her. Another reason for Tony D. to hate him.

'It's way cool to see you!' Francie said, holding his hand. 'And way cool you're here today because —'

At that moment, the front door opened and Margarite walked in. She stopped in her tracks when she saw him. The surprise on her face was quickly supplanted by a look of intense joy, which was just as quickly stifled.

'Lew,' she said in her low, creamy voice. 'What a surprise.'

That was an understatement worthy of note. The last time they had seen one another was just before New Year's Day, at Narita airport in Tokyo. Croaker had been seeing her off as she flew back to the States.

I want you to know something, she had said. *If I never see you again, I'll shrivel up and die.*

But you're going now, he had replied, his heart breaking. *Back to Tony D.* He had seen tears standing in her amber eyes. *It would help if you gave me the procedure for contacting the Nishiki network.*

That was Dom's only legacy, the perpetuation of all his power. I won't jeopardize it – even for you.

Now, standing in the doorway in jeans, cowboy boots and a stylish leather jacket, she seemed far more beautiful than he remembered her. Her face, with its prominent nose, wide lips and unusual amber eyes, filled him with the kind of joy so unexpected it was akin to pain.

'Mom. Hi.'

'Hi, sugar.' Margarite grinned at her daughter. 'How you doing?'

'Super!' She clung to Croaker with a childlike joy.

Croaker stood with his hands on Francie's shoulders, reluctant to let go of her. Why? Was she a shield for his intimate feelings or the connective tissue that bound him to Margarite?

Looking from one adult to another, Francie said, 'I'm gonna get some lunch. Anyone else get hungry, the kitchen's that way.' She gestured to a hallway to the left before disappearing down it.

Margarite came into the living room, threw down

her purse and car keys on one of the facing sofas.

'I didn't know you were back from Japan. How long –'

'Couple of months.'

'I see.' Her head went down. 'And in all this time not even a phone call.'

'Margarite –' He took a step toward her, then froze, the knowledge of what he was doing flooding through him. Since she had returned from Tokyo, he had had her under surveillance. Nicholas had given him the name of an operative whom the company used from time to time in New York to keep the corporate spies at bay. As soon as Croaker had returned to New York several weeks ago, he had taken up much of the surveillance himself. What he was looking for was anything out of the ordinary in Margarite's routine. He knew she must make periodic contact with a member of the Nishiki network that Okami had set up to provide Dominic Goldoni with dirt on prominent Washington figures. And she would go about it via the same procedure her brother had before her. The mechanisms had been in place for some time; they wouldn't be changed now.

He loved her and he was spying on her while trying to keep out of Tony D.'s way. Again, he asked himself the basic question: how could he be in love with someone on the opposite side of the law? But then he supposed she must ask herself the same question.

'How is Tony D. treating you?'

'Oh, Lew, don't let's spoil this moment by talking about him.'

Instantly, he was on guard. 'Is he hurting you?'

'No,' she said at once. 'Thank God that's over.' She attempted a smile. 'I think he's trying to turn over a new leaf. He wants Francie back home; he wants our marriage to be the way it once was.'

Croaker felt as if an iceberg were moving through him. 'And you believe him?'

Now her smile was genuine, warm. 'I haven't believed anything he's said for years.'

He took another step toward her, and it was as if he were magnetized to the pole star. One foot in front of the other and he just kept coming until he had wrapped her in his arms and his mouth came down over hers. Her lips opened and he heard her sigh, felt the tension melt out of her.

'Oh, God,' she whispered, 'I thought . . .' She closed her eyes. 'I don't want to say what I thought.'

'I'll never stop loving you.' His hand stroked her hair. 'No matter what happens.'

She was weeping silently. 'I never believed in hell, but that's where I feel I am now. I know you want me to tell you about Nishiki, but it's the one thing I can't give you. Is there some way you'll find to make me do it? I don't know, but I feel sure you'll try. I don't want you as an adversary; it's killing me. I feel as if I'm being torn in half.'

They clung wordlessly to one another. What could he reply? Anything he would say would be a lie, so he chose silence.

Both of them longed to be alone, but it was impossible – Margarite had only an hour to spare and Croaker needed to check the logs and go over her movements for the last twenty-four hours – and, in any event, there was Francie to think of. Instead, they went into the kitchen and had lunch together, all of them pretending there was no subtext, nothing odd, no hidden agenda, and in that way the real world was, for the moment, kept at bay.

The next morning, he was parked on the east side of Park Avenue at Forty-seventh Street, and yesterday's encounter felt like a dream. Movement at the corner of his eye brought him to full attention. Two cars behind him, a woman had stepped into the street to hail a cab. She was a handsome woman in her mid-forties, affluent, as attested to by her suede and fox-fur coat and black patent-leather Chanel handbag. As she raised her hand, a rail-thin black man on a bicycle lowered his helmeted head and, his thighs pumping, put on a sudden burst of speed. He swerved to his right, cutting off a car, whose horn blared angrily. At the point he was abreast of the woman, his hand hooked out, snatching the Chanel bag off her shoulder. She spun around, slamming her hip into the bumper of a parked car, went down on one knee.

The cyclist was just hitting his stride when Croaker flung his door open right into the bicycle's front fender. The cyclist went flying and Croaker was out of the car, sprinting along the tarmac. He kicked aside the bike, bent down to reach for the bag. The cyclist rolled over, grabbed the bag, and, in the same motion, slashed upward with a switchblade.

'Motherfucker, you want this back, you betta be ready to die for it.'

Croaker struck out with his left hand, luminous blue and matte black. The blade of the knife struck two fingers and sparks flew, metal on metal, and the cyclist's eyes opened wide.

'Oh, mama!'

Croaker curled his titanium and polycarbonate fingers inward, trapping the blade. With a quick twist of his wrist, he flung the knife from the cyclist's grip. Then he placed his hand in front of the man's strained face, slowly extruded the wicked-looking stainless-steel nails. He placed the tips against the cyclist's shirt, scored five rents in the fabric.

'Hand me the bag,' he rasped, 'or I'll put these right through you.'

'Okay, okay,' the cyclist said, throwing the bag at Croaker. He slithered up, never taking his eyes from Croaker's hand. 'What the fuck *is* that thing, anyway?'

'If you've got to ask, you don't want to know.'

The cyclist went warily to pick up his bicycle, but Croaker put a heavy foot on the rear wheel. 'This is mine now.'

'Hey, chill out, I'll lose my job without it. This is my livelihood, man.'

'You should have thought of that before you snatched this.'

Croaker watched the man slink off, then walked back to where the woman was staring at a run in her Fogal stocking. 'I believe you lost this, ma'am.'

'You should have beat the shit out of that animal,' the woman said, taking her Chanel bag. Her gray eyes were already searching for a taxi. 'Dammit, now I'm late for my meeting at Sotheby's.'

'You're welcome, I'm sure,' Croaker said, getting back into his car. He left the bicycle where it lay in the street.

Jesus, he thought. *What's become of this city?* It was here that he and Nicholas Linnear had met many years ago. He reached for the paper cup of cold coffee on the dashboard, regarding his left hand as he did so. In the course of their subsequent work together Croaker had lost his left hand. In its place, a team of clever Japanese surgeons had attached this biomechanical substitute. He still marveled at it. The fingers were realistically articulated like flesh-and-blood digits. Powered by a pair of special lithium batteries, the hand was sheathed in matte black polycarbonate, stainless steel, and blued titanium. Inside were the bones, muscles and tendons of boron and titanium. It was an altogether impressive construct, part implement, part weapon. It had taken him months to get used to it, a year to master the intricacies of its multiple uses, but now it seemed to him an integral part of his body.

Croaker was a big beefy man. In recent years, he had let his muscle run to fat, much like an out-of-work football player, but Nicholas had put him on a strict regimen of exercise and healthy food, and his softness was slowly burning off, leaving hard muscle in its wake. Croaker had always been enormously strong. The addition of his biomechanical hand had only made him more so. He had the weather-beaten face of a cowboy.

Some years before, he had prematurely retired from the NYPD to Marco Island in Florida where for the past several years he had been running a charter fishing boat service. Vegetating, in other words. Alix, the woman he had lived with down there, had claimed he looked like Robert Mitchum, an opinion he found amusing.

He glanced at his watch. Three minutes to ten. He saw Margarite a moment later in a tweed suit the color of ox blood as she got out of the taxi down the block. Her beautiful face was tense as she headed toward her weekly 10 a.m. meeting at her accountant's office. She had the look of a professional gambler, the successful integration of intuition and logic that was the key to beating house odds, no matter which house.

It was torture seeing her this way and not being with her, but what other choice did he have? At least, if he kept his distance he could maintain the thin fiction that this was just another job tailing a suspect, and thus keep his sanity.

Croaker unfurled a newspaper in front of his face like a wall. His relationship with Margarite was liminal. His sense of her was constantly changing, the layers of her personality and her role in his life peeling away to reveal others beneath. She was not only Dominic Goldoni's sister, but his successor. Through her husband, Tony D., she now ran the Goldoni empire as efficiently as Dominic had. But what had been Dominic's ultimate purpose? Through the course of his investigation Croaker had come to understand that Dominic Goldoni had been a good deal more than a cold-blooded gangster. He had had more lofty goals in mind than merely raking off his percentage from almost every major business sector in the east. His ties to the entrenched Washington establishment were exceedingly strong.

He and Mikio Okami had formed a clandestine alliance. But to what purpose? Neither Nicholas nor Croaker had yet found out. First, they had to find Okami. Periodically, the Kaisho had funneled useful information to Dominic Goldoni. Though Dominic was dead, the conduit was still open and Margarite was using it.

Nicholas and Croaker had together decided that this would be Croaker's dread assignment: to shadow the woman he loved in order to trace the information conduit back to Okami. As he watched her cross the wide, plaza-like sidewalk, Croaker knew he was at risk from a double-edged sword. Not only did he need to keep his work secret from Margarite, but he also had to be on guard lest Okami's enemies get wind of what he was doing and piggyback on his investigation, using him as a stalking horse to get to Okami.

Through large glass panels, he watched Margarite step into the elevator that would take her up to the twenty-eighth floor. That she could stay in the same house as Tony D. was a measure of how seriously she took her responsibility to her late brother, Dominic Goldoni. Tony had a history of abusing her; their intimate relationship was nil and, as a result, their daughter, Francine, was chronically depressed and bulimic. Still, it seemed strange to Croaker, when he was with Margarite, to know that she was married, bound to a man who was, in effect, her mask for the dark world she chose to inhabit. The words on the printed page were not registering, and he closed his eyes. But he could not stop his thoughts. The irony of his being in love with a woman on the other side of the law was devastating in its simplicity.

'Hey, buddy, this is a no-standing zone.'

Without looking around Croaker dug out the federal badge given to him by his former boss, the late and unlamented William Justice Lillehammer, the man who had put him in charge of the investigation into Dominic Goldoni's murder. He held it up at the window so the traffic cop would go away.

'Turn off your engine and get out of the vehicle, please.'

Croaker put down the paper. Instead of one of Manhattan's brownies, he saw a uniformed policeman, a young man with an unmanageable stubble and muddy brown eyes.

'You see this shield, officer? I'm on assignment, not in your jurisdiction. Give it a rest.'

Keeping his eyes on Croaker, the cop reached in, unlocked the door, opened it. 'Please do as I say.'

'Are you nuts? I'm a fed.'

'Now.'

Croaker found himself looking at the cop's right hand as it wrapped around the wood grips of his handgun. Where was this guy when the rich bitch was having her handbag snatched? He put the badge away, got out of the car. He could see the blue-and-white squad car parked just behind him, its revolving lights off. There was a uniformed cop behind the driver's seat, who seemed to be staring straight ahead, at nothing.

'Come with me, please,' the young cop said amiably but firmly.

Croaker shrugged, got into the back of the squad car

as blue-jaw indicated. The cop got in beside him and they pulled out into traffic. They did not use their lights or their siren.

Croaker sat back and said nothing. He was too much a veteran to ask questions he knew would not be answered. He'd be better off concentrating on these two and where he was being taken.

The driver was older, a heavy-set man with a mole on the side of his nose, and a wooden toothpick rolling back and forth between his liverish lips. He seemed uncomfortable, as if his uniform were a bad fit.

They went west, then downtown to the entrance of the Lincoln Tunnel. *New Jersey*, Croaker thought.

'Don't even think about it,' blue-jaw said. His gun was pointed at Croaker's rib cage.

Sure, Croaker thought. *What New York cops would be taking me across the river to Jersey?* No wonder the driver was uncomfortable in his uniform. This was probably the first time he'd had one on. Who were these guys?

They seemed to be a long time underwater. When they emerged, it was to a long sweep of fuel-stained concrete, the front porch of New Jersey.

The air had changed. It was sweaty, soot-laden, as if the entire area were one vast mill. Cars, concrete, steel and high-tension wires made an unappetizing mosaic, an environment devoid of color or life.

They turned off right away, heading toward Hoboken. But they never actually made it there. The blue-and-white pulled in past a rusting gas station that must have been a relic of the forties. An old VW Beetle, stripped and burned out, hunkered on the blackened concrete apron where underground gas tanks hadn't been filled in decades. A black cat scrounged indifferently through piles of litter.

Behind the deserted station was a junkyard full of rusted cars of no conceivable use to anyone. It was surrounded by a high chain-link fence topped with barbed wire. It had the appearance of a POW camp. Rubble was everywhere as if, at some time in the not too distant past, this had been a war zone. A couple of bundled-up homeless people trundled dispiritedly past, their backs bent as they pushed shopping carts full of brown bags, string, and old, soiled clothes. They crossed the street in a racket as the carts collided. A brief argument ensued, then one of them made a brief attempt to capture the cat, but it was too nimble, streaking away at the first clumsy lunge.

'Nice neighborhood,' Croaker said. 'You boys come here often?'

'Shut up!' blue-jaw said, jabbing him with the muzzle of the pistol.

'Careful, sonny,' Croaker said. 'You might get careless and shoot yourself.'

'I told you –'

'Clam up!' the driver snapped. 'He's here.'

Croaker turned in time to see a midnight-blue Lincoln Mark VIII gliding around a corner behind them.

The driver put the blue-and-white into gear and they went through open gates in the chain-link fence into the junkyard. The Lincoln followed them, its huge engine purring contentedly.

They jounced over a bed of broken-up brick and concrete, then stopped. The driver turned off the engine, got out without a word.

'Move!' blue-jaw said, and Croaker slid out of the squad car. He could see the driver with his back to them, taking a leak against the bole of an old scabrous plane tree that had somehow survived the industrial abuse and pollution.

The Lincoln slid to a halt several feet away. Its windows were tinted that odd dark color one saw all the time in Florida to keep out the sun and the heat.

A man emerged from behind the wheel, and Croaker let out a little breath. It was Tony DeCamillo, Margarite's husband. Tony D. came walking across the rubble. He was dressed in the suitably subdued chalk-stripe suit of the upscale show biz attorney he was. Only his silk shirt with his initials embroidered on one point of his collar betrayed his ambition. He would never be the criminal genius Dominic Goldoni had been. In fact, Croaker mused, now he would not be much of anything, except a figurehead, robed in the trappings of Dominic's vast power.

'Beat it,' Tony D. said to the phony cop contingent that had brought Croaker to him.

'But, Tony,' blue-jaw protested, 'this jamoke's dangerous.'

'Sure he is,' Tony said. 'But I have Sal in the car.'

The blue-and-white took off, backing out of the junkyard.

'This place one of your premier holdings, Tony?'

Croaker regretted the flip remark the moment he'd said it, but the truth was he hated this man, not only for the stink of corruption that followed him around, but because he was a violent man with his family. Croaker thought of the beatings Margarite had taken from Tony D. and his heart began to pound so painfully in his chest he had to take slow, deep breaths through his mouth.

DeCamillo was a good-looking Mediterranean. He was olive-skinned and his brown eyes were hooded, liquid, lascivious. He came up very close to Croaker and shot his cuffs.

'You're the man,' he said in a rumbly, breathy voice, 'who's been fucking the shit outta my wife.'

Nicely put, Croaker thought. To Tony DeCamillo, he said, 'I'm the man who doesn't lift a hand to her.'

Standoff.

There was nothing intellectual or even rational about their mutual hatred. They were like two bulls, blood-maddened and in heat, each determined to own the high ground, the prize female, and the herd.

'She thinks you're swell,' Tony D. said flatly. 'Nevertheless, I'm gonna blow your brains into this brick.'

'Don't you have any respect for her at all?' It was a funny line, but Tony chose to ignore it. Maybe he wasn't in the mood.

He lifted one hand, and the passenger door to the Lincoln opened. Out stepped Sal, no doubt Tony's body-guard. He handled a high-powered rifle the way an expert would, swinging it up, resting it on the top of the car, aiming carefully. Croaker could see that Tony had choreographed this with precision. Croaker was within range of a guaranteed hit, and Tony was not in the line of fire, would not even have to move unless he didn't want a spray of Croaker's blood all over his Sulka tie. No matter. With his attention to detail, he had probably brought a couple of replacements in the Lincoln.

Sal settled his cheek against the stock of the gun; his eye was in the sight.

'You ready to die, you sonuvabitch?' Tony D.'s voice was thick with emotion.

'Who is?' Croaker was thinking not about life and death, but about how Tony DeCamillo needed to learn the difference between thought and emotion. Perhaps this was why he couldn't help beating his wife.

Margarite. He thought of her and knew he did not want to die, most especially not at the hands of this jerk. But it was a shut-ended situation. He was in no position to deal and, even if he were, he suspected that Tony D. was in no mood to listen. He was angry for allowing himself to get into this position. Marco Island had blunted his instincts. Too much booze, carousing with customers, lolling in the heat. You went loopy, but long before that you lost your edge. This is what had happened to him, and now he was going to pay the ultimate price for his sin. How many good cops had he seen go down, the victim of one fatal mistake, one lapse? Now it was his turn.

Jesus.

He remembered Alix, sun-splashed in a Marco Island sunset, an impossibly beautiful woman, a model who had so improbably fallen in love with him. He remembered Margarite, so complex, strong-willed, incandescent, saddled with her brother's love and his legacy, an empire built on blood, influence, and vigorish. He remembered Nicholas, in Tokyo, their friendship bonded in battle, a mutual trust that stemmed from saving one another's life. He remembered his father, gunned down in a back alley of Hell's Kitchen, his policeman's uniform stained with blood. Croaker's mother had refused to have him buried in that uniform, had, in fact, thrown it out. But Croaker had retrieved it from the garbage, had reverently folded it into a plastic bag. He had taken it out, stiff and black with his father's dried blood, on the day he had made detective.

As if it were all happening in slow motion, Croaker saw Tony D. nod his head. He could almost feel Sal's forefinger tightening on the trigger, the marksman's eye staring at him through the magnifying lens of the scope.

The sound of a shot exploded, but no bullet slammed into Croaker. His heart hammered in his chest. He heard a little groan, and he and Tony D. turned at the same time. Sal was slumped on the rubble of brick and concrete, the rifle an arm's length away.

'What the fuck –'

'Don't try thinking it through, Tony,' a commanding voice said. 'It'll be too much for you.'

Croaker saw a figure striding across the junkyard. He

116

was somewhat older than Tony, nevertheless his shock of unruly, curling hair and his wide grin gave him something of the aspect of an adolescent. He bounded across the uneven ground on long, powerful legs.

Tony's jaw dropped open. 'Mary, Mother of God. Bad Clams.'

'In person,' Caesare Leonforte said, his jaunty grin in place.

'You got a fuckin' nerve stepping into my territory without permission.'

Leonforte peered curiously at Tony as if he were an exotic exhibit in a zoo. 'You think so? Yeah, I know, I had a deal with Dominic, rest his soul, that I'd stay on the West Coast and he'd stay in the east.' He shrugged. 'But you know how it is, counselor, human nature being what it is, Dom started expanding westward and I, well, I moved east.'

'You fucking *gavone*!' Tony screamed, red-faced. 'You come here, kill my bodyguard, you're looking for an all-out war!'

'Calm yourself, counselor,' Leonforte said. 'I'm only looking out for my interests. Just because you allow your balls to run your life doesn't mean I have to go along with your mistakes.'

He had the eyes of a killer. A film of red madness danced close to the surface of his irises. Croaker had seen it many times during his stint on the street. But there was a difference here; Leonforte had about him an air of calm and calculation that was at odds with the berserk look in his eyes. It was, Croaker thought, as if he were two men inhabiting the same body.

'What the hell are you talking about?'

'When are you going to wake up, counselor? You're a fucking amateur trying to make it in a game you can't even begin to comprehend.'

'I don't have to listen to this garbage. I have private

business with this bastard. What the fuck d'you want with him?'

'Let's not overtax that brain of yours. I tell you what, counselor, why don't you take the ride back across the river in your new Lincoln, which by the way I very much admire, and we'll discuss this another day.'

'What? You think you can waltz onto my turf and *order* me around?'

'Take it easy, counselor. You need either a dose of Halcion or a good blow job, preferably both.'

'You're a dead man, Bad Clams.' Tony D.'s voice was heavy with the kind of menace that impressed production executives at Paramount and MGM.

Caesare Leonforte, however, was unmoved. He clucked his tongue as two heavy-set men in overcoats appeared. From beneath their coats they lifted MAC-10 machine pistols.

'There's no need for an altercation, counselor. And to show my sincerity, I'll ignore the threat to my person. I don't want trouble –'

'Well, you've fucking got it, buddy.'

'– and neither do you.'

Tony looked from the MAC-10s to Croaker. 'I don't believe your luck.' Croaker's teeth grated. 'And neither should you.'

Reduced to parroting Caesare Leonforte, he retreated to the relative safety of the Lincoln. His face had drained of all blood now. He looked as if he were going to pass out. 'You'll wish you'd never set foot here, Bad Clams, that's my fucking promise to you.'

'Big man,' Leonforte said as Tony drove off. Then he turned to Croaker and laughed. 'Well, look at you. All ready for the wringer.' He shook his head. 'That boy was serious. He means to have your nuts in a sling.'

'Yours, too. That makes us, what, some kind of soul mates?'

Leonforte regarded Croaker for some time. 'My God, you're a cool customer.' He smirked. 'Or should I have one of the guys check to see whether you've wet yourself?'

'What, no babes around to do the dirty work?'

Caesare Leonforte threw his head back and laughed, but he sobered up quickly enough. 'Make a joke of it all you want, but you owe me your life, Mr Croaker. Now I want my quid pro quo.'

The vibrations filled Nicholas's frame with discordant music. He was in the back of Chief Inspector Van Kiet's military jeep. Blindfolded and bound tightly with metal flex, he made calculations based on the incoming sensory data. He heard Van Kiet shouting terse orders for vehicles to pull aside. He inhaled the scents of fresh eel, cut sugarcane, longan and rambutan, fruits with distinctive smells.

Even without opening his *tanjian* eye, he had deduced that he was being taken back to Saigon. Then he was not to be summarily executed, as Van Kiet had intimated. No doubt an interrogation was planned before they put him in front of a military firing squad. Forget about a lawyer or even a trial; he knew he was beyond such basic amenities of the civilized world.

He knew what needed to be done. Shindo was dead, and now, too, was Bay. At each step he was coming closer to the riddle of Vincent Tinh's murder. Now he knew the name of the theoretical-language cyberneticist who had put together the illegal Chi-Hive hybrid computer, a Russian national named Abramanov, who was in hiding somewhere northwest of Saigon. The Cu Chi tunnels were the halfway point.

He knew what needed to be done now. Shindo had been convinced that Chief Inspector Van Kiet knew more about Tinh's death than he was acknowledging. Nicholas knew he needed twenty minutes alone with Van Kiet to extract the information.

Twenty minutes.

He concentrated on the flex binding his wrists and ankles. He was half-lying across one of the backseats of the jeep. The flex was no problem. Though it had been wound tightly, Nicholas had expanded the muscles, tendons, and ligaments in his wrists when he was bound. Contracting them now gave him enough leeway to find the end of the flex with his fingertips and begin unwinding it.

He was careful about it, even though, with the jouncing of the jeep, he was certain no one would be able to tell what was happening even if one of them periodically glanced his way.

His hands were free within ten minutes. Then he began work on the flex around his ankles. When this dropped away, he moved his head back and forth against the seat back, as if being bounced by the terrible condition of the highway. The blindfold slowly rose until it slipped off.

And Nicholas found himself staring into Van Kiet's grinning face. The chief inspector, turned around in his front seat, was pointing a Russian-made pistol at him.

'No good,' he said. 'You see, I know who you are. Or, I should say, *what* you are. I know the things you are capable of, and believe me when I tell you I will not allow you to do any of them. I'd sooner put a bullet through your brain right here.' As Nicholas shifted, he said, 'Don't play brinkmanship with me. I mean everything I say.'

Opening his *tanjian* eye, Nicholas knew that in this, at least, Van Kiet was telling the truth. He relaxed, sat back in the jeep's rear seat. Even though he remained

120

unbound, he was now further from freedom than he had been when he had been dumped into the jeep at Cu Chi.

They remained in silence while the driver maneuvered through the cart-clogged outskirts of the city. Nicholas saw almost at once that Van Kiet had no intention of taking him to the police station. That was an ominous sign, and Nicholas began to speculate on whose orders Van Kiet was following. A man like him, in the thick of intrigue in Saigon and its environs, might conceivably be on the payroll of more than one major operator. If he was sufficiently enterprising and clever enough, Van Kiet could juggle these multiple responsibilities while keeping them separate. It certainly wouldn't do to let the Shan opium warlord who might be paying him off learn that he was also selling intelligence and protection to an international arms-trader in the area. Such a misstep could only lead to the kind of violent death that overtook Vincent Tinh.

Nicholas knew he had to concentrate on surviving in any way possible. Van Kiet appeared to be acting on someone else's orders, and in all likelihood someone who was in some way connected to Tinh's murder. Nicholas had set events in motion along this path. Tinh had been making money on, among other things, the illegal computer hybrid using the stolen Chi technology, a first-generation neural-net chip. Now Tinh was gone and so was the illegal computer, and Nicholas had established himself in Saigon with a second-generation neural-net chip. Surely, he had reasoned, this was the most potent bait for the people with whom Tinh had been in business.

Bay had given him one name, the Russian national Abramanov. But Abramanov was a tekkie, not a businessman. Besides, he would have no influence in Vietnam; Russians were universally reviled here. Who was behind Abramanov? Nicholas could not escape the suspicion that whoever it was, was the same person who had ordered Tinh's murder. Now, it seemed likely that Nicholas was being taken to that man or one of his group. If he could survive long enough.

At length, they pulled up in front of an anonymous building with only a number affixed to the crumbling stucco facade.

Something about the address seemed familiar. Bicycles and *cyclos* passed by as they climbed out of the jeep. Nicholas could appreciate the element of freedom these passersby had, for the first time separating that freedom from the extreme poverty that was ubiquitous. These people, poor and miserable as they were, possessed something invaluable he did not. When he had arrived in Saigon, he would have found it inconceivable to envy anyone here, but now he did, and he felt humbled by it.

Inside, the building appeared deserted. Then Nicholas turned and, peering back down the hallway, felt his memory engage. The address. This building was where Vincent Tinh had rented space to do his illegal business, according to Shindo. Now Nicholas felt another step closer to solving the riddle of Tinh's murder.

With the driver leading the way and Chief Inspector Van Kiet just behind Nicholas, they mounted a steep flight of metal stairs. But before they could reach the first landing, their way was blocked by a figure coming down from above.

'Chief Inspector,' a well-modulated voice said.

'You!' Van Kiet was as still as a statue.

'I'll take charge of this man now,' Seiko said.

'Impossible! Have you any idea what he's charged with?'

'I know everything.'

'Even so, I can't just –'

'This is me you're talking to, Van Kiet. You can and you will.'

Nicholas, listening to this extraordinary exchange, felt his heart skip a beat. This beautiful Japanese woman, Seiko Ito, had been his assistant. It had been she who had suggested he hire Vincent Tinh to be the director of Sato-Tomkin's new Saigon office. Apparently, she had also been involved in the smuggling of the Chi neural-net chip out of Tokyo to Tinh here in Saigon. In Nicholas's absence, and without solid proof, Tanzan Nangi, Nicholas's partner, had sent her here to take over the operations, hoping that he would give her enough rope to hang herself. If she was convinced that she was trusted by management in Tokyo, Nangi reasoned, she might become careless and give herself away.

Now she was here, in the building where Tinh had rented space, and was not only acquainted with the chief inspector of the Saigon police but was apparently also able to exert absolute influence over him.

Seiko took one step down the stairs, where Van Kiet's driver was blocking her path. She wore a black-and-turquoise raw-silk tank dress that left her shoulders and most of her legs bare. She was without earrings but wore a wide worked-silver cuff on her left wrist. She looked beautiful and fit and, at the moment, most determined. Her expression was one that Nicholas had never seen on her face before.

The driver looked inquiringly at his superior, who gave him a curt nod. The driver stepped aside.

'Come, Nicholas,' Seiko said, brushing against him as she went past. 'You must be exhausted after your long ordeal.'

He wanted to tell her no, that she should just leave, let him be now that he was so close to his goal. She thought she was saving him, but, ironically, all she was doing was setting back his investigation, perhaps fatally.

123

But how could he tell her all this with Van Kiet staring at them?

He had no choice. He went past the glum policeman, following Seiko along the corridor. Ahead of him, he could see the brilliant oblong of the open doorway to the street, where bicycles and *cyclos* whizzed past, free as the black birds in the sky.

'Tony thinks you murdered Dominic Goldoni.'

'But you know better, don't you, Mr Croaker.'

'Yes. As a matter of fact, I do.'

Caesare Leonforte poured them both refills from the bottle of Jordan cabernet he had ordered. 'There are many advantages to living in California, not the least of which is being so close to the best wine-producing country in America.' He sipped the ruby liquid. 'I was brought up on Italian wines and I still love them, but the wines of Napa and Sonoma . . .' He looked into the glass. 'A magnificent achievement! Like the Japanese, really.'

'The Japanese?'

Croaker and Caesare Leonforte were seated in the rear of a trendy TriBeCa restaurant on the west side of downtown Manhattan, just south of Canal Street. No homey checker-clothed table in Little Italy for Bad Clams. The long, narrow room had a vaguely industrial air with its factory windows, exposed pipes and waiters in black trousers and collarless shirts. The bareness of the cavernous room was mitigated only by a long, sleek cherrywood bar that rose from a polished wood-plank floor that looked old and scarred enough to have once been trod by Herman Melville. Presumably, the MAC-10-toting bodyguards were skulking somewhere out of sight on the pavement.

'In the fifties and sixties,' Leonforte said, 'the phrase "made in Japan" was synonymous with cheap junk.

124

California wines also, once upon a time. But now look!'
He lifted his glass. 'These wines are the envy of the
world. And the Japanese economy, well, despite their
present problems no one makes a joke about Toyotas,
only Cadillacs. I, myself, wouldn't be caught dead in a
Caddy.'

'You'll pardon my curiosity,' Croaker said, 'but how
is it you know about me?'

'It isn't all that difficult if you give it a moment's
thought.' Leonforte waved a hand in the air. 'I have
access to the same forms of electronic communication
as do most branches of what is euphemistically called
law enforcement in this country.' He sat back, feeling
expansive. And why not? He had just humiliated his
rival, run him off his own turf, and snatched someone
his intelligence had classified as a federal agent, saving
said agent's life in the process.

'Really? I would have thought most, if not all, of
those forms of electronic communication were impenetrable to unauthorized personnel.'

'Who says I'm unauthorized?' Leonforte laughed at
Croaker's stunned look. 'Well, okay, so I *am* unauthorized. Technically speaking. But not everybody thinks so
– or cares enough to keep me out. These government
people are overworked –'

'And highly underpaid.'

Leonforte grinned. 'That's it precisely, Mr Croaker.
Underpayment is the bane of the bureaucrat's existence.
To understand that is to understand everything about
these people.' He spoke about 'these people' as if they
were a different and inferior form of life. 'They move
the country along in its business, and gaining their trust
or – often more accurately – their interest is one of my
prime concerns.'

'Greasing the wheels.' Croaker got some bread and
olive oil into his mouth. All the wine was souring his

empty stomach. It wasn't every day you came back from the dead, especially in the company of one of the devil's disciples.

Leonforte raised a hand, indicating to the waiter that he wanted another bottle. 'It's a fact. Every car can use a lube job now and then, especially the ones that live on low-octane fuel.'

Up close, Croaker could see that Leonforte had a thin scar across one half of his throat. He made no effort to conceal it; on the contrary, a man like him would be proud of such a mark of what must have been youthful bravado.

'Okay, you know who I am. So what?'

Leonforte waited for the waiter to uncork the bottle and pour a sample of the Jordan into a fresh glass. He waved the waiter away without taking a drink. 'So here's what, Mr Croaker. What on earth are you doing tailing Margarite Goldoni DeCamillo?'

'You seriously expect me to tell you?'

Now Leonforte took the time to sample the wine. He made a great show of it, then poured for them both. 'I'll tell you something that may shock you. We have someone in common. Dominic Goldoni. We're both obsessed by him.'

Croaker said nothing, but despite the bread, the cabernet was doing nasty things to his insides.

'Maybe you think I'm full of shit, but if so, you better give the subject another think. Let me tell you something about myself. My father, Johnny, God rest his soul, was a man from the old school. What do I mean by that? He was heroic, bigger than life. He was interested in the elemental things in life: money, influence, respect. He also fucked a lot. He took me to a brothel when I was twelve. It was tradition. He watched while me and the whore got it on. Maybe he wanted to instruct me, maybe he just got off on it, who the

126

fuck knows? But from that moment on he considered me a man. Inside of six months he had put a gun in my hand and was training me to shoot, load, break it down even in the dark, very military in some ways, my father.

'Anyway, it was all fucking preparation. For what? Making my bones. "You ain't a man if you don't make your bones," the old man used to say. "And if you ain't a man, you're nothing." He had a fucking point, I'll tell you.' Leonforte sipped his wine, savoring it as fully as the tale he was spinning.

'So it was my father who told me to kill. Some wise-guy had gotten out of line, passed comments about my father in public. So he was to be killed in public – in the restaurant that was his favorite place, where he felt most secure. "I'll make a statement," the old man said, "to this man's friends and to everyone else. They'll get the point."

'I was just thirteen then, you understand, but my childhood was already a thing of the past. It's what my father wanted; it's what I wanted.' Leonforte looked at Croaker for a moment. 'I know you've killed men in your time, but I expect you found it difficult. I didn't. It was like I was a messenger of God, like angels sang on my shoulder. *Bam! Wham!* Blood and brains and clam sauce all over the fucking place; people screaming, the fucking guy's friends open-mouthed or vomiting outright. Christ, the sense of power was like nothing else in the world. And you know something, I wanted to whack them all, everyone at that table, like they were infected because of their association with him. But I controlled myself, dropped the gun and walked out through the madhouse.'

Leonforte, flushed with the residue of absolute power recalled, hunched over the table. 'Now here's the truth of the current situation: Dominic was a fucking genius.

I hated his guts, but I'd be a moron if I didn't admit the fact, at least in private. He was clever enough to keep me at bay even though I had more money, more people and more resources than he did. He thwarted me every time I tried to go beyond a certain geographical point. I never heard from him directly; there was never even a hint of a confrontation. But in one state a property deal fell through due to a convenient change in local regulations, in another the feds raided a company I was planning to buy, in still another a corporation I spent millions to take over had its assets mysteriously drained days before the signing. Over and over again. I know Dominic was responsible. Now how the fuck did he do that? Inquiring minds want to know, Mr Croaker, and my mind is exceedingly inquiring.'

'Fascinating. But what does all this have to do with me?'

Leonforte put his glass down with some force. 'You want to play hardball, okay, you got it.' That unsettling light in his eyes took on a bestial quality. 'He got to you, didn't he? I mean Dominic. Sure. He had that effect on everyone. You, my friend, tracked down Dominic's murderer and, so I understand, had a hand in whacking him. You also had a hand where it maybe didn't belong, mainly in Margarite DeCamillo's panties, and now you're hooked but good into the family.' He held up a hand in what was rapidly becoming a signature gesture. 'Not that I care; in fact, on one level it's pretty damn funny. Guys will be guys, right? Hell, it's another humiliation for him. Man like that must've come out of his mother's ass, you follow me?'

He pointed his finger at Croaker. 'But you do that, being who you are and all, it gives us a bad name. It's an *infamia*, like you insult us to our face, so at the moment I'm a little pissed off at you.'

You and Tony D. That makes two enemies today, Croaker thought. *Some days it just doesn't pay to wake up.*

'On the other hand, I have a weird feeling about Margarite myself. I mean, her brother gets whacked and he leaves the business to a knucklehead like Tony D.? Just because he married into the family? It doesn't add up. Dominic was too damn smart to make that classic mistake. So what's the story?' He held up the hand. 'So maybe you don't know, but I'm willing to bet my chadrool that Margarite does. You know I'm on the fucking right path because you've had the same notion. Why else are you tailing her and not Tony?

'Margarite was the only one close to Dominic in the years before his death, and she's one smart cookie, even though she's handicapped.'

'Handicapped?'

'She's a woman, schmuck. What would *you* call it?'

Croaker looked away. 'I want something to eat.' The two separate people inside Caesare Leonforte were driving him crazy.

Leonforte, smirking uncontrollably, signaled the waiter. 'Sure. Why not? That's why we came here, right?'

He ordered penne with vodka and a green salad. Croaker, whose mood had turned from sour to bitter, opted for the steak frites. Leonforte added another salad for Croaker.

When they were alone again, Leonforte lifted his glass, pointing it in the direction of a young couple who were being shown to a nearby table.

'Look at this putz, staring into her eyes. He looks like a heap of limp linguine. I tell you what, I'd sure like to be across the negotiating table from him this afternoon. He'll get back to the office, he won't know whether to say yes or no to anything.'

Leonforte broke off a crust of bread, dipped it into

the cabernet, stared at the ruby stain. 'Ever since the dawn of time women have had an evil effect on men.'

'Is that your opinion or a statement of scientific fact?'

Leonforte laughed briefly. 'You, my friend, should not be such a skeptic.' He popped the wine-soaked bread into his mouth, chewed reflectively. 'Take you and Margarite, for instance. A liaison – a mere dalliance – would not, objectively speaking, be for the worse. But you've developed an *attachment*. Now, when you should be clear-headed, your judgment has been impaired. You want to protect her, to be her savior.'

'You know nothing about it.'

The salads came, and Leonforte lit into his with the gusto of a man with a freed id. Croaker took one bite of his and his stomach closed up. He put down his fork.

'Fact is, I know *everything* about it,' Leonforte said between mouthfuls of mâche. 'Because I know what goes on between men and women. Men crave power and women crave men who are powerful, that's the nature of the human condition. End of story.'

He finished off his salad, then used a chunk of bread to wipe up the excess oil and vinegar. He pointed. 'You gonna eat that?'

'Help yourself.'

He did, finishing off Croaker's salad in record time. Then, with a heartfelt sigh, he pushed the plate away. The waiter appeared and cleared the table, setting out silverware for their next course.

Leonforte took some wine. 'Look, I can get over the fact that you're banging Tony D.'s wife because, God help you, I can see you got a real good hard-on for her. But this is a weakness, Mr Croaker, and now you see why I say that women exert an evil influence over men. You owe me big time and, unlike Tony the weeny ding-aling, I am no man to trifle with. You got the inside track with Margarite, and I'm convinced she has in her possession something I want very much.'

Croaker tried to still the heavy beating of his heart. 'And what might that be?'

'Dominic's list. The item that allowed him to intimidate almost everyone in the city, state and federal governments. Tony D. sure as shit doesn't have it, so that leaves Margarite. God only knows why she was the only person Dom trusted; no matter how smart she is she's only a skirt, no one will pay her any respect.'

The entrées came, and Leonforte started on his penne almost before the waiter had set the large bowl in front of him.

'Here's the way it is, Mr Croaker. You're gonna continue shadowing Margarite. You're gonna find out what she knows, Dom's secret, and then you're gonna give it all to me. Because you work for me now.'

'What if I say no.'

Leonforte looked up, and that red light of madness danced brightly in his eyes, and an awful grin burst across his face. 'Then, Mr Croaker, I put a bullet through Margarite Goldoni DeCamillo's brain.'

FOUR

Tokyo/Saigon/Washington

The girl with the almond-colored skin turned her dark eyes in Akira Chosa's direction and he saw the secrets floating there like islands in the stream.

Secrets were Chosa's stock in trade, so he felt an immediate bond with the girl. She was spread upon a black lacquered table, her long hair, glossy as the lacquer itself, fanned out across her small breasts, slim belly and firm thighs. The atmosphere at the intimate *akachochin* he frequented was thick with cigarette smoke and the musky intimation of sex. The girl, naked, streaked with indigo dye, watched him as she calmly opened her mouth in a perfect O.

Secrets were what allowed Chosa, the *oyabun* of the Kokorogurushii clan of Yakuza, to remain out of jail. Too many high-rolling financial traders, high-ranking politicians and senior bureaucrats were being investigated, hauled off to jail to face charges of embezzlement, tax evasion and making illegal contributions to political war chests.

A thin strip of a shiny Mylar-like material was stretched decorously across the girl's loins, but there was no mistaking the phallic shape of the large rubber device being lowered into her open mouth. This was the performance: while colored strobes probed her breasts and belly and thighs, only her lipstick-coated lips moved in a subtle dance. It was so still in the room that Chosa could hear the ragged breathing of the small audience of males who had come to this after-hours club from expensive and boozy business dinners, where the immense pressures of their daily work schedules could be obliterated for at least a few hedonistic hours.

Of all the secrets that Chosa possessed, the one he treasured most was the one about Nicholas Linnear. But, in truth, Linnear was only the central figure around which events whirled in their own peculiar rhythm.

Like the girl's lips, which pulsed, expanding and contracting as they worked their way up and down the shaft of the rubber device. She knew her business, this girl, her eyes closing slowly, as if in ecstasy, as her tiny pink tongue swirled around the head.

Nicholas's father, Colonel Denis Linnear, had formed a kind of sub-rosa alliance with Mikio Okami, during the early years of the American occupation of Japan. On the surface, there was nothing extraordinary in that. In those days, it was common practice for the American military to enlist the help of Yakuza to quell the Communist-inspired worker riots that plagued the big cities. Better by far, the Americans felt, to have Japanese nationals cracking the heads of protesting Japanese workers than to have American military personnel do it. And the Yakuza were more than happy to help out; they feared the Communists as much as the Americans did.

But it seemed as if the relationship between Colonel Linnear and Mikio Okami ran deeper than a mere business quid pro quo. The two, it appeared, had been fast friends. Beyond this point, Chosa's intelligence was rather sketchy. Just exactly what the two men were up to was still a mystery. But at least some inferences could be made. For instance, Chosa was alone among all the Yakuza *oyabun* who understood Tomoo Kozo's motivation for trying to kill Nicholas Linnear this past New Year's Day.

It was widely assumed that Kozo, who was then the *oyabun* of the Yamauchi clan, was terrified that Linnear would find out that it had been Kozo's orders to follow Linnear's wife, and that her fear of being followed had caused the accident in which she and her lover had been killed. Chosa had lied to Ushiba – Kozo had deliberately gone after Justine Linnear, he wanted her dead, just as he had wanted Nicholas dead. All because he believed that Colonel Linnear and Mikio Okami had killed his father Katsuodo in 1947 because Katsuodo had been against Okami's policy of appeasement with the Americans. Katsuodo despised everything Western; he was never able to surmount his humiliation at his country's defeat in the war of the Pacific. Consequently, he and Okami had constantly been at odds.

At the time an internal war had seemed inescapable even though all Yakuza *oyabun* knew this would deeply injure them all. Two weeks after Katsuodo spoke openly of going to war with Okami, his body was found floating in the Sumida River. There was not a mark on it, but a closely guarded secret was that the elder Kozo could not swim. The boy Tomoo Kozo theorized that someone somehow learned that secret, and he had made it his life's work to discover the perpetrators of his father's death. His suspicions led him to concentrate his investigation on Okami and Colonel Linnear, but Chosa had never found out whether Kozo had gathered sufficient evidence – or any at all – on which to base his conclusions.

The girl's muscular control astonished Chosa, but of course this was why she had been chosen to perform. It was her gift. Not a muscle moved on her body, though her skin was now burnished with a fine layer of perspiration. A single bead, glittering in the lights like a diamond, clung to one erect nipple. There was something ineffable about that one bead of moisture, like a tear or a cherry blossom about to fall, that spoke of life transfigured, unaltered either by time or by emotion.

In one important sense, Chosa found himself admiring Nicholas Linnear because he was entrenched in a purely Japanese dilemma, worthy of its most famous heroes. Nicholas loved his father, but believed that his alliance with the Yakuza – with Mikio Okami in particular – was morally indefensible. Thus his abiding hatred of the Yakuza. And yet, in order to honor the memory of his father, he was forced into service to Okami because the Colonel had made him promise to help the old *oyabun* should he ever need it. Last year Okami, having gotten word that a contract had been put out on him, had gone to Nicholas. To Nicholas's credit, he honored his *giri* to his father, though the cost to him, personally, must have been great.

A slender strand of saliva linked the tip of the girl's tongue to the end of the rubber device as it was withdrawn from her mouth. There was a low collective groan from the men surrounding her. The smell of sweat was strong on the air. Cigarettes were fired up. The show was over and the spell had been broken. Chosa signaled to one of his men to go backstage and wait for the girl while she showered and dressed. She would, he knew, be waiting for him in his bed when he returned later that night. But first he had an interview with perhaps the only person besides Mikio Okami who knew all the secrets of occupied Tokyo in the latter half of the 1940s.

Chosa climbed into the back of his armor-plated limousine and spoke softly to his driver. Beside the beefy man, Chosa's bodyguard sat stoically and so still he might have been asleep. Nothing could be further from the truth.

Within twenty minutes they were rolling through a worn-out district that paralleled the Sumida River. Stray dogs skulked on the edges of the headlights, and fires burned in trash cans. The black facades of the warehouses seemed forbidding in the night. The limo stopped outside a private residence wedged between two such structures.

It was raining lightly, the drops fizzing against the harsh sodium lights of the street. Chosa emerged from the car, pulled the collar of his overcoat up around his cheeks. After the thick, steamy atmosphere of the club it was good to breathe open air. He could smell the Sumida, but the effluvia of burning ash collected in the back of his throat, and he hurried up the steep flight of stairs to the front door of the private dwelling.

It opened immediately at his knock as if the woman inside had been waiting for him. She was heavy-set, a plain-looking woman in her late twenties with a thick mane of black hair, frizzy as the fibers in rice paper.

The interior of the house was Western and elegant, a small oval foyer flowering open to a grand central staircase. Sparkling light from a crystal chandelier burnished the warm tones of the rooms, and a marble console held a crystal bowl of flowers he knew were cut fresh every day.

He was led down a hall tastefully paneled in cherrywood, and was shown into the library. A very old and expensive Persian carpet covered the floor on which stood a velvet-covered sofa and a pair of high-backed upholstered chairs. Books on every conceivable subject lined one wall. Opposite was a glass cabinet displaying a full set of samurai armor dating from the seventeenth century that surely belonged in a museum. Next to it was a burlwood French secretary at which sat a woman who turned and rose as he was ushered into the room.

This was her sanctuary, and Chosa was at all times respectful of it. The woman, who must have been in her seventies, looked perhaps two decades younger than that. She had the kind of patrician face that spoke of pure samurai blood. Her skin was the color and smoothness of porcelain, but in her fiery black eyes was contained an entire world of emotion and intellect. This was no woman to trifle with, Chosa knew. She was the sister of Mikio Okami, and that alone placed her on a different level, but the force of her personality almost made her family connection irrelevant. Chosa, who had learned from his steel-willed mother to respect the quiet strength of a female, would not make the fatal mistake of thinking this woman to be an inferior being.

'Good evening, Kisoko-san,' Chosa said deferentially. 'I hope I haven't disturbed you at this late hour.'

Kisoko regarded him levelly. 'Time is irrelevant to me,' she replied in her well-modulated voice. 'As is sleep.' It was an exceptional voice, one that could be used as a weapon as well as a promise. In other words, this was a woman well used to the company of men. 'Would you care for a brandy?'

'A brandy would be perfect.'

Kisoko poured from a cut-crystal decanter. She wore a magnificent kimono of brocaded silk, black on indigo, in a water pattern. As tradition warranted, an under-kimono of soft black silk peeked out at cuff and collar, but her hair and makeup were strictly Western and as voguish as any model's.

She handed Chosa his drink and sat in her gilt Louis XV desk chair. Chosa went over to admire the suit of samurai armor.

'Magnificent,' he said. 'I'm envious of you.'

'Oh, that isn't mine. It belongs to my son, Ken. He's fascinated by the weapons of Japan's past.' Her eyes swept past Chosa to the armor. 'His sense of honor is, how shall I put it, preternaturally heightened.' She gave a little laugh. 'Perhaps he wishes he were back in the seventeenth century. At least then everything had its place. I sometimes suspect he's completely baffled by the complexities and subtleties of the modern world.'

It was a brave thing to say of a child who was permanently crippled. Or perhaps, like all mothers of impaired children, she could not see her son's disabilities for what they were. Even the most rational of people, Chosa knew, could be blinded by their love and desperate hope for their offspring.

She smiled benevolently. 'But I must apologize. You did not come here to listen to me talk of my son.'

Chosa turned and took some brandy on his tongue. He had never developed a taste for the liquor, but he could appreciate its medicinal properties. It was often this way with the many things required of him during his days and nights of business.

'I'd like to speak to you of Colonel Linnear and your brother.'

Kisoko turned her head as will a bird at the sound of a potential threat. 'Go on.'

'I do not wish to offend you.'

'Chosa-san, we go back a long way. I dandled you on my knee, took you for walks in Ueno Park, freed your kite from the branches of a cherry tree.'

'I remember, yes. It was a tiger.'

Kisoko nodded. 'A very fierce creature, who nevertheless needed all your love to survive.'

'My brother tried to steal him and I beat him badly.'

'He went to hospital, I recall. A fractured collarbone.'

'To this day that side of his shoulder is lower than the other. But when he came home he never tried to steal anything of mine again.'

'He also never told anyone what had really happened.'

138

Chosa was silent for some time, working on the riddle. He knew he dismissed these childhood reminiscences at his peril. Kisoko was famous for speaking in epigrams and oblique lessons that pertained to the subject of the moment. What was she telling him here?

At length, he said, 'I suppose you know that Tomoo Kozo tried to murder Nicholas Linnear.'

'Yes. The news media had nothing on it, of course. The police saw to that.'

'Kozo believed that the Colonel and your brother were responsible for his father's death in 1947.'

'Yes. I recall the day he was discovered floating in the Sumida.'

'Was Tomoo correct? Were they responsible for the elder Kozo's death?'

'Of course not,' she said without hesitation. 'Tomoo was mad, everyone knew that. How you tolerated him at council is anyone's guess.'

'But they were good friends, Colonel Linnear and your brother.'

'Friends?' She cocked her head. 'That's a rather odd way to put it. The Colonel was a Westerner, how *could* they have been friends?'

'Inside he was Japanese.'

'Was he? What an extraordinary notion.'

Chosa put down his glass. 'Are you refuting the evidence?'

'What evidence? You're mistaking popular myth for fact.'

'But surely it's a documented fact that Colonel Linnear actively worked within the Occupation machine to restore an equilibrium to the Japanese economic and political landscape.'

'That is without question.' Kisoko downed her brandy in one shot. 'But he also strove diligently to ensure that any trace of the prewar industrial-military complex was eradicated.'

Chosa stood stock still, fascinated and appalled. 'I don't think I understand you.'

'It's simple once you understand that there were certain elements within the Occupation machine who felt strongly that keeping a core of the best Japanese military minds would provide the kind of bulwark America required in those days against Communist aggression in the Pacific. Because this was our role in the postwar world: to be America's fortress in the Far East against the Soviet Union and mainland China. It was odd, don't you think? The Americans disarmed us and then told us to patrol their perimeter.'

'We're speaking now of war criminals.' Chosa wanted to make certain he got this right. 'Some Americans at SCAP headquarters wanted to keep Japanese war criminals out of the trials and use them for their own purpose.'

'They *did* keep a group out of the war trials. History tells us these generals were never found, but I know where they went. Underground. They became spies for the Americans.'

'And your brother and Colonel Linnear were involved in this scheme.'

Kisoko pursed her lips. 'In a way you could never understand.'

'But I need to know this!' He was startled by the vehemence of his voice.

'*Need*? But why do you need?' Her kimono made a sound like angels whispering as her arms moved. 'The *oyabun* commands and it is done.'

He closed his eyes for a moment; he needed a rest from her intensity. 'I cannot command you, Kisoko, you know that.'

140

'No. The Okamis are beyond even your powers. My brother saw to that.'

'But Nicholas Linnear is no friend of yours. Just answer this one question: are you telling me that your brother and Colonel Linnear did not have a close friendship?'

She offered him more brandy, but he declined. 'All marriages go through their bad patches. It's just that, in the end, some break up and others don't.'

'What happened to theirs?'

'One question, you said.' She put down the decanter, stood in front of him so close that he could hear her breathing. 'If Mikio were here, you could ask him yourself.'

Too late, Chosa understood the riddle she had presented him with. Her hand came up, her strong fingers curling around the side of his neck so tightly he could feel the pulsing of his blood through his carotid artery.

'But he isn't here. He's in hiding. Someplace far away from me . . . and from you.' Her eyes were fever bright, and Chosa had the curious and unpleasant sensation that at any moment she would turn into some great serpent that would unhinge its jaws and devour him whole. This was what she had meant: that no matter what Mikio had done or would do, he was still her brother, and there were some virtues – such as the loyalty Chosa's brother had shown him, such as the loyalty she was now showing toward her brother – that overrode any other moral consideration.

'Did you try to kill him, dear?'

Chosa was so startled by the question that he could not make his mouth work.

'Do you covet his power? Do you wish to sit in the Kaisho's chair? Do you want his influence diminished?' Her grip on him was inexorable. 'You were such a sweet child, so much like your playmates. You fit in. I used to sing you lullabies at night. Now look at you, part of the underworld. Well, dear, I must say the darkness fits you like a cloak. You grew into it, or it grew into you.'

Chosa knew that he had gambled and lost. He had used up the coin of the past with Kisoko, but recklessly he asked her one more question. 'If you won't talk to me about your brother and the Colonel, would you at least confirm something about Koei?'

'Koei?' He could see that he had startled her, and her grip loosened. 'Why would you think I would know about her?'

Typically, they used only her first name. With Koei, one always did.

'It is unthinkable that you wouldn't.'

Then he felt true pain as she dug her long nails into his Adam's apple. 'Despicable creature! It disgusts me to hear her name coming from your mouth! We don't speak of Koei here.'

'Why not?'

'You disgust me. That's your real reason for coming here.' Her eyes were eating him alive. 'It wasn't about Colonel Linnear and my brother. You thought you could get me to speak about her.'

'The secret − I must know −'

'I'd sooner see you dead −'

'Mother.'

In truth, Chosa did not know what the outcome would have been had Ken not rolled into the library in his wheelchair. He was a handsome man, with a long, brooding face and soft brown eyes that were ultimately deceiving. This man was powerful in body: wide-shouldered, deep-chested. He worked out every day in the specially made gym upstairs where he and his prize collection of ancient weapons coexisted.

'Yes, Ken.' Her hand slipped from Chosa's neck, leaving a white imprint that quickly turned red. But her

142

eyes did not leave Chosa's for a long, disquieting moment. Then she turned around, that benevolent smile on her face.

'You're needed upstairs, Mother.'

'I see. All right then.' She took a step toward her son but paused, as if remembering that Chosa was still in the room. She said to him, 'I trust I've been of some help.'

Chosa, the blood pulsing heavily in his neck and the pit of his stomach, could not think of a thing to say.

'The dead and dying are all around us, but I have saved a life.'

Seiko stood very close to Nicholas, the peaks of her breasts warm against his tattered clothes. She had taken him to a modern-looking apartment. Its windows overlooked a street crowded with shops selling cheap electronics, secondhand cameras (most of them probably stolen), and custom-made *ao dais*. The scents of manioc powder and *nuoc mam*, the fermented fish sauce ubiquitous in Vietnamese cuisine, wafted up from a restaurant on the ground floor.

The place was decorated in a jumble of wooden furniture and handicrafts made locally, as well as those imported from Burma, Thailand and India. A riot of colorful silk fabrics from northern Thailand covered the walls, except one spot beyond a beaded curtain to the kitchen where a poster of Jimi Hendrix from the 1960s held sway.

'He wanted to kill you. Van Kiet was trembling when you went past him; the passion was in his belly.' As she breathed, her nostrils flared and her bow-like lips quivered. 'You haven't bathed in a couple of days. You smell good.'

They had an odd history, incomplete and inchoate,

full of misplaced trust and repressed emotion. Justine had been wildly jealous of Seiko, had in fact accused Nicholas of having an affair with her. He had dismissed such paranoid speculation until, on the eve of his employment by Mikio Okami, Seiko had confessed her love for him. But was it love or simple desire? He suspected that even she did not know.

Her fingers pushed aside what was left of his shirt. 'There's blood all over your skin.' Her nails scored parallel tracks down his chest. 'I'd kill to get a chance to do this.' She leaned against him, her cheek like a silk pillow. Then she turned her head and her teeth closed over a wedge of skin, drawing it tight.

'What is it you want, Seiko?'

Her teeth opened and she pressed her lips to his chest. 'Use your *tanjian* eye. You tell me.'

But he suspected intuition would prove just as useful. 'Did you apply for the job as my assistant because of me?'

'Yes.'

'You'd seen me before.'

'Yes. At Nangi's club in Shinjuku where he takes you all the time. I was at the bar one night with my boyfriend. He wanted to get me drunk because I was angry at him and he wanted to take me to bed. I was halfway to being drunk when you walked in. I thought I was having a heart attack. There was a pain in my chest that made me dizzy. I excused myself. My boyfriend thought I was going to the toilet, but I was just trying to get nearer to you.' She was moving against him slowly, sinuously. 'I got lost in the crush of people. I knew you'd never see me, but I could stare at you for as long as I wanted. I was ecstatic. I couldn't keep the muscles in my thighs quiet and my breathing was ragged. I fantasized. In the end, I had an orgasm. I simply couldn't help myself.'

He could feel her heated body beneath the tank dress as completely as if she were already naked.

'I think I was there for hours. Maybe my boyfriend came after me to see where I'd gone, I don't know. He finally left, horny and out of money. But I no longer cared; I had you. Almost. Not until I applied for the job. Not quite. When you told me I had it. Then.'

'But by that time you knew I was married.'

'I knew all about you.'

'So you knew you could never have me.'

'On the contrary, it never occurred to me that I'd never have you. My fantasies were too real. I knew they were visions of the future.'

Perhaps she was mad, Nicholas thought. Perhaps it was as simple as that, but he doubted it. Real life was rarely neat and simple. 'Why is Van Kiet so hot to kill me?'

'He holds you responsible for killing the two soldiers in Cu Chi.'

'He executed Bay for those murders.'

'No. He killed her because it pleased him to do so. He'd still skin you alive if given half a chance.'

Nicholas looked down at her. 'But you won't give him that chance, will you?'

'That's right,' she said with a thorny smile. 'You're safe with me.'

He put his arms around her. 'And why is that? Who do you work for here?'

She squirmed in his tight embrace, reacting to the beginning of his interrogation. 'Why should I be working for anyone except you?'

'Because influence is everything here, and you're a female. Worse, a Japanese, a foreigner.'

'Not quite. My father is Vietnamese.' Her lips flowered as her head swung back. He felt the trembling in her as he extended his psyche, a kind of spasmodic

145

quivering that reverberated through her. What was happening? She was flushed, and perspiration broke out on her skin. 'Ohhh!' It was a long, stomach-deep groan, and she collapsed in his arms.

My God, he thought, stunned, *she's had an orgasm*.

She pulled herself against him, whispering, 'Again, again!' in a deep, guttural voice.

'Seiko —'

Her mouth closed over his, her pink tongue twining with his. At the same time her hand gently squeezed the bulge between his legs.

'I knew it,' she said breathlessly. A satisfied smile spread across her face. 'You can't hide how you feel about me. I felt it so strongly that night at the airport when you left for Venice it was almost a physical pain.' Her fingertips, the palm of her hand, were working on him, drawing him out to full length. 'Were you really so surprised when I told you how I felt about you?'

'Yes, I —'

'No, don't lie to me. I *know* what you felt, because your aura quivered. I felt its echo like a ripple in a pond that tells of something moving beneath the still surface. I could sense this unfurling even then.'

'Seiko, you're deluding yourself if you —'

'This is no delusion,' she whispered, sliding to her knees. She had unfastened his trousers, had him out, hot in her hands. What was happening? He could not control himself. The orgasm she had experienced without his physically touching her had inflamed him, and now her strange fire had infected him, and it was too late to stop.

She bent her head, her long hair sliding sensuously across her shoulders as she took him between her lips. He was engulfed in an exquisite wet heat. She moved slowly down him, and inside, her tongue was busy roll-

146

ing and flicking at all the most sensitive parts of him.

Without conscious volition his hands stroked her shoulders, pushed down the straps of her dress. She dropped her arms long enough to bare her breasts, and when his hands moved down to cup them, he felt the deep vibration in her throat as she groaned.

He did not want it to end this way, but he could not bear to make her stop. He rolled her nipples between his fingers as she took him all the way inside. He felt sensations down his shaft, then at the tip. They built to the point where he could no longer control his body or his thoughts. His *tanjian* eye opened as if of its own will, projecting itself outward in a rush as he exploded, bent over her, feeling the rhythmic sensations as she continued her ministrations.

To his surprise he did not lose his hardness, and now he pushed her roughly down, shoving her dress up her thighs. She wore no underwear, and she was very wet. He entered her to the hilt, and he knew that she was feeling him not just physically but psychically as well. One stroke caused her to cry out as she spasmed, her heart thundering, her tender flesh contracting wildly around him. There were tears in her eyes and her cries of excitement were so passionate that he knew instinctively that she was not mad, rather that she possessed a rare ability, a sensitivity to his psychic energy. This was what had attracted her so strongly at Nangi's club on the night she had first seen him, what had drawn her to him, what had caused her orgasm amid all those people.

Nicholas lost himself inside her, unable to help himself as she was unable to quell her ecstasy. He tried to control his *tanjian* power, keeping it tightly bound, but it was desperate to be loosed and would not obey him. It emerged from undercover, wrapping them in a protective cocoon that kept their desire aflame for far longer than it would otherwise have been possible. Afterward, they slept as if dead.

It was deep in the night when they awoke, and it was like returning to consciousness after a high fever. They were both disoriented, but part of this must have been the desire to keep a hold on a state of being that was fast evaporating.

From the open windows a riot of sounds drifted up from the streets: chickens squawking, motorbikes revving, trucks rumbling, rock 'n' roll blaring from a club down the block, the chanting of a Buddhist prayer. A heady mixture of incense, grilling meat, perfume, vinegar and cloves, fermented salt fish, human sweat and diesel fumes turned the atmosphere oppressive and cloying.

'Am I awake?'

He pushed damp hair off his forehead. 'Yes.'

Her eyes filled with tears and, covering her bare breasts with her hand, she rolled away from him. 'I'm sorry. I have no excuse for my actions. I –'

His hand closed over her haunch and he felt her shudder as she let go with a tiny cry. A muscle in her buttock quivered.

'Ah, Buddha, what is happening to me?' She was weeping now. 'I wanted you so badly, so desperately, that I would have killed, I would have done anything –'

He put his palm across her mouth. 'Hush, now.' He pulled her up against him, rocking her gently. 'I felt it, too, even – yes, you were right – that evening at Narita.'

She leaned against him. 'I feel as if I've drunk a quart of Scotch.'

Her breath came against his chest, and he could feel her heartbeat as if she were within him. Somewhere deep inside him he suspected that it was dangerous to allow himself this intoxication, to be this close to her, to involve himself in the form of magic he now believed

148

she represented. On the other hand the challenge was irresistible.

Apart from the fact that she was his best lead to Abramanov and the person or people behind Vincent Tinh's murder, and thereby Abramanov, the psychic union they had undergone had made her precious to him.

Now he was confronted with someone who responded to his psychic emanations on a wholly elemental level. What did Seiko possess that allowed her this gift? Was it *koryoku*? Her sensitivity to auras seemed to fit Celeste's description of Okami's power – the edge that had allowed him to keep several steps ahead of his enemies for more than ninety years. And Nicholas had learned that, contrary to popular belief, *koryoku* was not a discipline one learned, but was rather a natural ability lying dormant in a select few people, waiting to be born.

The aftermath of so much energy had left a metallic taste in his mouth. What they needed was to return to normality as quickly as possible.

While he showered, Seiko went to an all-night bazaar. She brought back fruit, vegetables and an enormous paper box of steaming noodles. She also had a handful of clothes for him that more or less fit: several sets of underwear, khaki trousers, a white, gauzy shirt, a pair of sturdy hiking boots, two pairs of sweat socks, a military-style, waist-length jacket.

She stir-fried the vegetables in sesame oil, and they ate in the yellow-and-chrome kitchen that looked as if it had been transplanted from an American house built in the early seventies.

They were both famished. They said nothing while they ate, eyed each other warily.

'You have some explaining to do,' Nicholas said as he pushed his empty plate away from him. 'There are too many things about you I don't know.'

'Then we're starting from the same place.'

'No, you know quite a bit about me – that I'm ninja, and *tanjian* as well. You made it your business to find out about Justine and my relationship with her.'

'All right. I plead guilty.'

She sat facing him. Her face devoid of all makeup was quite striking, softer, with a hint of innocence that he already knew was spurious. But he could feel their attraction as if it were a rope that glittered in his mind. Unaccountably, he was reminded of a film he'd seen with two Spanish gypsies engaged in a blood feud. Armed with knives, their wrists had been bound by a single length of cord, isolating them to the radius of a small circle. In that circumstance only one could survive.

'I want to ask you to do something . . . unorthodox.'

Her mouth pursed and she licked her lips. 'Haven't we already done it?'

'Perhaps, in a way. I want to look inside you.'

'No.' She stared down at the bits of food left on the plates. 'It would be something like rape, wouldn't it?'

'I don't know. I'm not qualified to say.'

Her head came up and her eyes locked on his. 'Why do you want to do this?'

He told her about *koryoku*, and a bit of why he was looking for it, that her reaction to the projection of his *tanjian* eye made him curious as to whether she possessed *koryoku*.

'I'm not psychic,' she said. 'I don't have visions or premonitions. In that area, I am perfectly dull.'

'Let me try, in any case.'

'What will you see?'

'I can't know that yet.'

'Everything? My life as it is, as it has been?'

'I don't have that kind of power. No one does.' He

nodded. 'Give me your hands.' She slid them into his; the fingertips were chill. 'Don't be afraid.'

His *tanjian* eye opened and her eyes closed just as if he had given her a spoken command. He felt her relax as his psychic energy flowed into her. He surrounded her in a shell of warmth and protection, until she relaxed further; her brain was almost in delta rhythm, a dreaming pattern of deep sleep. Then he went in.

In objective time, his probe lasted no more than a tenth of a second, but it was enough for him to tell that she did not possess the Illuminating Power. He would have to find Mikio Okami for that.

He closed down his *tanjian* eye and her eyes opened slowly. 'How do you feel?'

'Fine. I – feel good.' She squeezed his hands. 'Did you find what you were looking for?'

'No.'

'And my life . . .'

'I know nothing more about you than I did before. I told you, I can't read minds.'

She nodded, slipped her hands from his.

He looked at her curiously. 'You're not at all the woman I hired.'

'That was in Tokyo.' She rose, cleared the dishes. 'Here in Saigon my Vietnamese side takes hold.'

'You said your father is Vietnamese. He's still alive?'

She put a pot on for tea, got a paring knife and went to work on the fruit. 'Yes. He's a politician, although that word doesn't really apply here. Vietnamese politics is so inextricably bound up with influence-peddling, selling your services to the highest bidder, and changing ideology at the hint of a coup that the word has lost all conventional meaning.' She glanced up from the fruit, gave him an odd look. 'My father has worked for many different people. He's nimble, which is how he has survived and prospered for so long.'

151

'Is he why Van Kiet takes orders from you?'

'Partly.' She neatly skinned a longan. 'But I have my own influence here.'

'Does that extend to knowing the woman I was with?'

'Bay? Yes, of course. She was well known here as a rep for an international arms dealer.'

'She told me she was an independent go-between.'

Seiko laughed harshly. 'This is Vietnam. No female could have that kind of power.'

'You seem to.'

'I never said I was independent. Even with my father's influence that would be impossible.' She sliced a cinnamon apple, arranged it on a plate with the longan and two bananas sliced lengthwise. 'Women have no rights of their own here. If they gain any respect at all, it is granted grudgingly and, I'm afraid, temporarily.'

'So you have two employers: Sato International and . . .'

Bringing the plate over to the table, she set it between them. 'I work for a man named Shidare who has a number of interests here.'

'Shidare? Then he isn't Vietnamese.'

'Not many of power are.' She shrugged. 'But that's the way it's almost always been here. Nothing inherently Vietnamese has any permanent worth. We've only become important in world geopolitics because of our location. We've been a pawn for decades in a game we can barely imagine, let alone understand.'

'Now you sound bitter.'

'Do I?' She took a piece of longan between her fingertips, studied it. 'Vietnam has spent all of its modern history being invaded by one people or another. We've been left with no culture. Our music is French, our cuisine is an agglomeration, and we all

152

aspire to look American. What would you have me feel?'

'I can't say. To be frank, I can't imagine such a situation.'

'I suppose I feel it more acutely because I'm half-Japanese, and when I'm in Tokyo, I see the things I have, yet don't have at all.'

'Seiko, I can't have you working for two companies at once. That's a gross breach of security.' *And, to be frank,* he thought, *there's a good deal of suspicion back in Tokyo that you aided and abetted Masamoto Goei.* Here in Saigon, with all that had occurred, he was finding it all too easy to forget about what Seiko might have been accomplice to in Tokyo — Goei was one of the team leaders of his Chi Project, who was caught trafficking in the Chi neural-net chip with Vincent Tinh.

'Will you fire me then?'

'Only if you force me.' What good would firing her do? He needed to find out if she was telling the truth. Who was she really working for besides him? It was imperative he give her the impression that he trusted her. If he didn't, he feared he'd never find out the truth about her. 'You'll have to choose one job or the other.'

'I don't want to leave Sato — or you,' she said almost immediately. 'But I need — *we* need — an aegis for the time we're here. You've seen the value of such an arrangement this morning. When we return to Tokyo, I'll sever all other ties. Is that satisfactory?'

'Only if I can find the right person to run Sato-Tomkin here. Remember, Nangi sent you to Saigon to take Vincent Tinh's place.'

Seiko nodded. 'Agreed.'

Nicholas felt unaccountably relieved. What was it about this tough but strangely vulnerable young woman that drew him against his own better judgment?

He knew he'd better find the answer to that question as soon as possible. In the meantime, he decided to extend his trust of her another notch – or, as Nangi would say, increase the length of rope she would fashion into an incriminating noose.

'When I was with Bay, she mentioned something curious. I think it must be a place: Floating City.'

Seiko's head came around quickly. 'What did she tell you about it?'

'Almost nothing. Just that where we were in Cu Chi was a halfway point between Saigon and the Floating City.'

'She should not have mentioned it.'

'She was dying, Seiko. She obviously thought it was important. It's obvious you do, too. What is Floating City?'

Seiko got up, went to the refrigerator with the rest of the cut fruit. But after she'd put it away, she stood with her back to him. At last, she turned around.

'Some information is very dangerous here.'

'So Bay said. Yet she felt I needed to know.'

Seiko came back to the table, sat next to him. 'Floating City is a kind of citadel.'

'Citadel?'

She nodded. 'In the strict, old-fashioned sense. It's an armed city, a place of virtual sovereign independence within Vietnam.'

'Have you been there?'

'No, I haven't. And no one I know has.' She slipped her hand into his. 'Some have tried to break in, others have made attempts to steal in. None have been successful.'

'How do you know that?'

'Because all have been found hanging upside down in the jungle perimeter of Floating City, their genitalia removed and stuffed into their mouths.'

There was silence for a long time. The usually raucous street sounds seemed dim and remote as if, like the poster of Jimi Hendrix, they belonged to a different time.

At length, he squeezed her hand. 'You said Bay worked for an international arms dealer. What is his name?'

'Timothy Delacroix.'

Nicholas kept his face impassive but his mind was racing. Delacroix was a man he had heard about from Lew Croaker. Delacroix claimed to have done business with Vincent Tinh and a company he believed to be Sato International. As Nicholas understood it, Delacroix dealt in anything and everything in the ordnance game. And somehow he had access to even the most advanced American military weapons – the same inventory that Nicholas had pulled up on the computer screen at the Paris office of Avalon Ltd, where he had also encountered the entry for Torch 315.

'Is Delacroix here in Saigon?'

'Yes. It is rumored that he has regular dealings with Floating City.'

'You mean it's his arms source. Interesting.' *Is there some connection between Delacroix and Avalon Ltd, Torch and Floating City?* Nicholas asked himself. *Is this why the Kaisho directed me here?* He made a quick decision. 'I want to meet him.'

All the softness, the innocence, seemed to have drained out of Seiko's face over the last several minutes. 'I wouldn't recommend contacting him. Frankly, I wouldn't recommend trying to get in touch with anyone connected with Floating City.'

'Why not?'

'Abramanov, the man you were supposed to meet, lives there. You were betrayed in the Cu Chi tunnels. By whom I do not know, but it would be foolhardy not to suspect that the people of Floating City saw through your cover as Mr Goto.'

Nicholas knew she could be right, but what other choice did he have? He had to see Delacroix and find out if Floating City was Vincent Tinh's connection with the dark underside of the Southeast Asian black market, where Sato-Tomkin's corporate reputation had almost been destroyed. He had to find out what Delacroix knew of Avalon Ltd and Torch 315.

'Nevertheless, I want you to set up a meeting with Delacroix. It's critical that I speak with him.'

Seiko, drawing closer to him, bowed her head; he recognized in that gesture the emblem of her acquiescence.

Deplaning at Washington's National airport, Croaker watched Margarite head directly for a limo with darkened windows. A uniformed driver had the rear curbside door open for her. He touched the bill of his cap as she approached, slammed the door after her, then hustled around and got in behind the wheel. By this time, Croaker was already at the taxi stand and was using his federal badge to get himself to the first taxi in line.

As Margarite's limo pulled out from the curb, he tapped the cabby on the shoulder and, shoving the badge into the man's face, said, 'Keep that limo in sight, okay? There's a fifty in it for you.'

'For that kind of money you're the boss,' the cabby said, merging with the airport traffic outflow.

Croaker leaned forward, peering through the windshield. He jotted down the limo's license number, noting that it wasn't a rental. He thought that was curious; he had been here with Margarite before and he had expected her to pick up a rental car at the airport.

This unscheduled trip to Washington was the first blip

in her otherwise methodical and arduous program. It interested him for a number of reasons. She had made it without Tony D., who would otherwise have been needed to front for her with those who assumed he was running Dominic's operation. Also, recalling Dominic Goldoni's federal file, he had pulled up the fact that the dead don had made periodic trips to DC. Not that that was in itself suspicious. Quite the contrary. With Dominic's many deeply entrenched relationships with the country's political heavyweights, it would have been odd had he not made frequent trips to Washington. Still, the coincidence, imagined or not, lodged in Croaker's cop's intuition like a stone in a boot.

As his taxi dodged through the heavy traffic on Washington Memorial Parkway, he stared out at the flat gray Potomac and tried to dredge up the places Dominic had frequented while here. No doubt the don had been aware that he was being followed, so he'd known better than to meet with anyone who would trigger the feds' suspicion if he or she was investigated. Still, for many years Dominic had proved himself far more clever than the feds. Who knows what they might have missed?

He counted off the places he remembered: Dom's elegant brick house in Kalorama; his favorite watering hole, the Occidental Grill; the Museum of History and Technology; the Washington Hotel; Moniker's, a businessman's showgirl bar, where he picked up his one-night stands; a club called Omega in Georgetown; the restaurants where he took them: Villa D'Este in Alexandria's Old Town, Veneziano and Blue Angel Café in Adams Morgan; the private tennis courts in McLean belonging to the senior senator from Texas; the Belle Rive Country Club in Chevy Chase where he golfed with legislators, international bankers and lobbyists. Did any of these have a significance other than the one

Dominic had wanted his federal tails to see? Perhaps Margarite held the answer.

Croaker fully expected her first stop to be her step-mother's Georgian mansion in the rolling hills of the Potomac horse country. He had been to Renata Loti's house with Margarite and had learned that she was Dominic's mother. She was also highly connected to the complex machine of the government. But, to his surprise, Margarite's limo headed into town.

It was early evening, and the lights were already on along the parkway and the Arlington Memorial Bridge. Clouds had gathered as ominously as the rush-hour traffic, and the smell of incipient ozone was in the air. A light sooty rain was falling on the shoulders of the State Department joggers as they pounded the concrete footpaths along the bridge. One heavy-set man stood, winded, hands on his knees, bent over, head down. Poor bastard, Croaker thought, fighting the urge to give him a lift back to the office. Having had to battle bureaucrats almost all his adult life, Croaker had never had anything but contempt for them, but today he would gladly have changed places with even this oxygen-starved wretch.

He was trying not to think of Bad Clams Leonforte in whose service he now reluctantly toiled like a sinner in the depths of hell. Bad enough he was working against the woman he loved; now he was in the employ of her arch rival, a madman who would like nothing better than to see Margarite and Tony D. dead. And he had made it all too clear that he wanted to use Croaker to get that done.

Margarite's driver dropped her bags off at the Hay-Adams, then took her to have drinks at the Washington Hotel with Senator Graves of Indiana. Fifty minutes later, she met Renata for dinner at a hot new spot on Pennsylvania Avenue. Hot in DC meant that it was a favorite of the new administration. Scanning the menu while the women chatted over martinis, Croaker supposed they could run up a bill of over two hundred and fifty dollars. He gave the cabby a hundred-dollar bill, along with a ten spot, and sent him off for some fast food. Fifteen minutes later Croaker was wolfing down something that might have been a double cheeseburger, though he couldn't be sure. His stomach started to hurt almost immediately. Nicholas was right, he thought. How did people eat this crap as a steady diet? Next time, he vowed to duck into a sushi bar.

Margarite's dinner with her stepmother took just over two hours. Then she climbed back in the waiting limo and was off.

'How long you think you'll need me?' the cabby said over his shoulder. 'My shift ends in about an hour.'

'Hard to say.' Croaker handed him another hundred dollars.

'Thanks. I'd better tell the dispatcher to phone my wife and tell her to put my dinner in the freezer.'

They drove through the city, on the limo's tail. The rain was falling harder now, and the wind had picked up, gusting down the side avenues, shaking the trees like admonishing fingers. Croaker was trying to figure ways to nail Bad Clams without finding Margarite smeared all over the New Jersey badlands. Right now, on that score his mind was a blank.

'Not the greatest part of town your friend is going to.'

The cabby's nervous voice broke Croaker's train of thought. He could see that they were indeed in a sleazy neighborhood that might make the typical tourist think twice about taking a stroll at night. Honky-tonk bars, neon-fronted strip joints and cheap restaurants lined the streets, and the sidewalks were filled with hustlers, petty henchmen, whores and other assorted lowlifes.

Croaker watched as the limo slid to a stop at the curb outside Moniker's, the place Dominic had used for his white-meat pickups. Margarite went inside.

Now this *was* interesting, Croaker thought.

'What d'you think your classy broad is doing at this dump?'

Croaker wanted to know that himself. 'Wait here,' he said as he got out. Inside the club he found a pay phone outside the coatroom and, using the credit card Lillehammer had given him, dialed a number. He hoped that Looking-Glass, the American clandestine espionage organization Lillehammer had worked for, was still operating. Since the death of Leon Waxman, its director, it could have been dismantled. He was still using the large advance on expenses Lillehammer had given him last year, but it would help to be able to continue to tap into the agency's extensive resources.

The number rang twice before being answered. Croaker gave the voice the coded ID Lillehammer had provided him with last year, praying it hadn't been discontinued. The ID was his passport inside Looking-Glass; it had the highest classification. When the voice acknowledged the ID, he breathed a sigh of relief. He was instructed to punch in the last four digits imprinted on his card, then he waited while a series of relays shunted his call through God only knew what federal catacombs.

At length, he could hear a series of double rings. A female voice answered with a simple 'Yes.'

Looking-Glass was still in business.

Croaker read off the entire number on the card, then told the voice what he wanted: a trace on the limo's license plate.

'Forty-five minutes,' the female voice said.

'I need it in twenty.'

'It's after hours,' the voice complained.

160

'Just do it.' He hung up, went into the club proper.

Moniker's was pretty much what you'd expect: red and silver wallpaper, colored spots bristling off mirrored globes that had seemed old-fashioned even in the seventies, a stench of cigar smoke and sweat. Harsh and jarring rock spit out of banks of speakers hung from the ceiling by black cables. Lurex-wrapped dancers with long legs and top-heavy chests spent ten heavy-breathing minutes on a long stage running across the width of the room. It was mirrored so nothing was left to the imagination. Without the essential mystery, Croaker thought, there wasn't an ounce of eroticism in the place. But the babes, without a hair on their sleek bodies, knew their business, and there was a good goggle-eyed crowd bellied up to the stage shooting whiskey and beers at an astonishing pace.

A hostess who jiggled more than a bowl of Jell-O came up to him, and Croaker opened the federal badge in her face. She seemed unimpressed – maybe she'd seen too many of his kind in her time – but at least she didn't push the watered-down drinks on him.

He described Margarite. 'Sorry.' Her smile was as inviting as Medusa's. 'Nobody like that's come in here tonight.'

Croaker leaned toward her and, leering obscenely at her, said, 'How'd you like me to rip off those false eyelashes one at a time?'

'Shit.' All the same, she pointed the way backstage. She seemed disappointed she hadn't been able to snow him like the horny marks at the bar.

The music pulsed and moaned, the kind of grunge metal that with sufficient exposure could make you break out in hives. Croaker picked his way through the crowd toward the left side of the club. There he found his way blocked by a large black man with a bald pate shiny with sweat, and muscles bulging with years of steroids. This individual appeared to believe Croaker's badge was either a forgery or a mirage because he steadfastly refused to move aside.

'Everyone wants to get back there,' he said laconically. 'No one does.'

'I know you're just doing your job –'

'Get the fuck outta my face!' Bluto said with such ferocity it cut through even the grunge rock. He poked a meaty forefinger hard into Croaker's sternum, then spun him around. 'Out,' he hissed, 'or I'll eat your fuckin' liver for dinner!'

Without a word, Croaker grasped Bluto's right wrist with his biomechanical fingers and squeezed. It was interesting watching the changing expressions on the big man's face as Croaker applied enough pressure to contort muscle and shatter bone.

Still Bluto tried to get at Croaker, hammering out with his other fist. Croaker sidestepped the vicious blow, kicked in the side of the big man's knee. Bluto went down and more bones shattered.

'Hope you're not hungry,' Croaker said, stepping over him. He went to the closest door but it was locked. He dug out a rig of picks, popped the lock. He was in a storeroom. He went back into the hall, gripped Bluto under the armpits, dragged him into the storeroom and shut the door. Hopefully, he wouldn't be missed for the short time Croaker planned to be at the club.

The narrow hallway vibrated to the amplified bass. Bits of paint and plaster lay at the corners of the floor, and cheap green-shaded lamps swung on their chains as if attached to a ship on stormy seas.

A great deal of naked female flesh was flying about, but no one gave him a second look. He figured he had Bluto to thank for that. As the man had said, everyone wanted to get backstage but no one did. And now Croaker could see why. There were no doors to the

162

dressing rooms, so roving male eyes would not be appreciated. Having instant access to every room made his job easier.

He was three-quarters of the way down the corridor when the one door at the far end opened and he saw a flash of Margarite's ox-blood suit. He ducked into the nearest dressing room, gave the leggy blonde and red-head in residence a boyish grin, then turned back to peer into the hallway.

Margarite was exiting the back room, probably the manager's office, with a stunning young woman with pale blonde hair swept down over one cheek, huge cornflower-blue eyes and a heart-stopping figure. She could easily have been a dancer here and put all the others to shame, but clearly she was not. She wore an olive-and-ocher-striped Armani suit as if it had been made for her. In her left hand she carried a Nile-green crocodile attaché case that cost more than any employee of this club made in a year. Matching Bulgari earrings and a wrist cuff glinted sumptuously in the shifting overhead lights.

That makes two *classy broads at this dump*, he thought.

The two women made no attempt to come back up the corridor, but turned to their left, disappearing through a door. Croaker went after them, found himself in a dim, cold service corridor. It smelled of booze, garbage and urine. A red sign above the only other door said 'Exit'. He went through that, found himself in a dank alley lined with Dumpsters. Nocturnal creatures, probably feral cats, hissed at him.

He looked around in time to see a black Nissan 300ZX pull away from the curb. He had just enough time to ID Margarite and the blonde and get a partial on the license plate before the wall of the alley intervened.

He went back inside the club. There was no hope of following them so he did the next best thing: he broke into the back room where they had been closeted.

He closed the door behind him, careful to lock it against unwanted intrusion. It was a cramped, windowless space with a sooty air vent high up in one wall. A swaybacked Swedish modern couch in a fabric that was once whiskey-colored tweed was parked against a side wall. To its left was a standard fake-wood and metal desk and black vinyl executive chair. Behind that, a cheap metal file cabinet rounded out the office's mean complement of furniture. The walls were bare save for a poster, incongruous in this context, of John Singer Sargent's mysterious *Fumée d'Ambre Gris*, a painting of a woman in flowing white robes, in a vaguely Middle Eastern milieu, whose face was made somehow incandescent by shadows partially obscuring it. Croaker wondered what this said about the stunning blonde. She was classy *and* brainy?

He sat behind the desk. On it was a recent issue of *Strip!*. He thumbed quickly through it. Every industry had a trade magazine these days, he thought. Beneath was a contract with one of the dancers, several bills from vendors and the utility company, and a bound business checkbook. He began taking notes. The club's corporate name was Morgana, Inc. It had a Washington address.

He began methodically to go through the desk. The top drawer yielded the usual office supplies: pens, pencils, erasers, paper clips, rubber bands, blank lined notepads and the like. He felt all the way to the back to make sure there wasn't a false wall. He repeated this procedure in each of the other three drawers.

In one, he found some personal effects: the blonde's extra lipsticks and other makeup items, but apart from substantiating her expensive taste, it revealed nothing of value.

In another, he pulled out an accounting ledger. He

scanned it, but there seemed nothing out of the ordinary in it. The club's books were kept in meticulous order. He doubted whether even the most zealous tax auditor could find as much as ten dollars out of place. A lot of money was going through the club, but it was being generated by a franchised network of Moniker's strip clubs nationwide.

Returning the ledger to its drawer, he glanced at his watch, called the same number he had dialed from the club's coatroom. Going through the laborious security procedures, he got the female voice. When he identified himself via his card number, she said, 'That license is registered to Richard Dedalus.'

'*Senator* Richard Dedalus?'

'Let me check the address . . . Yes, it's one of the senator's cars.'

Croaker, taking down Dedalus's home address, was silent for a moment. At seventy-six, Richard Dedalus was the elder statesman on Capitol Hill. He had not only seen history happen over the decades but, unlike most others his age, had had a decisive hand in it. It was said that John Kennedy would never have been elected without Dedalus's support, that LBJ's tough time in office was for the most part engineered by Dedalus. It was even rumored that Dedalus had been Deep Throat. Certainly, it had been Dedalus who had kept secret JFK's serious illness – the lack of adrenals; and it had been he who had helped shape the committee . investigating the assassination of John Kennedy. Could this dean of Washington power brokers have been in Dominic Goldoni's hip pocket? On the face of it, it seemed incredible, but if the streets of New York had taught Croaker anything, it was never to discount the incredible – or even the impossible.

'Anything else?'

The female voice snapped his train of thought.

'As a matter of fact, there is. I need the long-distance telephone records for the last three months for Moniker's.' He gave her the address. 'Also, I have a partial DC license number on a black 1995 Nissan 300ZX ragtop. See what you can do.'

'It's a help that it's a ragtop; not too many of those around. Still, it'll take a while.'

'Tomorrow morning do you?'

'Not before six. All the info will be at the concierge desk at the Holiday Inn Central on Rhode Island Avenue and Fifteenth Street under the name Samuel Johnson.'

'You got it. Thanks.'

He sat for a moment, feeling momentarily defeated. He stared at the Sargent, letting the exotic aura of the painting flow over him, even though this was just a poster. It made him think of the blonde. In his imagination he conjured her up, watching her from the hallway as she came out of the office. He examined the clever glint in the cornflower-blue eyes and wondered again what she was doing here. Could she really be managing this strip joint? Not likely. What was far more plausible was that she was here because no one would expect her to be in a sleazy place like this. It was his experience that people left their secrets in places where they felt them most unlikely to be discovered.

He continued to stare at the woman in her billowing white robes. What were the secrets with which Sargent had infused her? What was she doing and why was she doing it?

Abruptly, he got up, went over to the poster. He took it off the wall. The blank wall leered at him mockingly. Then he put the poster down, looked more closely. The wall was cracked, so it was difficult to pick up, but there was no doubt he was looking at cracks that formed a right angle. He followed them down, found two more

166

right angles. He traced the lines all around with his forefinger until he had formed a rectangle.

Bingo!

Using the blade of a penknife, he dug into one crack, pulled up a corner. It peeled back, revealing a safe. Croaker produced a small key ring on which hung perhaps a dozen hooked implements. Eyeing the brand of safe, he selected one, inserted it in the lock. He put his ear to the metal housing, listened to the tumblers falling as he manipulated the probe.

The door popped open and he took a look inside. At that moment, he heard a sharp noise as someone in the corridor tried the doorknob. There was the muffled sound of a questioning voice and the door rattled.

Croaker went through the contents of the safe as quickly as he could. There was over a hundred thousand dollars in neatly stacked and wrapped bills, the lease for the building, which was owned by Morgana, Inc., the usual insurance documents, a second accounting ledger, and a small calfskin notebook.

The noise at the door had ceased, but he was not fooled. Whoever had wanted to get in would be back, and he knew he needed to be out of there before then.

He opened the ledger first, went through it. This one told the true story of the Moniker operation. Morgana, Inc. was funneling tens of thousands of dollars per month through the club. The monies that were supposedly coming from the nationwide franchise organization were actually originating overseas, specifically France and England. And unlike the false ledger that showed the monies to be in the tens of thousands per month, this one put the amount far higher. Moniker's laundered almost a million dollars a month for Morgana, Inc. No wonder there was no typical sleazebucket manager running this place.

Croaker slid the ledger back into the safe, opened

the calfskin notebook. It was filled with neatly printed letters interspersed with Arabic numerals. He recognized this as some kind of code.

He pocketed the notebook, closed and locked the safe, pressed the plaster-like rectangle back in place, then replaced the poster. He crossed to the door, put his ear to it. Then, carefully, he unlocked the door and, opening it slowly, peered out through the sliver between the door and the frame. He saw no one.

He slipped quickly out of the office, exiting the club as Margarite and the blonde had done. He walked through the refuse-strewn alley and around the corner toward the front of the club. The rain beat harder, soaking him. He climbed into the cab and told the driver to take him to the Hay-Adams, Margarite's hotel.

He dismissed the cabby outside the Hay-Adams, then took a room on the floor above Margarite's. The night manager, responding to his badge, was only too happy to give him the location of her room. He also agreed to phone Croaker's room when Margarite returned.

Up in the room, Croaker ordered food, took off his jacket and rubbed his wet head with a towel. Then he sat down at the desk in the room and opened the notebook. He took out a pad and pencil and went to work.

He had spent six months in the army in codes and ciphers and knew more than the rudiments of cryptography. He felt certain this was no spy network he was dealing with, so the chances were good that this code would not be an arcane one. Something easy to remember, such as a substitution code where one letter filled in for another, would be a logical place to start, he determined.

The first thing he noticed was that the number 9 kept repeating on several pages. In each instance, the 9 was preceded by five letters. He began the series substitutions, using the three most common ones, as he had been taught.

He had gone through them all without success when the food arrived. He stretched, stood looking out the window at the rain-swept Washington night while he munched his chicken sandwich and swigged on a bottle of beer. It was almost midnight. Somewhere out there Margarite was in conference with the woman with the pale blonde hair. For all he knew they were both with Senator Dedalus, discussing the fate of the world, but he doubted it. Margarite had arrived at Moniker's in Dedalus's limo – in fact, she had had use of it from the moment she stepped off the plane at National. If the two women were going to Dedalus's, why not use his limo? Instead, they had lit out from a dark alley in the blonde's Nissan.

It was really pissing down out there and the only good thing about the evening, as far as Croaker could see, was that he wasn't out in it. He finished off the sandwich, took the remaining beer back to the desk, sipping it while he stood staring from the open note-book to his attempts at crypto-busting. He had thought he'd cracked it with the third substitution system. What was he missing? He looked at the code again, not trying to read each group of characters, but looking at the whole to see if a pattern would emerge. Switch the *a* and *e*? Substitute the five middle letters of the alphabet for vowels? Work backward from the end of the alphabet? Substitute a letter for another?

Wait a minute! He sat down in the chair, took up his pen. The numbers! Each grouping had either one or two numbers as part of it. His heart was thumping. After several tries, he thought he had it. The number was the key. You subtracted the number in the groups that began with even-numbered letters, added the number in groups that began with odd-numbered letters. For

169

instance, the group DK3A decoded became AND — *A* was an odd letter, the first in the alphabet, and 3 was the key to go forward three letters, assuming the alphabet was a circle, so that *A* came after *Z*. In the instances where the groups contained two numbers it was now simply a matter of either adding those numbers together or subtracting one from the other in order to obtain the key for that cipher.

Having cracked the code, Croaker now began the laborious work of translating the groups into English. It took him the better part of three hours. What he found himself looking at was a series of entries for delivery dates and contract prices for a mind-bending array of top-flight international weaponry. All the latest ordnance was here, including American F-15 fighters, Lockheed SR-71 supersonic jets, Badger computerized flame throwers, Sioux infrared gunships complete with Wolverine A-322 air-to-ground heat-seeking missiles, Russian Tupolev-22 M bombers, T-72 tanks, SAM-13 anti-aircraft missiles, Python-600 mortars, Deyrael hand-held antitank bazookas.

His exhaustion evaporated as he drank in the implications of this comprehensive range of high-tech weaponry from the US armed services. It was illegal to export this ordnance outside the United States and yet here was proof of a steady source of supply. So Morgana, Inc. was in the same business as Avalon Ltd. Both were merchants of death operating beyond the law.

He rubbed his tired eyes. Everything was decoded except for the few groups that had the number 9 embedded within them. No matter what he did, he could not make them intelligible. Obviously, here the 9 was not the key; it must be part of the cipher itself. Then what *was* the key? Each group contained five letters plus the numeral.

Then he got the idea of breaking the number down into its additive parts. He started with three threes. That would make the first letter a *T*. But the second letter became *Z*, so that was out. He kept the *T*, the first three, decided to add one. That made TO – so far so good. He tried two, thinking that because there were five letters he needed five numbers to equal nine, but that didn't work. Adding three gave him TOT, but with only two ones left to make nine, he was back to gibberish. He tried five, got TOR. Three, one and five equaled nine . . . maybe – 315.

It hit him all at once, the partially unencrypted letters and numerals coalescing in his mind. His head throbbed and he heard a rushing in his ears. In a fever of apprehension, he finished decoding the groups, certain now of what he would find.

'Jesus.'

Here within this calfskin notebook of a vastly profitable arms merchant was confirmation of the enigmatic weapon that Nicholas had come across in the computer files of Avalon, Ltd.

TORCH 315.

Quickly, he decoded the following groups. He sat back, staring at what had appeared out of the ciphers. He could hardly think, his heart was hammering so hard in his chest. So he and Nicholas had guessed right. He read the terse notation again and again as if it were a mantra, and as he did so his blood ran cold:

'Torch scheduled March 15 at agreed site. Area chosen for proximity of target and density of population. Maximum impact assured.'

The moon-faced boy was eating a *banh chung*, a traditional Vietnamese sweet cake made from sticky rice. A smear of beans, onion and pork, the cake's filling, made his smile appear wider than it was.

Nicholas smiled back at the boy as he and Seiko approached the Giac Lam Pagoda. Sunlight glinted off the blue and white porcelain tiles along the roof of what was the oldest Buddhist temple in Saigon. Originally built in 1744, Giac Lam had last undergone renovations in 1900, sparing it the kind of modernist reconstruction that had ruined so many other temples in Vietnam.

The boy, his mouth filled with *banh chung*, ran behind the old *bo de* tree that dominated the garden in front of the pagoda. He was obscured by a pair of saffron-robed monks, a number of whom lived year-round at Giac Lam. In a moment, the monks disappeared inside the pagoda.

Nicholas and Seiko were in the Tan Binh district of Saigon, about ten miles from Cholon, the Chinese market district where Nicholas had first met Bay two nights and seemingly another lifetime ago. To the right of the pagoda were the heavily embellished tombs of the most venerated monks who had lived here.

This was the place that the arms merchant Timothy Delacroix had designated they meet him. It was now six minutes past six in the morning.

The sky was pale green. Birds in their bamboo cages twittered and cleaned themselves. Palm fronds clattered as the city awoke. The delicious scent of freshly baked baguettes filled the air, mixing with the incense wafting from inside the pagoda where the carved jackwood statues of Buddha in all his incarnations rose, surrounded by images of solemn judges and the fierce guardians of hell. For this moment, at least, when the late-night traffic had ended and the early-morning crush had not yet begun in earnest, the air possessed the peculiar sweetness that must have attracted the original Viet to this once paradisiacal land.

A chanting arose from the depths of the pagoda as

172

the monks' morning prayers began. The young boy smacked his lips loudly as he greedily jammed pieces of his sticky rice cake into his mouth.

'They are reciting Buddha's Four Noble Truths,' Seiko said. 'Existence is unhappiness; unhappiness is caused by selfishness; unhappiness ends when selfishness ends; selfishness can only end by devoting oneself to the eightfold path.'

'Yes. Understanding, purpose, speech, conduct, vocation, effort, alertness and concentration in a manner mindful of the Four Truths. Do you believe any of that?'

Seiko smiled. 'It doesn't leave much room for joy, does it? Life is already severe enough without that kind of mental shackle.'

'Is it a shackle if it leads to enlightenment?'

'Now you sound more like a holy man than a businessman.'

'I'm as much simply a businessman as you are simply my assistant. We all hide behind masks, Seiko, even from ourselves. Why is that, do you think? Are our true natures that difficult to face?'

The boy, perhaps bored because he had finished his *banh chung*, was playing peekaboo with them from behind the *bo de* tree.

'Here he comes,' Seiko said.

Nicholas turned, saw a tall, lanky man clad in a light jacket, gauze shirt and bush trousers. His sandy hair was overlong, tousled by the wind. The skin of his lean, almost vulpine face appeared to have been scoured rough and red from a life among the elements.

'You sure this is him?'

Seiko nodded. 'Positive.'

'Okay then, this is what I want you to do —'

But at that moment, Nicholas became aware of a movement in the periphery of his vision. The young

173

boy behind the *bo de* tree hadn't finished his sweet after all because he was tossing it toward them.

There was an instant when, with the help of his *tan-jian* eye, Nicholas became aware of it all: the black square sailing toward them; Delacroix, stopped in the quiet street, legs planted apart as in a marksman's stance.

In among the sensations of intense peril were the mundane sounds and smells of the early city morning: the incense burning more heavily, the monks chanting their right-minded sutras, the clattering cough of a *cyclo* starting up, the rumble underfoot of a convoy of trucks on the nearby avenue, the shouts of children, the calls of merchants as they opened their shops, the harsh screech of a bird, alarmed.

Then the object – not the boy's half-eaten sweet at all, but a square of shiny black plastic – hit the pavement near them. Delacroix's right hand appeared from within his jacket. In it was a small oblong device with a short rubber antenna, not unlike a mobile phone. Nicholas leapt at Seiko, away from the black square, which lay shining on the pavement like a rune.

His shoulder hit her, and they both went down.

Delacroix's finger depressed a button on his device.

The world exploded into ten thousand shards; the blast wave hit them and everything went white.

Demonology

The god is absent;
His dead leaves are piling,
And all is deserted.

Basho

110° E by 12° N, South China Sea

Abramanov was ready to die. The Tupolev-10 shuddered like a beast that had been shot, and the green sky canted over, making Abramanov's stomach heave. Dirty gray clouds blew past the Perspex canopy, and rain, hard as buckshot, slammed against the plane's fuselage.

'Prepare yourself,' said Fedorov, the pilot, from just behind him. 'I have lost partial control. If I can't regain it, we'll be going down hard.'

Into the high, curling swells of the storm-battered South China Sea. A long way down. Too long. Abramanov squeezed his eyes shut, the sight of the thin, red finger of land – Vietnam, Fedorov had told him – far closer in his mind than it was out the right side of the aircraft.

He began to pray.

Abramanov had been ready to die for more than a decade, the amount of time he had worked in utter secrecy and isolation in Arzamas-16, a city of atomic commerce found on no map in the world.

Less than two hundred miles east of Moscow, Arzamas-16 was, although the nation's collapse appeared near, still the site of the central nuclear weapons laboratories for what was left of the Soviet Union. Abramanov, despite being a Jew, had held a top post in Moscow's Kurchatov Institute of Atomic Energy, where he was viewed by his fellow theorists with equal amounts of awe and suspicion, mainly because he was a genius not only in atomic theory but in theoretical-language design. His contention was that it wasn't enough to develop new forms of atomic energy if one didn't have the means to harness and deliver them. Computer technology, he had argued, was the only viable method of doing this with such forms of energy that were potentially lethal to human beings.

'The Jew is brilliant,' his colleagues often said. 'Too brilliant for his own good,' said V. I. Pavlov, who had been dispatched to head Kurchatov by the Central Committee during the spring of 1981 after a particularly nasty purge. 'It is my opinion that the State is in jeopardy from such Jews,' he wrote in his report of his subsequent shake-up.

Apparently the Central Committee did not disagree with him, because in the summer of 1981, Abramanov had been demoted to Arzamas-16 by this vindictive superior, a notorious anti-Semite, purportedly as a means of squashing Abramanov's budding love affair with a beautiful assistant at Kurchatov. No official mention was made of nipping his career in the bud.

While V.I. Pavlov chuckled at the Jew's exile, Abramanov, until that time a brilliant but servile apparatchik of the Soviet regime, arrived at Arzamas-16 with a plan of his own. He was not only a genius in his own field of advanced nuclear theory and cybernetics, but was also the kind of visionary on a macro scale rarely seen among humankind.

Almost a decade before it would happen, he had already envisioned the death throes of Soviet Communism, the rabid divisiveness of ethnic strife, and the economic collapse of a world superpower whose leader, only some years before, had promised the West, 'We will bury you.'

But it was the Soviet Union, Abramanov was convinced, that was to be buried, and he was determined to be one of the first to place a wreath on its grave. All he had wanted was to be a scion of the State, but the State, grown dense and wanton with corruption, had at last beaten him down.

Also, it had changed him, and it was only now, at the point of death, that Abramanov could look at the past objectively and be grateful.

On his arrival at Arzamas-16 he began to de-emphasize the arms development and evaluation programs at the labs. In addition, he commenced a sub-rosa communication with Douglas Serman, a brother-in-arms working at the DARPA laboratory for experimental nucleonics in the American state of Virginia. DARPA was an acronym for Defense Advanced Research Projects Agency, which meant nothing at all to Abramanov, except that his American counterpart had as much money as he needed for his project while Abramanov increasingly had less and less.

Abramanov had met Serman, an American nuclear theorist, at one of the few international conferences he had been allowed to attend when he had been at Kurchatov. He had been able to strike up a friendship with Serman only because his KGB watchdogs had been intent on keeping him from being 'contaminated' by the Israeli contingent.

Continuing this covert dialogue with his DARPA pal was astonishingly easy for a man of Abramanov's talents. Day and night the Arzamas-16 complex was emitting bursts of telemetry and carrier-wave transmissions, and Abramanov found it a relatively simple task to hide his private coded communications within these transmissions.

By and large the subject of Abramanov's clandestine communication with Serman had been the creation of transuranic isotopes heretofore believed to be only theoretical. And this growing passion had led him to develop the premier high-flux neutron facility in what had then been the Soviet Union. It was within this facility that 114m had been born.

The Tupolev gave another shudder and began a long, sweeping arc downward through the buffeting grit of the gathering storm. The sky, black and lethal-looking, swung away from Abramanov, who wished now to peer beyond the clouds at the face of God. Instead, he twisted in his seat, stared back down the long empty length of the aircraft to where he knew were stowed on either side of the cabin the two cases made of DU, depleted U-238. He could not keep his thoughts from their abruptly malevolent contents.

The transuranic isotope 114m had been born in the hot cell Abramanov had had built at Arzamas-16. This was a windowless cubicle with five-foot-thick concrete walls. The material had to be manipulated via stainless-steel robotic arms, controlled from outside the hot cell, at the panel of dials, gauges and levers where an operator sat. The hot cell was equipped with the most extreme contamination control systems, including an inert atmosphere, and even the surrounding areas were fed by negative-pressure ventilation units in order to prevent the highly toxic particles of plutonium and 114m from migrating out of the primary confinement zone.

For some years now, scientists had been trying to create transuranic isotopes – that is, substances with higher atomic numbers than uranium – without much success. Isotope 114m had been created by bombarding a brick of plutonium with a high-density field of neutrons in an argon atmosphere. This had been attempted before, but Abramanov's brilliance had come in pulsing the neutrons at a frequency that overexcited the atoms of the plutonium, thus forcing a reaction.

A number of isotopes of element 114 had been observed forming, but they rapidly decayed because of their minuscule half-lives.

Only one isotope remained. Abramanov named it 114m because it was the fourteenth isotope created from the event. He estimated its half-life to be in the tens of thousands of years. Other surprises lay in store for Abramanov and his team. Because they found it possessed an inordinately high cross-section of thermal neutrons, 114m was an extremely potent fissile material. And because its critical mass was lower than both plutonium and uranium, its potential value sky-rocketed. Abramanov calculated that what he had discovered just might be the most powerful and efficient nuclear energy source on the face of the earth.

The unique nuclear criticality displayed by 114m led Abramanov to continue his experiments in his own time, keeping his own counsel – and that of Douglas Serman in Virginia. What he found both elated and terrified him, so much so that he dared not make his findings public – even to the rest of his research team.

When it came to the human race, Abramanov was no optimist. He saw the potential danger should even one brick of 114m fall into the wrong hands. The sins of greed, avarice, ambition and temptation paraded across the stage of his mind like tawdry whores vulgarly displaying their elemental wares. He could count from merely those around him the number who would be tempted to use 114m for personal ends.

It seemed to him then that he was in a hot box of his own making – trapped within a conundrum. He found it unthinkable to give over to his masters the terrible secret of this transuranic isotope. He would not even trust it to the minds of his colleagues in Arzamas-16; how could he deliver it into the hands of the Central Committee in the Kremlin? Besides, at that point there was no telling who was in power, and who would remain there for any meaningful length of time. There was no way to destroy the ingots of 114m he had already manufactured, and he could think of no place secure enough in his tremor-prone area of the country to bury them.

This was the trap he had so cleverly, if unwittingly, constructed for himself. Then, one night, he awoke from a dream that showed him how 114m was to be his savior rather than his doom. For months now he had been dreaming of getting out of the increasingly anarchic Soviet Union, but he lacked the nerve. Now he had the impetus because fleeing his homeland with the deadly ingots was his only logical egress from the hot box.

Working at night, he constructed two boxes of DU so that the ingots of 114m were shielded by three inches of the heavy metal. This was far from the ideal thickness, but Abramanov was driven by the constraints of time and portability. As it was, each container weighed nine hundred pounds, but he knew he must still maintain the two-foot physical space between the ingots of radioactive isotope. The consequences of bringing them in close proximity made him break out into a cold sweat.

The wild, dark sea was coming up from below, solid as a steel-clad door, and only now did he understand fully the extent of his folly.

He had enlisted the aid of a pilot friend of his, a colonel in the VVS, the Soviet Air Force, who, like Abramanov, had grown weary of and disillusioned with Communism, and together they had plotted their getaway. Then Abramanov contacted Douglas Serman and told him he would shortly be on his way.

Fedorov was scheduled to take a MiG-29 UB two-seat jet trainer across the country from Moscow to the military airfield outside Vladivostok. For Abramanov, who wanted to get to Virginia in the east of America, it was the long way around, but his options were limited, and he had had no choice.

Fedorov's main problem was how to avoid the Soviet and Vietnamese perimeter radar; Abramanov's had been how to deal with the size and weight of the depleted U-238 cases within which lay like the children of Behemoth the deadly ingots of 114m.

Fedorov had been in the Soviet Air Force for more than twenty years and he knew every flying trick in the book. At Vladivostok, he had logged in a refit flight on the Tupolev-10, an old long-distance military transport, had stayed within the radar fields, then, along the coast, had taken the aircraft to an altitude below effective radar range, putting out a spurious distress call that would lead Soviet search planes north while they headed steadily south.

The two four-by-five-by-eight-inch ingots had a total weight of just over three hundred pounds, and the DU cases themselves were each just under half a ton. Abramanov and Fedorov had replaced the guts of a pair of the MiG-29's AA-10 Alamo laser-guided air-to-air missiles with the cases, using the automated gantry servos used to load bombs.

At the Vladivostok airfield, the military was already in such chaos that it was a relatively simple matter for the two of them to transfer the cargo to the Tupolev in utter secrecy.

Having felt firsthand the power of the MiG-29's twin Tumanski jet engines, Abramanov had wished to continue their flight in that swift aircraft. But this had proved impossible. Besides the fact that he had to log the MiG-29 in with the field commander, Fedorov had pointed out that if the Chinese or Vietnamese radar picked up the configuration of a warbird outside Soviet airspace, they would initiate an international disaster of incalculable proportions.

Now, in the fierce grip of the subtropical storm, Abramanov wished for the 4,700-kph thrust such a plane would give them. At least they would have a chance to outrun the storm. In the wallowing Tupolev, they were completely at the sky's mercy.

Too late he thought of the consequences should the two 114m cases come in contact with each other or – just as terrifying – if their DU shielding should be damaged in the coming crash.

'I can't hold it!' Fedorov shouted, giving life to Abramanov's worst fears. 'We're going down!'

The colonel unstrapped, while Abramanov sat in his chair, paralyzed with dread. He was not thinking of himself, but of the 114m.

'Damn you, come on!' Fedorov grabbed Abramanov by the front of his flight suit, hauled him out of his seat.

The Tupolev was canted crazily, its nose dragged down as if by a lead weight. Rain pelted the cockpit cowling and the fuselage, setting up a fearful din. Great gusts of wind slammed the aircraft over and down.

'We have to jump now!' Fedorov shouted in Abramanov's ear.

As if in a trance, Abramanov hesitated, reluctant to part with the cases of 114m. 'Our cargo –'

'You idiot, fuck the cargo!' Fedorov screamed, hauling him toward the door. 'The autopilot won't hold us up for long. A moment more and we'll be too low for the chutes to open in time!'

Fedorov leaned on the cargo door, sliding it open. Wind and rain flew in, bouncing around the cabin like ricocheting bullets. The elements plucked at them like a living thing, taking Abramanov's breath away.

'Now!' shouted Fedorov at the edge of the doorway.

'I can't leave! I –'

But Fedorov had already released his hold on the fuselage, his body sucked out of the aircraft. Abramanov watched with an almost detached curiosity as Fedorov's dark form dwindled, tumbling over and over. Then the quick bloom, startling in its paleness, as his parachute opened.

The Tupolev was shuddering and groaning as the storm, let loose inside it, threatened to rip it apart. Abramanov's teeth were chattering. As if in a dream, he watched his fingers give up their white-knuckled grip on the edge of the doorway. He felt a sudden burst of kinetic energy, as if the hands of a giant had slammed into the small of his back, and he was hurled into the heart of the black storm.

Upside down, the wind howling in his ears, drenched to the bone, he scrabbled for the rip cord. He saw the underside of the Tupolev yaw away from him and wondered that he could not discern the massive roar of its engines above the primal howling of the storm.

Disoriented, he could not find the rip cord, and he panicked, tasting bile in his mouth. He thought of the ocean, so far below him, rising up to slam him into oblivion. His belly turned to ice, and he almost lost a grip on his bowels. Then his hands closed around the plastic handles and he jerked them down. The abrupt break in his downward momentum felt like the intercession of God. As he righted, he gave a prayer.

Below him was the sea and, to his right, the top of Fedorov's chute, a comforting flower in an inimical world, and Abramanov felt dissipate a measure of the tension that had racked him ever since they hit the leading edge of the storm.

In retrospect, it seemed as if he knew what would happen a split second before it actually took place. An eerie sense of immediate déjà vu gripped him as he saw Fedorov slice sideways, driven by a fierce gust of wind.

Almost simultaneously, a rent in his main chute appeared, a dark, grinning mouth, widening madly until the chute collapsed into segments and Fedorov commenced to plunge downward at a terrifying rate.

Abramanov tried to shout a warning, but the sound was snatched from his lips, lost within the violent whorls and eddies of the storm.

He was close enough to the heaving ocean to see what happened to Fedorov as his friend struck it. It was as if the sea rose up to meet him. Abramanov could see approaching a gigantic wave, shot through with darkness, a demon with glass teeth, a beast out of a nightmare, trembling with feral fury. Fedorov's head canted at an impossible angle as his body struck the leading edge of the wave and disappeared into that lost world. The passage of life into death was momentarily marked by the stain of the shredded parachute, before it, too, was sucked beneath the waves.

Abramanov felt an overwhelming urge to vomit. The sea was so high, so close now, that he could taste the salt and phosphorus it gave off as if it were radiation. Abramanov thought that perhaps his friend's fate was the better of two evils. Instantaneous death must be preferable, he told himself, to drowning. A sudden squall of wind caught him as it had Fedorov, jerking him from side to side as if he were trapped on a ride in an amusement park, and Abramanov thought for a moment that God was going to grant his wish.

But his chute held, driven sideways over the ocean, propelled by the wind. Above him, he could see, like a leviathan descending toward the ocean's floor, the Tupolev-10. The shadow of its passage was like an eclipse. Even the monstrous storm seemed to pause for an instant.

Then, like a celestial object thrown off course, the aircraft drove into the water nose first, and above the storm's incessant roar, Abramanov heard the squeal of tortured metal, felt the shock wave as if it were a bomb blast.

He swung vertiginously just above the waves, then, as the storm resumed its fury, he was dashed into the bosom of the South China Sea, closer to the Tupolev-10 and its unnerving cargo than he wanted to be.

Something tore, splintering. Pain lanced through his body. *Oh, God, my leg!* he thought as the first, enervating torrent of water engulfed him.

Rock breathed deeply of the sea air, scenting phosphorus and brine, decomposing seagrape and barnacles, fish heads baking in the sun. The boat rolled deeply in the green and indigo swells.

'We're almost there,' Abramanov said.

Rock looked up from his methodical cleaning of a black magic – an M16A1 army rifle – saw Abramanov hulking like a brown bear across the deck. Not so long a trip, he thought, but on the other hand before they were finished, it might be longer than a journey to the end of the world.

Rock had been in Asia for so long it was the only home he knew. He remembered another one, dimly and with a combination of rage and fear. In nightmares he experienced again his father looming over him, drunk and out of work again.

C'mon, his father would say to him in his nightmare. *Just you an' me, Junior, without your mother to save your stinking, worthless ass.* Then his father would strip the bedcovers off him, strike him beside his ear with such stunning force that Rock would almost pass out. Then again and again. Nightmare or remembered past?

Rock did remember the day he had faced his father down and – after years of beefing up at the gym, at army boot camp and on the first and only leave he had used to return home – with one stunningly quick left hook, had set him down on the pavement in front of the Pittsburgh ghetto tenement in which Rock had been brought up.

His father's only response had been to smile slyly as he spat blood. *I been waiting a long fucking time, Junior,* he had said. *Just remember I made you what you are.*

Now, as he stood upon the pitching deck of one of the many boats he owned, Rock watched the Russian crossing unsteadily toward him. That leg had been a mess when one of Rock's patrol boats had scooped Abramanov out of these storm-dark waters six months ago. Rock, who had access to the best of everything in Southeast Asia, had had his people do their best. But even so he lacked the facilities and the personnel of a Walter Reed Hospital. Bones had been reset but nerve damage was irreversible, at least in this part of the world. Of course, he hadn't told Abramanov that; the man had been grateful enough to be saved from drowning in an angry sea. Abramanov, like many people with thoroughly analytical minds, had an irrational fear. Rock supposed it was his good karma that Abramanov's phobia was drowning. He wasn't too crazy about sharks, either, which made him all the more grateful for the timely rescue.

Rock stood at the railing with Abramanov. He removed his sunglasses, squinted as the first line of nimbostratus occluded the sun. The light had abruptly turned leaden. 'If the weather holds,' he said, 'we'll have the robot down to the plane within an hour.'

He stared down into the ocean, trying hard to imagine the Soviet aircraft lying on an outcropping at the edge of an abyss of unimaginable depth. But already the water was darkening to the color of pitch.

The storm had blown in while they were too far out to sea. The captain of Rock's patrol boat was a small

Vietnamese who knew these waters better than many men twenty years his senior. 'The storm, when it comes, will be a bad one,' he said in his lilting voice. 'But if we turn back now, we will be heading broadside into the brunt of it, and I don't believe I want to do that.'

Rock nodded. 'Good, neither do I. Hold your position, then, and we'll go to work.' He turned to Abramanov. 'How will the robot perform in this weather?'

To prove his gratitude, Abramanov had spent the months of his rehab constructing a submersible robot, a seven-foot titanium shell housing a network of laser-guided telemetry, mini-computers, navigation transducers, sonar, a complement of turbo thrusters, articulated arms with sophisticated finger-like pincer ends, video cameras, tungsten spotlights, backup lithium batteries and the like, all connected with the shipboard computer via a fiber-optic cable bundle.

The complex creation appeared to be child's play for Abramanov, who cobbled most of the robot's component parts from Rock's vast storehouse of military ordnance. Part of the robot's design was based on the specialized manipulator 'hands' Abramanov had built for his high-flux neutron-field hot room in Arzamas-16.

'The robot will be fine,' Abramanov said. 'It will be six hundred feet below the surface and won't feel a thing. It's us that will be the problem if the storm really kicks in. If we can't hold our position and can't get the robot up in time, the cable could be severed and we'd lose the robot.'

'Get it over the side,' Rock said.

'But —'

'Now, before the swells get too high to get it in the water.'

Rain was spitting at them in irregular bursts and the ceiling had lowered significantly just in the time they had been talking. Clouds streaked past, dark and gravid with precipitation. In the distance it appeared as if the swelling sea was heaving up to meet the angry sky.

Rock gave the signal to the team manning the special winch and the electronic monitoring devices in their airtight housings. A moment later, a bulky chalk-white object was lowered over the side of the boat. There was a dull clang as the robot, caught in the rising current just beneath the surface of the sea, struck the hull of the boat. They all held their breath. Then it was clear, descending toward its destiny.

Abramanov had built this robot as a tabula rasa. It possessed great skills, but lacked the brain to implement those skills. It would be up to Abramanov to fill the steel, ceramic and fiber-optic networks with purpose.

'Halfway down,' Abramanov muttered to Rock as he clung to the coping of the hatch leading into the main cabin below. He was clearly uncomfortable with the rolling and pitching of the boat and appeared ready to duck into the safety of belowdecks at a moment's notice. 'Everything okay. The swaying has stopped. It's calm down there.'

Rock went to check their position with the captain. Despite the increasingly foul weather, the captain remained confident he could keep them stable. Rock told him to inform him immediately of any change in that status.

For the time being satisfied, he turned away, stood next to Abramanov as the Russian adjusted the remote transceiver he had clipped to his belt. Then, with a nervous glance at Rock, Abramanov slipped on the wire ear- and mouthpiece and switched the system on.

'It's very dark down there. Color values are nil. I'm switching on the tungsten floods.'

'Are you nervous, Abramanov?'

'Yes. I am very fearful. We are close to the objective now.'

'I can read you. You want this every bit as much as I do. Do you want the cargo to sit underwater until some undersea quake breaks open the DU casings?'

'God forbid! The consequences of such an event would be catastrophic.'

'So you've said. Is the robot on the ridge yet?'

'I am still suspended.'

Abramanov had a curious habit when connected with the camera eyes and claw hands of the robot to put himself in its place.

Rock pulled up the hood of his slicker, went out on deck. Seawater washed across his ankles as the deck canted, then righted itself; the water sluiced away.

He went back into the cabin, where Abramanov sat cabled to the descending robot. 'Where are we?'

'Almost there,' Abramanov said, checking his bank of portable computers. 'I'm twenty feet from the upper level of the ledge.'

'Too bad we couldn't drop it closer, on the lower level, but the outcroppings the discrete-image sonar picked up would almost certainly have cut the cable.' Rock shook his head. 'We don't even know whether he will be able to walk down to the bottom level.'

A spray of rain hit the windows with the force of a hammer throw. The boat rocked at its mooring. Rock glanced at the captain, but he was too busy giving orders to notice.

'I'm on the ledge.'

Rock returned his attention to Abramanov, who was rechecking the plethora of sophisticated telemetry coming in from the robot's remote sensors.

'What does it look like?'

'Slow. Serene. Unlike up here. I will show you.'

Abramanov switched on the video camera, made

191

some adjustments. On the twelve-inch monitor a perfect image appeared of the immediate environs of the shale ledge six hundred feet below him.

Awed, despite himself, Rock whispered, 'I see the ledge floor. Go forward.'

The image shifted, and Rock felt almost as if he himself had begun to walk that narrow shale ridge below that hung over thousands of fathoms of water under pressure so severe it would burst apart anything man-made.

'It's surprisingly easy,' Abramanov reported. 'It is not steep.'

'According to the sonar sweeps that will change very soon and very quickly.'

'Yes, yes. I know.'

Abramanov was locked into the wonder of his underwater world. Rock wondered what it must be like linked so completely into the sensors of a machine. He didn't care for the thought, but for a scientist like Abramanov it must be heaven.

'Be careful.'

Rock saw the image changing. Within the light field he could see the striations of the shale ledge, floating bits in the water: diadems of plankton, mixed perhaps with bits of shale and biological detritus the robot had disturbed as it moved along the ledge. A tiny translucent squid passing in and out of the theater of vision. Nothing else.

'The drop-off begins,' Abramanov informed him.

The rain was a constant hammering now, and the boat was bobbing on the gathering swells. 'Everything okay with the mechanical systems?' And when Abramanov nodded, he said, 'Is the drop-off continuing?'

'Accelerating. The sonar readings are off by point five percent.'

'Not too bad.'

'The difference might have caused serious injury to a human diver. See?'

Rock did. The irregular shale had come off in thick, long plates, creating a kind of rift in the ledge. 'Can the robot negotiate the chasm?'

'No problem.'

Rock was suddenly aware of a feeling of weightlessness, and he made a grab for the hatch opening. Then the shale ridge came up into the light again, and the eerie sensation was gone. He could see that though the ledge now sloped down at a far steeper angle, it was somewhat wider than it had been up top. He waited, tossed by the storm on the surface.

'Problem.'

Rock's stomach tightened, and not just from the increasingly frenzied motion of the boat. 'Nature?'

'I'd better show you.'

The image on the monitor shifted, and Rock experienced a disconcerting sense of vertigo. Then the image stabilized and he could see the phalanx of outcroppings, sharp as lances, that shot out just in front of the robot.

'Can the robot get through?'

'The ledge appears impassable for the next sixty-five feet. Beyond that is the abyss.'

No, Rock thought. *We're so close; I will not be stopped short. There must be a way.*

As if reading his mind, Abramanov said, 'I believe there's a way around the impasse.'

'Tell me.'

'If you use the cable to swing me off the ledge at the angle I calculate, the forward momentum will drive me past the blockage and back onto the ledge.'

'Do it.'

Abramanov hesitated. 'There is a caveat.'

Rock's stomach was now doing flip-flops. 'Only one?'

'When my momentum brings me in past the outcrop-pings, there's a chance the cable will be severed.'

'If that happens, the robot *and* the objective will be lost.'

'Yes.'

'What are the odds of us making it across intact?'

'About even.'

'Alternatives?'

Abramanov sighed. 'I'm very much afraid there are none. As we have seen, no diver can possibly make it to the aircraft, let alone return with the cargo. The robot's the only chance we have.'

Rock took a deep breath. 'Initiate the procedure.'

Abramanov surprised him; this was the moment that, looking back, he began to like and to trust the Russian. 'The calculations are already complete. I am feeding them into the computers.'

The captain was plucking anxiously at Rock's sleeve. 'What the hell is this data coming on-line?'

'Never mind,' Rock said. 'Just keep an eye on the storm and hold us steady at our present position.'

'But, sir —'

Rock hefted his black magic. 'If we move even a centi-meter off-line, I'll shoot you.' To Abramanov, he said, 'Are you ready?'

'Yes.'

'Do it now,' Rock said, feeling his heart seem to stop as he watched Abramanov hit the button.

The image blew out against the edges of the screen. Diadems danced crazily in the light as the image swung, shifting radically, illuminating a larger section of the ledge as the robot was hurled outward into the sea, overhanging the abyss.

Darkness below, and an eerie sense of weightlessness, then the image shifted again as the robot was hurled forward. The light fanned outward, careening over the

194

phalanx of lethal-looking shale, bunched like the frowning brow of a giant sea god.

And then they were coming in quickly with the shale spears looming like the weapons of an execution squad.

Are we far enough forward? Rock asked himself. *Has Abramanov made the right calculations? It looks like we're heading right for those spears, they're so close.* Tiny creatures milled around their points, transfixed by the alien light, then blown away by the fierce displacement of water as the heavy robot swung inward.

Whoomp!

'The cable is intact.'

Rock felt light-headed as his fingers gripped the Russian's shoulder.

'On the ledge,' Abramanov said.

The image on the monitor faded for a moment, then reassembled, as the robot continued its descent along the edge of the abyss. After a time, the image became stationary, and Rock knew that the robot had stopped.

'What's happening?'

He was shown the view forward. The pitch of the shale ledge was now near to vertical. At the far end of the shaft cut into the shale the light illuminated something cold, hard, shiny beneath the silty biological casing that was encrusting it.

'Primary objective.'

Rock's heart leapt. 'Any problems negotiating the underwater chimney?'

'None.'

The image remained unchanged.

'Then what's the matter?'

Abramanov partially unhooked himself from the telemetry, turned to Rock. 'I think at this point we must consider abandoning the project.'

'Why? Can you see any cracks in the casings? Is there any sign of gamma radiation leakage?'

195

'Telemetry indicates no radiation leakage what-soever.'

'Do you have moral misgivings then?'

Abramanov sighed, 'I wouldn't be human if I didn't.'

'Then try to be more like me. I have no misgivings whatsoever. We've got to get your 114m out of this danger area. I told you there was a quake here of major proportions just last year. Almost every month, there's a minor one.'

'Yes, this is why we are here today. As I have told you, 114m was created by massive and repeated bombardment of plutonium by a high-energy, high-flux neutron field in an inert atmosphere of argon gas.

'The inert atmosphere was necessary in part because 114m is an exceedingly energetic gamma-ray emitter, and exposure for even one minute is lethal to humans.'

Abramanov had explained that all radioactive isotopes emitted three kinds of radiation: alpha, the slowest and therefore most easily stopped, beta, and gamma. Gamma rays moved at the speed of light and were therefore the most difficult to deflect. Lead or depleted uranium-238, both very dense metals, were most often used to contain the emissions. In the case of 114m it was yet to be determined whether the DU casings would be adequate in keeping the deadly radiation contained.

'Quite apart from that,' Abramanov continued, '114m is more chemically toxic than its parent element, plutonium, and let me tell you that plutonium is a nightmare to deal with. Contact with fine particles by inhalation, ingestion, or absorption through the skin is lethal to humans. The argon atmosphere minimizes oxidation and surface instability. However, I must emphasize that even with the best containment measures, particulates of 114m can and will migrate out of confinement zones.'

Rock stared implacably at the Russian. 'What's your point?'

The Russian shook his head sadly. 'If I am required to explain further, it is useless.' He turned back to his telemetry. 'Let's get on with it.'

Rock felt his stomach lurch upward into his throat as the image on the monitor canted over and down. The robot sank into the chimney of shale, alighting on the floor of the lowest section of the ledge.

There was the Russian aircraft that had brought Abramanov into his lap.

'Beginning fuselage penetration.'

The robot's sophisticated mechanical arms emerged from its squat torso, its delicate fingers probing the side of the aircraft. They worked industriously for some time.

Rock waited, his heart pounding painfully against his rib cage. The turbulence caused by the robot's armor-piercing blades made it impossible to follow the procedure visually.

'Fuselage breached. Going in.'

A riot of images exploded on the monitor as the robot's spots illuminated the interior of the plane in disjointed segments.

Rock could not bear the tension. 'Do you see them?'

The images – flaring white light, impenetrable darkness – were impossible to decipher. Maybe the aircraft had shifted with the tectonic activity, spilling the 114m into the abyss; maybe they hadn't made it all the way into the water with the plane; maybe –

'Cargo located.'

Rock squinted at the screen, could make out the dull metallic boxes the robot's articulated arms were handling.

'Yes! Come to mama!' Rock was too elated at this moment to feel any fear. He hand-signaled to the crewmen standing by to be ready to deploy the automatic nets that would capture the robot and its extraordinary prize when it emerged on the surface.

But already the image had shattered, re-forming in a kind of slow-motion free fall as the robot, having backed out of the rent fuselage, was teetering on the shale ledge. The movement was putting it in danger of dropping down into the abyss that seemed limitless.

'Fucker, I told you to keep this damn boat steady!' Rock shouted at the captain as he hefted his black magic.

'It isn't the storm,' Abramanov said as his fingers worked frenziedly over the robot's remote controls. 'There's a tectonic shift in progress.'

'An undersea quake!'

The images on the screen shuddered, then splintered like sparks from a burning log.

'I've hit something! The fuselage or an outcropping. The thrusters are inoperable.'

'Get the thing out of there, Abramanov! Now!'

'I can't! I'm paralyzed!' The Russian was sweating. 'Use the backup electronic winch!'

Rock rushed across the cabin, out into the storm. He signaled to his men, who leapt to the gantry securing the robot's winch to the deck. Rock, at the controls himself, began reeling the robot in. He tried to imagine the scene deep beneath him. How severe was the quake? He stared at the gauges through the sheeting rain, shouted wordlessly as they registered the tension and weight associated with the robot.

He gave over the controls to one of his men, raced back inside the cabin.

'Sir, I can't hold us here much longer,' the captain said.

'With any luck you won't have to.' To Abramanov, Rock said, 'How're we doing?'

'We're off the ledge, at least. Now all we have to worry about is losing the casings.'

But Rock knew that would not happen now. Soon he'd have the 114m on board, and shortly after that the precious isotope and its creator would be safely secreted within the bunker-like containment environment Rock had had constructed for the purpose.

Then he would give Abramanov his final instructions – or ultimatum. Rock was fully prepared for that. He had no compunction about doing whatever had to be done in order to take this extraordinary raw material and make of it something unique. The way he saw it, 114m was not unlike the tears of the poppy his people harvested high in the Shan mountains of Burma. That substance was also extraordinary, but it needed the careful refining process to make it unique – and highly valuable.

Rock, watching the back of Abramanov's head as he monitored the ascent of the robot and the DU-cased 114m bricks through turbulent waters, knew that he must have an end product from the fissile isotope like no other.

He knew this because an eternally grateful Abramanov had revealed his creation's secret: that it was the most powerful portable nuclear-energy source imaginable. To Rock, that had implications that made his mouth water. Today's world was vastly different from what it had been even two years ago. The Cold War was dead, Russia was no longer the threat it had been. It was the time of the small, mobile ethnic battle, and that meant the rise of terrorism. Unwittingly, Abramanov had given him the most potent product he could sell to the new kind of customer that was, increasingly, demanding weaponry.

Rock was almost salivating in anticipation. He had in his hands the ultimate terrorist weapon – immensely powerful and compact. Even better, he had the one man who could manufacture it.

BOOK II: Ensigns of Betrayal

A lightning flash;
between the forest trees
I have seen water.

Masaoka Shiki

FIVE

Washington/Vung Tau/Tokyo

A woman in a bubblegum-pink angora sweater and a short, pleated skirt the color of the sky at dusk was waiting for Croaker when he walked into the lobby of the Holiday Inn Central on Rhode Island Avenue and Fifteenth Street. The color of her hair could only be termed violent black. It was blunt cut, perfectly straight, and came to just below her jawline. She had a heart-shaped face and wore wraparound sunglasses with mir-rored lenses. She lounged against the check-in counter; under one arm was a thick manila envelope, which she handed to him when he approached the concierge's desk.

'Samuel Johnson, I presume?' She had a low, husky voice that seemed more of a purr.

'And you are?'

'Just a voice on the other end of a coded line.' She regarded him as he opened the envelope. 'Shouldn't we do this somewhere . . . more private?'

He looked up. 'We? What are you doing here anyway?'

She shrugged. 'I was intrigued. These days I'm so bored I go Rollerblading all afternoon.'

'Yeah?' He took a look at her legs, which were very long and beautifully shaped. 'And what happens if you're needed?'

'I get beeped.' She smiled. 'Have cellular phone, will travel.'

He went through the documents quickly. 'What got you so intrigued?'

'I was wondering why you wanted me to run down my sister's car.'

'Your sister?'

'Yeah.' She pointed. 'The Nissan 300 ragtop's hers. Vesper Arkham.' She stuck out her hand. 'My name's Domino.' She laughed, looking at his expression. 'I often get that look. Don't worry. My father was a James Bond fanatic. He named his daughters after characters in the novels.'

'At least he didn't name either of you Pussy.'

'Thank God for small favors.' She hooked her arm through his. 'Now how about buying me breakfast while you tell me what you want with Vesper.'

At that hour there wasn't much to choose from. She took him to the restaurant at the Four Seasons in Georgetown. It was out of the way, but that was the point. He ordered orange juice, coffee, eggs and bacon.

Domino asked for coffee and toast, both of them black. 'I like my toast charcoaled and my meat bloody, who knows why.'

When the waiter had gone, he said, 'What do you know about Senator Richard Dedalus?'

'Dedalus? How is he connected with my sister?'

'He may not be. It depends.'

The waiter appeared with the coffee and juice, then disappeared behind some potted foliage. Across the expansive room sunlight flooded through a narrow garden and into the restaurant. There were few other patrons; the closest was a beefy salesman, busily scrolling through a notebook computer, and unless he was equipped with a directional microphone, he was out of earshot.

'Actually, I went out with him for a while.' Domino sipped her coffee. 'It was an assignment, really. Richie's so influential it was thought, well, it might be best to vet him in this rather . . . unorthodox manner. I mean, we didn't have access to flutter him or anything.' Fluttering meant submitting to a lie detector. 'It was for his own good.'

'Sure it was.'

Domino made a face. 'I didn't sleep with him or anything.'

'I didn't say you did.'

She put down her cup. 'You didn't have to.'

Their food came, and he was silent for some time, watching her take tiny bites out of her cindered toast. 'Do you think you could take off those glasses? The lenses are giving me the willies.'

Domino removed them and he saw a pair of wide-apart emerald eyes, fully as large as the startling cornflower-blue eyes he had glimpsed in her blonde sister.

'I like Richie,' Domino continued. 'He's smart and quick. There's nothing old about the way he thinks.'

Croaker broke one yolk, mopped up the mess with a slice of bacon. 'He have any unusual friends?'

'Unusual?'

'For a United States senator.'

'Richie has a lot of friends.'

Richie. She was speaking about one of the most powerful men in America. 'Was one of them Dominic Goldoni?'

'The Mafia boss? The guy who was murdered last year?'

'That's the one.'

Domino wiped her fingertips on her napkin. 'I guess so. I remember meeting his sister. What was her name?'

'Marilyn.'

'No. Margarite. I remember her very well. She impressed me; not like some Italian princesses I've met, if you get my drift.'

205

Croaker certainly did. 'So Margarite and the senator got together. What did they do?'

Domino shook her head. 'You first. What do you want with Vesper?'

Croaker wiped his mouth, took a swig of coffee while wondering how big a hole the acid was going to burn in his stomach. 'I saw her last night. At Moniker's. She and Margarite took off in the black Nissan ragtop.'

'Where did they go?'

'I don't know.'

'And Richie?'

'Margarite arrived at the strip joint in Senator Dedalus's limo.'

'So you're following Goldoni's sister.'

'No. Someone else who was at Moniker's.' No way he was going to tell this woman the truth. He had trusted Lillehammer up to a point and had been betrayed.

Domino turned her head toward the sunlight streaming into the room while she thought over his answers. 'My sister worked for Leon Waxman before his death.'

'I worked for William Justice Lillehammer.'

'Really? And you two never met? Lillehammer worked for Waxman.'

'Right. Same agency. I was recruited in the field. I never came to his office. In fact, I didn't know he had one.'

Domino pursed her lips. 'You sure you came by the codes legitimately? I'd hate to think I gave intelligence over to an interloper.'

'Lillehammer hired me as a freelance to look into Dominic Goldoni's death.'

'And you're still doing that? I had heard Goldoni was murdered by a crazy Vietnamese with a grudge – Duck something.'

Croaker couldn't help smiling. 'Do Duc, yes. But it's

206

never been made clear just who hired Do Duc. It's my belief that it was Waxman.'

'That would make sense since Waxman turned out to be Johnny Leonforte.'

It was becoming clear that this woman was no dim-witted bureaucratic clerk.

Croaker thought a moment. 'How did Dedalus come to hire Waxman in the first place?'

'He came highly recommended.'

'By whom?'

'I wouldn't know.' She contemplated him for some time. 'Maybe Vesper does.'

'Another reason why I need to see her.'

She leaned across the table. 'Who were you surveilling at Moniker's?'

'I'm afraid that's privileged information.'

She stood up. 'Then I can't help you with Margarite and the senator.'

'Sit down. Please.'

Reluctantly, she did as he asked. It was dawning on him that this woman was outmaneuvering him. That rankled. He knew he shouldn't feel that way. If she had been a man, he'd see this merely as an interesting adversarial confrontation. He wondered how to proceed. Perhaps a modicum of the truth was called for.

'The truth is Lillehammer brought me in because he was concerned about a traitor or traitors inside his agency. He warned me to trust no one; so far it's been sound advice.'

'The trouble with it is in order to get on with your investigation you've got to trust someone sometime.'

She was right, of course, but he hated to admit it. 'I am curious about Dominic Goldoni's relationship with Senator Dedalus. On the face of it, it's odd enough to warrant investigation.'

'I agree. But when you know that Dedalus was in charge of a subcommittee looking into re-regulating interstate trucking and municipal bidding for new construction, Goldoni's motivation for sucking up to the senator becomes clear.'

'And Margarite is continuing the relationship.'

'I imagine so. I can't think of any other reason she would want to see Dedalus.' She gave him a playful smile. 'You see? A little trust isn't such a terrible thing to give away, is it?'

Nicholas opened his eyes into whiteness. He blinked rapidly, tears coming to his eyes, as he became aware of his breathing: in, out, in, out. The whiteness was everywhere, as if he existed, weightless, within a cloud. He could hear his heart beating like the *ki* of the sky, the blood coursing through his arteries and veins like the wind.

The harsh cry of a seagull took him out of himself; the soft rolling susurrus of the surf stole into his consciousness. He was very near an ocean; perhaps along a shoreline. Where?

'Have you ever had the recurring dream where you're in a building – an office or a private house, it doesn't matter which. Anyway, there are people all about – you can't see them but you can feel them like lice on your skin, and you know you've got to hide from them. You don't know why but you *must*.'

'I never have, no.'

'Well, I have – all the time.'

Nicholas recognized Seiko's voice, but who had answered her? A male voice, well modulated, educated. They were speaking Japanese.

There was the soft clink of ice against glassware, and Nicholas was aware of sweat on his bare skin, the whisper of a thin cotton sheet covering him from the waist

208

down. White mosquito netting was tented over him so that he appeared suspended within a cloud.

'What happens in your dream?' the male voice asked.

'I'm desperate not to be seen. I run through the rooms of the house, banging on the walls looking for a trap door. Then, as I am about to be overtaken, I turn a corner, reach up to the ceiling, and find one.'

'So you're safe.'

A soft sound of fabric, a whiff of perfume, and Nicholas knew Seiko was moving around. 'No, they find me anyway in that dark, cramped space.'

'I'm no Freudian, but –'

'I know, I know, it's a birth dream. That's one interpretation.'

'What's *your* interpretation?'

'I'm ashamed of what I am doing.'

The man laughed. 'Are you serious?'

'Perhaps not. Someone once said that all dreams are jokes, anyway.'

'I should hope so. Try as I may, shame is a sentiment I cannot connect with you.'

Nicholas groaned.

Seiko caught her breath. 'He's awake. Thank God.'

'I told you it wouldn't take long.'

'And how would you know?' She reached the bed on which Nicholas was lying. She looked down at him and smiled, obvious relief on her face. 'Thank God,' she said again as her hand gently passed across his forehead. She leaned down, pressed her lips against his.

'Where am I?' Nicholas said hoarsely.

'Give him a drink, for God's sake,' the male voice said, slightly vexed. 'Kisses can come later.'

Seiko, kneeling beside the bed, brought a tumbler of cold water to Nicholas's mouth. He drank avidly.

'I want to get up,' he whispered. He was aware of his

209

cheek resting against Seiko's shoulder. It was as cool as alabaster.

'I don't think that would be a good idea.'

'Oh, stop mothering him,' the male voice said. It was on the move, coming toward them. 'He can do whatever he tells you he can do. I told you that.'

Nicholas felt rather than saw Seiko look up at this man. He was curious about the stranger, but instinctively he did not want to look into his face until he was on his feet.

'Where are we?' he said as Seiko helped him off the bed.

'Never mind. It's someplace perfectly safe.'

He saw, much to his astonishment, that all he had on was a batik-print bathing suit.

'Look at him,' the man said. 'Whatever superficial scrapes and bruises he had are all but gone.'

He was right, of course. Just as strenuous physical exercise caused important chemical changes within the mind and body, so Tau-tau could manipulate the body's chemicals – endorphins, nucleopeptides – to aid the healing process.

Nicholas, on his feet, swung his head around. 'Who the hell are you?'

'Nicholas Linnear, this is Tachi Shidare, the new *oyabun* of the Yamauchi clan.'

Shidare bowed, but not, Nicholas noticed, very deeply, being careful to limit the respect offered in the gesture.

'I know how you feel about Yakuza,' Seiko said. 'But I was desperate. I needed to call on someone I could trust, someone without a hidden agenda.'

'You are Tomoo Kozo's successor,' Nicholas said to Shidare.

The *oyabun* smiled thinly. He was young, perhaps only in his mid-thirties, tall, and had the avaricious black eyes of a crow. His long and narrow face had a deeply defined nose with flaring nostrils that were disturbingly feminine. There was about him the air of controlled menace, as if he were a fully stoked furnace carefully locked behind an iron door. Something told Nicholas that whoever sought to open that door did so at his peril.

'Already I feel the sins of my predecessor scourging my flesh.' Shidare's expression indicated he did not mean a word of what he said.

He appeared to Nicholas as if he was one of the new breed of Yakuza – brash, arrogant, as secure in his license beyond the law as he was in the privilege of his formal education. In his manner and bearing it was clear that, unlike Chosa or Akinaga, he had not come from the streets, but was the product of a major university, perhaps even Todai – Tokyo University – and therefore could not share their peculiar outsider's sense of isolation from society.

'I see you've come through your ordeal in remarkable fashion.'

'Nicholas,' Seiko said, 'you saved us both, but I still don't know exactly how. I felt your body on top of mine, and then a kind of liquid warmth, almost as if I'd been dipped in wax. For a moment, I couldn't breathe, I couldn't see. I panicked. I tried to squirm away, but the percussion came and I thought we'd be blown to pieces. I heard a howling as if from a long distance away, then I lost consciousness.'

Shidare was moving elegantly across the polished tile floor of the large sun-lit room. He wore a handsome off-white linen suit in the voluminous Italian fashion. Nicholas was finding it increasingly difficult to ignore him.

'I used Tau-tau,' Nicholas said softly. 'I projected my *ki* outward to form –'.

211

'A kind of shield.'

'Not really. Think of the design of an aerodynamic vehicle – a car or a plane. The force of wind is encouraged to slide up and over the vehicle. Think of us as that vehicle. I did much the same thing with the shock wave of the blast.'

Shidare was close now. His glossy black eyes focused directly on Nicholas. There was nothing there; not a hint of emotion nor a glint of intent. He cocked his head to one side. 'I am told, Linnear-san, that you study aikido,' he said in the old formal manner. 'Tell me, are you familiar with *jiyu waza*?'

'Tachi –'

'It's all right, Seiko-san,' Nicholas said. 'The *oyabun* has spoken and so has chosen his path.'

But she did not want her warning to go unheeded. 'This is not what we agreed upon, Tachi. I beg you not to flex your muscles. Not here. Not now.'

'Please be still, Seiko.'

Nicholas regarded Shidare with increasing interest. He had silenced Seiko with a simple phrase. Was she intimidated by him because of his stature as one of the three Yakuza *oyabun* on the Kaisho's inner council, or was she merely respectful of a man she admired?

'I regret that I have no *gi* or *hakama* to offer you as traditional garb for aikido, but your bathing suit will do.' Shidare gestured with a long-fingered hand. 'Shall we go outside onto the sand?'

'He's been asleep for thirty-three hours, healing.' Seiko's tone was more accusation than plea. 'What is the matter with you?'

Shidare glanced at her briefly. 'I told you to be still.'

They went outside, into the red sun that squatted just over the horizon. A late-afternoon breeze stirred the palm trees and cooled the humid air. The sky was that yellow-blue hue Nicholas associated with

212

Vietnam; blue-green waves crashed onto a wide, white beach. He tried to calculate exactly where they might be. Then there was no more time for contemplation as Shidare, gliding forward in a blur, delivered a vicious *mune-tsuki*, a low blow to the abdomen that Nicholas only partially deflected.

Nicholas went down, and Shidare locked onto his right wrist, twisted it and, using Nicholas's own rising momentum, spun him over and down. Nicholas felt some pain come into his body, but he welcomed it as a wake-up call. He had been asleep too long; the intense projection of *tanjian* energy that had shielded him and Seiko from the brunt of the small antipersonnel explosive had drained him to the point of total exhaustion. It was good to feel alive again.

He rolled, avoiding a kick that would otherwise have struck him in the ribs. He scissored his ankles, but Shidare danced away.

In what seemed like the same movement, the *oyabun* grabbed Nicholas's right wrist with both his hands. Nicholas, still off-balance, took a chance, beginning a *tenkan*, pivoting on his right foot, dragging his left backward, putting enormous pressure on his lower back and thighs, reducing the leverage in his arms. But now, as he spun back and to his left, he had Shidare stretched out and vulnerable. Nicholas completed the turn, went into *tsugi ashi*, coming across in front of the *oyabun*'s body, sliding under his extended arms. Dropping to his right knee, Nicholas flicked his wrist, launching Shidare up and over him. At the apex of the arc, his left fist shot upward, burying itself in Shidare's right side just above his kidney.

He could hear the *oyabun*'s surprised grunt of pain even before he hit the sand and skidded away. Nicholas rose, but Shidare was already regaining his feet, the grimace of pain quickly wiped from his face. He came at Nicholas with his right hand dragging behind him, the shoulder slightly lower, as if he were struggling to regain sensation.

He was very close when his right hand whipped in front of him and the miniature *naginata* swept toward Nicholas with appalling speed. The short, curved spear that the *oyabun* had somehow concealed beneath his baggy Italian suit was an instant from cracking Nicholas's forearm.

Nicholas was left no other choice. He opened his *tanjian* eye and, projecting his psyche outward in one violent push, caused the *oyabun*'s arm to falter just long enough for Nicholas to counter the unexpected strike with a *tegatana*. Using the outer edge of his massed fingers as a sword blade, he chopped at the inside of Shidare's wrist.

Shidare stepped back, a look of stupefaction on his face. His weapon fell to his side as his black crow's eyes focused on Nicholas. Then the world seemed to shift on its axis, colors bleeding like neon in the rain, gravity and perspective warped out of time, and the space around them darkened with the fall of an unnatural night.

In disbelief, Nicholas saw the blank rock face of Shidare's eyes cracking open. He had the sensation of spiraling downward. Beyond, swimming in their depths, he recognized the color—no color that established the astonishing kinship. Then he felt the projection from Shidare's psyche, and a moment later their *tanjian* minds met in the space between them in a form of wary greeting invisible to all onlookers. It had been several years since Nicholas had come across another true *tanjian*. They were so rare that after Kansatsu, his *tanjian* mentor, had died, he had searched in vain for another skilled mind. To find one here, now, in such an unexpected place, was both exhilarating and profoundly disturbing.

Nicholas saw Shidare's hand come up, the *naginata* extended between them. He raised his own arm and carefully closed his fingers over the end of the weapon. The *naginata* had once been used by itinerant priests who needed to defend themselves against bandits and other brigands. Now the flow of *tanjian* energy surged through the forged steel as, centuries ago, the Buddhist *ki* – the life force – had empowered it.

Shidare bowed abruptly, deeply and formally. 'Tomoo Kozo was a fool,' he said in a clipped fashion that left no room for interruption or contradiction. 'You did us all a service by killing him. I, for one, am in your debt.'

Seiko's eyes, narrowed in confusion, moved from Shidare to Nicholas and back again. Just a moment ago these men had been determined antagonists, and now they were motionless, the fierce tension of hand-to-hand combat all at once drained out of them. Nicholas had opened his *tanjian* eye, of that she was certain. But what had happened after that? Wouldn't he have used his psychic energy to defeat Tachi? But she sensed no victory here, no defeat, only two men moving toward one another.

Seiko touched Nicholas's arm briefly, as if in the young *oyabun*'s presence she was abruptly shy. 'Three times death has brushed you, Nicholas. Four is an evil number. In Chinese, it is synonymous with death.'

Nicholas looked past Shidare to Seiko. 'Can't we enlist your father's aid?'

'I'm afraid that's out of the question.' Shidare gestured. 'Let's walk along the beach.'

They strolled down the white sand toward the turquoise surf. Salt and phosphorus were thick on the air, and Nicholas could see fishing boats far out on the water.

'In case you're wondering, this is a part of Vung Tau, the Bay of Boats.' Shidare pointed. 'We are about two hours by fast car southeast of Saigon. This is quite a cosmopolitan part of Vietnam. As far back as the fifteenth century, when Le Thanh Tong was busy dismantling the kingdom of the Champa, Portuguese merchant ships were plying their trade here. For decades afterward, foreigners in Vietnam came here for R and R.' He pointed behind them to a tile and stucco villa. 'My house was built in the 1930s. Seiko's father arranged its reconstruction for me a year ago.'

Wondering how much more there was to Seiko that he did not know, Nicholas said, 'How well do you know her father?'

Shidare gave a grunt. 'No one knows him well. I suppose that is his wish. He is like one of the old kings here, or a statue of a king, so far removed from what we consider human existence that it is difficult even to find a way to connect with him.'

Nicholas turned to Seiko. 'Why won't he help us?'

'Because he and I are cut off from one another.' There was a look on Seiko's face that Nicholas had never before seen. 'He has never been able to deal with my . . . emancipation. As far as he's concerned, I should have been married long ago, with two children and another on the way. "Where is my grandson?" he would shout at me. "You have destroyed my future!"'

She turned her head away from Nicholas, into the breeze off the South China Sea, and sunlight spun off her hair. 'That was some time ago, of course, when we were still speaking. Now he's remarried, and his twenty-one-year-old wife has given him two fine sons, who, I am certain, he believes will be fruitful and multiply. Thus will his future be salvaged.'

'He won't even speak to you?'

Seiko shook her head. 'He views the way I lead my

216

life as a personal insult to him. As far as he's concerned, he has no daughter.'

Nicholas looked past her to where Tachi Shidare strode beside them. Tachi shrugged, as if to say, Yes, it's sad, but it's her karma. What can one do?

'After this third attempt on your life, Seiko asked for my help.' Tachi had the easy Western style of an increasing number of young Japanese. This automatically made him more worldly but also, perhaps, less deeply dependent on the fundamental sensibilities that made his country unique. Nicholas, seeing the future encapsulated in this man, wondered how beneficial the trade-off would be for the Japanese and for the rest of the world.

'Good. The way things are going I can use all the help I can get,' Nicholas said. 'To begin, everything I've learned so far points to a place known as Floating City.'

Tachi nodded. 'I've heard of it, but, like Seiko, I know of no one who has been there and survived. Even the mountain tribes are terrified of it. Trading is done through third-party intermediaries.'

'Like this woman Bay, who Chief Inspector Van Kiet shot to death.'

'Apparently.'

'I think we should talk to Van Kiet.' Nicholas felt the creaming surf rush over his bare feet and ankles, its soft coolness refreshing him. 'Seiko, you have influence with him. Could you set up a meeting?'

'I could try, but Van Kiet despises me – I have no doubt because I am a woman doing what he considers a man's job.'

'Far better to let me contact him,' Tachi said with a smile. 'He'll be willing to speak to you when I get through with him.'

*　　*　　*

217

It happened in the middle of the night when not even the rubber-booted fishmongers at Tsukiji market were up and about. Frankly, Naohiro Ushiba had sunk so deeply into the cynicism that was a byproduct of his disease that he had ceased to believe that the police were capable of such an audacious gambit.

Ushiba had known Yoshinori for most of his adult life. Dubbed the 'minister's sword', Yoshinori had had a say in the making – and, in several cases, the breaking – of the last eight prime ministers.

That he had apparently been under investigation for some time and had now been arrested said a great deal about how Japan was changing, and how even the most powerful figure of the leading Liberal Democratic Party was not beyond the clutches of the Tokyo prosecutors.

Ushiba had responded to a call from Tanaka Gin, the Tokyo prosecutor with whom he had been working on cleaning up the scandal-ridden investment and business sectors.

'We have detained Yoshinori,' Tanaka Gin said in his customary laconic style.

Ushiba's heart raced. This would send enormous shock waves throughout the LDP and, indeed, all of Japanese politics. 'On what charges?'

'Tax evasion, donations to secret political accounts he controlled, payments to businesses suspected of being owned by the Yakuza, possibly in exchange for services rendered or favors granted.'

Ushiba was so stunned he could think of nothing to say. His shock was not in the revelations but in the fact that Yoshinori had been caught in these transactions.

'I may be out of line telling you, but this is the real thing,' Tanaka Gin continued. 'We have Yoshinori with ironclad evidence. You know what that means: an ever-widening investigation. I can envision a mad scramble within the right-wing factions of the LDP to distance themselves from him, because who knows where this inquiry will lead? Proclaiming themselves the only guarantor of a democratic and free-market system won't save them these days as it has in the past. This embarrassment can't be swept under the rug like the Recruit and Lockheed scandals.'

'You have been investigating Yoshinori for some time.' It was not an accusation, but a statement of fact.

'I have many inquiries in my jurisdiction. You know that.'

Ushiba's mind was racing. Tanaka Gin was not one to cavalierly bend the rules of his tempered-steel world. He had kept the Yoshinori investigation secret until the moment he had been ready to move. Now he was telling Ushiba more than he, Ushiba, really needed to know. What was his purpose in carefully laying this groundwork?

'This is something more than a courtesy call,' Tanaka Gin said. 'Yoshinori wishes to see you. You and he are old friends, are you not?' Ushiba, recovering quickly, did not miss the warning tone in Tanaka Gin's voice. He had spent enough time with the man over the past several months to know that he was exceedingly clever in his dogmatic way, and absolutely incorruptible. In short, he was quite astoundingly the right man in the right job.

'Yes,' Ushiba said. 'He and my older brother were classmates. He's like an uncle to me.'

'He loaned your brother money once, didn't he?'

'That's right. It was a personal favor. My brother's business fell apart, leaving him with a mountain of debts. Yoshinori put him back on his feet. My brother repaid the loan within two years, but Yoshinori refused the interest fee. My brother bought him a car instead.'

'We have that, too,' Tanaka Gin said without a trace

of irony. 'I'll pick you up myself in twenty minutes. Will that be satisfactory?'

'Of course.'

There was a silence between them, and Ushiba was about to hang up when Tanaka Gin added, 'The charges are likely to be quite severe. We've just uncovered more than one hundred million dollars in gold bars and diamonds in Yoshinori's house.'

The two men rode in silence through the rain-slicked streets of Tokyo. Neon lights gathered in the gutters. Enormous billboards to the twin temples of industry and consumerism winked and rolled, devoid of meaning without the crowds to ingest their messages.

Ushiba sat huddled beside Tanaka Gin. He was cold and his stomach felt as if he had swallowed battery acid. He had taken two pills before he had left his apartment, but they had done nothing to ease the pain. Power is indeed fleeting, he thought as he watched Tanaka Gin's dark profile. Once, men like Yoshinori would have brushed off this kind of police probe with a contemptuous wave of their hands. No more. Greed had made even the most influential people careless, and the ensuing scandals had made waves reaching out to the media and, worse, the public. Now there was an outcry from the populace against greed and the endemic corruption they did not understand. Now the police and the prosecutors had the weight of the people on their side and the balance of power was tipping in their favor. Ushiba, so close to the personal hand of the law, knew his one duty: to keep safe the secrets of the Godaishu.

Tanaka Gin pulled into the driveway of his office building, sat with the engine idling for some time. There was not a soul about. The slap and thwack of the windshield wipers were the only indication of time passing.

Tanaka Gin cleared his throat. 'I have decided to take a chance and ask of you the impossible.' His eyes met

Ushiba's. 'I need your help in prosecuting Yoshinori. Will you give it to me?'

Ushiba said nothing, unable even to form a coherent thought.

'I know what matters to you.' Tanaka Gin's slim, dark face was filled with crags. Reflection from the windshield filled his face with rain. 'Light, form, poetry. Honor.' His voice was abruptly gentle. 'There comes a time in every man's life when certain priorities present themselves above all others.'

Ushiba's heart skipped a beat. 'That's true. Old age becomes one's bedmate without one's quite knowing how it got into the house.'

'Old age and disease fell even the mightiest cryptomeria in the forest. But before they do, they transform one's perceptions.' Tanaka Gin stirred. 'You might ask yourself how one as young as I might know this. My father died of lung cancer. Perhaps it was from living on the outskirts of Nagasaki, perhaps from other environmental pollutants of our age. In any case, I spent some time with him toward the end and discovered that he had been transformed by his illness. His mind, freed of the bonds of time and death, was more lucid, more structured in a way than it had ever been. He became, for me at least, an entirely different person.'

Ushiba could not still his heart. All this oblique talk of disease, transformation and death had a purpose. Tanaka Gin knew that he did not have a bleeding ulcer but stomach cancer. Damn him, the prosecutor was too clever by half. Did he know as well the real relationship between Ushiba and Yoshinori? Ushiba shuddered inwardly.

Tanaka Gin's gaze was implacable. 'As I said, I know what is important to you.' His hands upon the steering wheel were strong, heavily veined and callused. They were beautiful instruments, like the hands of a great

221

pianist or a surgeon. 'Yoshinori has betrayed the trust of those who believed in him most. Will you help me prosecute him?'

Ushiba looked into Tanaka Gin's eyes and saw a great deal that he had not been allowed to see before. He opened his mouth to speak, but what was the point? Both men knew the nature of the reply.

Inside the building, Tanaka Gin ushered him down a long dimly lit hallway guarded by two men in suits who clearly knew Tanaka Gin but nevertheless asked to see his identification badge.

They took an elevator to the sixth floor, where Tanaka Gin was again obliged to show his ID. He did not give Ushiba's name or title and no one asked. They went down another anonymous corridor, stopped before a wooden door painted an awful shade of green.

'I can give you forty-five minutes. No more.' Then Tanaka Gin walked quickly away, disappearing around a corner of the corridor.

Ushiba looked around as if he might be secretly observed. Then, taking a deep breath, he turned the doorknob, went in.

Yoshinori was seated at one end of a polished wooden table. He stood up when Ushiba entered, and a small smile broke out on his lined face.

'My friend.'

The 'minister's sword' looked every day of his seventy-eight years. His face was ashen, his clothes were in disarray, as if he had been forced to dress in a hurry. The room stank of smoke, and Ushiba saw a large brass ashtray full of ground butts next to a pack of cigarettes and a thick gold lighter.

The room looked more like a boardroom than a detention cell, and perhaps that was what it was. Twelve matching chairs ranged around the table. A pair of credenzas stood against two walls, on which were trays with tea and ice water, cups and glasses. The room was windowless and chilly.

'I was told you wished to see me.'

'The worst has happened, Ushiba-san.'

Yoshinori collapsed into a chair. He took out a cigarette and lit up. The ambient smoke was already irritating Ushiba, and he went to one of the credenzas, poured himself some water.

'I have pulled all the strings I have left,' Yoshinori said, 'but times have changed. The LDP is no longer what it once was – a bastion of sanity against the Communists and Socialists. It seems our entire raison d'être no longer exists. Once the LDP was the only choice for voters wanting a free-market economy. We were installed thirty-nine years ago as a bulwark for the people, to ensure their freedom and prosperity – for the good of Japan! Now, there are splinter parties to the right and left. There are many choices for voters, but is that good? I doubt it. Politically, Japan now may well go the way of Italy: a revolving door of weak parties trying to muster alliances that will allow them majority rule.'

He shook his gray head like a wounded animal. 'There is bitterness all around me. And, of course, that great beast envy. I do not think I will escape Tanaka Gin this time.'

'Do not give up hope that easily.'

Yoshinori gave him a wry smile. 'If I am to fall upon the sword, I wish to do so with a pure heart.'

Ushiba took his glass and sat down near Yoshinori. The watery eyes could still blaze with the old energy when needed and, as Yoshinori pushed his fingers through his tousled hair, a semblance of the man he used to be even a decade ago began to break through the bleak visage of the tiger in winter.

'People are expecting a political revolution here now that the LDP has lost its majority, but I know the truth,'

Yoshinori said. 'These reformers have come from our ranks; they have suckled at the breast of "money politics", they have participated in government by bribe. It is all they know. I am not naive enough to believe people – especially politicians – can change in the blink of an eye.'

Yoshinori turned away for some time in silence. At length, he took a deep breath. 'I, too, have done questionable things,' he said in a reedy voice just above a whisper, 'and committed what some might think unpardonable sins. My break with you, for instance.' He pulled on his cigarette thoughtfully, let out the smoke in a hiss. 'Sitting here alone at the end of a long and eventful life sets one to contemplation. For instance, let us take love. Such a complex emotion, so riddled with, at times, affection, guilt and unbridled lust. But what is love's other, darker side? What happens when love is poisoned, affronted? It seems to me now that the deeper one loves, the greater is one's potential to hate. Now isn't this what happened with us?'

Yoshinori took another drag on his cigarette, and for a moment the glowing end of it was the brightest light in the room. When it had waned to gray ash, he continued, 'It isn't whether we hated one another, is it, Ushiba-san, but how *deeply* we came to hate one another.' He stubbed out the butt, lit another. 'A sad ending for an uncle and his nephew, don't you agree? I never forgave you for not backing me, not donating your share to my coffers . . . and you?' He shrugged his thin shoulders. 'I can only speculate, but knowing you as I do, you disapproved of how I did business. You no doubt called it corruption, just as Tanaka Gin does.' He smiled, not unkindly. 'In many ways, the two of you are similar. It's quite extraordinary really. Being taken into custody by him, I thought of you and I knew what I had to do.'

He smoked for some time in silence, apparently gathering his thoughts. Ushiba rose, poured himself more water. While his back was to Yoshinori, the old man said, 'Of all the questionable acts or supposed sins I have committed, I regret only one. It was something I did only days ago, and I did it against my better judgment simply because of my hatred for you.'

Ushiba put down his glass and turned around.

'As I said, I want the end to come with my heart pure. I have to exorcize the poison of my hate. Tonight, I have forgiven myself for hating you, but I know more is required of me. I must confess this one act to you.'

'So that I will forgive you?'

Now Yoshinori did smile. 'That is not required of you, nephew. I only want you to listen. Several days ago, Akira Chosa came to me. We have done business together for many years. You never suspected, did you, Daijin? Well, no matter. Chosa and I are partners in gambling parlors, insurance and construction companies. We've made fortunes together so, when he wanted a favor from me, I was inclined to grant it. He of course knew of the enmity between us and used that. He said he wanted to use a certain man as a weapon to get to an enemy's Achilles heel. Does this sound familiar?'

'Yes,' Ushiba said, thinking of Chosa's vow to find a way to destroy Nicholas Linnear.

'He said you were against his plan. Is this true?'

'It is.'

Yoshinori's eyes had begun to tear, perhaps because of the acrid smoke. 'Because of that I granted him that favor. I allowed him to use my influence to convince the newly appointed *oyabun* of the Yamauchi clan, Tachi Shidare, to become this weapon.'

SIX

Vung Tau/Washington

The skeleton was enormous, over thirteen feet long, Nicholas estimated. Firelight flickered off the glass case in which it was housed, causing odd shadows and distended fingers of light to play over the rib bones.

'This one was caught in 1868,' Tachi said. 'All the whales here at Lang Ca Ong have a special significance.' Lang Ca Ong, the Temple of the Whales, was built in 1911 and had about it a distinctly non-Buddhist air, with its cases of cetaceous skeletons. The whale cult, to which Lang Ca Ong was consecrated, was appropriated by the Vietnamese from the Champa, one of the indigenous peoples they had defeated in founding their nation.

'Whales have for centuries played the part of savior in local folklore.' Tachi put the flat of his hand against the glass case. 'Not surprising in a nation of fishermen.'

The sky was bright with stars, and a moon the color of bananas floated in the sky like a ship one could imagine setting sail against the shadows cast by the ghostly skeletons of these enormous beasts.

'What time did Van Kiet say he'd meet us?'

Tachi looked at Nicholas. 'Have patience. We are here early for several reasons. I wanted you to see this place because it is unique in Vietnam. I also wanted us to catch a scent of the meeting ground. It's not that I don't trust the chief inspector; I don't trust any Vietnamese.

I think they've learned to lie to everyone – including themselves.'

They walked through the temple grounds. Surrounded by the massive forms of the whales, Nicholas felt the spatial harmony of life. The great sea mammals provided a kind of context that made the stars seem less remote, the moon appear closer.

'From what I know of the Yakuza it's unusual for someone so young to be made *oyabun* of a full clan.'

Tachi smiled. 'Yes, well, you know far more about the Yakuza than any of my fellow *oyabun* would believe.'

Nicholas paused in the shadow of the beast; his face was striped by the strips of darkness thrown from curving bones, bleached by time and the elements. He refused to be drawn out in this manner. 'I know that you are now one of the Kaisho's inner council.'

'That's right. And you have sworn yourself to protect Mikio Okami. But Okami may already be dead. Some of his inner council would undoubtedly rejoice at the news, since one of them ordered his assassination. At the very least the former Kaisho is in hiding.'

'Has he already been stripped of his title?'

'So it would seem from my limited knowledge of the current workings of the inner council.'

This response intrigued Nicholas. 'You don't sound as if you're really part of them.'

'Why would I be? Just because I've inherited Tomoo Kozo's position? I don't yet have his influence, though I'm working on it.' Tachi glanced upward to the stars. 'I have a theory: I believe I was chosen to succeed Kozo precisely because I am young and do not yet have the influence of either Akira Chosa or Tetsuo Akinaga. What could be better for them? I need help and they are only too eager to provide favors, knowing that once I am in their debt I will be tied to them forever. The power of the Yamauchi has been effectively stifled, so they believe.'

'You have other plans I take it.'

'I do.'

They went on through the temple, and on the edge of a small stone garden, they sat, their legs dangling over the side of the veranda like boys at ease. Tachi broke open a satchel, pulling out cold grilled meat, rice and a whole baked fish. They ate by the light of the stars and the moon, the hulking masses of the whales at their backs.

When they were finished and had packed the remains away, Tachi said, 'My plans include you, assuming I could discover a way to interest you.'

'The Yakuza hold little interest for me.'

'I know otherwise,' Tachi said, rising. 'Your father's best friend was Mikio Okami. Through Okami he used the Yakuza to achieve certain goals.'

'Those years after the war were pure chaos. Everything and anything had to be considered in order to restore political order and economic balance to Japan. It was Occupation policy to use Yakuza on occasion. This was part of my father's job.'

'Yes. He was a great man in the founding of the new postwar Japan. I doubt we would be where we are today without his help.'

But from his tone Nicholas was quite certain this was not at all what Tachi had meant to say. *Shicho*, the current of thought, played between them like heat lightning. And now Nicholas saw how their elemental affinity through Tau-tau could be a two-edged sword. While it could bring them together in spirit and purpose, like the carcasses of the leviathans arranged beneath the stars, it could also betray them, revealing more, perhaps, than either was consciously willing to divulge.

They both became aware of the figure at the same time. Slowly, almost hesitantly, it detached itself from the shadows of the temple columns, padding toward them. It was small, willowy, the narrow hips swaying in an age-old rhythm that seemed out of place, even grotesque.

It was a girl, not more than nine years old, too young even for her breasts to have begun to bud. Yet she swung her hips like any seasoned streetwalker the world over.

'Let me handle this,' Tachi said, as the girl held one hand out to them. She was beautiful, if one could imagine her without the bruises on her face and bare shoulders.

She said something in Vietnamese that sounded to Nicholas like, 'Want to fuck here? Do it now. Only five dollars American.' But he could not believe a child so young could sell herself this way.

Nevertheless, Tachi rose and, pressing several bills into her fist, bent to slip his jacket across her shoulders. He spoke to her quietly in the same dialect she had used. In time, the suspicion on her face dissolved enough for her to allow herself to be led to where Nicholas was.

She sat between them, this filthy, wretched child, and ate in the large famished bites of a wild animal all the food they had left between them. She picked the sweet meat of the cheeks from the fish's head, chewing slowly in a kind of euphoric daze. Then she slipped the head into her mouth, devouring it completely. Finally she took the bones and crunched on them contentedly.

Her eyes were dark and luminous, the deep color of her skin like burnished bronze where it was free of bruises. While her limbs were delicate they were already developing out of the shapeless appendages of a little

229

girl. Her youth made her bruises and scrapes seem all the more abominable.

Between swallows she answered Tachi's gently probing questions. Nicholas found it fascinating to watch this Yakuza boss tenderly minister to this creature of the nighttime streets.

'She says that her father taught her how to give pleasure to men,' Tachi told Nicholas softly. 'Her family is very poor and without the money she is bringing in they would have nowhere to live. Her baby brother is ill, and what her father earns goes on medicine and food.' He looked at Nicholas. 'In her company it would be easy to hate such a father.' He reached out, wiped the child's lips free of grease. He said something to her and received a lopsided grin in return. Then she scrambled up and, clutching his jacket tightly around her, scampered off, seemingly as carefree as any child her age, into the shadows of the temple and the whales.

'We've given her only a temporary respite from her life,' Tachi said sadly. 'Tomorrow she'll be back at it, turning tricks, lying about her virginity so foreign businessmen won't worry about contracting AIDS. No one thinks about how soon it will be until the disease finds her.'

The night had become very still. The moon was turning fiery as it descended through the layers of exhausted air surrounding Vietnam's new industrial future. Soon soot would cover this tiny garden, clinging like glue to stone and tree alike.

Shorn of his jacket, Tachi's arms were bare. Nicholas could see a series of what appeared to be long concentric circles spiraling down his right arm. Tachi, who had little body hair, was devoid of it on this arm. Instead, the skin was pale and puckered, shiny as melted wax, though it was clear these scars had been inflicted long ago.

Tachi did not look at Nicholas, but continued to rummage in his satchel. 'I imagine you're curious. I know I would be in your situation.'

Nicholas said nothing. He thought of Croaker and his biomechanical left hand. Fabulous as it was, Nicholas wondered whether his friend ever missed having two flesh-and-blood hands. He missed Croaker. They had spoken by phone earlier via the prearranged schedule they had set up, bringing one another up to date on the progress of their parallel missions.

'I've been trying to make contact for two days,' Croaker had said, 'signaling, then waiting for your return call. Nothing. What the hell happened? Are you okay?'

'Just barely. Remember Timothy Delacroix?'

'The arms dealer, yeah, sure.'

'He's in Saigon and I tried to set up a meet with him. The bastard tried to blow me off the street.'

'Christ! You sure you're okay? You want me to come out there?'

'I appreciate the thought,' Nicholas said, 'but I'm all right. Besides, it sounds to me you're needed right where you are.'

'I'm not so sure.' Croaker told him about the break-in at Moniker's and the Morgana ledger. 'I found out the truth about Torch, and it's worse than we thought. It *is* some form of new weapon – and it's of a sizable scale. It's scheduled to be detonated on March 15, but I have no idea where. What I do know is the site was chosen for – and I quote – "proximity of target and density of population".'

'That means a major urban center,' Nicholas said, his heart filled with dread.

'Right. But where? It could be any large city in the world.'

'We'll have to put the pressure on: we only have

231

three weeks left. But from what you've told me, I think our best bet is for you to pursue your end.'

When Croaker had told him about Domino, Nicholas had said, 'I think you'd be well advised to learn more about her as quickly as you can.'

'I agree,' Croaker had said. 'What was a supposed Looking-Glass clerk like Domino doing with all the information she gave me?'

'Exactly. And if Vesper Arkham is part of Okami's Nishiki network, I find it highly alarming that she also worked for Looking-Glass's late boss, Leon Waxman.'

'Of course. Waxman was Johnny Leonforte, Bad Clams' father,' Croaker said.

'The implications are more and more ominous as far as Vesper is concerned,' Nicholas had said. 'What if she's the Godaishu's mole inside the Nishiki network?'

'I had been thinking along the same lines. Nishiki is Okami's method of keeping the Goldonis – Dominic and now Margarite – up to date on the peccadilloes of Washington's power elite. If Vesper is already inside Nishiki, she could travel without too much difficulty back along the network to Okami.'

The possibility that Okami's enemies possessed a means of finding him even while he was in hiding chilled both men.

'This makes your mission even more urgent,' Nicholas had told Croaker. 'You've got to find Okami before Vesper does.'

'Soon,' Nicholas said now, bringing himself fully into the present with Tachi, 'she'll be an outcast in her own land.' He watched the shadows into which the girl had disappeared.

'An outcast, yes.' Tachi raised his right arm until the moonlight flooded the skin in a pearlescent glow. The glossy ridges of his ropy skin stood out whitely like embroidery upon a dark quilt.

'Linnear-san, you better than anyone else I know understand the meaning of the word *ijime*. Being half-Caucasian you must have encountered some form of it growing up in Japan.'

'Bullying by other children because I didn't fit into the group, because I was different.'

Tachi nodded. 'Precisely so.' Showing off his right arm as if it were a trophy, he said, 'This is from *ijime*. Outside Kumamoto, where I was raised, my family was different from most others. For one thing, my father had a lot of money. He owned fabric-dyeing mills in the area. We had moved there when I was six because it was a depressed area and my father determined he could make a greater profit by lowering his overheads.

'Whereas all my classmates lived in small, ugly ferro-concrete houses, we lived in a sprawling two-story wood-frame house. It was beautiful really. My mother was an artist, a fabricator of the most fantastic art. I wanted desperately to follow in her footsteps but, sadly, I had no aptitude for art. Form and perspective were as alien to me as quantum physics was to my mother.

'Also, my skin was light, another strike against me. My earliest memories are of my mother bathing. Her skin was as white as milk, or so it seemed to me, and so translucent I often believed I could see through it. When I was older, I read magic tales and myths of the snow fox that lives high in the Japanese alps, who on the last day of the year comes down to the levels where mankind lives and, transforming itself into a maiden of milky skin, plays tricks on farmers and townsfolk alike.

'From that moment on, part of me believed that my mother was a magical creature. The worse for me, since this only served to further my sense of specialness and isolation from those around me.

'It goes without saying that I was despised at school, not only by my classmates because I was foreign, rich and light-skinned, but also I believe by the teachers and the principal, who found my presence alien and disruptive. In fact, there's evidence that these officials felt I bore the brunt of the responsibility for my troubles. The fact was my family *was* wealthy, we *did* live in a grand house by the standards of the area, I looked different from the stunted, dark-skinned trolls of the town, and I had never bothered to master their dialect. In short, I did not conform to the strict tyranny of the group. I was as different as if I were half-Western.'

Nicholas thought of the difficulties he had had in school and then in the martial arts dojo until he had proved himself more than capable of defending himself. In fact, for the first time he wondered whether his batterings in school had led him into martial arts. The fact that he had chosen aikido as his first discipline of study was telling, because its governing theories were essentially defensive.

'I was bullied constantly,' Tachi said, 'in the classroom and on the sports field. I was by turns kicked, beaten, insulted and snubbed. How many times my poor mother was dragged away from one creation or another to sew my upper lip or the inside of my cheek. She did take me to the doctor once, but since two of his sons were often the instigators of my injuries, he refused to acknowledge that I needed medical assistance. My mother's hands, so adept at wielding a horsehair brush or a sculpting knife, were equally confident with surgical needle and thread.

'When my father went to school to plead my case, the principal greeted him coldly. After all, my father had been educated in Tokyo. He made in one week what the principal earned in a year. The principal told my father that instead of complaining about his son he should have compassion for the boys who were, he said, only acting out of a well-developed instinct for the survival of the group. When my father threatened to take my story to the local paper, the principal pointed out that both the editor and publisher had children at the school, that they would understand even if my father didn't that the rights of the other children needed to be protected. Nothing could be allowed to interfere with their futures.'

Tachi sat very still. It was clearly not easy for him to allow the past its due. It seemed to sit on his shoulder like a demon, huge eyes gleaming like kaleidoscopes.

'I did try one act of defiance. I set my right arm on fire as I sat in the auditorium with the entire school listening to what amounted to a tiresome sermon from the sanctimonious principal. I suppose it was brave of me, but it did no good. Predictably, the school officials closed ranks, terming the incident an accident. They wanted nothing more than to end a thoroughly unpleasant incident.

'So I did the only thing that would save me, the only thing I seemed suited for: I joined the Yakuza. I went to Kumamoto and with the brashness of youth – and I suppose the urgency of desperation – I sought out the local *oyabun*. When I told him the story of my arm, he understood immediately. He had no son of his own, only daughters. That was my lucky break, and I used it.'

Tachi now brought his left hand into the light. The end of his little finger was missing. He looked at it with such compassion that the demon on his shoulder vanished. 'I made one mistake with this man. I thought it was the end for me. He assigned me to protect his eldest daughter on the day of her wedding to the son of the *oyabun* of a neighboring town. There were those against such a wedding because they saw a future where both clans would be joined into a single, far more powerful entity, and this they could not abide.

'There was an attack, and in the melee the bride was struck by a stray bullet. Even though I knew there had been nothing more I could have done to protect her, I had failed. Six hours later, she died on the operating table and I went before my *oyabun*, certain of my fate.

'Instead, he spoke to me of happenstance and loyalty; he spoke to me as if I were his own child. In the end, I gave him this part of me and he forgave me, not only in word but with his heart. That is a lesson I have never forgotten. In the real world – the world of my youth – there was no honor, but among the ranks of the Yakuza I found what I was looking for. I discovered what was important in life.'

The first thing Croaker did when he woke up was check to see if Margarite was in the hotel. He was told she wasn't. Once again, he used his Looking-Glass ID to log onto the number given him by Lillehammer. A man answered with the light, chirpy voice of youth. When the voice acknowledged the ID, he asked to speak to Domino.

'I'm sorry,' the voice replied. 'There's no one here by that name.'

'But there must be. I spoke with her last night,' Croaker said, but his mind was already running several steps ahead, and he could see his folly.

'On this line? Impossible. I was on duty then. I didn't speak to you.'

'But I called –'

'Hold on. All calls are electronically logged in by the central net. Let me access . . . Here we go. What time was your call?'

'There were two of them.' Croaker gave him the times.

'I don't know where you called, but it wasn't here. I

236

have no record of your ID logging in at all this year until right now.'

Croaker closed his eyes, his mind continuing to race. Who was Domino and how had she known he was going to call? Just as importantly, how had she interrupted the federal net so he wouldn't be logged in? Maybe she was a cyber hacker. Or maybe . . .

Croaker gave a description of Domino to the OD operator, and the man laughed. 'I don't know. Except for the hair and the color of her eyes, I'd almost say you were describing Vesper Arkham.'

Croaker gave a little choking sound, and said, 'She was Waxman's assistant, right?'

'Well, yeah, but now she works directly for Senator Dedalus.'

'Doing what?'

'Whatever he asks. Rumor is she's trying to keep together the remnants of the active agents from Looking-Glass so they can all be thoroughly vetted. The news of Waxman being Johnny Leonforte literally devastated the agency. A clean sweep and all that.'

'But wasn't Vesper just an administrative assistant?' Croaker asked.

'Yes, but again rumor is now she was much more. Maybe Dedalus's mole, who knows?'

Croaker considered this for a moment. It was looking more and more as if he and Nicholas were right about her. She was a mole and Dedalus's woman. If she was also part of Okami's Nishiki network, was she working both sides of the street? According to the agency rumor mill, she was used to a double role. Clearly, he needed to find out more about her. If she was putting Nishiki at risk, then Margarite was in danger.

'Does she have a sister?' Croaker asked.

'Vesper? Not as far as her personnel file is concerned, and that's as thorough as they come.'

237

'Okay then.' Croaker pulled himself together. 'I need two things: Vesper's home address and a complete telephone record for the last three months for a strip club called Moniker's. Also I want a trace on all the numbers.' He gave the voice the address. Domino had lied to him, so it was logical to assume the documents she had given him were falsified. Even if by some miracle they weren't, it was only prudent to doublecheck whatever she had provided.

'I'm sorry,' the male voice said, 'the addresses of agency personnel have been reclassified strictly Director Only. However, the phone records will be no problem. A courier will deliver the hard copy to you within two hours at the location of your choice.'

'My hotel will be fine. You wouldn't be bringing them yourself, would you?'

'Are you kidding? That's strictly against agency policy.'

But it hadn't been against Domino's policy. Croaker said, 'By the way, who *would* have the proper authorization to requisition home addresses?'

'Mr Lillehammer would have, for example. But, of course, he's dead.'

'Who else?'

'Well, Senator Dedalus, naturally.'

'How so?'

'It hasn't been made public knowledge, but he is head of the Senate committee investigating Leon Waxman, who ran this federal agency until his death late last year.'

'Did the senator request his involvement be kept out of the press?'

'I'm not sure, but I'd guess so. He's so busy overseeing DARPA I doubt he'd want it known he was dividing his time.'

'What is DARPA?'

238

'The Pentagon's Defense Advanced Research Projects Agency.' The voice chuckled. 'You wouldn't believe the kind of sci-fi crap these boys are funding. Walking robots, weird weapons, all kinds of shit. Where they get their money is beyond me – probably black budget, you know, off the public record, like the NSA.'

That was interesting, Croaker thought. The woman who identified herself as Domino had told him of Dedalus's involvement with interstate trucking and municipal-bidding re-regulation but not this.

'Who's your boss now?' he asked.

'I suppose Senator Dedalus is making policy decisions until a new director can be found.'

'And who will appoint the new director? The president?'

'I doubt it, presidents never have before. This agency has always been Senator Dedalus's baby.'

Croaker cradled the phone, looked at his watch. It was almost four in the morning. He slept for just under two hours, too exhausted to take off the rest of his clothes. The alarm he had set woke him at six from a dream in which he was sitting on a stool, dressed in a jester's baggy clothes, being interrogated by officials of the US government who sounded suspiciously like Bad Clams Leonforte. He tried not to think of Bad Clams' threat against Margarite, but that was like trying to tell a surgeon operating on his wife not to think about his patient. He put a call in to Nick, leaving his electronic marker.

In a moment, the phone rang and he jumped, then snatched up the receiver.

'Nick?'

'Lo, Lew.'

Croaker was stalking back and forth across the carpet, unable to sit still. Despite his exhaustion his adrenaline was at full throttle. 'Senator Dedalus is seemingly now

239

in control of Looking-Glass. I've got to find out whose side he's on – the Goldonis' or the Leonfortes'. He was supposedly Dominic Goldoni's friend, but a Leonforte ran his agency. And, as we know, Johnny Leonforte was a leading member of the Godaishu.'

'Interesting,' Nicholas said. 'The Godaishu is a Yakuza-spawned organization.' He filled Croaker in on the possible linkup between the Yakuza, Avalon Ltd, Torch and Delacroix.

'Still,' Croaker said, 'I'd like to know who is manufacturing Torch.'

'I think I may have an idea,' Nicholas said, and told him what little he had gleaned about Floating City.

Croaker said, 'Could be whoever's taking possession of Torch is the same person or persons responsible for putting the death sentence on Okami. I'd put my money on the Godaishu.'

There was a pause while the two men hit upon the same conclusion at once.

'What if Okami is Torch's target?' Nicholas said.

'It makes sense, doesn't it? And Okami's smart enough to suspect it, but because he's deposed and in hiding, he lacks the power to prevent it.'

'That's just it, he doesn't lack the power. That's why he's been feeding us clues, Lew. He's got us.'

The darkness of night was reluctantly lifting by the time Croaker cradled the receiver. Twenty minutes later, clean, deodorized and shaved, he went out of his room. On the way downstairs he began to see a possible pattern forming. While in the bathroom he had deliberately blanked his mind, doing deep-breathing exercises to keep his forebrain occupied, giving his unconscious time to work. Now he re-engaged.

What had happened to him from the moment he had connected by phone to Domino had the smell of a classic vetting set piece. While he was busy trying to pump

240

her for information, she had been doing the same with him.

He hit the lobby running and grabbed a taxi outside. He gave the cabby Senator Dedalus's address.

It was looking more and more as if Domino, the imaginary sister of Vesper Arkham, was Vesper herself. It all made sense once he added one fact to the scenario: Vesper was Dedalus's mole inside Nishiki. Spinning the scenario out further, it appeared as if Dedalus was the power behind Johnny Leonforte, which neatly answered the question of how Leonforte as Waxman passed the agency vetting.

He also needed to ask Vesper who owned Morgana, Inc. The books at Morgana and Avalon Ltd both made mention of the weapon Torch 315. If these competing arms companies were after Torch, it must be hot indeed.

Those two hours he had slept were the first in the last forty-eight. His face was red and sore from the hurried scrape of the razor, and despite his fresh clothes he felt unkempt. Not the best way to meet the senator for the first time; he'd just have to rely on his charming personality.

A light drizzle was falling. Every so often the chill winter wind metamorphosed it into sleet, which pattered against the roof and windshield of the cab like the scratching of a homeless mongrel. Within the complex web in which he and Nicholas were enmeshed he was desperately trying not to think of Margarite, but he couldn't help himself. If she was involved with Vesper, who ran Morgana, Inc.'s illicit arms dealings, it threw a whole new spin on the situation. His sense of Dominic Goldoni was that the man had been far more than chief racketeer of the East Coast. Goldoni had been a visionary. He had thrown his lot in with Mikio Okami, breaking with the highly lucrative Godaishu, in order to run an exceedingly dangerous counterplot that had led to

241

his death and to Okami's near-assassination. Why? What had been so urgent to the two men?

Against tradition and logic, Goldoni had trained his sister in secret to take over his end of the operation. And yet Dominic's arch rival Caesare Leonforte had begun to smell a rat. Maybe he knew Tony D. too well, or maybe he was more clever than Dominic had anticipated. In any case, he now had Croaker just where he wanted him: as a hunting dog who had already caught the scent of his quarry.

Croaker shuddered in the back of the jouncing cab, unpleasantly reminded that the closer he got to Margarite and the Nishiki network, the closer Bad Clams came to destroying her.

Increasingly, he felt like a rat in a maze, one that had been diabolically devised just for him. He was unused to being powerless, manipulated by unseen forces beyond his comprehension, and this worried him for a number of reasons. He had to be careful not to let his anger make him careless. He had seen enough street cops blown away by lapses in vigilance caused by their emotions running rampant to know he didn't want to die that way. Also, he was beginning to glimpse a picture so large in scope that he already felt the intimations of fear. This emotion, too, he had to fight, because just as anger could make you reckless, fear could paralyze you.

Assumption number one: Dominic and Okami owned Morgana, Inc. Assumption number two: Vesper, with her ties to Looking-Glass, the supersecret federal agency run by Johnny Leonforte and now Senator Dedalus, was a major player in this game. Croaker and Nicholas had been pointed in the directions they were now headed by clues delivered obliquely by Mikio Okami. Information they had gleaned had sent them after Avalon, after Torch, had made them aware of the

Nishiki network and its purpose to keep power in the hands of Dominic Goldoni and now Margarite. For an instant, Croaker had an image of Okami hidden in shadow, pulling strings on the immense stage of the world.

Senator Richard Dedalus seemed to be the key, and Croaker was looking forward with dread fascination to his meeting with the man who had effectively created Waxman's agency, and who now apparently ran it as he saw fit.

Dedalus lived on a twelve-acre estate in McLean, Virginia. The manor house was an imposing stone and slate affair that somehow managed to conjure up the atmosphere of an old English castle without being in the least pretentious. The curving granite-set driveway was a quarter-mile long. It was lined on either side with majestic Aristocrat Bradford pear trees, which, with their very upright habit, gave the impression of the sentries on guard at Windsor Castle.

On his way to the house, Croaker passed an immaculately tended fruit orchard and a cleverly concealed tennis court. A figure in cap and overalls he took to be the gardener moved slowly through the periphery of the orchard in a golf cart, its back loaded with pruning equipment. Despite the early hour, the gardener paid the taxi no notice. No doubt he was used to the odd hours his employer must keep.

Croaker paid the cabby and got out in a porte-cochere large enough to accommodate the president's bullet-proof limousine and a pair of staff cars side by side. The carved front door was high enough for a basketball player to enter without stooping.

Croaker's insistent ring on the bell was answered by a young woman in her twenties. She was dressed in a neat Donna Karan suit. A string of pearls around her neck set off the color of her skin, which was the hue

243

of hot chocolate. Her large black eyes regarded Croaker with a mixture of curiosity and good humor. Her thick hair was woven into a series of sinuous braids that wrapped around her head.

'May I help you?'

He showed her his federal badge. 'I'd like to see the senator.'

The young woman looked from the badge to Croaker's face. She had taken the time to read the thing, which impressed him. Most people didn't; they were too intimidated by the trappings of authority.

'Won't you come in?' She took a step backward. 'I'll see if the senator is out of bed yet.'

She led him through a vast oval entryway, floored in white marble blocks. It was dominated by a crystal chandelier and a wide, curving teak staircase that was obviously new and custom-made. A small ebony table, its shape echoing the larger oval, stood beneath the chandelier. On it, an evocative Bennett Bean sculpture in granite, stainless steel and fired clay rose to just beneath the lowest crystal.

'Would you care for some coffee or tea?' the woman asked him as they went down a short hallway.

'Coffee would be my choice.'

She smiled at him over her shoulder. 'I think I'll join you.'

She was well built, with a narrow waist and good legs. The contours of her shoulders and upper torso, visible beneath the suit as she moved, were square, the muscles well developed. Croaker found himself wondering whether he was being escorted by one of the senator's security contingent.

She led him into an enormous kitchen, painted in a pale-yellow enamel that reflected the myriad copper pots hanging from French-style metal ovals chained to the ceiling. A professional Garland stove

244

was complemented by a stainless-steel refrigerator with glass doors for which many a restaurateur would sell his soul.

The young woman poured two cups of steaming coffee from a complex maker on one of the many counters. She brought it over to him in a glass set into a metal holder. Very European. She had a wide, flat face with inquisitive eyes and a ready smile. She was as alert as if it were three in the afternoon instead of a quarter to seven in the morning.

The entire rear of the kitchen was a series of windows and French doors leading out to a lawn dotted with a progression of curving flower beds. These earthen cut-outs were arrayed with the architectural precision one found in the gardens of the châteaus of France. They were splendid even in the dead of winter.

'Magnificent, isn't it?' The young woman had moved beside Croaker as he stared out at the empty garden. 'Gardens are so austere in winter, and rather melancholy, I think.'

'I don't know. I don't have enough experience with them to have an opinion.'

She turned to him and extended a hand. 'My name is Marie.'

He took it, found it cool and firm. Exactly as he had expected. 'Lew Croaker.'

Marie nodded. 'It's awfully early to see the senator.'

'My business with him is urgent. Will I get to see him?'

'He'll be down in five minutes.' Croaker did not know how she could know this or even how she had conveyed his presence to Dedalus. 'I'll be with the two of you during the interview.'

'Are you his lawyer?'

She laughed. 'The senator doesn't need a lawyer. He *is* one.'

245

He studied her carefully. If she was carrying a weapon, he couldn't detect it. 'Don't you trust me? I'm with a federal agency. The *senator's* agency.'

'Mr Croaker, I am paid an exorbitant amount of money to be suspicious. Believe me, it's nothing personal.'

'Terrific. I feel a whole lot better now.'

She had a good chuckle, deep and genuine. Even better. He liked people with a sense of humor. 'You been with the senator long?'

'I'm too young to have been with him long. Just over a year.'

'What happened to your predecessor?'

Marie showed him a set of magnificent white teeth. 'He wasn't as good as I am.'

'Uncle.' Croaker raised his hands palm forward.

'Marie, have you been entertaining our friend?'

'Yes, sir.'

Croaker turned to see a tall, rangy man with white hair and a long, lugubrious face. The kitchen, large as it was, had changed its aspect the moment he strode into the room. He did not move like an old man, but rather with the enviably practiced step of the sailor upon a pitching deck. He was slightly stooped as if any space he occupied was too cramped for his personality. He had clear blue eyes, a large nose and a wide slash of a mouth. Dressed in casual slacks, a flannel shirt and a melton wool coat, he seemed more the gentleman farmer than one of the most high-powered men in the capital.

'He went through the electronics,' Marie said. 'No weapons, no bugs. He's clean.'

Dedalus nodded, then stuck out a hand, pumped Croaker's aggressively. 'Richard Dedalus, Mr Croaker. I understand you're from the agency.'

So there were microphones throughout the house;

probably closed-circuit video cameras, as well. 'Yes and no,' Croaker said.

'Oh?'

'The fact is, Mr Lillehammer hired me to look into the murder of Dominic Goldoni because he was becoming suspicious of someone inside the agency.'

Dedalus nodded. 'Probably worried about Leon Waxman, his director. Quite right, actually. Waxman was a mistake.'

That was the understatement of the century, Croaker thought, since Leon Waxman had turned out to be the supposedly deceased Johnny Leonforte.

'If you're finished with your coffee, I need to take a look at the tennis court. This wet weather is playing havoc with the surface.'

The three of them moved toward the door. 'Is Marie's presence necessary?'

'After the debacle with Waxman, I'm very much afraid it is.'

They went out into the misty morning. Marie kept several paces back, her eyes constantly moving from the two of them to the landscape through which they walked. In the distance, Croaker could see the gardener. He had stopped his golf cart and was bending over to tend to an evergreen beside one end of the fenced-in tennis court.

'Better to talk about certain matters out of earshot,' the senator said, though whose earshot he didn't make clear. Perhaps he was referring to his own electronic surveillance system. If so, that would be interesting.

'I'm looking for a woman,' Croaker said, 'and since she works for the agency – or did when Lillehammer was alive – I've come to you.'

'Her name?'

'Vesper Arkham.'

The senator continued on, walking vigorously, but

Croaker could see by the clouds of exhalation that he had begun to breathe hard.

'And what would be the nature of your business with Ms Arkham?'

'It's all connected with my ongoing investigation of Dominic Goldoni's murder.'

The senator stopped abruptly. 'Good God, man, Lillehammer has been dead more than three months. Who gave you orders to continue?'

'No one ordered me to stop.'

Dedalus peered at him through the mist. 'You intrigue me, Mr Croaker.' He began to walk again. 'Not many men would be so tenacious. Who, may I ask, is paying you?'

'No one.'

Dedalus grunted. 'You're either exceedingly curious or a man of principle. I'll find out which soon enough.'

'I suppose you'll order me to quit my investigation.'

Dedalus glanced at him sharply. 'What gave you that idea?'

'It would make sense. You were a friend of Goldoni's, you often entertained him and his sister Margarite. In fact, you sent your limo to meet her at the airport two days ago. He was up to something of a global nature, and I'm convinced that Vesper and perhaps Margarite as well are involved.'

'So I must be involved as well, is that it?' Dedalus shook his head. 'I'm the big bad wolf with all the power to run things as I will, is that how this scenario you've built goes?' They came to the gate to the tennis court, and the senator opened it. 'As you said, I was a friend of Dominic's. That may sound odd to you – even hypocritical of me, a member of the United States Senate. But you didn't know Dominic Goldoni. He was one hell of a man. Calling him a racketeer does him a great disservice. He was responsible for a lot of good, but don't ask me for a list, I'm not the one to justify or rationalize what he did or was accused of doing.'

They went onto the rain-slick court and Dedalus stared gloomily at the clay. 'I knew I should have laid Har-Tru. Look at this.'

'What do you know about Vesper Arkham?'

Dedalus produced a palmtop computer, punched in an access code. 'She was born in Potomac, Maryland, thirty-two years ago to Maxwell and Bonny Harcaster. She graduated Yale, summa cum laude, did her doctorate work in clinical psychology at Columbia, postdoctorate work in parapsychology at –'

'*Para*psychology?'

Dedalus looked up. 'Yes. She's Phi Beta Kappa and a member of Mensa.'

'The brainiacs.'

'The national genius-level-and-beyond club.'

Croaker looked at Dedalus. 'She ever married?'

His eyes flicked down to the palmtop, but Croaker could see he was not reading the screen. 'Once, to a man named John Jay Arkham, a local Washington businessman, industrial demolition. It lasted just over a year.'

'And yet she kept his name.' Croaker took a look around the court. 'Senator, did Margarite and Vesper come to see you two nights ago?'

'No.'

'Is that the truth?'

Dedalus put the computer away. 'I may be in my seventies, but by God I don't need Marie to throw you off my property. I'll do it myself.'

'Just asking, Senator.'

'Yeah, yeah, save it for someone half my age.' He turned to Marie. 'What do you think? Har-Tru?'

'Har-Tru.' That was the answer the senator wanted and she gave it to him without hesitation.

Croaker was beginning to get the measure of the man. Provoking strong emotions was just one of the tricks of the trade. Keen observation could be just as effective.

'Don't make a mistake now. I'm not your enemy,' Dedalus said to Croaker. 'I want you to continue your investigation precisely because Dominic was a friend of mine. If you want to speak with Vesper Arkham, I'll arrange it. Just tell me when and where.'

'All right.' Croaker took a last look around. Marie was staring fixedly at him as if she might turn into an attack dog at any moment. The gardener had finished his inspection of the evergreens and was climbing back into the golf cart. 'Noon today. As for where, I'll phone you at eleven forty-five with instructions. Will you be here?'

'No. I'll be in conference then.'

Croaker regarded him evenly. 'If you're sincere in wanting to help Dominic, you'll take my call.'

Dedalus handed Croaker his card with his office address and phone number. 'Just give my secretary your name; she'll do the rest.'

The young Vietnamese woman was naked. She stood upon a low wooden platform draped in silk the color of the ocean. She wore no makeup save for lipstick – the scarlet bow of her mouth startlingly erotic against the copper color of her unblemished skin. Her legs were spread and her hands were on her hips. Her entire body was hairless, the skin shining in the lamplight with rose-scented oil.

In front of this vision was another woman, also naked, on all fours. Her head was down so that the long cascade of her black hair fell to the floor and obscured any sense of individuality or identity.

'Go on,' Rock said, to give himself the sense that they needed his encouragement. His eyes were slitted, his breathing slow and even as if he were in a meditative trance. Outside the walls of this locked room the business being transacted in Floating City spun on, in sunlight or in monsoon-like rain, he didn't know which and didn't care. Let his partner take care of business. The only reality was in here.

The standing woman took her hands away from her hips, placed them on the buttocks of the second woman, who faced Rock. She licked her full lips as her hands disappeared between the other woman's buttocks. Her knees bent as she went about her work. Rock stared at them, his eyes glittering, imagining what was taking place. After an interval, the woman on all fours gasped and the cascade of her hair swung back and forth across the silk.

'Is she ready?'

The woman with the hairless body nodded wordlessly. Her dark nipples were erect.

Rock stepped onto the platform. He was as aware of the sensuous feel of the silk beneath his bare feet as he was of the tightness in his groin.

He put his hands on the woman's hairless body. 'What about you?'

It was difficult not to be intimidated by Rock. He was tall, well muscled, with the shoulders of a weight lifter. His hair, still dirty blond, was cut so short on the sides the scalp beneath had been burnished by the sun. He was tan, which made his blue eyes appear unnaturally luminous. The tan failed to completely mask the parallel lines of scars on his cheeks, the product of a severe case of untreated adult acne. But rather than making him ugly, they increased the fierceness of his appearance, as if he were an African tribal chieftain ribboned with crude facial tattoos.

'I need you.' Her mahogany eyes held his as she continued to work on her companion. 'Make me ready.'

Rock reached up, unwound her hair, pulled it gently so that her head came back. He kissed her but did not like that he could not press up against her, so he pushed the second woman roughly away. He heard her little cry of surprise and disappointment and he was immediately hard.

The woman with the hairless body reached down and pulled him between her thighs, trapping him there. She swung her hips provocatively from side to side so that he felt the exquisite friction of the soft skin on the insides of her thighs. His blood was on fire.

Then he felt a tickling sensation between his legs. Without looking he knew that the second woman had crawled up to him. It was time. He thrust himself into the woman with the hairless body, hearing the breath go out of her, feeling one leg lifted, curled around his hip.

The tickling progressed up and down his legs, teasingly, reaching higher with each progressive wave, until the second woman's fingertips and tongue reached the apex. Lights exploded behind his eyes as he felt the pressure. His thrusts were deep, ragged, almost uncontrollable. Fingers and tongue insinuating, penetrating as he penetrated. It was all too much, and he howled over and over in heartfelt release.

The three of them collapsed in a sweaty mass. He smelled their musk, watched, his heart still palpitating, as the two women entwined their bodies like serpents, slithering, tongues flickering, pleasuring each other, watching as he grew hard again. They used him as he had used them, doing to him whatever they wanted, whatever gave them pleasure until right up to the end, when he took charge again, rearing up as they fell back, accepting his seed as if it were wine.

Afterward, saturated with their fluids, he dropped into a sleep that was, unfortunately, not dreamless.

There, in a place he could not name and a time he preferred not to remember, his father stalked him through dark tenement rooms, cloying with putrefaction, inhabited by cockroaches and rats.

Just remember I made you what you are. His father's fierce voice echoed off the filthy walls, becoming more and more of a physical presence, until the room Rock found himself in was filled with blood, and he drowned.

He awoke with such terror that he screamed at the drowsy, naked women, beating them insanely until he drove them, tearstained and bloody, from his presence.

SEVEN

Vung Tau/Washington/Tokyo

When Chief Inspector Van Kiet arrived at the Lang Ca Ong, it was with the face of the devil himself. If he were fuming any harder, steam would have been pouring out of his ears.

'It's difficult enough having a semblance of a private life without people like you dragging me out of my home at all hours,' he said to Tachi. This was before he saw Nicholas and let out a groan. 'You're an evil omen, you know that?' He turned back to the *oyabun*. 'If you ever owe me a favor, I swear I will ask you for permission to kill this man.'

'Thanks for the warning,' Tachi said dryly. 'I'll try to keep it in mind.'

The skeletons of the whales loomed above them, dark and grotesque.

'Must we stay here?' Van Kiet glanced around nervously. 'I like to keep moving, especially at night.'

Nicholas took careful note as they went out of the temple and along the street. This man's manner was markedly different from the last time they had met when, surrounded by his men and their weaponry, he had seemed totally in control of the situation. What had changed?

'There was something of an incident two days ago,' Tachi began, 'at the Giac Lam Pagoda.'

'Christ, don't I know it.' Van Kiet was clearly agitated. 'I'm under tremendous pressure from the government to find the perpetrator. The problem is I know who ordered it and he pays me far more than the government ever would.'

'This man here was the target of the bomb,' Tachi said, indicating Nicholas. 'It was only by extenuating circumstances that he survived.'

'The worse for all of us, I can tell you,' Van Kiet said sourly. He glanced over his shoulder as if he were longing for a bulletproof vest.

'Who ordered me killed?' Nicholas asked.

'Jesus, Rock, of course.'

Nicholas looked at Van Kiet. 'Who is Rock?'

'The emperor of Floating City.' Van Kiet grunted. 'He built the damn place, carved it out of the jungle and solid rock. God alone knows how he did it, but money can buy you anything, they say, and Rock has so much of it he can't spend it fast enough.'

'If he owns you, why are you telling us this?' Nicholas asked. 'If Rock wants me dead, you should have taken one look at me, pulled out your sidearm, and shot me yourself.'

Van Kiet gave Tachi a sidelong glance. 'Is this guy kidding?'

Tachi shrugged, then said, 'Tell him.'

Van Kiet's eyebrows raised. 'Really?'

'Really.'

Van Kiet shifted his gaze to Nicholas. 'I get rented out, not owned. I may be a whore, but I haven't yet sold my soul.'

Tachi rolled his eyes. 'You're starting to chew the scenery. No, I meant tell him the *truth*.'

Van Kiet shivered. 'I'm not comfortable here. Can we go somewhere?'

Somewhere meant Van Kiet's boat, a twenty-one-foot ketch with a white fiberglass hull, a teak deck and gleaming brass fittings. It was hardly an item a policeman – even a chief inspector – could normally afford. Van Kiet brought the engine to life, turned on the running lights, while Nicholas and Tachi untied the boat from her mooring. They had reached her by a dinghy, which bobbed at the ketch's side.

Van Kiet took them out about half a mile, until the crescent of lights from Vung Tau made a bracelet in the night. Then he dropped anchor, broke out a chest full of 33 beer. They all drank, sitting in the velvet night, luxuriating in the feeling of being apart from everything and everyone.

'The real truth,' Van Kiet said at last, 'is that Tachi and I have been working for two years to infiltrate Rock's Floating City.'

'Rock owns the poppy fields in the Shan States,' Tachi said.

Van Kiet nodded. 'As far as I can tell, he's a US veteran of the war here. He stayed on after the troops went home. How he managed this particular feat without his superiors knowing about it is a mystery. Maybe he faked his death – he wouldn't have been the first, I can tell you. Maybe he just disappeared himself. Whatever, he apparently got the idea that opportunity presented itself here, so he took himself to Burma and systematically muscled into the drug trade. He hired himself out as an assassin to those warlords willing to listen. He murdered their main rivals in exchange for a fee. What they didn't know was that part of the fee was an alliance with Rock. He wasn't just in it for the money – he wanted the trade itself.'

Van Kiet sipped his beer thoughtfully. 'Those who wouldn't acquiesce, he did in.'

'All by himself?' Nicholas was clearly skeptical.

'Listen, the man was a monster during the war. Who knows how many people he blew away and how much he came to like it? Killing can become a kind of addiction in those circumstances. He could handle any sort of ordnance. To this day, he carries a LAW. Do you know what that is? An M72 light antitank rocket launcher. Can you imagine having one of those beasts leveled at you? And word is he has modified the thing so it's even more deadly. Plus, he's a clever bastard. There's a pretty nasty rumor that he destroyed the last remaining major warlord by killing his most prized possession – a young girl – and serving her severed ear to him in a stew.'

'*Monster* seems to be the right word for him,' Nicholas agreed. 'Have you been inside Floating City?'

'No, but I think I was close. And then you showed up with your computer-chip scheme. Rock saw through that one right away, which is why he's marked you. It's why you pissed me off so badly.' Van Kiet hawked and spat over the side of the boat. 'Don't expect an apology. I would have blown your brains out just like I did that woman you were with after I'd had a chance to interrogate you to find out who you really were and what you were up to.'

'Same thing as you, it would seem.'

Tachi twirled his beer bottle between his hands. 'Tell me, does this second-generation chip actually exist?'

'It does,' Nicholas said. 'But it's safe in a Tokyo lab. I wouldn't have taken the enormous risk of bringing it with me.'

'What were you going to show Abramanov?'

'Then Abramanov exists?'

'Oh, yes,' Tachi said. 'He exists and he's working feverishly in Floating City on a project unrelated to Rock's drug trade.'

'Rock isn't merely into drug trafficking,' Van Kiet interjected. 'He's also one of the main suppliers of illegal arms worldwide. I mean these days just about anyone with cash can buy any weapon they want, within

257

reason, from the Russians or the Chinese. But then you're stuck with basically shoddy equipment. That's all right for some minor despots and terrorists, but the big boys want more. They play for keeps and want to come out on top. They want American weapons – and the latest ones, to boot.'

'That's where Rock comes in.' Tachi pulled another beer out of the cooler, popped the top. 'He somehow has a pipeline into – what? The US military? The Pentagon? The arms manufacturers? Who knows? The point is, he's the only source. Middlemen come to him and him alone and pay top dollar for his consignments. That's what happens when you have a monopoly. Where are you going to go when you get gouged?'

'And if you are stupid enough to complain?' Van Kiet cocked his thumb and forefinger like a gun, pulled the trigger.

'Is that what happened to Vincent Tinh?'

'Possibly,' Van Kiet said. 'But my own theory is the little bastard just got too greedy and Rock decided to make an example of him. In Rock's business it pays to do that every once in a while. Keeps the citizens from getting restless.'

'How can the Vietnamese government allow such a place to exist?' Nicholas asked.

Van Kiet grunted. 'Are you kidding? Rock's made his life's work a gold mine for them. Floating City got its name because Rock has managed to make it into its own miniature city-state; he pays key officials in the government so much that they deny the existence of his independent kingdom – his Floating City.'

Nicholas finished his beer, but declined Van Kiet's offer of another. Despite his rapid recovery, it felt like a long day, and he was noticing the accumulated effects. There was a buzzing in his head he suspected only sleep would finally conquer.

'Have either of you heard of something called Torch 315?' He told them how he had come across the entry in the Avalon Ltd computer, and what Croaker told him it meant. 'We're talking a major bang here; a disaster for what could be a large number of innocent bystanders.'

'It could be what Abramanov is working on,' Van Kiet said.

'Isn't he a cyberneticist and theoretical-language technician?'

'That's right,' Van Kiet said. 'But apparently that's not all he is. Disturbing rumors surfaced about six months after Abramanov appeared that Rock was transporting enormous quantities of lead and depleted uranium-238.'

'Do you know what that stuff is used for?' Tachi asked.

'Usually to contain radioactive material,' Nicholas said with mounting excitement. 'This could be it. Have you done some background digging on Abramanov?'

'Yes, and I've gotten nowhere.' Tachi grunted. 'We're speaking of Russia. Bureaucrats are far too busy trying to survive to dig out bios of former citizens. And every time I've found a less than distracted bureaucrat over there, he's been replaced a week later.'

Van Kiet was tapping his upper lip with his empty beer bottle. 'You know, there is someone in Saigon who may be of some help. He arrived four days ago from Bangkok via Osaka, but according to his passport his original point of departure was Moscow. I remember the memo coming in and noting it because these days we get so few Russians. The people here hate their guts, will spit at them, curse them, try to beat and rob them. We get a fair number of complaints from Americans who have been mistaken for Russians.'

'So he's Russian,' Nicholas said. 'That doesn't mean he'll know anything about Abramanov.'

'Oh, but he will.' Van Kiet showed his yellow teeth in a discomfiting grin. 'If Abramanov is a nuclear scientist, this man will know him. He's the head of the Kurchatov Institute of Atomic Energy in Moscow.'

'What's he doing here?' Nicholas asked.

'In Saigon, he's looking for only one of two things.' Van Kiet rose, turned on the engine and began to raise the anchor. 'Money or opportunity.'

'Maybe both,' Tachi said, stowing the cooler underneath a bench. 'And that could mean he's headed straight for Rock and Floating City.'

Croaker got out of the taxi at the building demolition site. After the countrified Gordian knot of Senator Dedalus's estate the damp urban wind seemed to cleanse him. It was good to be amid the clamor and grime of the city; he'd had enough of Senator Dedalus and his odd James Bond manqué. Dedalus must have been born understanding how to manipulate people. His control of power was quite extraordinary. Croaker, whose business had been to size up people in an instant, did not know what to make of the senator. Was he sincere as he professed to be, or was he hiding behind a mask of seamless manufacture? Had Vesper and Margarite been there two nights ago as Croaker suspected, or was Dedalus telling the truth?

Croaker stopped the first man he saw at the demolition site. 'I'm looking for John Jay Arkham. His office said he was here.'

The worker pointed into the abandoned office building. 'He's inside, directing the placement of the charges.' He meant the explosives that would implode the building, bringing it safely down upon itself. 'Big guy, blond hair. You can't miss him.' He handed Croaker a hard hat. 'Here. Wear this while you're on the site, even if you have to go pee.'

Croaker thanked the man, settled the hat on his head, and went inside. It hadn't been difficult tracking down Arkham; his demolition company was the largest in the area. Since he was often on-site, his office was used to directing potential clients to the field.

The inside of the building was eerie, all empty vaults, creaking wood joists and half-exposed metal girders. The air was filled with drywall dust and paint flecks. Here and there, exposed pipes and ductwork attested to the diligent work of the homeless, who had torn loose pieces of insulation as blankets to huddle beneath during the long winter nights. They might not freeze to death, but God only knew what the exposed asbestos and torn fiberglass was doing to their lungs.

Croaker made his way through the rubble until he spotted a small group of men bending over an area where four girders met at the concrete subfloor. The sound of a high-speed drill could be heard intermittently as concrete dust billowed up. One man, oversize and blond, gave terse orders.

'Mr Arkham?' Croaker had to shout several times. It wasn't until the drill stopped that the big man looked over. 'Lew Croaker.' He dropped his badge open. 'Can I have a minute of your time?'

The blond said something to one of the men and the drill started up again. He walked over to where Croaker was standing and took off a pair of thick plastic safety goggles, pushed the filter mask down off his nose and mouth. The skin of his face and hands was covered in a fine powdering of whitish dust.

'I don't have a lot of time, I'm afraid. I have a deadline to make here and we're already a day behind schedule.'

'I understand. This won't take long. I need to speak with you about your ex-wife.'

Arkham eyed him for a moment, sizing him up. He was huge, perhaps six foot five with brawny shoulders

261

and narrow waist and hips. He had the winning good looks of a college quarterback in whiteface with all the paraphernalia of his trade hanging off him. Croaker supposed he could see the appeal this man might have had for a woman of Vesper's unusual beauty.

Arkham pointed to his left. 'Let's go out here so we can talk in peace.'

He led Croaker through the ruins, out of a side doorway into a gray alley with a rivulet of water. Far away at one end Croaker could see part of Arkham's team assiduously positioning charges from a set of plans.

'What do you want to know about Vesper?'

'Everything.'

Arkham grunted. 'Then you've come to the wrong place. I loved her but I hardly understood her.'

'Too brainy?'

'Shit, maybe. Your guess is as good as mine.' Arkham took out a cigarette, lit up. He blew out some smoke, looked disgustedly at the end of the cigarette, and ground it out beneath the thick rubber sole of his construction boot. 'I know I can give it up, I've done it so many times.' He wiped his forehead with his sleeve. 'All I can tell you about Vesper could fit on the head of a pin. I think she loved me in her own way, though God knows what that was. See, I was just a part of her life. She'd disappear for days, sometimes weeks, and when I'd ask her where she'd been, d'you know what she'd say? "Jay, I have a life independent of you. That's the way I am. Accept it or leave me."'

He looked down at his feet. 'In the end I did. She gave me no choice, although I'm sure if you'd ask her, she'd tell you differently.' He sighed. 'Yes, she loved me, but in the end what did that mean? I'm sure I can't tell you because she's still a complete mystery to me.'

'Maybe you liked that about her.'

'Yeah, sure, what man wouldn't? Up to a point. But the mystery was far more than a game to her, I'm positive of that. When she got serious, she was *deadly* serious. So much so that she frightened me. I've never been scared of another human being.' He cracked a wry smile. 'A benefit, I guess, of being so damn big. But there were times I admit Vesper spooked the shit out of me.'

'In what way?'

'She was so *smart*.' He shook his head. 'Actually, the word *smart* doesn't even come close to defining what she is. There were times when I was convinced she knew me so well she was right inside my head. And then, there were other times when it seemed as if' – he shrugged, in its resignation a peculiarly anguished gesture – 'she wasn't aware I existed.' He glanced at his watch. 'I gotta get back to work.'

Croaker let him get a few steps away before he said, 'There's more, isn't there?'

The big man turned toward him. 'There's no more.'

'Mr Arkham, it's likely that Vesper is in serious trouble.'

'How serious?'

'Quite frankly, it could be terminal.' Croaker felt a twinge of remorse trapping Arkham this way. But he had no choice; most often he didn't. People were not in the habit of spilling their guts to investigators, so you needed to find their vulnerable spot and press as hard as you could. Without knowing it, Arkham had revealed his soft spot: it was Vesper. Despite whatever had happened between them, he was still very much in love with her.

Arkham came back to where Croaker stood. 'Look, what if there *is* more? How will it help her now?'

'I need to understand her, Mr Arkham. She's still innocent until proven guilty. The better I know her, the

263

better my chances of saving her in the end. You'd want her to have that chance, wouldn't you?'

The mist filtered down on them, the filthy water ran in the alley, and far away now, the drill continued to bore through the concrete subfloor. Croaker was aware of all these things, but they had been shifted into the background, as if they were no more than hiss on a bad cassette tape one needed to ignore in order to enjoy the music that had been recorded.

Arkham put his big hands in his pockets, nodded at Croaker's biomechanical hand. 'That's some piece of work. It do well for you?'

Croaker looked around, pulled up an old rusty crowbar from the rubble close to the building. He wedged it between two exposed girders and, gripping one end with his biomechanical hand, exerted pressure. The bar bent, then wrapped itself around the girders in a U-shape.

'Nifty. But I'll bet you'd still rather have the real one.'

It was clear from the way Arkham spoke that he felt he had lost something fully as valuable as a hand. *Maybe that is to the good*, Croaker thought. *It'll make it easier if he thinks we have something in common.*

Arkham took a look around, as if he were worried they would be overheard. 'Shit,' he said softly. Then he raised his head, looked Croaker in the eyes, and began. 'One time when she disappeared, I was so frantic I tried to find her. I went to her parents' house.'

'The Harcasters.'

Arkham nodded. Beads of moisture were building on his hard hat, slipping like tears off the metal surface. 'I didn't know what to expect because, well, Vesper hardly spoke of them. There had never been any talk of being with them at, you know, Easter or Christmas or Thanksgiving. We always spent holidays with my family, and she seemed happy to be there.

264

'Still, I was unprepared for the reception I got from her parents. It was openly hostile. I told them I was Vesper's husband and for a moment I thought her father was going to get his shotgun off the wall. Then his wife put a hand on his arm. His face was white. She asked me what I wanted and I told her that I was looking for Vesper. Do you know what her father said, Mr Croaker? He said, "Why have you come here?" Can you imagine a parent saying that about his child?'

Arkham had a stunned look on his face, as if he were living the terrible incident all over again. '"Our child doesn't live here anymore," Vesper's mother said. "It's been many, many years." Neither of them would use her name. They had kicked her out, disowned her. They wanted no part of her. I could see her mother's heart was still breaking, but her father's was stone cold.'

'What happened?'

'For one thing she was adopted . . . and she was gay, or at least bisexual.' The sentence had been squeezed out of him, and Croaker was aware of how much the admission had taken out of him. 'When the Harcasters found out, they freaked out.'

'When did that happen?'

'According to Mrs Harcaster, when Vesper was a senior in high school.'

A warning bell went off in Croaker's head. 'I'm curious about something. Vesper is exceedingly well educated — Yale, Columbia, postdoctoral work. All of that schooling takes a whole lot of money. Obviously, she didn't get it from mommy and daddy. Where *did* it come from?'

'She went to New York, scammed her way into a job working for the Democratic mayoral candidate. You know Vesper, once she was inside an organization, she would find a way to make it open up like a flower.'

'But the pay wouldn't have been enough to put

her through a community college, let alone Yale and Columbia.'

Arkham nodded. 'She once told me that she had been very lucky. The candidate got elected. He was so impressed with her he recommended her to a foundation that helped deserving students in financial need.

'Has she been scamming again? She can't help it, you know.' The man's pain was palpable, and Croaker felt sorry for him. He'd never stop bleeding for his ex-wife.

'I can't say yet. Tell me, do you know the name of the foundation?'

Arkham's face was lined in thought. 'Acton? Andover? I remember it started with an *A* just like my name.' He snapped his fingers. 'Avalon! That's it! As in King Arthur.'

Croaker stood stunned for a moment. Avalon Ltd was the name of an international arms merchant concern. It was also the name of a foundation that had put Vesper through years of higher education. Coincidence? In Croaker's world, coincidence did not exist. Was Dedalus stealing from his own organization, DARPA, and getting rich selling the booty through Avalon Ltd?

'Mr Croaker, she's not a bad person,' Arkham said desperately. 'Bad things have happened to her. That's not the same thing, is it?'

'No, it's not.'

Croaker watched the big man melt into the shadows of the building that would soon come crashing down upon itself in much the same manner as Arkham's world had come down on him.

Ushiba went to see Tetsuo Akinaga, the *oyabun* of the Shikei clan. Given the Daijin's clandestine relationship with Akira Chosa, this was a most difficult decision to make. But Yoshinori's revelation that Chosa had enlisted Tachi Shidare, the new *oyabun* of the Yamauchi clan, to destroy Nicholas Linnear had given Ushiba no choice.

The truth was that Ushiba did not trust anyone – least of all a revenge-minded Chosa – to have success against a man such as Nicholas Linnear. The truth was that Ushiba did not believe any of Chosa's well-reasoned arguments for Linnear's demise. Not that they didn't have validity – far from it. But Ushiba knew Chosa well enough to understand that, like the doomed, mad Tomoo Kozo, who had tried to kill Linnear on New Year's Day, he had his own personal reasons to see Linnear destroyed. And the ultimate truth was that Ushiba did not believe in personal revenge. It went against every tenet of *kanryodo*, the creed of the samurai-bureaucrat, by which he lived his life. It also went against everything he had observed in life. How many men had he seen consumed by their need for personal revenge? More than one was often too painful to remember.

In his lifelong battle against the Americans, Ushiba had tried with varying success to remember the painful penalties of obsession. Surely those who chose to define morality to suit their own vision were doomed. Tomoo Kozo and Chosa came immediately to mind. There had to be an absolute morality, Ushiba believed, like the tenets of *kanryodo* or Buddhism, upon which the world worked and the human heart flourished, or else it would merely survive like an organ preserved in formaldehyde.

After the debacle with Kozo, Ushiba thought that Chosa had learned his lesson. But Chosa was hardheaded; more, he still had the arrogance of youth, whose chief illusion was that mortality and disaster could be kept at arm's length merely by force of will. Ushiba could detect nothing but danger in such a cavalier attitude, and he had no desire to be pulled into the vortex that must surely ensue from Chosa's irresponsible actions.

Ushiba stared out the tinted window of his car, but he saw nothing of the passing panoply of Omotesando, one of Tokyo's beautiful wide avenues. Instead, he continued to gaze inward, thinking of Chosa and Akinaga, and how much the inner council had changed since the attempt on the Kaisho's life had forced Okami into exile.

Tetsuo Akinaga ran many large and complex businesses in Tokyo, but his favorites were his smaller boutique companies. These he took a direct hand in starting up and multiplying like crickets all over town. His current interest was Big White Men.

Ushiba's car had come to a stop without his knowing it. He got out when the driver opened the rear door for him. He suppressed a wince as his stomach regurgitated pain like rotten food.

This particular Big White Men was in Harajuku, near the Meiji Shrine. Ushiba went across the busy sidewalk, into the store. Of course, Big White Men wasn't really a store. It was a discreet laundry service specializing in men's underwear. For a monthly fee, the patron received the key to an anonymous-looking box, approximately the size and shape of a mailbox in the post office. The patron paid one hundred yen per item, then deposited the soiled garments in the box and, forty-eight hours later, returned to find them laundered and neatly pressed. Business, Akinaga said, was booming, particularly since underwear was being stolen off clotheslines in apartment blocks. 'Who would have thought it,' Akinaga said jocularly. 'I'm getting rich protecting people from fetishists.'

Ushiba and Akinaga spoke in one of the back rooms of Big White Men. The smell of detergent and bleach permeated the air, and the low thumping din of the machines was felt as tremors through the floor.

Akinaga, looking particularly gaunt, poured tea for them both. They were sitting on low chairs, a stubby-legged table between them. These sparse furnishings were of modern Japanese design and manufacture and, as was typical, they displayed a bizarre hybridization of traditional Japanese sensibilities and European flair.

On the table was a phone and a small plate with sweet pastilles to counteract the extreme bitterness of the *macha* green tea. The two men drank in silence, each immersed in the ritual, savoring the confluence of two extreme tastes in their mouths. When they were finished, the young woman who had brought the tea cleared the low table.

When they were alone, Ushiba said, 'I have a matter of the utmost urgency to discuss with you.'

Akinaga inclined his head slightly, the only indication he would give of his surprise. 'I am honored that it is to me you have come, Daijin,' he said with great deference.

'I have most recently received word that Chosa has taken a most incautious path.'

'Chosa is often rash and hard-headed about personal matters.' Akinaga's perpetual frown lifted slightly, as if he were talking of a wayward child. 'What has he done now?' As if he were going to be asked to provide the cloth to wipe this baby's behind after an unfortunate accident.

'It seems that he has somehow enlisted the aid of the new *oyabun*, Tachi Shidare, to carry out his desire to destroy Nicholas Linnear.'

If Akinaga had been capable of dropping his jaw in astonishment, he would have done so now. Instead, his frown deepened so that two vertical lines appeared between his eyes. 'Yes. That was a most foolhardy decision to make. I cautioned him against any such act

269

after you and I had our last talk. But it seems as if Chosa is not a reasonable man when it comes to the subject of Nicholas Linnear.'

'Apparently not,' Ushiba said, disheartened. 'Is Shidare so vulnerable to such pressure?'

Akinaga shrugged. 'Undoubtedly. He is quick-witted, ambitious, but young. His mentor was an *oyabun* from Kumamoto. The sticks. He cannot possess the power that Kozo had before him, and it will take him some time to consolidate his own. Easier if he were to agree to align his clan with Chosa's at council. He'd have instant access to Chosa's contacts and influence. At least, I imagine that is what Chosa offered him.' Akinaga's bony hands turned over on the table. 'It will take him a while to understand how he has been lied to. But by then it will be too late. He will have ceded too much control of the Yamauchi to Chosa, and Chosa will own him.'

The pain in Ushiba's stomach flared so badly he was obliged to press his hand against it beneath the table. 'Mikio Okami set up the inner council just so this kind of power grabbing could not happen,' he said. 'The position of Kaisho was established to bring an end to the perpetual territorial wars between the major *oyabun*. Now, it seems, without Okami to keep you in line, there will be war again.'

'Not if I have anything to say about it. We have to deal with Shidare and Chosa, but in separate ways.'

Ushiba nodded, bowing to the inevitable. 'I have come to the same conclusion.'

'Now I am doubly glad you came to me with this matter,' Akinaga said warmly. 'It is urgent, indeed.' He thought a moment. 'Here is what I propose. Let me deal with the youngster Shidare. I'm afraid if I start meddling with Chosa at this delicate stage he could easily become hostile. If he's in the midst of grabbing power, he'll be paranoid about any inquiries from another *oyabun* of the inner council.'

Ushiba was not happy, but he said nothing. It was not his place. While he was a respected senior member of the Godaishu, he was merely an adviser and ad hoc peacemaker to the inner council. He had hoped to have Akinaga deal with Chosa because he did not care for the idea of doing it himself. On the other hand, his anger at Chosa for continuing on a path that could wreck the entire Godaishu was intense. How could Chosa have betrayed a trust that Ushiba considered sacred? At the very least, he should have consulted Ushiba before he put his plan into play. It made no difference that Chosa must have known what the Daijin's response would be. He clearly did not want to be tempered.

Ushiba listened to the dull throbbing of the washing machines. He consoled himself with the thought that there would be a measure of satisfaction in devising the method of bringing Chosa to heel.

He rose, thanked Akinaga for his time. They worked out a timetable for their parallel missions and, promising to keep each other closely informed, they parted company, Ushiba to return to his office at MITI, Akinaga to oversee the laundering and bundling of thousands of snowy white undergarments.

When Croaker returned to the hotel, he ascertained that Margarite still had not put in an appearance. Neither had she checked out. He picked up the agency hard copy waiting for him with the concierge.

He took the elevator to the floor below his, went down the corridor to Margarite's room. He looked both ways; the corridor was clear. He got out his set of picks, went to work on the lock, popped it without trouble.

Inside, the room was completely spotless. Two chocolate mints in gold foil lay on the coverlet of the unslept-in bed, along with a printed sheet for room service breakfast. He went into the bathroom. The soaps were unwrapped and the outer leaf of the toilet paper roll was still neatly folded. Nothing had been used. He went back into the room, crossed to the closet. No luggage. He pulled out the desk chair, sat on it thoughtfully.

Margarite had never been in here; her bags hadn't been brought up despite the fact that he had seen Dedalus's limo driver drop them off at the hotel. Also, the driver had checked in for her. That could mean only one thing: Margarite knew she was being followed from the moment his taxi had swung in behind the limo on the way from the airport.

He went out of the room, took the elevator up. Back in his room, he splashed cold water on his face and ordered room service. Then he lay down until the food arrived. He still had two hours before he had to call Dedalus's office with the directions to his rendezvous with Vesper.

He closed his eyes but his heart was pounding so heavily he was obliged to sit up and take long, slow breaths. His mind was filled with Vesper. The more he learned about her the more fascinating – and dangerous – she seemed to him. She was Dedalus's woman, it appeared, from the moment she set foot at Yale with Avalon's money. It seemed to him that Avalon must be owned by the Godaishu. But then what was she doing running Morgana? Was there a connection between the two?

He licked his lips; they were salty. That was when he realized that he was in trouble. Thinking of Vesper Arkham he had broken out into a cold sweat. He hadn't done that since he had shot his first human being, an addict who had felled his partner with a vicious blow

272

of a crowbar to the back of the head. That had been his rookie year on the force, a long time ago.

The food came, and he wolfed it down while looking over the twelve sheets the phone company had provided for Moniker's last three months of calls.

He didn't know what he had been looking for, but whatever it was he hadn't found it. There was nothing unusual. No calls to Senator Dedalus, the president or anyone connected with organized crime. He had been most interested in calls that repeated both within any one month and from month to month. There were a number of those, none of any immediate interest: caterers, carting, liquor distributor, laundry service and the like. Just what you'd expect in any legit business. However, a series of calls to a number in London caught his attention. According to the trace, it was listed to Malory Enterprises in Hammersmith. It could be nothing, or . . .

Croaker glanced at his watch. It would be late afternoon in London. He picked up the phone, accessed an overseas line, dialed the number.

'Malory,' a bright female voice with an English accent answered.

'Oh, hello, this is Philip Marlowe. I'm with Morgana, Inc. Just come on board, in fact. I was told to –'

'Hold a moment, won't you?'

Silence, then, 'Marlowe? Philip Marlowe, like the American detective?' It was a deep, booming baritone with a mid-Atlantic accent, a combination of English and American.

'Uh, that's right. But no one gets us confused.' Croaker tried a small laugh.

'I never heard of you, Marlowe. When did you say you were hired on?'

'I didn't,' Croaker said, hanging up. He stared down at the telephone records. So Malory Enterprises was linked in some way to Morgana, Inc. On a hunch, he opened the hard copy the woman he believed to be Vesper had given him. The phone records matched except, as he had suspected, the Hammersmith number of Malory Enterprises was nowhere in evidence. She had falsified the material. Clever girl, but not, it seemed, clever enough.

He finished up his food, then took out the card Dedalus had given him, dialed the senator's office number. The secretary told him that Dedalus had not yet arrived, but had phoned to tell her that Croaker would call. He gave her the place where Vesper should meet him, then hung up, deep in thought. Where had the senator gone after Croaker had left?

He stopped at the concierge's desk, asked to have a rental car waiting for him as soon as possible. Then he took a cab to Dupont Circle. He walked the several blocks to the Phillips museum. Originally the private home of Duncan Phillips, an heir to the Jones and Laughlin Steel Company, the building became a museum for impressionist and postimpressionist paintings in 1921.

Croaker stood beneath the most famous acquisition of the Phillips Collection, Renoir's *The Luncheon of the Boating Party*, which Phillips had had the extreme good fortune to purchase for $125,000 in 1923. The scene was lush and vivid, like the best of Renoir's works, saturated with sumptuous summer colors and a typically Gallic joie de vivre. The muscled men were masculine, the women frilly, flirtatious and round. Everything was as it should be.

Croaker lost himself in the painting. For him, at this moment, it became a meditation and a comment on the baffling modern life he was living, filled with chimerical people such as Margarite, Vesper, Dominic Goldoni and Caesare Leonforte who defied traditional classification.

The old ensigns of persona with which he had grown up had changed – and more: they were mutating at such a rapid rate that he needed to form an entire new mindset to understand them.

At length, he became aware of the passage of time. It was well after noon, and still no sign of Vesper. He strolled through the museum, only marginally aware now of the art hanging on the walls. He waited ten minutes in the lobby, then another five outside on the front steps. The sky was still dark and gloomy, but at least the mist hadn't changed to rain or, worse, snow.

He called a cab at twelve thirty-five and was back at the hotel ten minutes later. His rental car was waiting for him and he filled out the forms hurriedly, surrendered his credit card for a moment, then took possession of the keys.

Before one, he was on his way to Senator Dedalus's office. He got caught in the seemingly ubiquitous traffic. He needed another inning with the senator, and this time he did not want Dedalus to have any advance warning. Vesper had failed to show and that could be for a number of reasons. She might not have wanted to come, or she might not have been given the message. Dedalus had told Croaker he'd be at his office – or had he?

Croaker, staring at the cars in front of him, thought back to their conversation. Dedalus had merely said he'd be in conference, then had handed Croaker the card with his office number on it. Croaker had assumed . . . Shit!

Ten to one the good senator was still at home, deep in conference . . . with whom?

Croaker turned off at the next light, went back out of town. He arrived at Dedalus's McLean estate just before two. He pulled into the granite-set driveway, then ran the car over the Belgian-block curb, across an expanse of lawn, into the trees. There, he turned off the engine, got out and headed toward the manor house.

The mist had thinned and the ghosts of shadows could be seen on the ground. A moment later, the sun broke through the banks of clouds and blue sky began to appear. Up ahead he could see the gardener in his golf cart. Croaker automatically went behind a tree, beginning an arc to take him around the gardener.

He kept the man in view as he made his way through the trees and underbrush. The gardener had stopped and, wiping his forehead with his sleeve, he took off his cap.

Blond hair shone like gold in the sunlight. It was pinned up flat against the gardener's head. Croaker, who had come up short, now melted deeper into the glade of trees. He moved cautiously toward the golf cart. The gardener turned his head, as if, like a deer, he had caught a whiff of an unfamiliar scent.

And Croaker's heart skipped a beat. The intense blue eyes, the line of the nose coalesced in his mind with that unforgettable hair color. Unless he was hallucinating from lack of sleep and spoiled food, Senator Dedalus's gardener was Vesper Arkham.

EIGHT

Saigon/Washington

As it happened, the Russian from the Kurchatov Institute of Atomic Energy was not difficult to find. Van Kiet, from his office, told them that he had been checked into the Cho Ray Hospital six hours before Nicholas and Tachi had returned to Saigon from Vung Tau. Of course, they had come back with Seiko, but the chief inspector did not know this.

The Russian, whose name was V. I. Pavlov, had been brought into the hospital's emergency room at about the time Van Kiet, Nicholas and Tachi were having their meeting aboard the chief inspector's ketch. He spent seven hours in surgery before the doctors got him near to stabilized.

'What happened to him?' Nicholas asked over the phone.

'Plenty.' Nicholas could hear the rustling of papers and knew Van Kiet was looking at the official admission report. 'The surgeons spent three hours picking lead out of him; they spent another three probing for the bullet that was supposed to enter the base of his brain. Apparently, the top of his spinal cord got in the way. He's completely paralyzed – and he may not make it at all. I think you'd better get over there right away. I'll dispatch one of my men to get you through the red tape. Keep me informed.'

Cho Ray Hospital was on Nguyen Chi Thanh Boulevard in Cholon. It was well known throughout

Vietnam as an excellent medical facility that employed a number of English-speaking doctors. Though it was hardly up to Western standards, it was said one had a decent chance of walking out in good health.

The tenth floor was given over to foreign patients, and Van Kiet's sergeant met them here, guiding them past protesting nurses, doctors and the hospital security.

The room was as stained and yellowed as sun-bleached paper. When they entered, Nicholas thought they were too late. V. I. Pavlov lay in his bed, tubed and tented, as white as paste. His lips were purple and the rise and fall of his chest was barely discernible. He was a big man. Time had turned youthful muscle into a thick girdle of fat. Those outer layers lay loosely on him like bags of suet tied to a pole.

'They really did a number on him.' Tachi circled the bed like a boxer sizing up his opponent.

'Whoever *they* are.'

'You know about Russians in this part of the world.'

'A bullet to the base of the skull is not the MO of a street criminal. A knife to the belly or a sock filled with coins to the temple is more like it.' Nicholas pulled an old wooden chair to the side of the Russian's bed, sat in it. 'We need some answers from Dr Pavlov.'

Tachi, peering at the array of monitors, said, 'I don't think he's in the proper frame of mind.'

'He will be.' Nicholas bent forward, pulled the plastic of the oxygen tent away. One part of him was aware of Tachi observing him, another part was already deeply in Tau-tau, concentrating on V. I. Pavlov. Nicholas almost recoiled the moment he projected his psyche. The Russian was in an almost unimaginable amount of pain, and Nicholas enfolded the man in the strength of his *ki*. Then, with the methodical precision of a micro-surgeon, he worked on the overloaded pain receptors, restoring their ability to transfer the correct messages to the brain. In this way, it began to manufacture the endorphins and nucleopeptides that would naturally reduce the pain to bearable levels. Then he hit a wall.

Without breaking his connection, he said to Tachi, 'There's a heavy-duty narcotic in his system; morphine, I think.'

Tachi nodded. 'I expected as much. As long as it's there, he won't be of much use to us.'

'I can do something about that.' Nicholas increased his connection to Pavlov. The colors in the room sparked, then dimmed as if the light had been sucked out. Shapes shifted and jumped as Nicholas, sunk deeply into Tau-tau, caused the transformation of thought into deed. The darkness pulsed around him, and time, a beast with ten million eyes, seemed tethered to a stake in the earth. Nicholas, outside the dictates of time, began the manipulation of life on a cellular level.

So gradually he had to strain to be sure of it, the Russian's blood chemistry began to alter as he drained the morphine from Pavlov's bloodstream. This was a dangerous procedure. He had to hypermetabolize the morphine – in other words, speed up its breakdown. If he went too fast, he would overload Pavlov's lymph and renal systems and the patient would go into shock.

Pavlov groaned, his head moving from side to side on the damp pillow.

Tachi dragged his chair a few inches closer. The scraping sound caused the Russian to open his eyes. They were an opaque blue, bloodshot, the whites as sickly yellow as the room.

He said something unintelligible. Nicholas gave him water. He sucked it up, staring at Nicholas and Tachi.

'Are you doctors?' he said in Vietnamese.

'I'm the surgeon who worked on you,' Nicholas said. 'And this is Dr Van Kiet, the hospital administrator.'

'He looks Japanese,' Pavlov said vaguely.

'My misfortune,' Tachi replied. 'Can you tell us what happened to you?'

Pavlov closed his eyes and, for an instant, Nicholas thought they were going to lose him. His pulse rate jumped, and his blood pressure rose. Nicholas, enfolding him in comforting warmth, said, 'You'll feel better in a moment.'

Pavlov's breathing slowed. He opened his eyes and looked at them mutely. Nicholas suspected what was going through his mind.

'The police are naturally interested in your case. There are officers outside this room, in fact. They seem very anxious to speak with you.'

There was sweat on Pavlov's fat, white cheeks, but neither man made a move to wipe it off. 'You can't let them in here,' Pavlov said in a quavery voice.

'Don't worry about that.' Nicholas patted the padded arm. 'I won't let anything happen to you. I worked too hard to save your life.'

Above them both, Tachi was shaking his head. 'I don't know. I'm getting a great deal of pressure from the chief inspector of the Saigon police. I don't know if I can —'

'But you must!' Nicholas said it sharply, his head turned toward Tachi. Then he returned his gaze to the patient. 'But you understand Dr Van Kiet's predicament.'

'What am I to do?' Pavlov whispered. 'I can't talk to the police. *I can't.*'

Tachi leaned menacingly over the bed. 'But I'm afraid you will have no choice —'

'Wait!' Nicholas raised his hand. 'Doctor, there may be a way. If Dr Pavlov tells us what happened, perhaps we can work out a way to bypass the police. After all, his health is in the balance.'

Tachi was shaking his head. 'I don't know. The irregularity –'

'But I would tell you,' Pavlov whispered hastily. 'If you can help me with the police.'

'You can trust us.' Nicholas smiled. 'We have only your best interests in mind.'

'All right then.' Pavlov was sweating again, his heart rate fluctuating frighteningly. Nicholas did not know how long they had. He extended his psyche, wrapping the Russian more tightly in warmth.

Pavlov licked his blue lips. 'I never would have come here except that my institute needs money. I'm the head of the Kurchatov Institute of Atomic Energy in Moscow. That used to mean something. I led a life of privilege . . . a gleaming Chaika to take me to and from work, a beautiful dacha on the Baltic where my wife took the children in the summer, a large apartment in Moscow.' He paused to gather himself; even talking was an enormous effort for him. 'All that changed when the Soviet Union died. Now I am reduced to the level of a simple mendicant, traveling thousands of miles in order to obtain money for the institute.'

'You came to Saigon for funding?' Tachi asked.

Pavlov tried to smile, but it turned into a grimace of pain. He paused for a moment, panting. Nicholas gave him more water.

'Saigon is where Abramanov is. He was to be my benefactor.' The Russian made an odd sound, somewhere between a gurgle and a cough. Perhaps it was meant to be a laugh. 'He used to be my bête noire, Abramanov. Perhaps he still is, who knows? You see, he used to work for me at Kurchatov. Some said he was brilliant in his field of study, but I knew he had a mutinous mind and a disruptive personality. He's a Jew, after all, and we all know about them.'

The Russian's eyes closed, and Nicholas and Tachi

exchanged glances. Nicholas said, 'Just what was Abramanov's specialty, Dr Pavlov?'

The Russian let out a long sigh. 'High-flux neutron fields.'

'What does that mean?' Tachi asked.

'You should know. You're a doctor!' Some of what must have been Pavlov's old fiery personality came briefly to the fore, before he subsided in a coughing fit. Nicholas was aware of a seepage of blood somewhere deep inside the Russian, and he knew what that meant. Death was waiting in the shadows, and no surgeon on earth could hold him at bay.

'Doctor, please,' he said, 'you'll do yourself no good. Calm down.'

'Yes, yes, I know. But after what's happened to me . . . where was I? Oh, yes, high-flux neutron fields. As simply as possible, Abramanov was hellbent on creating a stable transuranic isotope. His hope was to find an atomic substance that could be used as the ultimate fuel, cheap and virtually limitless.'

'Was he successful?' Nicholas asked.

'Not at Kurchatov. But after I exiled him to Arzamas-16, the atomic city, I lost track of him. But now . . . now I suspect that he has been successful. Because, you see, I came here to sell him something he needs very badly. He was supposed to pay me a great deal of money for it. Twenty-five million dollars.' Tears began to leak from Pavlov's eyes. 'Was I naive in believing I'd get it? Now it's gone and I have nothing.'

A discreet knock on the door interrupted the interrogation. Van Kiet's sergeant beckoned Tachi outside. Nicholas wanted to wait until Tachi returned, but he knew there was no time to spare.

'It was stolen?' Nicholas asked Pavlov.

'Yes, stolen. But I'll tell you this, I blame Abramanov because whoever shot me and took it must have known its worth. He was waiting for me at the rendezvous point Abramanov himself gave me. No one else knew where I was going.'

Pavlov began to weep in earnest. 'It was a usurious price, I know, but what was I to do? The institute needed the money and I knew Abramanov had nowhere else to go. Besides, that damn Jew . . . bolting the country. I got pleasure from the thought of squeezing so much money out of him.'

Tau-tau made Nicholas aware of the blood spilling inside Pavlov, filling him with his own fluids. The coughing fits were becoming more pronounced.

'What was stolen from you, Dr Pavlov? What did Abramanov want so desperately?'

The Russian spasmed so badly that Nicholas could not hear what he said. Only the continued projection of Nicholas's psyche had allowed him to live this long.

'It was part . . . part of a new type of contamination-control field to counteract the extreme toxicity of plutonium,' he managed to get out.

'Why was Abramanov so desperate to have it? Is he dealing with plutonium?'

'I believe it's far worse. If . . . if he has created this transuranic isotope it will no doubt be even more highly toxic than plutonium, both chemically in . . . in flaking particulates . . . ah, ah . . . and energetic gamma radiation.'

Tachi returned. He bent over, spoke urgently in Nicholas's ear. 'That was a messenger from Van Kiet. He wanted me to see the bullet they dug out of Pavlov's spine. Van Kiet had never seen anything like it before, but I had. It's a .308 caliber, and by the markings on it I can tell it was fired from a Steyr's rifle. That's top-of-the-line sniper's equipment, usually comes equipped with a scope with about a six-hundred-yard range.'

'Then the Russian was right,' Nicholas said. 'He *was* set up.'

Pavlov's head was lolling on his neck and sweat was streaking his face. His eyelids fluttered and blood began to leak from his nostrils. Nicholas tried to keep his grip on the Russian, but now not even Tau-tau was enough to keep him from slipping away.

'Dr Pavlov, we need to get to Abramanov.' Nicholas gripped the Russian's arm, digging his nails in. 'He's your enemy. Tell us how to get to him.'

There was a film across Pavlov's eyes, the blue already glaucous. But the pupils were still focused on Nicholas.

'Pavlov, can you hear me?'

'Y-yes, I –' He began gasping for breath; blood was filling his mouth with pink bubbles. He was literally drowning.

'A name! We need a name!'

'Zao.'

'What's he talking about?' Tachi said urgently. 'That's Japanese!'

Nicholas looked at him. 'Remember what Van Kiet said about his passport? He came here via Bangkok . . . and Osaka.' He turned back to Pavlov. 'Who is Zao?'

But the Russian's eyes were fixed on a point far beyond Nicholas, far beyond the walls of this peeling hospital room.

Nicholas let go of Pavlov's arm. 'Christ, he's gone.'

Rock rarely left Floating City these days; it was his sanctuary and he was its absolute monarch. When he did leave, it was for a good reason. He met Timothy Delacroix at one of the new Western-style restaurants that seemed to be popping up all over Saigon. Delacroix was one of a handful of the world's successful middleman arms merchants dependent on Floating City for his matériel.

Delacroix was waiting for him. Rock had made certain of this by being forty minutes late. In fact, he had arrived early at the rendezvous point that he had insisted upon. Paranoid by nature, made even more so by the war and by his hard-won battle to found Floating City, he slowly and methodically reviewed every back alley, shadowed doorway and open window overlooking the restaurant's entrance and every parked car. Since he knew the restaurant's owner, perhaps it was not necessary to vet every member of the staff, but he did it anyway. Rock was an exceedingly careful man. Before he went back into the street by the rear entrance, he handed a small package to the owner.

Though Delacroix was sitting at a table against a rear corner of the dimly lit restaurant, Rock picked him out immediately. Perhaps it was his eyes, which were so pale as to be virtually colorless. Delacroix had about him the air of an adventurer who had spent all his forty-odd years in the bush or the outback. His skin was like leather, lined and permanently reddened. His sandy hair was long and unruly. He licked his lips incessantly, as if he were always parched.

Rock could see Delacroix's clever, colorless eyes scrutinizing every inch of him as he made his way around the clustered tables filled with diners in trendy Western clothes, and he was glad he had come in unarmed.

Delacroix was nursing a beer when Rock came up. They nodded to each other wordlessly. A female Vietnamese singer warbled a Jacques Brel tune, the French lyrics world-weary and death-conscious.

A whiskey was placed in front of Rock before he had a chance to order. Then the two men were left alone.

Rock took a sip of the liquor, then said, 'How did that little piece of business I gave you work out?'

'Why ask me,' Delacroix said sullenly, 'when you no doubt already know?'

'Oh, is that it?' Rock raised his eyebrows. 'And you think I'm pissed that you didn't blow Linnear to kingdom come?'

'That's about the size of it from where I sit.'

Rock laughed. 'I only wanted to put the fear of God into him. *This* god. The god of Floating City.'

'I think I did that, all right.' Delacroix seemed to relax somewhat.

'Good.' Rock appeared content to sip his whiskey. The singer was hitting her stride now, wailing over the percussion of the three-piece band. The sounds ricocheted off the walls like bullets. At last, he said, 'You know, I was worried for a while. That sonuvabitch Vincent Tinh was running scam after scam while he was working for Sato International. He was buying weapons from me, posing as a middleman, then turning around, making a huge profit posing as a supplier to you and other arms merchants. And the fucker had the balls to claim he was an emissary of mine!' Rock grunted. 'He claimed Floating City's aegis once too often. I made an example of him, blew his brains all over that drug warehouse – but not before I dipped him in acid.' He chuckled. 'Now there was a sight!'

Delacroix said nothing, but seemed to shrivel into the corner.

Rock, who was trained to pick up and analyze the slightest nuance, smirked. 'What's the matter, Tim, the real world too much for you? Christ, you're part of it by your own choice, don't be complaining now that your stomach's weak. I won't believe you anyway. You've been through too many microwars, seen too much blood spilled.' The smirk widened to a knowing, sardonic grin. 'You know the contribution you've made to the way the world is today.'

Delacroix finished his beer. 'I didn't expect you to pay me yourself. The usual method would have sufficed.'

'But this is so much more pleasant.' Rock had to raise his voice in order to be heard over the music. 'I rarely have the chance to get out these days. It's good for me, you know. I sometimes have difficulty remembering what the world outside Floating City looks like. You've done me a favor.' He reached inside his jacket, pushed a white envelope across the table.

Delacroix picked it up, pocketed it without opening it.

'It's good that you trust me, Tim. I like that in my independent contractors. It gives me confidence in the long-range nature of the relationship.' Rock turned and a waiter was at his side. He ordered dinner for both of them.

'I need some advice,' Rock said confidentially. 'Recently, my partner's becoming something of a pain in the ass. I think he's getting ideas of a nature I can only describe as grandiose.'

'Grandiose?'

'Yeah, grandiose. What do you think I am, a fucking moron, sitting here with more money than you could ever imagine?'

'No, Rock, I was just . . . startled that there was any friction.'

Rock chuckled unpleasantly. 'Yeah, well, shit, you know what marriages are like. Sooner or later you get stir-crazy and you gotta cheat.'

They each had another drink, and Delacroix offered some advice to which Rock barely listened. By that time the singer was into covering rockier up-to-date Mylene Farmer songs, and the food had come. 'I hope you like the fare,' Rock said, spreading his hands. 'It's not as fancy as some of the places you eat at in Paris, but for this part of the world it's first-rate.'

Halfway through the meal, Rock put his cutlery down and excused himself. He went back past the rest rooms into the kitchen where his friend, the owner, was staring into a pot of gazpacho.

'Too much heat for the people who come in here,' he said morosely. 'Now what am I supposed to do?'

'Shoot the chef,' Rock said.

They both had a good laugh. Then Rock held out his hand and the owner slipped a .25-caliber Colt pistol into it, along with a small ceramic cylinder. Rock screwed the Vitek-112 induction-coil silencer onto the end of the Colt's barrel.

'What's that going to sound like?' the owner said, nodding at the weapon.

'Just like a cork being pulled from a bottle.'

The owner nodded.

'Thanks for holding on to this stuff. I owe you.'

'What are friends for?'

Rock went back to his seat. Keeping his hands beneath the table, he leaned forward. The singer was just hitting full stride; a couple of slender Vietnamese with electric guitars had joined her, raising the noise level considerably.

'Tim, I want to ask you a question.'

Delacroix leaned toward Rock, who pointed the pistol and fired three quick shots just as the music hit a protracted climax. There was thunderous applause. Tonight, as always, there would be an encore, Rock thought, as he rose and went out the back of the restaurant, throwing the pistol in the trash. It seemed a shame that Delacroix wouldn't get to enjoy it. Just as well. The moment he had hired on to lob the explosive at Nicholas Linnear, he had become a liability, a way to trace the attack back to Rock.

Feeling fit and energized, Rock prepared to spend the rest of the nighttime hours prowling Saigon's back streets for whatever human oddities he could unearth. The prospect was enough to make him whistle a jaunty tune.

That hair! It shone in the sun like spun gold, like caramel being pulled, like cream spilling from a glass pitcher. Croaker, skulking in the trees like some part-time poacher, followed Vesper as she drove the golf cart slowly along a rutted dirt service track.

Deeper and deeper they went into Dedalus's estate. He noted that she gave a wide berth to the main house, looping around a pond and a conifer garden, over a ridge tawny with the roughage of dead summer grasses, down into a glen where a smaller house sat, made of fieldstone and logs. It looked like an elegant fishing cabin. Blue smoke curled from the stone chimney, and teak furniture in the traditional Adirondack style of the thirties and forties was ranged along a wraparound porch. The cabin overlooked a rough-seeded lawn that ran down to thick patches of underbrush and large zelkovas, whose upper reaches towered over even the old oaks that dominated much of the property. Beyond, Croaker could glimpse slivers of a rushing stream that, no doubt, Dedalus yearly stocked with trout.

Vesper ran the golf cart to a dirt area at the side of the house and stopped it beside her black Nissan 300ZX ragtop. She climbed out and, dusting off her overalls, went up onto the porch and into the cabin.

Croaker detached himself from the trees and, running in a semicrouch, made his way to the edge of the porch, where he carefully and silently climbed the wooden steps. He crept from window to window until he saw Vesper. She was standing beside an oversize stone hearth within which flames flickered. Someone was pouring her a glass of white wine. When the figure turned to put the bottle on a side table, he caught a glimpse of the face: it was Margarite.

Edging closer, he put his ear against the cold glass. In this manner he could hear what was going on inside.

'I don't understand why you have to go to London,' Margarite said. 'You've given me the latest intelligence from Nishiki.'

Vesper smiled at her. 'I told you, this is different. I'm not merely a Nishiki courier. I have other duties. There seems to be a problem and I have to be briefed in person. Besides, that bit about Congressman Martin I just gave you is incomplete. I know he's important to you because he's drafted the new banking regulation bill that could hurt your family's interests. Before you move on it and put pressure on him to amend the bill, you've got to have *all* the dirt on him. So sit tight until I get back.'

'How much danger are you going to be in over there?'

Vesper put down her glass, went to where Margarite stood. 'Why worry about it? This is what I was trained to do.' Her laugh was oddly carefree, making her seem nothing more than a happy schoolgirl. 'Nothing is going to happen to me.'

'But the danger inherent in the Nishiki network —'

'You really must curb this morbid streak, darling.'

Margarite shuddered. 'I was thinking of Lew. Everything is so much more dangerous since I met him.'

Vesper looked at her archly. 'I don't think "met" is the operative word.'

'Are you jealous?'

Vesper laughed. 'Do I still make you uneasy?'

'When it comes to sex, you can be omnivorous; you're not going to deny that.'

Vesper drew a lock of Margarite's hair away from the side of her face. 'I don't have designs on you. You'd know if I did. As to sex, I admit to having a certain facility with it. Dedalus saw that right away. It's at the heart of our relationship.' She kissed Margarite on the cheek. 'Like your brother was, he's tremendously intuitive. It was one of his great strengths.'

'God, I miss Dom. But sometimes I think I hate him for saddling me with his responsibilities.'

'You don't hate him.' Vesper squeezed Margarite's hand. 'He's given you a chance to be something more, something greater. He saw that spark in you and he nurtured it. Give him credit for seeing you as more than merely female.'

Margarite went across the room, stared into the fireplace. 'I see something more, some special quality in Lew, too.'

Vesper faced Margarite. 'Let me remind you that because of your Lew we could all be killed. Caesare —'

Margarite's eyes flashed in abrupt anger. 'What are you doing? Are you trying to poison my emotions?'

Vesper shook her head. 'I'm doing my best to protect you.'

'From Lew? Don't be absurd. He'd never hurt me.'

'Not intentionally, perhaps. But how long do you think you can keep him balanced on the edge of the law that is so important to him? He can't stay there forever, and when he goes off either side, darling, odds are he'll take you down with him.'

'You are presuming on our relationship. And now I think you're something of a hypocrite.'

'I made love to your brother because it pleased me to do so. I admit I formed a strong attachment to him, and he for me; because of that perhaps I became too involved in your struggle with the Leonfortes.' Vesper shook her head. 'Still, with all that, he never would tell me the origin of the enmity between the two families.'

'Nor will I.' Margarite turned away.

'Really? That's curious. I'm the one who delivers the

Nishiki intelligence to you, and that intelligence is what allows you to maintain your advantage over Caesare Leonforte and all the other Family dons.'

'Family is family. You'll miss your flight,' Margarite said with crisp finality.

After a moment, Vesper nodded and said, 'You're right. I'd better get changed.'

When she disappeared from view, Margarite sat on a sofa lost in thought for some time. Then she picked up the phone and called her daughter, Francine. Croaker felt a pang. His visit with her had been all too short, and her sadness at the continuing plight of her parents had been all too palpable. But he knew that pang was for Margarite as well. Hearing how her voice changed when she spoke with Francie reminded him of how desperately he missed her and of how much he despised himself for continuing to spy on her.

Margarite finished her call, rose and brought out two small valises, lined them up beside the front door. For some time, she stood still and silent, staring down at them as if by a supreme act of will she could make them disappear, turn the present course of events on its ear, and perhaps change the future.

Then she turned, and Croaker knew that Vesper was coming. He stretched to get a better view, then froze. The figure who now approached was dressed in black jeans, a man-tailored white shirt open at the collar, an oversize Claude Montana leather jacket. A thick red jade choker was around her throat.

He stared in disbelief at her black, lustrous hair, close cut: a superb wig. Her large, brown, doe-soft eyes, altered with colored contact lenses, flashed with life and a highly developed sense of wit. Only the pouty mouth, devoid of lipstick, was the same.

I'd better get changed.

Now he understood the irony of her seemingly

innocent statement. The chameleon had changed its appearance again. Just what kind of a creature was she? Croaker remembered the old ensigns of persona he had contemplated while waiting for her to appear at the Phillips gallery. And he recognized this was the moment when he had to tear them up and start all over again. His traditional notions of gender and motivation no longer applied to this world he was burrowing into. If he could not let go of his basic prejudices, he knew he would never solve the riddle of Vesper Arkham.

Sex and Fear

For me who go,
for you who stay –
two autumns.

Buson

Tokyo

SUMMER 1962–AUTUMN 1971

In 1962, Colonel Denis Linnear made the mistake of introducing his son to Tsunetomo Akinaga. In the many melancholy autumns after the one in 1971, Nicholas had cause to wonder what his motives might have been. But, of course, by then it was far too late, for the Colonel had been killed in 1963.

In the summer of 1962, Tsunetomo Akinaga was a vital man, bursting with energy the way a peach is ripe with juice. He had been *oyabun* of the Shikei clan for many years. *Shikei* meant 'capital punishment', and in those days Nicholas often wondered why a family should bear such a designation. No one seemed prepared to tell him, least of all Tsunetomo, who had all the good humor of a professional comedian. The old man – for he was far older than he appeared – told strings of hilarious jokes that kept the boys howling with laughter.

The boys were Omi and Hachi, Tsunetomo's middle and youngest sons, and Nicholas. Tetsuo, the eldest son and the one destined to supplant his father as *oyabun*, was already out of the house, cutting his teeth, as Tsunetomo said with a grin, running a Shikei subfamily in Kobe.

Whether Omi and Hachi liked Nicholas was debatable, but because of his aikido prowess they accepted him. As for Tsunetomo, he respected Nicholas, at first because he was Colonel Linnear's son, and then because he recognized Nicholas's innate intelligence.

'You are a half-breed,' Tsunetomo said to Nicholas one afternoon over tea and soybean sweets, 'and so your life will not be an easy one.' They were alone, kneeling on tatami in a room that overlooked a small garden composed exclusively of azalea and rocks. The azalea were exquisitely sculpted into the shapes of rocks, so the garden itself became a complex meditation on the relationship between nature and artifice.

The *oyabun*, who led a hectic life, liked to spend an hour with one of his boys late in the afternoon after school and martial-arts lessons were over. He said it had the same effect as meditation, which he claimed he was incapable of ever since his father had been murdered in a territorial war a decade before.

'But I will waste no sympathy on you, young man,' he said as he crunched down on a sweet, 'because you need none. You will overcome your burden. In fact, it will teach you much about the people you meet, and you will be a shrewder person for that knowledge.' Then he told a joke about a farmer and an itinerant priest that made Nicholas burst into laughter.

Tsunetomo smiled. 'Laughter is good for my azalea. They drink it up as they do water and sunlight. When there is a wilt in my garden, I know it is because they lack the sound of laughter.'

'Is that why you tell jokes?'

Tsunetomo nodded. 'Partly.' He gestured to Nicholas to pour more tea. 'My father was a great prankster. Did I ever tell you about how he snuck into the inn where my wife and I were honeymooning and set off a string of firecrackers under our window? Ha, ha! Yes, he was a master, and it was a tragedy for many people when he was killed. My jokes are a way of keeping him alive, you see. In your laughter and the laughter of others

298

here he returns again and again to light firecrackers beneath my window.'

This conversation was made all the more poignant in Nicholas's memory because it occurred in the spring following the Colonel's death. For months, Tsunetomo had not called Nicholas, and though Nicholas regularly saw Omi and Hachi at the dojo, they never invited him home with them. For much of that time, Nicholas was too busy to think much about it, but there were days when he missed those afternoon encounters with the *oyabun* with a sensation as acute as pain. And it was only then that he understood how much they had come to mean to him.

He had loved and revered his father, but the Colonel was, after all, a Westerner, and this fact separated him from his son, no matter how attuned the Colonel was to the oriental mind. Tsunetomo provided what, in the end, Colonel Linnear could not: a wholly Eastern sensibility, and perhaps this was why the Colonel had introduced the two.

In the spring of 1964, Tsunetomo appeared at Nicholas's dojo. He spent an hour and a half watching only Nicholas, as the aikido *sensei* put him through his paces. By this time, Nicholas was well advanced and had, at another dojo entirely, commenced his training in *ninjutsu*. Some of this ancient secretive discipline could be seen in his unorthodox and often astonishing solutions to the aikido attacks the *sensei* had devised for him.

The *oyabun* waited patiently for Nicholas while his phalanx of bodyguards remained out of sight so as not to disturb the harmony the *sensei* had diligently labored to produce in his class. Nicholas, overjoyed to see Tsunetomo, was only too happy to receive an invitation to share tea and soybean sweets.

Later, after Tsunetomo's words reverberated in his mind, Nicholas understood how deeply the *oyabun* had been hurt by the Colonel's death. Perhaps it reminded him too keenly of his own father's brutal murder. Both he and Nicholas needed to heal from the wound before they recommenced their meetings. A strict sense of respect was also involved. Tsunetomo did not want to give Nicholas the idea that he was in any way aiming to supplant the Colonel in Nicholas's affections.

'I am Tsunetomo,' he said that afternoon, staring at the tender azalea buds on the verge of opening. 'And your father was the Colonel. I am *oyabun*, but he was far more than that. Your father was an architect of dreams. I do not expect you to understand this now, but one day you will.'

Tea was an endless ritual with Tsunetomo. It was sacred time; as long as he was at tea, his men and advisers knew that he could not be disturbed. In this way did Tsunetomo draw the demarcation between commerce and what he referred to as the business of life.

'As you can see,' he said, 'this garden is enclosed by four walls. Three are fusuma doors into the house; the fourth is the inner wall of this estate. Everything is low in the garden; this is deliberate. Not even the wind can disturb the components. I have caught sunlight and shadow like ships in a bottle. To sit here in the morning or the afternoon and watch how the shapes are transformed with the light is to understand the nature of life and time, for in the end nothing is ever transformed here. At the end of each night the garden starts afresh at the beginning of its cycle.'

Nicholas, who had been too long alone with his memories of his father, felt an inner door unlocking. 'I can see my father here.'

'Sooner or later, everything exists in the garden,' Tsunetomo said, obviously pleased. He watched Nicholas drink his bitter green tea as he crunched on a sweet. In the silence that ensued Nicholas imagined that both of them were thinking of the Colonel.

Tsunetomo, kneeling on the tatami with the regal aspect of a shogun, said, 'I want to tell you a story about the past. When I am finished, I want you to tell me what it means to you.' He cleared his throat. 'In the days before the first Tokugawa shogun united Japan, there was a feudal lord who was a great wencher. In all ways, he was an honorable man, and his retainers loved him. He had many sons out of wedlock, but he had only one legitimate son. This boy had won his father's heart when he had pushed himself out of his mother's womb despite being turned the wrong way. "He should have died," the astonished doctors told the lord, "and your wife with him, but his will to live was too great."

'The lord watched as his son grew from childhood into young adulthood. During times of war, the lord protected his son with his own forged armor and his own valorous heart. But there were times when the lord could not take his son with him on long and dangerous trips, and at these times he left him in the care of a young retainer who the lord trusted as if he were a member of his family.

'On his twenty-first birthday, the lord's son took ill, and despite the lord's pleas and imprecations, nothing the doctors did could save him. On the day of his funeral, when the incense burned with a steady glow and all the priests of the lord's fiefdom were at the burial site, the young retainer rode to the temple grounds and, dismounting, proceeded to commit ritual suicide before the altar of Buddha.'

Three plovers flew into the garden. Two of them alighted on a sheared azalea, but the third, who sat above and apart from the others, twittered on the curving top of the highest rock.

Nicholas watched the lone plover for a moment before he said, 'What the story tells me is that duty is not only familial. It is a sense of time and place; but mostly it is a definition of self.' He looked at Tsunetomo. 'Is this the right answer?'

The *oyabun* smiled. 'I am no Rinzai Buddhist priest. There is no right or wrong answer by which I must judge you. I merely wished to know your response when my words touched your mind.'

Over the years, Nicholas had cause to remember many times this story of feudal Japan. While it was the Colonel and his mother, Cheong, who had instilled in him his sense of honor, it was Tsunetomo who honed that sense as Nicholas reached for maturity.

In the autumn of 1971, when Nicholas was a young man, he entered Tsunetomo's house just as he had twice weekly for eight years. But this time, Tsunetomo was not alone in the six-tatami room he used for tea and the business of life. A young woman was with him. She seemed not much more than a girl really, and Nicholas was surprised to learn that she had just reached her majority.

His experience with women had been both stormy and ultimately disastrous. He was therefore understandably somewhat withdrawn around them, and these days rarely dated.

Tsunetomo turned when Nicholas entered the room. 'Ah, there you are. Nicholas, I want you to meet the daughter of an old friend of mine. Her name is Koei.' He rose. 'I wonder if you would make tea for her. Unfortunately, I have been called away for an hour or so. Do your best to entertain her in my absence.'

Koei was not an immediately striking woman, especially when one looked at each feature in turn. Her mouth was small and expressionless, her large eyes were withdrawn, and the angles of her face seemed too

302

hard and unforgiving. Her skin was as pale as that of the legendary nineteenth-century geisha who never went out in sunlight without the protection of an umbrella.

As she knelt with her hands primly together in her lap, she gave the impression of frailty or, if one was not in the mood to be charitable, infirmity. Nicholas initially wondered whether she might be crippled.

Nicholas bent to his task of preparing the tea. While he did so, he was silent, as was customary, but when they drank, he spoke to her of the sheared azalea and the rocks of the garden, and how only light and the occasional bird were free to move about in it.

'I suppose this must be difficult for you,' Koei said as if she had not heard a word he had said. She did not meet his eyes.

'What do you mean?'

'Being left alone with someone you don't know and being told to entertain her.'

'Well . . .'

'Especially since Tsunetomo is not someone you can say no to.'

He smiled. 'That's right. But even if he were not *oya-bun* of the Shikei clan I would have done what he asked.' He cocked his head to one side. 'It's not difficult . . . or onerous.'

She was still bent over, her eyes lowered. When she spoke, she barely moved her lips, and her hair, bound tightly to her head, reflected the light from the garden as if it were a lantern. She possessed a kind of ethereal stillness he had only previously seen in accomplished *sensei*, but there was a subtle difference here he could not pinpoint.

'I do not want to be a burden on anyone.'

'What makes you think you would be?'

'Who am I?' She put her cup back on the table. 'I am

303

not pretty, or particularly clever. I cannot imagine why anyone would want to be in my company.'

'But surely that can't be true. Obviously, Tsunetomo cares deeply for you.'

She raised her head, her expression a bit bewildered, as if she were a doe caught in the beam of a headlight. 'Do you really think so?'

'Of course. He invited you here to his tea room. He doesn't do that with just anyone.'

'He invited you here as well.' She seemed to become aware of him for the first time, like a snail emerging from its shell just after a predator has passed close by.

'Tsunetomo is like my second father.' Nicholas told her about Colonel Linnear and his death. She seemed oddly unmoved, as if he had told her a bird had flown through the garden.

She shivered, said to him, 'I am uncomfortable here.'

Tsunetomo had not yet returned. Nicholas decided to take Koei home; she seemed so fragile he could not imagine her being able to manage it on her own. They passed through the layers of bodyguards surrounding the *oyabun*'s compound. Outside on the street, he discovered a limousine complete with driver and two burly Yakuza waiting for her. These were not Shikei clan members. So Koei was the daughter of another Yakuza *oyabun*. An old friend, Tsunetomo had said, leaving it at that.

She stood still as stone on the sidewalk, staring into the interior of the limo as if it were an open grave. 'I don't want to get in there.'

'I'll take you home.'

For some time, she did not move or indicate that she had heard him. What he liked about her was that she obviously disapproved of what her father did. When Nicholas was with Tsunetomo and was a beneficiary of his great wit, generosity and affection, it was impossible

304

to dwell upon his profession. And, after all, some of the Colonel's closest friends had been Yakuza *oyabun*. And yet deep inside him Nicholas heard a voice of warning, felt a hard lump of sin forming like a pearl within an oyster's flesh. Most days, he ignored both and continued with his life.

Koei lived within a walled compound not too dissimilar to that of Tsunetomo. Her father, Tokino Kaeda, a saturnine man of prodigious size, was chief under-*oyabun* of the Yamauchi clan, which, since the untimely death of Katsuodo Kozo, had been in turmoil. Katsuodo's eldest son, Tomoo, who was in his early thirties, was still too inexperienced to assume the *oyabun*'s mantle. Thus, Koei's father, as the senior of the under-*oyabun*, had been elevated to head the clan until Tomoo came of age. Until then, part of his responsibilities was to teach Tomoo everything he knew.

Koei's mother was a neat, small woman, nearly as delicate as her daughter. But she had not aged well. There were unmistakable lines in her face, her hair was gray and her eyes were turned inward. As she served them tea, she spoke of her flowers – she taught ikebana, flower arranging – and how each season was marked by what lived and died. She seemed neither happy nor unhappy when Koei introduced Nicholas, merely vaguely surprised. But then, considering Koei's innate shyness, perhaps that was to be expected. On the other hand, she never directed her words to either of them, but spoke as if into empty air, or to herself.

Tokino Kaeda had the look of a stern disciplinarian. He returned to the compound with one of his sons. He glanced at Nicholas and his daughter, handed his briefcase to his son, and told him to take it into his study. 'Work until you get it right,' he said to the young man. 'If you make another mistake, you'll pay dearly.' He never looked at his son as he spoke, but gazed fixedly

305

at the couple having tea. His wife retired into the kitchen, presumably to make him something to eat.

'What have we here?' Kaeda said, coming toward them.

Koei looked down into her empty teacup and introduced Nicholas. 'He is a good friend of Akinaga-san's,' she added hastily. 'We met at Akinaga-san's house.'

'You are not Yakuza,' Kaeda addressed Nicholas. 'By the look of you, you're not even Japanese.'

'I am half-oriental, half-Western. My father is Colonel Denis Linnear.'

'I suppose saying that has gotten you into many a door that should have been closed to you.' The big man stabbed a quick glance at his daughter. 'I am not Akinaga. It won't do you any good here.'

Nicholas said nothing.

'I am cautious about who my daughter spends time with.'

'Father —'

'I understand,' Nicholas said, trying to head off a family argument. 'Most *oyabun* feel the same way. It's part of the territory.'

'I am not most *oyabun*. And my daughter is special.'

'I am only trying to be her friend.'

The big man grunted, then went into the kitchen.

'I'm sorry,' Koei whispered. She seemed to be trembling.

'For what?'

'My father's manners. He was brought up on the street. I am his only daughter. He lives with blood and death all the time and it . . .' She broke off, shuddering. 'It frightens me. What if he should be killed? There is so much infighting among the Yamauchi, so much envy and jealousy. Someone could slip a *katana* through his ribs and puncture his lung or his heart. It would be terrible.'

306

There was a kind of quickness to her breathing, to the rhythm of her words, that could be mistaken for vibrancy. Intense fear could do that to a person, Nicholas knew. It could animate even the half-dead. He was startled by this thought. Is that how he thought of Koei?

In the weeks that followed, he saw Koei with increasing frequency, and in that time the only thing he could say for certain about her was that she was a complete enigma. He was also falling in love with her. Perhaps that love was not perfect, touched as it was by the intrigue of the unknown, but what young love is without the imperfections of lust and a strong sense of danger?

The truth about Koei was that the longer one spent with her the more beautiful she became. She was like a camellia that has opened its dew-spattered petals slowly to an insistent sun. He no longer saw each feature separately, but had become entranced by the whole. Now the angles of her face seemed neither hard nor unforgiving, but rather an exotic backdrop that perfectly set off her eyes and mouth.

And then there was the darkness of her enigma. It hung above her brows, shuddered in the shadows as they sat huddled together against the autumn wind sweeping through the streets, clearing rust and gold leaves from the maples. It was always with them, and it drove Nicholas farther down a path he should have abandoned long before.

Koei looked into the cloud-filled sky. 'Have you ever wondered why life is as it is? Why there is so much pain and suffering? Why people can't find peace?'

'I suppose it's part of the human condition.' She was often inexplicably melancholy, like an old woman who has come to the end of her life and, looking back upon it, weeps bitter tears. 'There would be no religion, otherwise. Besides, humans need to struggle. Without it, they'd wither and die.'

Koei hugged herself. With any other woman Nicholas would have put his arm around her, but not Koei. She did not like to be touched. In fact, their sitting so close was something of a novelty. Nicholas did not mind; he'd already had his fill of promiscuous women.

'When I look at the future I see nothing,' Koei said.

'You mean you have no profession? Surely, you'll get married, have children, your own family.'

She shuddered, looked bleakly at the crisp leaves dragged along the ground by the wind. 'I don't think I could ever . . .' She shook her head from side to side. 'I don't even like being with men, except for you. I feel comfortable with you, Nicholas. I . . .' She seemed unable to continue. He could feel her breathing, the quickness of her pulse. 'Put your arm around me.'

'Koei . . .'

'Please.'

He did as she asked. Her eyes closed. Her breasts rose and fell beneath her coat. Then tears began to leak from the corners of her eyes. They rolled down her cheeks, fell into her lap.

'Koei, what's the matter?'

Her eyes opened, stared into his. 'Oh, Nicholas, I like you near me.'

It went further, slowly, painfully. He remembered vividly the moment when their lips first met. It was a night when the moon was dark. The sky, swept clean of clouds, was drizzled with stars. An owl hooted from across open fields. On the outskirts of Tokyo, away from her house and his, they felt the giddy freedom of explorers setting foot on a new continent.

He was aware of her trembling flesh beneath his, and a tiny whimper caught in her throat. Then, she broke away, as if she could not bear their shared heat a moment longer. She took deep breaths as if she had just completed a marathon run.

'Koei?' he whispered in the night.

'Yes, yes. Kiss me again.'

She seemed drawn to the devastation the war had wrought upon her city. Though almost all of the rebuilding had already been done, there were still places throughout Tokyo that bore the scars of the bombing raids and the napalm-induced firestorms. Afternoons, golden in the burnished autumnal atmosphere, she took him to these places as if they were intimate gardens whose exquisite existence she was willing to share. She seemed most at ease in these maimed sites, as if the protection of her shell was not necessary here. Thus, in an unconscious way, she presented to Nicholas the existence of her own scar, though not its mysterious nature.

Of course, by then he knew that she must have been hurt sometime in the past. But this wound ran deep, so it was probably not merely a last-minute rejection by a suitor or a callous remark by a lover. That it was sexual in nature he had no doubt whatsoever. It often seemed to him that Koei burned with a sexual ardor that was quite intense, and that she lived in mortal dread of that ardent part of her. She was split off from herself, two people at once, struggling to regain a semblance of balance after a trauma of unknown proportions.

'You're my savior,' she whispered to him one night. They were entwined in each other's arms, lying within a blanket they had laid at the edge of the open field where, sometime before, the stars had lit them, an owl had hooted mournfully, and their lips had met. 'Save me.'

What did she need to be saved from?

The terrible thing was Nicholas suspected that he

knew. He did not want to know, and yet he desperately wanted to understand it all because he wanted more than anything else to end her pain and suffering, to make her whole again. It was that time of his life. His belief that he could do this was absolute.

'Save me.'

By *save me* she meant 'take me'. He knew it and she knew he knew it. It was what she wanted. It was what he wanted. It was right.

Carefully, he unbuttoned her blouse. She arched slightly and he unhooked her bra. His head bent and his mouth enclosed one hard nipple. She gasped, ran her fingers through his thick hair. He could hear her ardent heartbeat, and it was as if he were dipped in fire. He wanted more than anything to enter her and, in doing so, enclose her in warmth and protection. He wanted an end to her suffering.

He kissed her breasts, white as milk, as he unfastened her skirt. He pushed it down, along with her underpants. Then he rose up over her.

At that moment, she cried out and, rolling away from him, drew her legs up to her chest. 'Oh, my God. Oh, my God,' she sobbed.

From behind her, he whispered, 'It's all right.'

'No, no.' Her head whipped from side to side. 'It's all turned to ashes, everything I've dreamed about for weeks.' Her shoulders shook. 'I have no explanation. I can't —'

'It's all right,' he said again, and turned her gently toward him. 'Don't worry. It will be fine.'

'No,' she whispered as her hand found him and enclosed him. 'It isn't all right.' She caressed him lightly.

'Koei, you don't have to —'

'No, no, I want to.' Her hand stroking so softly. 'Oh, Nicholas, I want what you want, please believe me, but I can't —' She gasped as his seed exploded on her fingers

310

and wrist. 'Yes,' she sighed, her head against his heaving chest. 'Oh, yes.'

In the night, with only the wind and the birds, they seemed suspended in time, wafted on currents and eddies only they could see.

Nicholas, working up his courage to say what needed to be said now, held her tightly. 'I know you won't tell me on your own, so let me say this for you.'

'No.' She put her hand over his mouth. 'Please, no.'

He took her fingers firmly away. 'You know it's for the best, Koei. Because if I don't, you will never be healed, and the darkness will remain between us and we will never recover. We'll come to distrust and hate one another, and I won't allow that to happen.'

He paused for a moment, heard only the wind and the wild beating of their hearts. She had acquiesced, finally, in the only way she knew how now.

'You were raped, weren't you?' He felt a tiny spasm go through her as if he had pricked her with a needle. 'How long ago did it happen?'

'Three years, five months, six days.' She stared up at the night sky, and her voice was as dry as that of an economics professor. The door was at last open.

'Your parents know, don't they?'

'Yes.'

That explained her mother's disengagement, her father's almost paranoid caution when it came to Koei's relationship with Nicholas. Her mother was still in denial and her father's rage had not abated.

'Who did it?'

She rolled away from him, but he caught her in his arms, forced her back. 'Koei.' He made her look at him. 'This poison that's inside you must come out. It's killing you, don't you see? You're only happy when we're together, and then only sporadically.' He thought of the raped parts of Tokyo where she felt free to display her

311

own terrible scar. 'We've lanced the wound and the poison is oozing out, but we've got to get it all or the infection will go on and on until you'll lose all will to live. I can't believe that's what you want. Not now.'

For a long time she gazed mutely into his eyes. She opened her mouth to speak, then closed it abruptly. He knew she wanted to cry, but it was too late for that. He was witnessing the last barrier she had unconsciously erected to keep herself sane after the rape. The split was not yet complete.

'Who raped you?'

'Please don't make me do this.'

'It's for your own good. You know it as well as I do.'

'He was . . . a friend. Yasuo Hideyuke. My . . . a boy from school . . . a senior.' She put her head down, sobbing so inconsolably he could only hold her, rocking her back and forth.

After a time, there were no more tears, only her voice, thin and reedy as she regurgitated the horror that now had to be fully exorcized. 'He was . . . older than I. I looked up to him . . . for protection, you know. I trusted him. I never suspected, but when he attacked me, it was very quick. I was asleep, I didn't know at first what was happening. I could smell the liquor on his breath, and then I felt his hardness pushing against me. It was like a pole or a spear, I . . . I didn't know what to do. I was wild, I think, then my mind went numb. I couldn't be there, this couldn't be happening, not to me. So I shut down. I remember my legs opening as his hands grabbed me.' Her fingers clutched Nicholas as if she were afraid of drowning in her memories. 'The pain roused me. I cried out, but this only seemed to spur him on, looming over me, pounding up and down on me. In me. There was something – I don't know – horribly aggressive, as if rage drove him, not lust. And that's when I snapped. I could have borne his lust, I suppose, because it would have been understandable in a way. But rage? How had my trust incited this in him?

'I tried to fight him, and he hit me. He seemed to like that, too, beating me while he was . . . inside me, and he reared up over me and . . . *God!* No more. No more!'

The next morning, Nicholas went through classes like a zombie. At his aikido dojo he barely heard his *sensei*'s lesson, and when he was thrown to the tatami by a second-year student, he knew that he was in trouble.

In the end, he knew whom he had to see and it wasn't Koei. It was the man who had cut her life in half before she had gotten to full flower.

He found Yasuo Hideyuke, who had graduated from school only to become a fisherman. He had taken over his father's boat and now ran it with the precision of a drill sergeant. He was, as Koei had said, a big man, with the musculature of a weight lifter. A surly, taciturn creature, perhaps he felt trapped in a business he didn't care for but that paid the rent for him and his widowed mother.

He did not like Nicholas's looks and made this plain without preamble. He was a political radical, hating both the Americans and the Communists with equal enthusiasm.

'Whether or not I dated Koei is no business of yours,' he said, with his spread-legged stance barring Nicholas from coming onto his boat. 'This is my property; you're trespassing.'

'The past will not go away,' Nicholas said. '*That* isn't your property.'

'I have work to do,' Hideyuke said dismissively. 'Leave me alone.'

Nicholas began to step on board. 'Not until I get some answers.'

'Here's the only answer you'll get out of me,'

313

Hideyuke said, grabbing a curved fishhook and swinging it with precision toward Nicholas's face.

Nicholas reacted instinctively. He stepped into the attack, rather than away from it. He ducked, the fishhook flashed over his head, and he struck Hideyuke in the stomach with an *atemi*.

The big man grunted, sucked in his breath, and slammed the wooden handle of the fishhook down onto the back of Nicholas's neck. Pain exploded in Nicholas's head and he went down across the space between the dock and the side of the boat.

Hideyuke kicked him into the crevasse, so that Nicholas was holding on to the gunwale of the boat with both hands while he dangled over the water. The fishing boat, though tied up, jostled in the water, moving dangerously close to the dock.

'How do you like *this* answer?' Hideyuke said as he brought the barbed end of the fishhook down onto Nicholas's left hand. Nicholas let go with that hand, and the hook buried itself in the gunwale of the boat.

That gave him his moment, and he swung upward. Hideyuke was caught between trying to punch him and letting go of his weapon. He opted for the weapon, concentrating on freeing it.

His muscles bulging, he ripped it free, but by that time Nicholas had kicked out, slamming the sole of his shoe into the side of Hideyuke's knee. The big man went down but, reaching out, took Nicholas with him.

They crashed onto the gunwale, and then, still struggling, tumbled over the side. Nicholas, on the bottom, reached up, grabbing a hawser, slippery with seaweed. Hideyuke, still clinging to his weapon, slid down, clutching Nicholas's left leg with his free hand.

Nicholas looked down, saw the big man swinging back his arm, readying another slash with the fishhook. He did the only thing he could: he drew back his right leg, slammed his shoe onto the top of Hideyuke's head.

Hideyuke's attack aborted in mid-swing, and he lost his grip on Nicholas. He went straight down, into the black water, churning with the movement of his boat as it jounced against the dock, bounced back out again.

The police held Nicholas for three hours for questioning, but he was finally released. Witnesses could not agree on how the fight started, but they all praised Nicholas's courage in plummeting into the water at considerable risk to himself in an attempt to rescue Hideyuke. Besides, he was Colonel Denis Linnear's son.

'There is something I need to tell you,' Nicholas said to Koei when they met at sunset at one of her bleak, scarred places in the city. 'I saw Yasuo Hideyuke today.'

Koei stood so still she might have ceased to breathe. All the color drained from her face, and the look in her eyes he had only seen in prey at last trapped by its hunter.

'Did you speak with him?'

'He wouldn't answer my questions.'

Some of the extreme tension that had gripped her dissipated, and he thought for a moment she would collapse in relief. He held her in his arms.

'Koei, he's dead.'

'Who's dead?' She had that bewildered look he had seen in her so long ago.

'Hideyuke.'

'What? How?'

Nicholas looked at her for a long time. 'We got into a fight.'

'He fought with you? You're . . . my God, I've seen what you can do.' Then, as if a switch had been thrown inside her, she gave a little moan. 'Why were you there?'

'You know why.'

315

Now she cried out in earnest. 'Retribution. That's what you wanted, isn't it?'

'No, I . . .' In truth Nicholas did not know, and the question had been haunting him ever since he hauled himself out of the water. Had he gone to see Hideyuke in order to confront him? For what reason? To hear him confess and gain a measure of satisfaction? Or had it been to seek retribution for the hideous crime he had committed? No, it couldn't be. He was incapable . . . Then he recalled one of his conversations with Tsunetomo when the *oyabun* had recounted the story of the loyal retainer who had committed seppuku because his lord's son had been killed. *Duty is not only familial*, he had said to Tsunetomo in response. *It is a sense of time and place; but mostly it is a definition of self.*

'I don't know,' Nicholas said.

'You don't know,' Koei repeated. Then anger filled her face, turning it into something he could never have imagined. 'Yasuo was an innocent boy. He and I held hands, once or twice. That's all.'

Nicholas was so stunned there was a buzzing in his ears. 'But you told me —'

Koei put her fists against her ears. 'I know what I told you, but I didn't know what else to say. You were making me talk about it, and maybe you were right, part of me wanted to. But I couldn't tell you the truth.'

'What truth!' He shook her so hard her teeth rattled. There was a taste of bile in his mouth and his bowels had turned to water. He had a glimpse of Hideyuke losing his grip, falling into the roiling abyss between dock and boat. '*What truth!*' he roared.

In the face of his pain and rage the cyst of silence and lies burst at last. 'It was my father! My father raped me!'

And now, as reality shifted, he saw in a flash all the interactions that he had so neatly misinterpreted: Koei

316

looking into her father's limo as if it were an open grave, the mother's disaffection, the father's jealousy, Koei's strange animation at describing an imagined violent death for her father, *I was asleep, I didn't know at first what was happening*, she had been at home when she was raped. The half-truths and the clues; the silence and the lies.

She collapsed at his feet, her hands over her eyes. But it was too much; even she could not block out the past and the present. 'Oh, Buddha, save me!'

But Nicholas, looking down at her with a mixture of pity and rage, knew that there would be no salvation for any of them. His heart was broken, but what did that matter now? He had made his choice. He had lain down with Yakuza and had gotten up covered in blood.

BOOK III: Skull and Bones

Banked fires; night grows late —
then comes a sound of rapping
at the gate.

Kyoroku

BOOK II: Skull and Bones

NINE

Kyoto/Washington

Nicholas awoke to the soft calls of the fishmongers. He had dreamed of Koei, and now his mind was filled with her. He had not had that particular dream in a long time. What had triggered it?

All his days and nights with her were preserved in his memory as if suspended in time. Sights, sounds, smells and, most of all, feelings were as vivid now as they had been when he had been with her. If Koei had been his right arm, he could not have felt her loss any more profoundly. His love for her had transcended the mere physical; it bloomed in the night when he was alone like some exotic and ethereal flower, even during the years he had been married to Justine. And, of course, the circumstances of that loss made it that much more painful. He had been betrayed by his surrogate family, by following in his father's footsteps, by his own instinct in befriending members of the Yakuza.

He had destroyed an innocent young man in his stumbling attempt to right a wrong. In the process, he had uncovered a nest of unpardonable sins. But he had yet to discover which had been *his* unpardonable sin: causing Yasuo's death or living in the Yakuza world? Little wonder he had grown up hating them so.

He felt a stirring beside him, turned and saw Seiko's face as she lay on her side beneath the covers of the futon. Silently, he pushed the covers aside, walked to the sliding doors that opened onto the window of the

321

room. They were on the second floor of a *ryokan*, a traditional inn on a side street off the Shijo-dori, one of Kyoto's wide, bustling avenues. The Shijo-dori might have been as modern as any avenue in Tokyo, but take a turn off it on almost any side street and, like this one, you'd find a semblance of the old Kyoto, with its wood-framed houses and narrow lanes.

Before leaving Saigon, Nicholas had temporarily installed a cousin of Van Kiet's in the Sato International branch office to monitor the local factories' output but to make no policy decisions. Considering the suspicions he harbored, he did not want to entrust the job to Seiko.

He, Tachi and Seiko had flown into Osaka, then had taken the fifty-minute shuttle bus to Kyoto because Van Kiet had discovered two receipts in V. I. Pavlov's wallet – a testament to the meticulousness of the Russian – one a roundtrip for transfers by bus to and from Osaka airport and Kyoto. The other was for a Kyoto nightclub called Ningyo-ro, the Doll Pavilion. Oddly, Pavlov had been carrying no receipt for a hotel or *ryokan*.

Outside, small trucks laden with fresh, glistening fish were being off-loaded onto the street as the morning sorting began. The fish market, just around the corner, was only open until noon, and six days a week the narrow street here ran with blood and brine.

Nicholas, standing at the window, looked down on the rubber-booted fishmongers and saw a dark crevasse, black water roiling and empty of life. So many years had passed since he had learned his lesson; so many years since he had turned his back on the Yakuza and Mikio Okami, his father's best friend. And then, last year, Okami had popped up, wanting Nicholas to make good on the promise he had made to the Colonel to come to Okami's aid should he ever need it. Now, in an insane twist of fate, he was sworn to protect Okami. In so doing, he had been drawn into a world he

322

could no longer define. That eventually brought Lew Croaker and Nicholas in contact with Okami's would-be assassin, a Vietnamese named Do Duc, whom Nicholas had killed.

'Nicholas.'

He turned, saw that Seiko had arisen. The room was redolent of broiling fish, which the kitchen downstairs was no doubt preparing for breakfast. Soon he would have to confront Tachi, the Yakuza *oyabun*, the *tanjian*.

'You look so sad. Would you like some tea?'

'Very much, yes. *Domo*.'

She went out of the room, filled an iron kettle with water, then returned to a hibachi sunken into the tatami and began to heat it. He watched her take green cut leaves out of a canister, spread them like a carpet into the kettle. When the water was ready, she poured it in, then closed the lid, letting the tea steep.

They sat facing each other. She handed him a full cup. He drank first. He could feel her wanting him to speak. He missed Lew. Their periodic phone debriefings were necessarily terse and to the point, underscoring the synergy the two men produced when they were together.

'The number of women in this puzzle is interesting,' Nicholas had said to Croaker. 'We have the two sisters, Margarite and Celeste, one based in New York, the other in Venice, where she works for Okami; Dominic's mother, Renata Loti, who is a major influence-peddler in Washington; now this woman Vesper, who's involved with Dedalus. What's odd is how all of them are in positions of, if not outright decision-making, then of real power.'

'Do you have a theory?' Croaker had asked. 'Right now I could use all the help I can get with Vesper because she doesn't fit any of my preconceived notions.'

'Neither do any of the other women. But I have the

323

impression that in some way neither of us are seeing, Vesper is a key. Keep that in mind when you get to London.'

'You will never trust me, will you?' Seiko's voice broke into his thoughts. She was looking at him over the edge of her cup.

'Nangi uncovered evidence that Masamoto Goei, the theoretical-language team leader on my Chi Project, was involved in stealing the Chi neural-net chip. There is suspicion that you helped him smuggle it into Vietnam to Vincent Tinh.'

'I'm guilty.'

'What?'

She nodded. 'I helped Goei, but not for money as Tinh thought, and not for ideology as Goei believed. It was to help Tachi and Van Kiet get inside Floating City. The illegal clone Tinh had Abramanov cobble together from stolen elements from the Chi Project and the American equivalent Hive computer gave them a foot in the door. Or so they theorized. Unfortunately, Tinh – who was the key, the liaison with Rock – refused to cooperate, even when Van Kiet put pressure on him.'

Nicholas thought about this for some time. Was she lying or telling the truth? The sexual vibrations she set up in resonance every time he projected his psyche made it impossible for him even to make a guess. Everything she said seemed plausible, but did that make it the truth? Was he among friends or in a nest of deadly vipers?

'Then who murdered Tinh? It seems to me that from what you and Tachi have told me, Rock had motive and opportunity. Yet I have no tangible proof.'

'Does it really matter? Vincent Tinh is dead. Nothing you can do now will bring him back.' She took a breath. 'He deserved his fate.'

'The truth matters a great deal to me.'

She put her cup down. 'I've told you the truth.' She put out her hands, palms up. 'Use your Tau-tau.'

He said nothing, made no move, but his eyes bored into hers until she was obliged to blink.

She swallowed more tea, then said, 'I want to tell you something. I had a brother, Matsuro. I'm going to tell you about his death because he died under . . . particular circumstances.' She paused then, as if she might reconsider.

Carefully, she put down the teacup, stared at it fixedly. At last, she said, 'Matsuro was special; his mental and physical ages were not synchronous.' She blinked once, as if she saw him now, in the mirror of the teacup. 'He was two years younger than me, but inside he was just a little boy. He did not understand . . .' Her voice faded out as her eyes clouded with tears. 'He did not understand the world.'

Her fingers laced and unlaced themselves in her lap. 'At that time, five years ago, I lived with them – Matsuro and my mother. At night I was in charge of him. My mother works nights; she runs a Kyoto *akachochin*.' An after-hours bar. 'Every night I would give Matsuro his bath before he went to bed. It was a kind of . . . ritual that he loved. I would tell him stories and we would talk and he was so relaxed he would almost seem normal.

'I was seeing someone then, a Vietnamese commodities expert who taught me a great deal about the foreign stock markets.' She stopped again, her throat clotted with memory and emotion. She swallowed hard, reached for the teacup, then stopped midway. 'You see how it was, he called that night. I hadn't seen him in two months – he had gone to Saigon on business. He phoned me the moment he returned. I . . . I only meant to leave Matsuro for a moment, to get the phone. But it was him, and I had missed him so much and he had so much to tell me, I got caught up . . .'

Her head went down, and slowly tears fell onto her hands, unmoving now in her lap.

'I have no excuse . . . none that will suffice for my inattention. It was only, I don't know, seven, eight minutes when I remembered my brother, alone in the tub half full of water. I dropped the phone, ran into the bathroom.' She had to stop again. Like a mountain climber who has ascended to heights where the air is very thin, she had to adjust to the harshness of a new reality.

'There is an image in my mind, and like a diamond in rock it endures. There is Matsuro lying face-down in the water. Water from the spout is rushing over his hair, moving it back and forth like the tendrils of a beautiful sea anemone. Otherwise, he is not moving.'

The tears dropped, one by one in an inexorable rhythm onto her lap.

'This is what I remember; the persistence of memory like a diamond that cannot be shattered. So hard, so cold. The rest is a blur: my pulling him up out of the tub, turning him over, giving him mouth-to-mouth resuscitation, calling an emergency medical team, hugging him to me even when they came for him, the ride to the hospital – and, after, my mother's wails, her screams, her anger at me. Because, you see, he was already dead when I came into the bathroom and I could not – *cannot* – accept what I'd done.'

Nicholas said nothing; words were inadequate in the presence of her profound grief. At once he understood a great deal about her: how cut off she felt from her parents, why she had found her way into this shadow world, filled with betrayal, fraught with terrible danger, and what she knew would inevitably happen to her when she had gone too far or had made one mistake too many: the ax would fall, her head would roll, and her guilt would at last be expunged.

Her grief was real; the memory had been pulled from her, of these things he could be certain. But what was her motive for this confession? Was she sincerely trying to prove her innocence with this vulnerability? Or was she a consummate actor dredging up a terrible personal tragedy in order to fool him into trusting her?

She loved him and she was deeply troubled. In the end, these were the only two things he could trust absolutely. It was not enough to evaluate the situation. Somehow he had to find a way to make it enough.

Nicholas rose, went to the window. The fishmongers were gone, and all that was left was the smell of eviscerated fish. Of course, the memory of Koei would haunt him now. Every instinct in his body screamed a warning. He knew firsthand what happened when one got involved in the affairs of the Yakuza. And yet here he was sworn to protect the head of all the Yakuza *oyabun*, in the company of a half-Japanese, half-Vietnamese woman, who may or may not have been involved in corporate espionage against his company, and a young, ambitious Yakuza *oyabun*, steeped in the lore of the *tanjian*. Wasn't there anyone but Lew and Tanzan Nangi whom he could trust?

'As long as you're in a confessional frame of mind,' he said, 'you can tell me if you have any doubts about Tachi Shidare.'

Seiko did not immediately reply. He could hear her rummaging around the room, but he did not turn to look at her. At length, she appeared at his side, dressed but as yet unmade-up.

'Tachi is not like the other *oyabun*.'

'You mean he's not infatuated with being beyond the law? He's not obsessed with power and influence?'

She put her head down. She stood close to him, but he knew she was aware of the deep gulf between them. He had hurt her, perhaps irrevocably, by so harshly

327

voicing his suspicions and then not believing her. But that couldn't be helped now. The situation they were in – the need to find Okami before his enemies finished their order of assassination, the necessity to discover the nature of Torch 315 before it was unleashed on the ides of March – overrode any personal considerations.

'No. I didn't mean . . . Of course, he's like them in those respects. But . . . let me tell you a story. I was waiting on tables at my mother's *akachochin* when he found me. He set me up in business in Tokyo so I could hone my skills.' She reached out to touch Nicholas, then, her hand in mid-air, thought better of it.

'I will tell you this now because I know that I must. I cannot bear your distance. Your distrust is like a knife blade through my heart, and toward morning when you tossed in your sleep and said her name, "Koei", my soul shriveled like a leaf in autumn.'

'Forget Koei.'

'But how can I? Because she was someone in your past? But it was she who you dreamed about last night when you could have had my flesh-and-blood arms around you.'

'It was a dream, nothing more.'

'You ejaculated against my stomach when you said her name.'

He gazed down at her with an ashen face. How long would Koei haunt him? As long as he remained in the company of Yakuza? No, no, impossible. Her memory must be put to rest.

There were tears standing in the corners of Seiko's eyes, and she bit her lower lip in order not to burst into tears. 'It was Tachi who sent me to interview for the job as your assistant. It was a wonderful job and I was so grateful to him. Then came the request to be the middleman between Masamoto Goei and Vincent Tinh.'

328

'Then the story you told me earlier about how you saw me at Nangi's club was a lie.'

'No, not a lie, just not the . . . entire truth.' She took a breath. 'I wanted to approach you myself, but I was paralyzed with fright. What if you rejected me? I was sure I couldn't bear that. So I did nothing. But I spoke of you to Tachi, and several months later he told me there was an opening for your assistant. He urged me on, prepared me for the interview.'

'So by that time Tachi had moved from Kumamoto to Tokyo. He was working for Tomoo Kozo.'

Seiko nodded. 'He was smart, everyone knew that, and he rose quickly in the ranks of the Yamauchi. It wasn't long before he had Kozo's ear. Kozo liked him, I think, because he knew Southeast Asia; soon enough he began running that sector for the clan.' Despite her best efforts, tears were rolling down her cheeks. 'Tachi is obsessed with infiltrating Floating City. Don't ask me why, I don't know. But now I've told you everything. I'm empty, except for my guilt over my brother's death and my love for you.'

'The fact is you know next to nothing about Tachi. You see his direction as a kindness when it might very well be nothing but artifice.' There came a discreet knock on the door, but he ignored it. 'What if he trained you, deliberately set you up to interview for a job inside my company?'

Then the sliding fusuma was swept aside and Tachi was standing in the hallway, looking at them both.

'Time for breakfast,' he said cheerily.

'Hey, you look great in a uniform, you know that?'

Croaker, striding purposefully toward Gate 19 in the international departures lounge of Dulles airport, was brought up short.

'Yeah,' said Bad Clams Leonforte. 'You look like you

belong in one of those ads, you know, "Fly the friendly skies." '

'Wrong airline,' Croaker said, looking beyond Leonforte. He was anxious to get on his flight. Besides, he couldn't stand the sight of the man. But he had threatened to put a bullet through Margarite's head if Croaker didn't cooperate, and Croaker had to grit his teeth in order to keep himself in check.

'No, really. A million bucks. I oughta think about having a pilot's uniform made for me. My mistress would sure get a kick out of it. I can imagine – '

'I'm late. What are you doing here?'

The wide, mad grin. The hands spread wide. 'Why, I'm looking after you, Lew.' He gestured, the image of sartorial elegance in his putty-colored Armani suit, a camel-hair overcoat thrown across his shoulders. His six-hundred-dollar loafers gleamed in the airport lights. 'C'mon, we're gonna have a little talk.'

'Much as that fills me with delight, I can't. Some other time, maybe.'

'*Now*.' That dark band of red flickered in Leonforte's eyes as his jaunty grin disappeared. 'What do you think, I'm gonna make you late for your plane? Forgetaboutit. It won't go anywhere without you, I promise. It's got highly valuable cargo, right? And I got influence.'

Croaker could see at least three of Leonforte's gorillas lounging around the terminal at strategic locations. It was all very professional, this box they had him in. He allowed Bad Clams to lead him through a door that read AUTHORIZED PERSONNEL ONLY.

He found himself in a spartan-looking room without windows. An old swayback sofa in green Naugahyde, three or four chairs, and a folding table on which stood a coffee maker, paper cups, plastic stirrers, sugar, Sweet 'n' Low and Cremora made the place seem cheap and mean.

'All the comforts of home,' Bad Clams said, expansive again. His changes of mood were abrupt enough to give you whiplash, Croaker thought. 'Christ, you'd think they'd treat their pilots better than this.' He ran his fingers through his tangle of curling hair as he swung around to face Croaker. 'So how's it hanging?'

'Fine. Just let me do my job without your greasy fingers getting caught in the gears.'

'Touchy, touchy.' Bad Clams waved a forefinger. 'You gotta learn to take my fraternal interest in you in the spirit in which it's offered.'

'Come off this crap, will you. It's bad enough you have me over a barrel without my having to put up with this circus sideshow.'

He knew it was a mistake when he said it, but this man set his teeth on edge. Bad Clams was in his face in one long stride. He slammed the flats of his hands against Croaker's chest, sending him reeling back against one cinder-block wall. Croaker curled his biomechanical hand into a fist but did not raise it.

'Don't dis me, bro, as the *mooinyan* uptown say.' Bad Clams nodded, stepped back. 'And speaking of sideshows, what the fuck are you doing following Vesper Arkham around? You spend any more time with her, you're gonna need my help bad.'

'That kind of help I don't need.'

'No? Right now, I'm your magic godfather – pun intended. And where you're goin' I do believe you're gonna need all the help you can get, even from this goombah.' Bad Clams sneered. 'Fuck you, buddy. I know just what you think of me, that I'm one small step above a gorilla in a zoo.' He pointed his forefinger at Croaker's chest. 'Fact is, I don't give a rat's ass what you think of me, okay? Just so we got that straight. You got your right to be an asshole just like everybody else, I won't lose sleep over it.

'The only thing you gotta keep in mind from now on is I got my eye on you, okay? Just 'cause you're flying the pond don't mean I won't know where you go and what you do. Don't try to cross me in London or wherever the fuck you wind up with this thing, because I'll come down on you with both my hobnailed boots strapped on and it won't be a pretty picture, all right?'

'I'm reading you loud and clear.'

Bad Clams laughed. 'Yeah, you even sound like a pilot. What did you do, wave your fed badge in front of the airline's nose?'

'Something like that. They loaned me this pilot's uniform and I'm deadheading with a couple of flight attendants on the second London run of the day.' He watched Leonforte carefully. 'Are you done intimidating me? Can I go now?'

Bad Clams waved a hand in the air. 'Do whatever the fuck you want, Lew. Just remember that every action has an equal and opposite reaction. Think of the consequences before you leap, not after. I take no prisoners.'

The giant aircraft was late in taking off, and sitting in the back of the plane, Croaker wondered whether it had anything to do with him. He had been the last person boarding, checking on Vesper from the doorway area. She was seated in first class, along with all the other millionaires.

He didn't want to think about Bad Clams Leonforte, but the madman just would not go away. How had he known when and where Croaker would show up unless he was having him followed? And if he could be believed, he was able to keep an international flight on hold while he psychologically twisted Croaker's arm.

It was beginning to look as if Bad Clams was as unusual in his way as Dominic Goldoni had been in his. What kind of world had he fallen into where underworld figures wormed their way into a highly clandestine bureau of the federal government, engaged in international economic warfare with Japanese Yakuza, and pretty much had the run of legitimate businesses? These people were not your normal *gavones* from Sicily who broke heads to intimidate their enemies and indiscriminately spilled blood when they didn't get their way. These were not crude men, but rather calculated thinkers with the kind of prescience that allowed them audacious leaps of deduction that went beyond mere canny business sense. Goldoni's successes had entered the realm of legerdemain, but he seriously doubted that Bad Clams, the egotist, the pseudo-philosopher with the hair-trigger temper, was in the league of either Goldoni or his own father, the brilliant Leon Waxman.

Waxman, the man of a thousand faces and identities, had been known as Jonathan Leonard when he served in the US Army during the occupation of Japan in the mid-forties, but he had been born John Leonforte.

Johnny had had three children: Bad Clams, Michael, and a daughter, Jaqui, who had died in a car accident when she was twenty. Michael was the real mystery. A genuine rebel who could not deal with authority on any level, he had been put to work in Special Forces in Vietnam. Soon thereafter, he went AWOL somewhere in the Laotian backcountry where even the superspooks in Special Forces had not been able to find him. Whether he was dead or alive was anyone's guess.

As for his father, Mikio Okami believed he had killed John Leonard when they had clashed in Tokyo in the spring of 1947, but Leonard had survived, had made his way to a hospital, and had had reconstructive surgery on his face after having his wounds patched up. When he recovered he had become Leon Waxman. How he had come to the attention of the spymaster Senator Richard Dedalus was a mystery for another day, but the fact remained that he had become the head of Dedalus's agency until his unmasking and death late last year.

Croaker had learned most of what he knew about Bad Clams' father from Faith Goldoni, Dominic's mother, who had known him in Tokyo. She also had changed names freely. Now known in Washington power circles as Renata Loti, she was a lobbyist of extraordinary influence. Margarite had taken Croaker to meet Faith, and he had seen what an extraordinary woman she was. She had been responsible for bringing Leon Waxman down.

Curiously, Faith had made no mention of Senator Dedalus. But what interested Croaker most now was Dedalus's relationship with DARPA, the Pentagon's Defense Advanced Research Projects Agency. He wondered if anyone there knew of Torch 315, whether they knew where it was going to be detonated on the ides of March, or whether he was making an interesting fiction out of a stew of disparate clues. He hoped this next step backward along Mikio Okami's Nishiki network would provide some answers because he had a distinct premonition that Okami and the late lamented Dominic Goldoni were tied up with Dedalus. At the very least, they had been involved with Morgana, Inc., the shadow corporation that dealt in illegal arms trading.

The merry-go-round was getting filled up, Croaker thought: Dominic introduces his sister Margarite to Senator Dedalus, who oversees DARPA. Margarite, it turns out, is also cozy with Vesper, who is working for Morgana, Inc. And Vesper was also a member of Mikio Okami's Nishiki network. All the players were there; it was now up to Croaker to figure out their roles.

He closed his eyes, and, in a moment, he was asleep.

334

That was a mistake. He awoke with a start, a thin film of sweat riming his upper lip. His underarms were damp. He was still half in the dream, where like a magnificent stage drama, his worst fear had come to life: two women moving on a shadowed stage, intimate whispers, the erotic slide of satin against skin. And then, like the sudden advent of a key light, a familiar voice piercing the semi-darkness as Margarite orders Vesper to kill him.

Blue smoke like mist.

Copper shadows curling toward the ceiling, stirred by music from the semicircle of matte black speakers surmounting a mammoth karaoke machine. The computerized machine was fitted with a chromium grille so that it looked like the front end of an old American car. Its aggressively retro look was currently the rage in Japan. In three months that all-important look would change, out would go this karaoke machine, in would come a new one.

A small man in a business suit was attempting to sing 'Be My Love' as he ran the flat of his hand along his temples to sleek his silver-streaked hair back like that of the moving image of Jerry Vale behind him.

As Nicholas and Tachi entered Ningyo-ro, the ultramodern nightclub in Kyoto that V. I. Pavlov had visited, they were engulfed by the tremoloed sounds blasting from the karaoke's speakers. They stood, transfixed for a moment by the shimmering atmosphere, tangible as the cacophony of a construction site at full bore. The combination of dark colors and chrome rails and seatbacks, all lit by a thousand pinspots, gave the room its own outré form of shadow and light. Beyond the main room was a smaller counterpart lit with black light. Shades of the seventies.

Ningyo-ro, the Doll Pavilion, was crowded, filled with

smoke and gimlet-eyed Japanese all cross-referencing their contacts in industry, government, the bureaucracy and the Yakuza. All these sectors were inextricably entwined in an elaborate institutional dance of favors met and payoffs proffered, intimidation exerted and face saved that invariably bewildered any Westerner exposed to even a small part of it.

Nicholas and Tachi moved slowly through the crowd, making their way to the bar at the far end of the room. It was constructed of frosted glass, lit from below by tubes of fluorescent light, which threw into high relief the carvings of female No figures seen through a forest of bubbles not unlike those in old-fashioned Christmas lights or sixties Wurlitzer jukeboxes.

As they neared this deliberate film noir artifact, Nicholas watched a slender waitress as she delivered drinks to a table of thick-set Japanese businessmen. She looked like a doll in traditional white makeup. They turned their sweat-streaked faces toward her briefly, laughing among themselves. One reached for a beer, and Nicholas saw a thick swath of elaborate *irizumi*, the tattoos favored by Yakuza.

Nicholas and Tachi ordered Sapporo beers. Another foolish Japanese businessman was trying out his awful Elvis impersonation, singing 'Viva Las Vegas'. Try as he might, he couldn't get the hip swivel. It was really quite laughable.

Tachi grunted. 'It's a big "if" as to whether this Zao is here at all.'

'I don't think so,' Nicholas said. 'The Russian was fastidious with his accounting. He kept a receipt for this place. That means if he stayed overnight in Kyoto, he didn't pay for it.'

'Maybe Zao put him up.'

Nicholas nodded. 'Right. It makes sense.'

'But how are we going to find him in this din? It

336

would be like looking in a haystack for a plastic needle. Not even a metal detector would help.'

Nicholas gave Tachi a grin. 'We're *not* going to find him; we're going to let him find us.' He signaled to the bartender and, when he came over, leaned in so that he could be heard. 'Tell Zao that Pavlov sent us. The deal didn't go through and Pavlov's unhappy. *Very* unhappy.'

'I don't know anyone named Zao,' the bartender said.

'Be that as it may, Pavlov's sent us with a message for him.' Nicholas tapped the spot beneath his jacket where a gun would have hung in a shoulder holster. 'I think you understand.'

The bartender shrugged, slid away from them as if he were on roller skates. He poured three whiskeys, a couple of sakes, filled some beer glasses.

'What do you think?' Tachi asked.

Nicholas shrugged. 'Toss-up. But if Zao's a regular here, the bartender's sure to know him.'

The businessman was into a truly awful rendition of 'Feelings'. Uptempo karaoke was bad enough, but ballads should be banned altogether, Nicholas thought.

Tachi finished his Sapporo, and Nicholas looked around to order refills. The bartender had disappeared. That might be a good sign, or the guy might just have had to take a leak.

A Yakuza strode into the main section of the night-club from the black-lighted interior. By the size and quality of his retinue of *kobun* – foot soldiers – he was something less than an *oyabun*. He was wearing the uniform typical of such men: wraparound sunglasses, black sharkskin suit, white shirt with an embroidered crest on the breast pocket, striped tie, polished loafers.

'He's coming this way,' Nicholas said, and when Tachi began to turn, added, 'You'd better let me handle this. We don't want to start a clan war.'

337

By the time the Yakuza was three paces from the bar Nicholas could sense his intent and he prepared himself for it. The man, who was broad-shouldered and narrow-hipped, with an angry, closed face full of pockmarks, pushed his way to the bar, brushing up against Nicholas and overturning what was left of his beer.

He said nothing, did not even turn his head in Nicholas's direction, but proceeded to order a Kirin from the newly returned bartender. Nicholas waited for the bartender to place the tall glass of beer in front of the Yakuza, then reached over, plucked it up and drained it. When he was finished, he smacked his lips loudly, set the empty glass back down in front of the man.

Nicholas began to turn away when he felt an iron grip clamp his right arm just below the biceps. He turned just in time to see the surprise register for a fleeting instant on the man's face as his fingers took the measure of the muscles in Nicholas's arm.

'You have no manners, *iteki*,' the man said in Japanese, his face dark with his loss of face.

Nicholas shook the man's hand from him, then bent his knees, extending his right hand palm upward toward the man.

'I beg you to countenance my words,' Nicholas said, beginning the ritual Yakuza introduction exchange.

The Yakuza's face again registered surprise, then renewed anger. 'Do you mock our traditions, *iteki*?'

Nicholas ignored the question, repeated his introduction.

The Yakuza assumed the responding pose. 'I have words of my own.'

'I beg you, since your position is higher, to hear mine first.'

The Yakuza nodded, straightened up, and Nicholas did the same.

338

'Speak, then, *iteki*.'

'My name is Nicholas Linnear. I was born in Singapore. I have no clan affiliation.' The Yakuza smirked at this. 'You have been deliberately insulting to me, knocking over my drink, pushing me, using epithets. I wish redress.'

The smirk on the Yakuza's face widened, and he thrust out his chest so that his jacket opened enough for Nicholas to see the butt of a pistol snug in its shoulder holster. 'And what form would you propose this *redress* take?'

'I have been polite. I have told you my name, birthplace and clan affiliation.'

The Yakuza, taken aback, was silent for a moment.

'My name is Kine Oto. I am also known as Zao. I was born in Kyoto, and I am an underboss of the Dokudokushii clan.' He stuck out his chin. 'You bring a message for me from the Russian.'

'Now we understand one another.' Nicholas bowed. 'I propose we play a game of *karuta*.'

Again, there was a hesitation on Zao's part. *Karuta* was a card game originally played by the elite families of Japan. When these families turned to other, more modern diversions, it had been championed by the Yakuza as their main form of gambling.

'Oh, this should be good,' Zao said with a half-stifled laugh. He gestured to a free table. 'By all means, let us play *karuta*.'

Karuta was based on seasonal flowers and was won or lost on certain number combinations. A deck of cards was produced from behind the bar and placed on the table. Nicholas asked the bartender if he knew how to deal. The man nodded, a bit fearfully. His fear escalated when Nicholas asked him to be the dealer.

Zao, sitting across from Nicholas, appeared to have no objection. He tapped the top card on the deck. 'Since you have chosen the game, I will decide on the stakes. Is this acceptable?'

'It is,' Nicholas said, even as he was aware of Tachi shifting nervously at his elbow.

Zao looked about the room shrewdly. 'When I win this game, you will forget who sent you to me and why you were sent. Also, you will ascend the karaoke stage and publicly apologize to me.'

'And if I win?'

'You won't.'

'If I win, you will tell us everything you know about the Russian and why he was here.' Nicholas ignored the Yakuza's stare, which was meant to be intimidating, and concentrated on the man's body language. This would tell him what he needed to know during the game.

Zao ordered the bartender to deal. The first hand, both were dealt winning combinations; the second proved a bust for both men. But on the third hand, Nicholas exposed a winning combination. Zao held an eight, a nine and a three. This was a losing hand and an ironic one, because those three numbers formed the kanji for the word *Yakuza*.

'I have won,' Nicholas said, standing. 'Remember the stakes, Zao-san. You must tell me what you know of the Russian Pavlov.'

'In one hour I will leave here. We will talk outside then.'

Nicholas nodded, and he and Tachi rose. Zao glared at them as they walked back to the bar.

'I don't trust this fellow,' Tachi said. 'He didn't like losing, especially to you.'

'I agree.' Nicholas ordered drinks for both of them. 'But we have no choice now. We attracted him, now we have to make sure he doesn't pin us both to the wall.'

340

It was late when Zao left the nightclub. Nicholas and Tachi followed. A cold wind was blowing, the red lanterns along the narrow street rocking crazily on their iron rings. There were few people about, but several cars were parked half on the sidewalk.

'Where did he go?' Tachi looked from one end of the street to the other. 'He's not going to talk to us.'

Nicholas had the same feeling.

The headlights of a car facing them were switched on, bathing them in brittle light.

'*Iteki!*'

'Zao,' Tachi murmured.

He watched the powerful figure of Zao emerge like a black bird from out of the blinding sun.

'You owe me my winnings,' Nicholas called out. 'Time to pay up.'

'I want a rematch.' Zao's voice boomed and echoed across the deserted street.

'Forget it,' Nicholas said. 'You lost. Accept the inevitable.'

'I cannot forget that you, a half-breed, caused me to lose face.'

'And you will not remember your word.'

Zao, close now, laughed harshly. 'My word is worthless to an *iteki*.'

'Then you are without honor,' Nicholas said.

'Stupid joke! What would a barbarian know about honor.' The pistol bloomed in Zao's huge fist like a malevolent creature. 'You are no more to me than an insect who has had the stupidity to crawl into my path.' He took another step toward Nicholas and Tachi. 'Get out of my way or I will crush you.'

Nicholas was moving – so fast that even to Tachi's trained eye he was a blur. Nicholas had heard the hammer snap back on the pistol, and his instincts had taken over.

341

The natural human reaction to an attack was to move directly toward it. The aikido Nicholas had learned as a child broke that instinct, replacing it with others that dealt with evading an assault and redirecting the intrinsic force of that attack away from you.

And instinct was the only thing that mattered. At the split instant of attack – perhaps a hundredth of a second – there was no time to consider options, work out strategies and employ them. There was only time to act out of pure instinct.

This Nicholas did. From his own sense of power, of the centralization that is *hara*, Nicholas struck out, an extension that was known as *ki*, the inner force.

Instead of advancing toward Zao, Nicholas engaged the extended pistol with his right hand as he swung to his right. As he did so, he brought his left hand against the Yakuza's hip, using the heel of it as if it were a meat cleaver chopping into Zao's exposed hipbone.

Zao gave a little grunt as his left leg began to collapse beneath him. Nicholas swept the pistol from his right hand, twisting the wrist as he did so until he heard the bone snap. With Zao semiconscious at his feet, Nicholas heard the grate of leather soles on the cement sidewalk – Zao's *kobun*.

Tachi spun, went into a crouch as he swept the Yakuza's gun into his hand, and shattered the car's headlights with a brace of shots. Dimly, then, he could make out the faces like pale satellites in the night.

'This is not your fight,' he told them softly. 'Your *oyabun* broke his oath; what has happened is his responsibility alone. This is an affair without honor. You are not required to take any action on his behalf.'

Nicholas felt the tension humming through the air like heat lightning. The foot soldiers had not yet retreated; they stood their ground. Nicholas began to speak to them. He pitched his voice just so, using that primeval sound that came from the back of the throat, the one the best hypnotists could just touch, the one that Tau-tau had taught him to master.

He kept talking to them, a kind of litany, until he felt the psychic tension resolve into a tolerable level. He knew they had about twenty seconds to do what had to be done. Without breaking his concentration, he motioned to Tachi to pick Zao off the ground and throw him into the backseat of his car.

Tachi got behind the wheel, gunned the engine. Nicholas jumped in beside the groggy Zao, slammed the door behind him, and they took off into the deepening night.

TEN

Tokyo/London/Kyoto

'She's not here,' the man in the wheelchair said. 'My mother's away for several days. Can I be of some help?'

Ushiba smiled. 'That is very kind of you, Ken. But I wouldn't think of imposing.'

'On a cripple?' Those powerful shoulders shrugged. 'I have time enough to spare for you, Daijin. I know you didn't come all the way out here just to exchange idle gossip with Kisoko.'

Ushiba nodded. He was used to Ken's odd ways. What others might term impolite was merely Ken's shorthand. He had little patience with proprieties – admittedly, an odd quirk in a Japanese – considering them nothing more than long-windedness. But perhaps this was nothing more than an affectation, one more attribute that was remarkable about him.

Not that he needed it; Ken was quite remarkable without it. He was powerful, and an accomplished martial artist even without considering that he had no use of his legs. He was a fanatic collector; he had an astonishing collection of museum quality antique weapons – many of them arcane – from Japan's past.

Ushiba actually liked the younger man, though it often seemed to the chief minister that Ken tried his hardest to be disagreeable. He liked to probe and prod, Kisoko had once told Ushiba with an odd kind of pride, because he was interested in what lay beneath the facade of people.

344

In his own way, Ken was a master sociologist, and Ushiba often thought of this house where Ken and his mother lived as one vast laboratory for his unorthodox experiments.

'I'd be pleased to stay a while and talk,' Ushiba said now. 'I could use a respite from the outside world.'

'Yes,' Ken said as he led the way down the corridor into the kitchen at the back of the house. 'Time seems almost to stand still here, doesn't it?'

He was a handsome man, with a long face and soft brown eyes that belied a tenacious personality forged by the trauma of his condition. But there was always a sadness about him that, perhaps unconsciously, touched Ushiba, that seemed almost familiar to him, as if Ken were a kindred spirit adrift like the Daijin in a world of pain.

'Outside, however, time is inexorable,' Ken continued. 'The Liberal Democratic Party is finished as the major political force in Japan.' He made a face. 'Good riddance to them, I say.'

'They had a crucial role to play in the development of this country. And I wouldn't exclude them so quickly from our future.'

'I understand your sympathy for your old friend Yoshinori,' Ken said astutely. 'But you see where he is, this symbol of the greedy past.'

'Yoshinori fought many battles on many fronts when you were just a child, Ken. Japan is strong today – a major world power – because of him and men of vision like him.'

'Men like yourself, Daijin.'

Ushiba said nothing. This man could be extraordinarily exhausting. His intellectual capacity was almost limitless, and one never knew whether he believed the point of view he espoused or whether he wanted merely to provoke a spirited debate.

'I was fixing myself lunch,' Ken said as he rolled to the counter. 'Would you like something to eat?'

Ushiba gave his assent and watched as Ken deftly put together two plates of fresh-cut sushi with lots of wasabi and pickled ginger on the side. He handed one of these, along with a bottle of beer, to Ushiba, and they went to the oval oak table in the left section of the kitchen. There were many non-Japanese touches to this house, a place where East and West met in, if not perfect then acceptable, harmony.

They ate in a companionable silence for some time. Ushiba prided himself that Ken felt so comfortable with him. Ken's forte was not interpersonal interaction, being more of an observer of reaction than a participant. Perhaps his infirmity had conferred upon him this observer status, Ushiba thought, and Ken clung to it because in society some status was better than none at all.

'How are things in your world of politics?' Ken said at length. 'It seems to me that a Daijin must be adept at that game in order to gain his position and keep it.'

'To be truthful, it's become wearying. Too many factions, too many battles to be fought on too many fronts.'

'You're getting old,' Ken said in his blunt fashion. 'People who feel the way you do should know better.'

'Know better?'

Ken nodded. 'You should get out before you make a fatal mistake and the force of your own politics runs you over.'

Ushiba suppressed his natural instinct toward anger at such brash and impolite analysis. The fact was, if he were to be brutally honest with himself, Ken was being considerate. He was telling Ushiba what Ushiba was too prideful to recognize on his own.

'You're right, of course.' Ushiba put away his half-eaten plate of sushi. His appetite wasn't what it had been even six months ago. 'When the game becomes a burden, the rules change and the hunter is most in danger of becoming the hunted.'

'Animals are bred to smell blood,' Ken said, one cheek distended with fish, rice and ginger.

Ushiba smiled. 'I remember when that could be said of me.'

'It still could, if you want the rewards of the game badly enough.'

Ushiba looked at him with renewed interest. Ken must surely be in his early forties now. Despite this, his face remained unlined, his hair as dark as it had been when he was twenty. His passions certainly burned just as brightly as they ever had.

Ushiba straightened his back, unmindful of the pain that emanated from his gut. 'One is born smelling the blood.'

'That's right,' Ken said, finishing off his sushi. 'It's bred in the bone, taken in with mother's milk.'

It was an odd phrase, and something in his tone caused Ushiba to wonder whether Ken was referring to Kisoko. She was Mikio Okami's sister, after all. She must have been born smelling blood, too.

Ken pointed to Ushiba's food. 'Are you going to finish that?'

Ushiba shook his head and watched with dismay as Ken reached over and happily began to chomp the sushi. One had to make allowances for people not used to the conventions of the outside world.

'So what brings you here, Daijin?' Ken said around a mouthful of food. 'You obviously need my mother's advice. Which faction is plaguing you today?'

'There is someone who has made a mistake,' Ushiba said carefully. Kisoko knew of his secret affiliation with the inner council because she was the Kaisho's sister, but Ken was another matter entirely. 'A grievous, head-strong error that must be corrected.'

'We're talking now of punishment, I imagine.'

There wasn't much that got away from the young man. 'Punishment, yes. But it is difficult for me because of my . . . relationship with this man.'

'He deserves punishment?'

'Without question.'

Ken nodded as if he took the Daijin's verdict on faith. 'Then devise a punishment to fit the crime.'

'I wish I could. But the truth is my mind is blank.'

Ken was silent for some time, as he consumed the last of the Daijin's sushi. At length, he said, 'Come upstairs with me. I want to show you something.'

They took the small elevator at the back of the house to the second floor where Ken's private dojo and weapons collection took up almost half the space.

The old windows had been replaced when the dojo had been built. In their stead, oversize panes of glass had been installed that let in light without sacrificing any of the privacy that both Kisoko and her son held dear. The highly polished hardwood floor gleamed. Ranged along one wall were rows of *katana*, *dai-katana*, the large samurai's swords; *wakizashi*, long knives for committing seppuku; shorter *tanto*; and other more eso-teric weapons, some of which Ushiba had never seen before.

Ken rolled himself to the wall and, using his heavily muscled arms, levered himself out of the wheelchair and onto the floor. He tucked his useless legs into the lotus position, then moved on his knuckles, his muscles rippling tightly. His torso acted as a pendulum, swinging back and forth, making his progress seem smooth and effortless. Nothing, Ushiba knew, could be further from the truth.

Ken set himself down in front of a series of *kyoki*wood

dansu, long low chests made to house *katana*. Ken opened a top drawer, pulled out a spherical object wrapped in silk. As he unwrapped it, Ushiba padded in stocking feet to where Ken sat and knelt beside him.

Ushiba watched in wonder as the object cradled in Ken's palm was revealed. It was a skull, burnished by age to a deep ocher and sienna. It gleamed, so Ushiba knew it had been periodically waxed in order to keep it from becoming brittle.

'This,' Ken said, holding the artifact aloft, 'is the skull of Masamoto Musashi, whom I consider the finest swordsman in the history of Japan.' Musashi had gained worldwide notoriety for writing *The Book of Five Rings*, a seventeenth-century text on *kenjutsu*, the technique of swordsmanship and strategy.

Ken's nimble fingers turned the skull around. 'Do you know that it was Musashi's closest friend who stripped his head of flesh and brains and sold the skull? It was all he had to keep himself alive.' Around the skull rotated, revealing in turn each noble view. 'Was he a villain, Musashi's friend, or merely a victim of expediency? Or, again, did he do Musashi the ultimate service by seeing to it that his memory would not be buried with him, but would remain alive and revered centuries later?'

Ken brought the skull down, delivering it into Ushiba's hands. 'Hold it, Daijin. Feel Musashi's power undiminished by either death or time. Is this not the meaning of immortality?'

The skull weighed more than Ushiba had imagined, its density perhaps due to its aura of power and influence. Ken was right. In its contours, indentations and ridges Ushiba could visualize the complex electrical patterns that had made Musashi's brain unique, and for this moment, he was without the pain of his cancer or the certain knowledge of his imminent death. Here was,

349

as Ken had said, existence beyond death. And if it was not existence precisely as humans knew it, perhaps it was something more, beyond the mind's imagining.

'It has moved you, Daijin.' Ken made no attempt to take back the skull. 'You feel what I feel. This close to Musashi there is no suffering.'

'No.' Ushiba was transfixed. 'There is no pain, no death, no time.'

'Daijin,' Ken said quietly, 'you must punish Akira Chosa for his crime.'

For a moment, Ushiba, dazed by the aura pushed out by Musashi's skull, did not believe what he had heard. Then he raised his gaze to Ken's face and knew there had been no mistake.

'How did you know?'

'Intuition fed by fact. Chosa was here not too long ago to see my mother. I believe she might have killed him had I not intervened. She thinks he ordered Mikio Okami killed.'

'Perhaps she knows something I do not.' The skull was abruptly too heavy for him, and he transferred it back to Ken's waiting hand. 'Too many people are eager to claim responsibility for an act that remains unfulfilled.'

'And yet the Kaisho no longer sits in the seat of power. He has been banished. Isn't that enough to gain stature from the act?'

Ushiba nodded. 'In our less than perfect world I imagine it is.' He looked searchingly at Ken. 'Why did Chosa come to see Kisoko?'

'To ask her what she knew about Okami's relationship with Colonel Denis Linnear . . . and what she knew about Koei.'

'Koei? Why would he want . . . ?'

'Punish him.' Ken was staring at the skull of Musashi. 'Who better than you to devise the fitting penance?'

'I told you, my mind is blank.'

'Then may I suggest a path.' Ken's soft eyes swung from contemplation of the skull to appreciation of the Daijin's beautiful face. 'It is sitting right in front of you, Daijin, like Musashi's skull. If you see it, you will recognize the path.'

'What . . . ?'

'Your friend, the Tokyo prosecutor. Tanaka Gin.'

Being in London at this time of the year was like living inside a cloud bank. Mist rose from the Thames, obscuring the office buildings of the City and putting the enormous ravens of the Tower into a pet. There had been a bombing in the City that morning, and Harrods had been cleared by threats of another. As it was the streets around the blast site were cordoned off while work crews labored to sweep the debris away and forensic specialists combed the twisted girders of the bank to discover the methodology of the terrorists.

The perpetual mist sometimes lifted to reveal the scraggly tops of bare trees in Hyde Park and St James's, sometimes occluded into a rain so invariable it seemed to have no beginning, no end. Through it all, indefatigable Londoners plowed through the slick streets and stalled traffic, their black umbrellas as crisp and neat as public school uniforms. Rising and falling like a tide from the underground, they performed their chores with the stoic precision of a drill team.

For all that, parts of London seemed to have taken on a decidedly American look. Whereas once Piccadilly Circus had been both tacky and quintessentially English, it now sported enough American stores hawking their wares at a frenetic pace to make a fair stand-in for New York. It had gone beyond the pale, from garish to a kind of queasy forgery, and like all counterfeits it had taken on a frightening life of its own.

351

Once again, Vesper had surprised Croaker. He had expected her to go straight from Heathrow to Hammersmith, where Malory Enterprises was located. Instead, he had followed her into Belgravia, where she got out of her taxi on the King's Road, then walked southwest to Eaton Square. The town house she entered had an excellent view of the spires of Holy Trinity Church just north of Sloane Square.

He had almost missed her at Heathrow. On the way to baggage claim she had stopped in the ladies' room, and the only thing that had tipped him off was the square carry-on that swung from one hand. Ten minutes later, she had reappeared in a shoulder-length blunt-cut red wig. She had ditched the doe-brown contacts and her amazing cornflower-blue eyes blazed in her heart-shaped face. Her makeup was decidedly grunge: aubergine lipstick and heavy black kohl on her lids and lashes. Though the red jade choker was still around her throat, she had replaced her shoes with a pair of shiny black plastic boots that came up over her knees, her jeans and shirt with a clingy black rayon dress that ended where her thighs began. When she bent over to retrieve her luggage, any man behind her would have an instant heart attack.

The problem with London was that his federal badge was useless here; worse, flashing it might actually get him into trouble with the local constabulary, who, he knew from experience, could become testy about Yanks poaching on their turf. He almost regretted turning down Bad Clams' offer of help here. On the other hand, he had made the acquaintance of a chief inspector in New Scotland Yard when the chief inspector's quarry had split to New York, where Croaker had tracked him down and had expedited extradition with the federales.

The chief inspector's name was Tom Major, though

behind his back Croaker had not been able to resist referring to him as Major Tom. Major was a ruddy-complexioned man in his late forties with the closed, hard face of a Yorkshireman, a handlebar mustache, and the kind of mien one found only in retired boxers; as it turned out he had been one during his stint in the army. He had a ready smile and a willingness to consume ale in quantities even Croaker had found astonishing. He also had an inexplicable fondness for overstuffed pastrami sandwiches.

Major was not at New Scotland Yard, but when Croaker identified himself a sergeant directed him to a site in Flood Street in Chelsea. Croaker was obliged to take an exorbitantly expensive taxi – though he reminded himself that he was back on Senator Deda-lus's expense account – because the tube didn't run into Chelsea, and he could make neither head nor tail of the bus routes.

Flood Street, not surprisingly, ran southward into the Chelsea Embankment which snaked along that section of the Thames. Perhaps owing to its relative inaccessibility, Chelsea remained one of the last enclaves of civilized residences that had once made London famous the world over.

He found Tom Major overseeing a contingent of police engineers digging up a front yard where a body had been unearthed by the new owner planting an elm tree. Neat rows of iris and tulip bulbs, sleeping during winter, were laid out atop piles of earth. Sheets of plastic had been set down upon which at least three partial skeletons had been painstakingly arranged as the bones had been unearthed.

'No wonder this garden grew like the devil,' Croaker heard one of the police excavators say.

Major was crouched over one of the plastic sheets, moving earth and roots away from a skull with the end

353

of his pen while a photographer shot a series of photos from every conceivable angle.

'Thomas.'

Major looked up, an annoyed expression on his face, which evaporated as soon as he saw Croaker. 'Christ Jesus,' he said, standing and brushing off his trousers. 'Will you look who's risen from the grave.' A couple of the engineers stopped to glance over at the two men, but were soon back at work. 'What brings you to sunny London, old son?' He stuck out his hand, gave Croaker's hand a firm squeeze. 'It wouldn't be pleasure, not at this time of year.'

'Business, I'm afraid.'

Major looked Croaker up and down, then sniffed loudly. 'Didn't bring me a pastrami from the Stage Deli, did you?'

'Sorry, no. I didn't think I could get it past Customs.'

Major laughed. 'It's all right, old son. My cholesterol's sky-high. All that steak and kidney, although my doctor reckons I've got to cut down on the stress.' He pointed to the remains at his feet. 'Look at this. Remarkable what one human being can do to another, isn't it?'

One of Major's minions came up. 'We've finished the prelims on all the neighbors, Guv. What now?'

'Go home, get some sleep.' Major gestured. 'Tell the lads the same. But have the new owner in DCI Hollworth's office in Lucan Street at nine sharp tomorrow. I'll have to liaise with him before this case turns nasty.'

'What are you going to give him?'

'Only as much as I have to, that the first body to be brought out has been identified as a foreign national, which is why our lot have been brought in.'

Major turned back to Croaker. 'Been at this charnel house since before sunrise. Less stress. My doctor must be as mad as a hatter.'

'Look, Tom, I can see you've got your hands full, but do you have a minute to talk? I need some help.'

'Help, is it? Fancy a drink? There's a pub on the King's Road.' He rubbed his eyes with his thumbs and, with a heartfelt groan, stretched his back. 'Glad you came along. I could use a break. Brain gets stale working in the same mode for hours at a time.' He told one of the remaining engineers where he'd be, then he and Croaker set off up Flood Street.

'D'you have a place to kip for the night?'

'If you mean a hotel room, no. I just got in.'

'A rolling stone, eh?' Major grinned. 'Just like you, Lewis.'

Major was the one person Croaker had ever known who called him Lewis. Even his father had called him Lew. They reached the King's Road and turned right.

'Well, you can bunk down with me if you've a mind to.'

'I don't want to upset the missus.'

'I wouldn't worry about that, old son. Moira moved out more than two years ago.'

'Sorry.'

'It's the frigging job.' Major opened the door to the pub and the familiar beery smell hit them. 'Can't be married to a person and a job all at once. At least, not a job like this one.' He shrugged. 'Her most common complaint was that the phone was more important than she was. Quite right she was, too. I miss her, but the truth is I'd miss the job more.'

They sat at a wooden table stained dark with age and smoke. Major ordered pints of ale and plates of food, sausage rolls to start, then shepherd's pie. Croaker closed his eyes and tried to mentally calm his stomach.

Over the meal, Croaker outlined whom he was following and a heavily censored version of why. Basically, he told Major that he was working on a case involving

355

illegal international arms traders. This story had the twin virtues of being a half-truth and of particular interest to Major, who, when he was not helping the Metropolitan Police in sorting out mass murder sites, was most often involved with arms brokers who used London as a staging area for illicit shipments to the Middle East.

'Eaton Square is a pretty posh spot,' Major said when Croaker told him where Vesper had gone from the airport. He had, of course, mentioned nothing about her frequent changes of disguise. 'There's pots of money involved, anyway.' Major forked up a mouthful of shepherd's pie. 'You say this woman's somehow involved with an American company called Morgana, Inc.?'

Croaker nodded. 'It's a very good bet they're somehow linked with Malory Enterprises, in Hammersmith. Morgana's books say they're in the arms shipment business. And the kind of merch they move comes straight from Uncle Sam's storehouse, which is closed up tighter than a duck's ass.'

Major took a long swig of ale and his gaze turned inward. He was silent for so long that Croaker was prompted to say, 'What's up, Tom?'

Major's eyes refocused on Croaker. 'I was just thinking . . . It's odd, really . . .'

'What is?'

'The names of the companies. Morgana and Malory. They've put me in mind of a legend. Morgana was Merlin's sister and, it was said, a powerful magician in her own right. Only her magic was far more elemental, derived from the tradition of the druids. The legend has been told and retold many times, but the most renowned version, *Morte d'Arthur*, was written by Sir Thomas Malory. Not many people know this, but he was something of a blackguard – a poacher, extortionist and, finally, a murderer. He wrote the book in prison.'

Major looked at Croaker. 'What's bitten you, old son?'

Croaker had gone white. The heavy food seemed to have congealed in the pit of his stomach. 'Tom, according to Malory's legend, where did Arthur have his court?'

'Camelot. Everyone knows that.'

'And the secret place where he was meant to rule?'

'Avalon.' Major cocked his head. 'It was a kind of fairy city, floating in the mist. Some say it was druidic, Morgana's home. What are you on about?'

Croaker's mind was running at full bore, but the rational part of him was having a hard time keeping up with the intuitive side. He remembered John Jay Arkham telling him that Vesper's education had been funded by the Avalon Foundation, *as in King Arthur*.

'There's a company my partner infiltrated that's also in the arms racket,' Croaker said. 'It's tied into an international cartel that's made up of members of the American Mafia and the Japanese Yakuza.' His eyes locked with Major's. 'What's worse, last year my partner and I discovered that certain members of the US government are also implicated. This company's name is Avalon Ltd. I have been under the impression that Avalon and Morgana-Malory were competitors.'

Major was shaking his head. 'Looks to me as if it's just the opposite: they're all part of one gigantic organization.'

Croaker knew he had come upon a major breakthrough. Ever since he had gone into hiding, Okami had been directing him and Nicholas toward Avalon Ltd. Why? He had been assuming that Avalon was owned and operated by the Godaishu. Then, when he had come upon Morgana, his first thought was that Okami and Goldoni had put into play their own arms network to try to put Avalon out of business. Now that he knew Avalon, Morgana and Malory were all one, he had to ask himself who was cornering the market on international arms shipments. The most obvious answer was the Godaishu. It fit. This would also be why Okami would be directing them toward Avalon. Vincent Tinh, the head of Nicholas's company in Saigon, had been murdered – by Rock, Nicholas had told him. The man who had spirited the body away had been a Yakuza giving Avalon as his company and a fictitious address in London. It was now virtually certain that the Godaishu had direct ties to Rock and Floating City.

But Johnny Leonforte had been the Godaishu's American head and he had been killed last year. Who was directing the continued pipeline of stolen US government weapons out of DARPA? It had to be the man who had hired Leonforte in the first place, and who oversaw DARPA: Senator Richard Dedalus.

'I don't know.'

The old woman, her back bent, hobbled down the stone path, stopped before the red torii and pulled the thick hemp rope, setting the bronze bell to tolling.

'Even if I knew, I wouldn't tell you.'

The old woman, standing before the Shinto shrine, clapped her hands twice, bowed to the *kami* she had just awakened and began her prayers.

'You're dead men.' Zao looked from Nicholas to Tachi. 'You have no idea –' The under-*oyabun*'s jaw dropped open as Tachi pulled back the sleeve of his shirt, revealing his *irizumi*.

Zao looked up into Tachi's face. He was seated in a chair, his wrists tied behind its back. Then his face screwed into a mask of hatred. 'Whoever you are, you're no one here in Kyoto. You don't matter to me.'

Nicholas, who had been looking out the window at the old woman praying at the shrine, now gave Tachi a look and they retreated to a far corner of the room.

They had come to this Love Hotel because it was anonymous and traditionally no questions were asked of its patrons. It was on a small side street in the Gion quarter, an ugly ferroconcrete building in a neighborhood otherwise made up of old restaurants that surrounded the beautiful, park-like Shinto shrine, one of Kyoto's many local surprises.

'This is getting us nowhere,' Nicholas said. 'And we're working against time.'

Tachi nodded. 'I know. You can be sure his people have been mobilized and are combing the city for him. If his *oyabun* has been informed —'

Nicholas knew the end of that thought. If Tachi should somehow be implicated in Zao's abduction it could cause a major struggle for face between him and Zao's *oyabun*.

'He knows time is on his side,' Nicholas said. 'We have to get him to give us the information and get clear of Kyoto before his people find us.'

Tachi turned to him and said, so softly that Zao could not hear, 'Don't worry. He'll give us what we want to know, and when it's over he won't remember he told us a thing.'

Tachi stood with his legs slightly apart, his hands at his sides, the fingers loosely curled. He took deep breaths. Meanwhile, Zao stared up at him as if he were a lunatic.

Nicholas, concentrating, could feel the marshaling of Tachi's psyche, an edgy curling as of an adder about to strike. But it was only when Tachi began the chant that Nicholas began to sense the enormity of what was about to happen.

In his mind's eye he could almost see the confluence of two streams, the light and the dark, Akshara and Kshira, the two polar opposites of Tau-tau. And now, magically, he saw swimming before him *kyu*, the sphere

359

of Tau-tau. Within it, he saw Akshara, the path of light, his own discipline, as well as its dark counterpart, Kshira. And now as he watched the two halves curling and twisting like strands of DNA, he recognized both and all his worst fears were realized. Because there were dark beads within the structure of Kshira that he recognized. Kansatsu, his teacher, his enemy, had indeed spiked his teachings of Tau-tau's Akshara with kernels of Kshira. Like deeply buried time bombs set to detonate on proximity, these precepts had become part of him, and only integrating the light with the dark would save him now.

Nicholas was transfixed. He was certain that what he was witnessing was Shuken. Tachi possessed *koryoku*, the Illuminating Power, the one path to integration, to Shuken. Nicholas had longed to learn the secret of *koryoku* from Mikio Okami, but the Kaisho had disappeared too quickly.

Shuken. The sphere, *kyu*, swirled in coruscating patterns as Tachi tapped into *koryoku* to conjure the Dominion. The chanting continued; the atmosphere of the room turned gluey and fluid. But Zao, for his part, was aware of nothing. His eyelids fluttered and his breathing became regular, then deep. Nicholas was aware of his brain activity slowing through alpha, then into delta and theta.

That was when Tachi indicated that Nicholas should ask Zao the questions he would not answer before. Zao spoke as if awake and alert. He was not in a trance nor was he hypnotized. He had, Nicholas realized, been incorporated into the sphere that he could not see but which rotated in the thick atmosphere just in front of his face. Within the sphere, where Akshara and Kshira were no longer estranged enemies but rather two halves of one whole, Zao believed what Tachi wished him to believe. Perhaps he thought he was asleep and dream-

360

ing, or that he was speaking with V. I. Pavlov. It did not matter; Zao told them how Pavlov had come to see him at the Ningyo-ro, how he had taken the Russian home with him and, the next day, driven him to where he needed to go. Names, places, deeds, he revealed everything.

At length, when Nicholas was done, Tachi ceased his chant. The sphere, *kyu*, spun away into ten thousand strands, which broke up into a million fragments, winking like fireflies in the room before vanishing altogether.

Nicholas and Tachi looked at one another across the body of Zao and what passed between them even Nicholas could not describe.

They left Zao in the room alone, the door ajar so that someone would eventually find him.

Seiko watched Nicholas and Tachi leave the Love Hotel. They appeared in a hurry. She had on an ankle-length raincoat and was carrying a large handbag. She stood well back in the shadows of the Shinto shrine, and they did not see her. She resented the fact that the two of them had apparently bonded. She was jealous of the psychic link between them, but she also felt cheated because when it came to the crunch, they had both treated her like a woman. Apparently, the interrogation of the Yakuza Zao was too dangerous for her.

She left the grounds of the shrine and entered the hotel. She went upstairs, found the only open door. Zao was twisted in his chair, trying to free his wrists. He stopped when he became aware of her, jerked around. She turned down the lights so that the room was almost dark.

'Who are you?'

She said nothing, just stood there regarding him levelly.

Zao gave her a twisted smile. 'Sweetheart, I'm awfully

uncomfortable. Do you think you could do something about that?' He spread his legs lewdly. 'That's why you're here, aren't you? To soften me up. Do your business, then leave.' The smile turned into a sneer. 'And when you go, tell the shits who hired you that it won't work.'

Seiko went to a table, set her handbag down on it.

'Who the hell are you, anyway? I know all the whores in Kyoto.'

He watched as she dug deep into her handbag, extracted a pair of rubber surgeon's gloves. Lightly powdering her fingers, she snapped on the gloves with practiced motions.

Zao had gone silent. He was watching her with the paralytic fascination a rodent has for a poisonous serpent.

She put both hands into her bag, rattled around in there for what seemed a long time.

At length, Zao said, 'You're not a prostitute, are you?'

Seiko gave him a long, slow smile. 'I'm a doctor.'

'Doctor?' He said it as if he were repeating a word wholly alien to him. 'I don't need a doctor.'

'You certainly won't when I get through with you.'

'What does that mean?' His gaze was riveted on her forearms at the spot where they disappeared into her bag.

It was interesting seeing the expression on his face as she removed her hands from the bag. One was holding a long, thin object.

Zao gave a tiny indrawn gasp. 'A hypodermic. What are you going to do?'

'Don't worry. You won't feel a thing.' Seiko smiled again. 'Ever.'

Zao recoiled, almost tipping the chair backward.

'Now keep those legs open, dear.'

Zao clapped his knees together. 'Don't touch me.'

Seiko paused, holding the object high. She looked down on him as a reproving schoolmaster would on an unrepentant truant. 'What's the matter?'

A smattering of Zao's old bravado surfaced. 'If you kill me, you'll be hunted down with those two shits outside.'

Seiko laughed. 'Kill you? What purpose would that serve? No, you have broken your word and without that you are nothing — not even a man.' She took another step toward him, the object held menacingly in front of her. 'I am going to inject you with a substance that will affect your prostate.'

Zao goggled at her. 'My prostate? Why?'

'Remember sex, dear?' She took another step. 'That's all it will be when I'm through with you, a memory.'

'No!' Zao shouted so loudly that the lampshades shuddered. 'You can't.'

'Ready or not, here I come.'

Later, when an exhausted Zao had told her everything he knew about the Russian, V. I. Pavlov, she relinquished her hold on the long, thin object and, reversing it, put the mascara applicator back in its plastic pouch inside her capacious handbag.

ELEVEN

Vietnam Highlands/London

'I've lost another one.'

'No matter,' Rock said, staring down into the chamber with the hot cell made of depleted uranium-238. 'There's plenty more where he came from.'

'Jesus.' Abramanov stood before him in his lead smock and thick rubber gloves. 'That makes twenty.' His eyes were bleak. 'Pavlov's miracle shield doesn't work.'

Rock grunted. 'What a surprise. You Russians haven't been able to get anything right for years.'

Abramanov shook his head, for once trying not to be intimidated by the huge man. 'You don't understand. Element 114m is dirtier than any isotope I've ever worked with.'

'What do you mean? You guaranteed me the fission detonation would be absolutely clean.'

'Of course it will be. But in this state the isotope is deadly. In order to work on the project it must be handled, moved in and out of the hot cell. That's when the leakage occurs.'

Abramanov shifted uneasily on his feet. 'What are you going to do with him, the latest man with radiation poisoning?'

Rock stared at the Russian, pursed his lips, and gave a piercingly jaunty rendition of Be-Bop Deluxe's 'Sleep That Burns'. He waited long enough to enjoy Abramanov's squirming, before he said, 'We'll do what

364

we did with all the others: string him up by his ankles and hang him in the forest along the perimeter. It's a good object lesson for the locals. I don't like waste.'

The Russian was shaking his head. 'I'll have to train someone new and I don't have the time.'

'Work double shifts.' Rock's pale eyes blazed. 'We've got ten days to March fifteenth. Torch must be ready by then.'

'I don't know whether that's a realistic date. I hadn't counted on losing so many men.'

Rock pulled Abramanov off his feet with such abrupt force the Russian's teeth clacked together painfully. The vise-like grip of Rock's huge paws held him fast. 'Doctor, I didn't save your life, retrieve your precious cargo, get you everything you wanted, just so you could fuck with me now.'

'But I had no idea then how dirty element 114m is. I would not have –'

'Spare me your sanctimonious bullshit, Doctor, I've heard all the rationalizations the petty human mind can dream up, and they're all drivel. You'd have done the same thing you're doing right now, and d'you know why? Because you love it here in your scientific womb. I've given you your heart's desire. Your former Soviet masters didn't do that. They belittled you and held you down because you're a Jew. If you'd made it to the States instead of crashing off the coast of Vietnam, the US government would have spent a year picking apart your brain, and even then they never would have fully trusted you. You know you're best off here. Me, I don't give a shit what you are. You're a fucking genius and that's all that matters to me.'

'But I have nightmares. This project has terrible ramifications –'

Rock abruptly turned away. 'Get it done any way you see fit. Just get it done. Otherwise, all this – your dream playland — will disappear. Is that what you want?'

'I —' Abramanov hung his head. 'No.'

People are so pathetic, and so easily manipulated, Rock thought with satisfaction. 'Torch will be detonated ten days from now,' he said. 'I've never yet reneged on a promised delivery date, and I don't plan to start.'

Rock left Abramanov to work on the final stage of Torch. He went out of the hot-cell observatory, down two flights of stairs and across the compound. Various outbuildings, barracks, storehouses, guard posts and the like fanned out from this nexus point, all enclosed by twenty-foot-high walls of interlocking cut trees of massive girth, anchored in six feet of cement footings. The tremendous number of heavily armed men gave the impression of being inside a military installation.

Rock paused beside the cage. It was six feet high, four feet by four feet, painstakingly constructed from Viet Cong design. He had made it of fire-hardened bamboo lashed together with nylon cord reinforced with an almost unbreakable monofilament. It was currently occupied by a man who was slowly wasting away from lack of water and food. He had been caught trying to smuggle a kilo of half-refined opium out of Floating City, having reported it ruined by an excess of sulfuric acid.

Rock watched him slumped on the hard-packed earth, no longer strong enough even to stand on his feet. The foul stench coming from him had turned him feral, and there was a look of madness in his eyes that Rock could appreciate. He had been taught the nature of torture by Do Duc. They had shared many things, rituals, murder, intimate knowledge that few men could understand. But Do Duc was dead, killed by Nicholas Linnear. Do Duc had been as dear to him as a wife or a best friend, though neither had been able to acknowledge their relationship; they had merely accepted it as fact. When Rock thought of Nicholas Linnear, ideas, irrational and profane, forested his mind. These ideas lay in the peculiar penumbra between life and death that, together, he and Do Duc had for years explored, plumbed and, finally, mastered. He knew how dangerous Nicholas was, but this made these ideas all the more stimulating to him.

Squatting down by the side of the cage, Rock pushed one arm through the bamboo bars, took the emaciated man by the throat so he could drink in the growing madness, confront its ragged edge and so feel close again to Do Duc.

At length, he rose and continued across the compound, entering a building that faced the laboratory. He went into his office and sank into his leather swivel chair. It was a relief to be out of the air-conditioning. Almost two decades in the jungle had thinned his blood. He turned on the stereo. The Pink Floyd flooded the room with psychedelic rock. 'Arnold Layne'. The early stuff, Rock thought, was always the best. He sang happily along.

'You're having trouble with him,' the familiar voice said from a corner of his office.

'Who?'

'Abramanov.'

Rock swiveled in his leather chair. Years ago, a four-star general had sat in this chair and had given orders that made no sense in an insane war. Now it was Rock's chair; he figured he was making better use of it than the four-star ever had.

'Abramanov will get it done,' he said.

'On time?'

'Yes.'

'We have clients I don't want to disappoint.'

'I needn't remind you we have one particular client

367

we can't afford to disappoint,' Rock told him. 'Don't worry. We won't disappoint any of them.'

There was silence for a long time. In the brief space between album tracks a wild bird called from the forest beyond the vast city-like compound. Tropical sunlight filtered through the wide bamboo awnings over each window, striping the interior of the office like a tiger's back. The room smelled of oil and sweat.

'I think you're getting soft,' the man said from the shadows.

Rock peered into the corner at the figure who, over the years, had become more familiar to him than any of the girls he slept with. He smiled. 'You're full of shit.'

'Think so? You let Niigata go.'

'I didn't let him go; he got himself out of here. But by that time he was mad. He was dying of radiation poisoning. Why should I have wasted my time going after him? He couldn't have gotten far. His bones have long ago been picked clean out there in the jungle.'

The figure shifted. 'You shouldn't have meddled in the rendezvous at the Cu Chi tunnels.'

'That bitch. D'you know what *Bay* means? Seven. She was the seventh child, the unlucky one. She was fucking that bastard Vincent Tinh. She deserved to die.'

The figure clicked his fingers. 'Her death hooked Linnear; he took it personally, as I warned you he would. Then, to compound your error, you used Delacroix – a *client* – to try to put Linnear away.'

Rock turned up the volume on the Floyd. 'A client was the perfect choice. Like a cutout, only better, because he's freelance, he doesn't work for us so he can't be traced back to us. What are you getting at, you signed off on the hit.'

'It was a mistake.'

Rock shot forward, a sudden rush of blood making his scars go white beneath his tan. 'Bullshit! Now it's a mistake because it failed. Don't try your revisionist crap with me, it won't wash.'

'The locals take to it well enough.'

'They're uninformed and uneducated,' Rock said contemptuously. 'Bugs Bunny could brainwash them.'

'In any case, deconstructing the past is not brainwashing. It's merely the freedom to express an opinion.'

'History is not opinion, my friend,' Rock said flatly. 'It's memory and fact.'

'Really? I wonder whether the recollections of the general in whose chair you're now sitting would jibe with yours when it comes to the war in 'Nam.'

Rock waved a hand. 'I'm not going to debate this with you. It's giving credence to something that is without merit.' He stood up. 'We're going to string up another one.'

'Another? My, I guess I'd better get out my lead-lined pajamas.'

Rock glowered darkly into the shadows where the figure lounged. 'That's right, make a joke of it.'

'I don't like the idea of Timothy Delacroix hanging around Saigon.'

'Don't worry. He's not going to be talking to anyone.'

'What did you do, sew his lips together? That would be your style.'

Rock took up a coil of rope and his ever-present LAW, then paused. 'You know, I hardly recognize you anymore. When I first met you, I was sure you'd gone completely native, but I see now I was wrong. It's those fucking French philosophers, those crypto-Nazis you read all the time. They've got your head screwed on the wrong way.' He shrugged. 'What the hell. I guess we've both changed since those long-ago days in the Laotian bush.'

'Not you. You know what your problem is?' The figure reached over to turn off the stereo. 'You're stuck in a time warp. Still the Wild Boy, living in the seventies. Wake up, buddy boy, it's the nineties now. It's a whole new ball game out there.'

At the doorway, Rock turned back, grinned over his shoulder. He began to whistle the first few bars of the Rolling Stones' 'Gimme Shelter'. Then, in a surprisingly well-modulated voice, he took up the lyrics, 'War, children, it's just a shot away, shot away . . .'

Eaton Square was as still as a tomb this hour of the night. The sleet clattered against the sidewalk, drummed on the top of the unmarked car on loan from Major as Croaker pulled up on the King's Road. His headlights had been off for a block and a half.

Croaker's concern over Vesper had now reached full tide. If she was managing Morgana, Inc. she must be deeply involved with the Godaishu. This was yet another confirmation that Dedalus was the Godaishu's mainstay in America, since Vesper was so closely tied with him.

He turned the corner onto Eaton Square and, hurrying through the evil weather, came to the five-story white town house with its formal quoined facade. He hesitated only a moment, then went up the stairs beneath the protection of the columned portico, and rang the brass bell.

Major had used his computer to search for the owner, who turned out to be an elderly woman who had moved to the country to ease her emphysema. The place was on the market but, according to the realtor whom Major had roused on his pager, it was currently vacant. There seemed no point in disabusing him of that notion.

After what seemed a long time, the door opened a wedge. A young woman with bright eyes and short hair peered out at him quizzically.

'May I help you?' Behind her he could make out a

slice of a marble-floored vestibule and the crystal facets of a chandelier.

'Ah, I believe I'm lost,' he said in a rush. 'I'm looking for' – he pulled out a map of London – 'uh, Eaton Terrace.'

'You've been given duff directions, I'm afraid. This is Eaton Square.'

'Oh, damn.' He glanced anxiously at his watch. 'Is it far from here? I'm terribly late for an appointment.'

'No. D'you have transport?'

'A car, you mean? No. A taxi dropped me off.' He looked out at the sleet. 'I wonder if I could ask you to phone for another taxi?'

Those bright eyes regarded him for some time as if he needed to pass some test. 'Wait here,' the woman said and, affixing a short chain to the door sash, left him.

As he heard the click-click of her heels over the marble flooring he quickly pulled out a roll of electrician's tape Major had given him and, stripping off a piece, ran it over the latch on the edge of the front door, so that it could not lock.

She returned a moment later. 'Your taxi will be here shortly.'

'Thanks so much, Ms –' But the door had already been shut in his face.

He went back down the steps, hunched his shoulders, and waited for the taxi. He did not know whether the woman with the bright eyes was watching him now but he could not take the risk that she was. When the cab came, he climbed in and told the driver to take him to Eaton Terrace. But within a block, he had paid his fare and was hurrying through the clattering sleet up the street. When he reached the head of Eaton Square, he kept to the shadows, slipping under the portico of the white house.

Holding his breath, he turned the knob on the front door. As he slipped silently inside, he stripped the tape off the latch.

He moved through the vestibule, listening for anyone, including the woman with the bright eyes. The place was not at all what he had imagined from the outside. No overstuffed furniture, Victorian sconces or ornate fireplaces here. Instead, the entire interior was cold and modern, painted in black, white and an icy shade of gray. Everything had clean lines, precise angles. Everything was geometric and symmetrical. Two of everything, wherever it was possible. Identical mirror images. It made you want to rearrange or steal something just to restore the natural random order of nature.

He crossed to the foot of a circular, black, wrought-iron staircase. He could hear a clock ticking, then muffled voices coming from upstairs. He took off his shoes, went up the metal treads that would magnify even the smallest sound.

The voices became clearer: two women. He paused at the head of the stairs, looking at the hallway, which branched in two directions, four doors each way, perfectly symmetrical. Light streamed into the hallway from the last door on the right.

He crept down the hallway, chose the door on his left just before the end. The room was dark, and he took a moment to allow his eyes to adjust. He saw a bed, dresser, night table, and a door on the wall closest to the room with the light. He went through this, found himself in a vast bathroom. Marble blocks and mirrors everywhere. On the far side of the bathroom was a connecting door to the far room. He went to it, put his ear against it. Then, his hand on the knob, he turned it, allowed the door to open a fraction at a time until a sliver of the lit room beyond was revealed.

Someone crossed in front of the lamp. Vesper? No,

someone else; a flash of a face that was instantly familiar.

Croaker could see her shadow moving on the wall. Then, in two strides, she had reached the bathroom door and had pulled it open. Margarite's sister, Celeste.

TWELVE

Yoshino

Yoshino was a sacred place. It was where, over the centuries, heroes had been forged in blood and sacrifice, where *yamabushi* made arduous pilgrimages across the steep mountain fastness, where Shugendo, the syncretic and vibrant amalgam of Shintoism and Buddhism still survived, despite the best efforts of the two-hundred-year reign of the Tokugawa shogunate to stamp it out. The Tokugawa, obsessed with power and the abasement of all perceived enemies, real and imagined, had favored Buddhism's formality. If all Japanese were Buddhists, the shoguns reasoned, they would be registered at their neighborhood temples and, therefore, be easy to keep track of. Shintoism made no such demands on its followers. Its only tenets were those dictated by the seasons and by the *kami* – the spirit – of the area where the Shinto shrine was built. For Shinto, there is no God, no Buddha, but, rather, the spirit guardians who dwelled in every atom of the universe.

The slopes of Yoshino's mountains were covered by, it was said, a hundred thousand cherry trees, whose splendid blossoms of the palest pink were, for three days in the spring, the most magnificent and moving sight in all of Japan. It was to Yoshino that a profusion of Japan's emperors over the centuries had made pilgrimages in order to worship the mountains' *kami*, and it was here the information provided by the Yakuza

374

under-*oyabun* Kine Oto, also known as Zao, had brought Nicholas and Tachi.

'Zao took V. I. Pavlov to see a man here named Niigata,' Nicholas said, as they headed up the narrow mountain road. This time of the year, Yoshino was shrouded in mist so deeply one had the impression that the mountain rose to a level just below heaven.

'According to Zao, this Niigata is something of a recluse and has become a Shugendo monk.'

'I take it that means he used to be something else,' Tachi said.

Nicholas nodded, noting that Tachi had only sketchy recall of the interrogation of Zao. What had the invocation of Shuken done to him? 'Yes. A nuclear physicist. If that sounds odd, it gets more so. Niigata returned to Japan six months ago after a lengthy stay in Vietnam.'

Tachi's neck cracked as he turned from watching the road to glance at Nicholas. The car jounced violently into a rut and out again, and Nicholas said, 'Watch it, Tachi!'

'Vietnam,' the *oyabun* said. 'He wouldn't have had contact with Floating City?'

'Zao didn't know. But he knew that Pavlov and Niigata talked about Abramanov.'

'We've got our connection to Rock!' Tachi said triumphantly as he pulled into a narrow ramped driveway in front of the *ryokan* where they planned to stay the night.

Blue mist gathered around the slopes of the mountains with such tenacity that they had virtually no view from the windows in their rooms. The place was one of those new-style *ryokan* where everything that had once been wood was now either tile or plastic. There was a TV in the room's tokonoma instead of a vase with a fresh flower. One paid for it by feeding coins into a slot to view half-hour intervals. The walls were papered green instead of hand-painted, and the hallways to the toilets were lined with vending machines dispensing everything from hot sake to iced cappuccino. It was not a restful place and had none of the rustic charm that made traditional *ryokan* desirable places to stay.

This supremely practical side of modern-day Japan was often tough to take. There seemed no connection at all with the culture that turned the manufacture of even everyday items such as combs and hairpins into high art, until one understood that Japan was a country of facades. Like lacquered walls, paper screens, translucent *noren*, which hung in open doorways, there was in all things Japanese the impression that something else lay just beneath the gauzy layer one had come through; if one sensed the truth was beyond the next layer, it was an illusion, and the cultural imperative to project secrets inward had accomplished its purpose.

According to Zao's information, Niigata lived at the bottom of a deep valley that lay between two Yoshino hills. They ate a quick meal, then left the *ryokan*, walking up the main street of the village, ascending toward the main Shugendo shrine where, it was said, dwelled the remains of the rebel emperor Go-Daigo, who in the fourteenth century set up a southern imperial court here.

The road forked at the foot of the steps to the shrine, and they took the right-hand route that led down an increasingly narrow street, past isolated stores and residential houses until it petered out at the edge of a flight of steeply winding steps overarched by a procession of vermilion torii gates.

They had been driving almost all day, and they were tired. It was nearing evening, and the twilight turned the heavy mist to jewel tones. As they descended, the light became aqueous and a chill emanated from the forest floor, seeping through the lichen, moss and ferns. Tachi shivered, pulling his coat closer around him as they descended the seemingly endless stone stairway.

'This place gives me the creeps,' he said.

They paused, hearing an eerie sound echoing through the woods that now rose far above their heads. It came again before the echoes of the previous sound had died away.

Tachi looked around. 'What is that?'

'The priests are calling the evening service by blowing through giant conch shells,' Nicholas said. 'They've done it this way for centuries.'

They continued down through the dense wood, accompanied by the otherworldly sounds echoing through the trees like the cries of Yoshino's awakened *kami*. Ahead, they could see that the stairway made a forty-five-degree turn to the right. In a niche just before the corner they came upon an enormous sword, its massive butt set into moss-covered stone. Metal flames struck off the edge of the blade, serving as poignant reminders that Yoshino was filled with the *kami* of long-dead heroes such as Minamoto no Yoshitsune. It was here that Yoshitsune hallowed his sword in a Shinto ceremony of fire purification.

For Nicholas, Yoshino was forever infused with the special melancholy conjured by the doomed romance between this thirteenth-century hero and his favorite mistress, the dancer Shizuka, widely renowned as the most beautiful woman of her time. It was to Yoshino that the couple fled after an aborted attempt on Yoshitsune's life by his enemies. Shizuka was almost magical in her dancer's abilities. She was supposedly able to end droughts with rainstorms and bring grown men to tears with her ethereal dances. And it was here that the legendary lovers were parted by fate, where Shizuka was betrayed and captured by Yoshitsune's enemies.

In his mind, this twilit winter's afternoon, Shizuka and Koei were inextricably entwined, and the deeper he descended into the Shinto valley, the more his personal memories were caught up in the tendrils of history that endured here, overcoming the advent of plastic geta and television tokonoma.

As they advanced down the last flight of stairs, they glimpsed the shrine. It was set beside a swiftly flowing stream that cut obliquely through the floor of the valley. Its peaked crimson roofs and massive polished cedar columns rose up through the trees, seeming a natural part of the terrain.

They passed over a small wooden bridge beneath which the stream rocketed over a bed of stones worn smooth by the water's passage. Beside the bridge was a thick column perhaps three feet high on which stood a bronze figure of a curled snake-dragon. This was Noten O-kami, a manifestation of Zao Gongen, the avatar of Yoshino.

'Tell me a bit about Seiko,' Nicholas said as they crossed the bridge.

Tachi, looking at the image of the coiled Noten O-kami, said, 'I think that would be most dangerous for our friendship, given that the two of you are sleeping together.' He turned to Nicholas, his lips curled in the ghost of a smile. 'Weren't we taught in Tau-tau that three is the number of conflict?'

'She says you're not like other *oyabun*.'

Tachi raised his eyebrows. 'Well, perhaps that is so. I am *tanjian*, and that alone sets me apart, doesn't it?' Beyond the other side of the bridge stands of tall, ancient cryptomeria marched along the floor of the valley, then upward along the far slopes. 'But you don't really mean to ask me about Seiko. I sense that you already know more about her than you'd like to.'

Nicholas stopped. 'What does that mean?'

'Knowing Seiko is bad enough, but caring about her is the same as getting caught in quicksand. She is a woman who has no sense of herself at all. She is, quite literally, what men have convinced her she is. If she seems strong now, it is because men have taught her to be so – I among them, I'm afraid. Inside, however, she has lost contact with who she is. To be brutally honest, it is likely she was never in touch with it at all.'

'And that makes her dangerous?'

'Oh, yes. A person who has no self-worth lacks the ability to put value on human life – any life. Seiko is likely to do the expedient thing, listen to the last compelling male voice she hears. Most people can be persuaded by money, sex, ideology or the promise of power, but not Seiko. She's motivated by whim, a capricious breath of air, and this makes her wholly unpredictable.'

'Let's be clear about this,' Nicholas said, wondering if Tachi knew the story of her brother's terrible death. 'Are you saying that she is incapable of love or of experiencing any human emotion?'

'No. What I am saying is that her definition of love or of any other human emotion is unlikely to be close to yours or mine. And, in a very real sense, this is the more difficult and perilous possibility, because she can easily communicate what appears to be the real thing. It will come as quite a shock, I can tell you, when you realize it isn't anything like what you thought.'

To their left the priests, their conch shells beneath their arms, were congregating for the evening service. Nicholas and Tachi moved off, down a hump and between two of the shrine buildings toward a road that wound into the rear of the valley.

Nicholas said, 'Why did you say before that I didn't really want to talk about Seiko? I did.'

'Perhaps. But we both know what is foremost on your mind.'

Shuken.

379

The word stood between them like a ghost at a feast, turning food into ash and wine into stagnant water. Shuken was what Tachi had over Nicholas, and now a future that seemed to have had many branchings just a day ago had been narrowed to two. Because Shuken would be present, invoked or threatened to be invoked, at every decision, confrontation and opinion. Everything they did now was prejudiced by it, and either they would be friends or they would be enemies. This was what Shuken had done to their futures; there was no room for compromise or a middle ground.

'Yes,' Nicholas said, not wanting to utter a word. 'Shuken.'

'And of course you want to know whether I will teach you how to reach the sphere.'

Nicholas said nothing, continuing along the road that was actually no more than a dirt path. They had quickly left the more civilized area of the shrine compound and had now plunged into the raw countryside. Birds twittered in the treetops, lost in the maze of cryptomeria needles.

'I already know your answer by what you have just said.' Nicholas turned to Tachi. 'You are right. I have no love of the Yakuza – far from it in fact. But with you I was willing to make an exception because . . .' Nicholas looked into the trees, cloaked in the coming of night. Their pitchy smell pervaded the area. 'Because our minds touched and there was a chance we could learn from one another. Tachi, we live such isolated lives that I . . . I lost a wife because of that isolation. I imagine I have lost someone else special to me for the same reason. In my youth, the splendid isolation of my internal art was enough for me. But that was a long time ago, and I was another person entirely.' He shook his head. 'You're right to believe that I have sought Shuken almost ever since I became aware that I was

380

tanjian – and I have compelling reasons to seek it that you could never fully understand. But I will not play power games with you or anyone in order to possess the integration of Akshara and Kshira.'

Tachi was motionless as he contemplated Nicholas for a long time. A black bird flew above their heads, disappearing into the forest of cryptomeria. At last, Tachi said, 'Who told you that Shuken was the integration of Tau-tau's two paths?'

'No one. I just intuited . . .'

'The theory of integration is a myth, Linnear-san. Do not be deluded. Shuken exists and *koryoku* is its only pathway, but what Shuken does is hold the two paths, light and dark, separate in one mind. The perfection of integration is, like any other form of perfection in human existence, an impossibility.' Tachi saw the look on Nicholas's face but had no inkling of what it might portend. He could not know of the Kshira time bombs ticking away in Nicholas. 'But I will willingly teach you everything I know. I pledged to do as much with each *tanjian* I met, but even had I not, I would give you what I have been taught. We are friends, are we not?'

'Yes,' Nicholas said, thinking of Seiko's warning about Tachi's obsession with Floating City, 'we are.'

They pressed on. Niigata lived in a small cottage at the end of this lane, and up ahead they could see lights in the gloom. Soon a small thatch-roofed house came into view. It was hewn from timbers in the traditional Japanese farmhouse style, all locked together by notches and dowels with no nails or glue used.

As they came up to the front door, Tachi said, 'Let me handle this. I know how to deal with Rock's people.'

'How do you know Niigata's been to Floating City?'

Tachi slapped his belly with his fist. '*This* tells me.'

His face was grim as he struck the door with his hand. A moment later, a lanky man in his mid-sixties stood peering out at them. He was so emaciated he recalled photos of concentration camp internees.

'Yes?'

His skull was absolutely hairless. Baldness in a man his age would not be particularly remarkable except that Nicholas could see that he had no eyelashes or eyebrows.

'Niigata-san?'

'*Hai.*'

'We have a message for you from a friend of yours.' Tachi took a step toward the threshold. 'His name is Rock.'

Nicholas took a swift step forward, catching Niigata before he fell to the floor. They took off their shoes, and Nicholas set the thin man on his feet. He seemed to weigh less than a child, and his skin was red and blotchy, shiny as vinyl.

'Forgive me,' Niigata said, 'but I had never thought to hear that name again.'

'This man's suffering from radiation poisoning,' Nicholas said to Tachi, then turned to the older man. 'Niigata-san, are you being treated? You should be in hospital.'

Niigata gave him a rueful smile. 'There is no treatment for what I have. I am better off here than being the object of scientific curiosity.'

'Then you've been to Floating City?' Tachi asked.

Nicholas was aware of Tachi's heartbeat accelerating.

'Come.' Niigata gestured to the dim interior. 'I was just sitting down to dinner. Won't you join me? It's been quite some time since I had guests. The priests visit me regularly, but they never stay. I would welcome the company, even if Rock did send you.'

Nicholas gave Tachi a quick glance, but the *oyabun* contrived to ignore it. 'That would be most kind of you,' Tachi said, the urgent note in his voice undiminished.

They followed the emaciated man into the interior of the house. As Niigata moved slowly around the sunken hibachi hearth, Nicholas said, 'You have been to Floating City and yet you're here now.'

'I escaped,' Niigata said simply. He stirred the root vegetables that were simmering in a soy broth. The stew was in a large iron pot hung from a hook above the hibachi.

'And yet you seem unconcerned about our appearance.'

Niigata looked up. 'I am already dead. What more could Rock do to me?' He took down a stack of rough wooden bowls, ladled out generous portions of the vegetable stew. His hands shook and, once, he almost spilled liquid onto the tatami, but neither man moved to help him. 'Sit,' he commanded.

The three men ate in silence. In fact, only Nicholas and Tachi appeared to have an appetite. Though the food was rich and flavorful Niigata barely touched it. Nicholas was not surprised.

'You worked on Abramanov's project, didn't you?' Tachi asked.

Niigata put down his chopsticks, abandoning all pretext at eating. 'You're not from Floating City.'

'No,' Tachi said. 'We want to stop what's going on inside it.'

'Then you don't know.' Niigata's voice was abruptly so weary that Nicholas might have thought it was emanating from Methuselah.

'The truth is we've come to find out.'

Niigata nodded. 'The truth is important.' His head came up and his fevered black eyes bored into theirs in turn. 'I find that these days nothing else has meaning.'

'It *is* the truth,' Nicholas said.

'Yes.' Niigata nodded. 'I suppose I have no choice but to believe you.' He shrugged his thin shoulders. 'It's a

383

good illusion anyway.' Then he told them everything he knew. How Rock had picked Abramanov out of the South China Sea in November of 1991, and how Abramanov had persuaded him to return to the site the following spring, when Abramanov's wounds had healed sufficiently, in order to retrieve the Russian's precious cargo. How Rock then built the lab with its hot cell for Abramanov's experiments with the highly toxic radioactive isotope.

'Just how powerful is this 114m?' Tachi asked.

'How to answer that?' Niigata's head bobbed on his stalk of a neck. 'No one really knows. Even Rock dares not test it inside Vietnam, so the prototype has been made on pure speculation. I know firsthand that the isotope is more chemically toxic than plutonium. It's a nightmare material. Direct contact with particles is invariably fatal. Since fine particulates are always present on its surface because of oxidation and surface instability, extreme contamination controls are essential. So it is handled within a negative-pressure-ventilated hot cell with an inert atmosphere of argon to prevent oxidation. But not always, and this gives rise to the transport of toxic dust. Then there is the gamma radiation to worry about. Element 114m is such an energetic gamma emitter that standing unshielded within ten meters of it for five minutes is lethal.'

'If it's such a nightmare, why bother with it at all?' Tachi asked.

'Several reasons. Element 114m has a very high cross-section for thermal neutrons, making it a most potent fissile material. It has a critical mass far below that of either uranium or plutonium. Plus, its half-life is exceptionally long. Do you know what all this means?'

'I think I can guess.' Nicholas felt chilled through to his bones. 'The isotope that Abramanov discovered will make an excellent weapons material.'

Niigata nodded. 'That's right. Abramanov claims that the criticality factor is so high that if one were foolish enough to bring two small bricks of the isotope – say five inches by eight by one – within three feet of one another spontaneous fission would initiate a full-scale criticality event.'

'A fission chain reaction.' Nicholas's throat seemed filled with lead. 'How large?'

'With just those two small bricks Abramanov estimates four square city blocks.'

'Good God.'

The three men sat in silence for some time. A bird sang in a branch just outside the window and then fell still. It was so quiet they could hear the rushing of the stream some distance away. Niigata stirred, moving his stiff limbs about. He was obviously in pain.

'The isotope was too hot even for the hot cell,' Nicholas said.

'Yes. We had to train locals, mountain tribesmen. It's exacting work, and we did not have enough time. Mistakes were made – small ones – but with 114m they were enough. While I was there, fifteen men died of radiation poisoning. You can see how its extreme toxicity makes it inappropriate for commercial use.' Niigata shook his head. 'Such a shame. Otherwise, Abramanov would have fulfilled one of mankind's most cherished dreams: a safe, cheap, virtually inexhaustible fuel.'

Tachi leaned forward, the firelight licking at his taut face. 'Is Abramanov being held against his will in Floating City?'

'Yes and no.' Niigata stirred the wood with a poker, put another log on. He had great difficulty handling the wood, but again neither man would shame him by offering to help. 'I don't believe Rock is keeping him captive; he doesn't have to. Abramanov is doing a first-rate job of it himself.'

In the flickering light it appeared as if all flesh had been stripped from Niigata and what now sat before them was an animated skeleton, yellow bones still shining with the remnants of a lost life.

'Abramanov has convinced himself of the worthiness of his work at Floating City. The project, which Rock has called Torch, is the price he believes he must pay for continuing his life's work. Like a lunatic, he listens to Rock and does his dirty work. A highly compact, portable, clean nuclear device. It makes the blood run cold. But Abramanov is oblivious. He is fixated on one point on the horizon, and it is this for which he lives – the eventual recognition he will receive from mankind.'

So this has been Okami's objective for me all along, Nicholas thought. *Floating City is making the nuclear device, and it's almost certain that someone plans to use it against him on the fifteenth of March.* But where was Okami, and who was buying Torch from Rock?

'But doesn't he see the terrible inevitability of its use for destruction?' Tachi was asking Niigata.

'What scientist does? Did the team at Los Alamos allow such considerations to deter them on the Manhattan Project?' Niigata stared at the charcoal that coated his fingertips. 'I assure you that the nature of the beast does not allow for such rational thought.'

Nicholas addressed Niigata. 'Do you know who is buying the first Torch?'

'A Japanese,' Niigata said without hesitation. 'I overheard Rock at one point. He mentioned the Yakuza. An *oyabun.*'

'Which *oyabun*?' Nicholas's heart was pounding heavily in his chest.

'I don't know. But he did mention the Kaisho.'

Nicholas's voice was abruptly hoarse. Okami was Torch's intended target. That meant whoever was buying it knew where he was hiding. 'I believe I know the target,' he said. 'Why would they use Torch in this way?'

Niigata shrugged. 'My guess is it's twofold. First, the location of the target has been established but not pinpointed. With a weapon like Torch, identifying the target's location in a particular house or even on a block is unnecessary. The entire neighborhood will go. Second, the resulting disaster in the heart of a densely populated urban center will send the most potent message imaginable to all potential buyers. Torch's price will skyrocket. And, believe me, every terrorist, warlord and ethnic cleanser will fall all over himself to purchase it.'

Nicholas shivered at the thought. He had to find out where Okami was hiding. 'I have information that Torch's detonation will be in a major city. Have you any idea which one?'

Niigata's breathing was becoming labored. 'I doubt that even Abramanov knows. Only Rock. And, of course, his partner. But my advice would be to get to Torch before the fifteenth. Once it leaves Floating City the chances of finding it — especially in a big city — are virtually nil.'

'His partner?' Tachi whispered, ignoring the terrifying implications of what Niigata had just said.

Tachi's voice was so strangled Nicholas threw him a sharp look.

'Rock's partner is alive?' he asked again.

'Of course he's alive,' Niigata said. 'Nothing short of being too close to the Torch detonation is going to kill that bastard. Mick, Rock calls him.'

'Yes, Mick.' An eerie light had come into Tachi's eyes, and his frame was vibrating so violently that even Niigata had become aware of it. 'You fucking sonuvabitch, I have you now, Michael Leonforte.'

THIRTEEN

London/Tokyo/Yoshino

The sleet had stopped, and silvery light from a full moon sliding through the last of a low-riding cloud bank, spilled through the bathroom, illuminating Celeste's face. Her hair slid across her cheek as she bent, upending the trash can into the toilet and flushing away the burned contents.

Croaker, standing breathless behind the shower curtain, found the tub porcelain cold. He had seen Celeste's shadow moving on the wall, enlarging dramatically as she began to head his way. That was when he had left the door, racing across the tiles to the tub. Celeste hadn't bothered to turn on the lights and so hadn't noticed the small spots of water that had fallen from his wet shoes.

Now, as he crept back to the door, he absorbed them with the soles of his socks. That had been too close, and his heart was thudding heavily in his chest. Celeste had been near enough for him to smell her perfume. He could have reached out and touched her. And if she had bothered to look down at the wet tiles . . .

Croaker had met Celeste late last year in Tokyo when they were pursuing Do Duc, the Vietnamese who had murdered her brother, Dominic Goldoni. That Celeste was part of the Nishiki network did not surprise him because Nicholas had first met her in Venice where she worked for Mikio Okami, but that Vesper was deeper and deeper inside it terrified him. It was beginning to look as if, like all the most successful moles, she was privy to the highest levels of Okami's clandestine network.

'For the first time since we began I am starting to have doubts,' Celeste said. 'The forces arrayed against Okami are so vast, so well entrenched.' She shook her head. 'You saw what happened after Leonforte was unmasked and killed – Dedalus took over and now it's as if nothing has changed. The Godaishu is like the Hydra – a monster with so many heads, lopping off one or two had no effect.'

'That was part of Okami's plan when he built up the Godaishu. Now that he's fighting it, it's like battling your own mirror image.'

Celeste looked up at Vesper. 'I'm terrified they will penetrate his defenses and kill him. If he doesn't get help soon –'

'I think you have to have faith in Okami,' Vesper said softly.

'But I haven't seen him in so long. And I feel as if the Godaishu's power is growing every day.'

Vesper said nothing, but her look of concern startled Croaker. Again he was witnessing the expert psychologist at work. Was it an act, or genuine, as it appeared? Could she care for these people – Celeste, Margarite and Okami – while in the act of betraying them? The more he saw of this woman the less he knew her. She was a unique creature, of that much he was certain.

Celeste shook her head, worrying her lower lip. 'We have another crisis. Serman hasn't delivered his last update on Torch. Without him we're dead in the water and the entire penetration is at a risk level we can't tolerate.'

Penetration of what? Croaker strained to hear every word.

Vesper nodded. 'Yes, there's got to be a problem at DARPA. I don't know what's in Serman's mind.'

Celeste looked worried. 'Do you think he's hit a wall? What if he can't deliver the element 114m analysis in time? Floating City will have its weapon, and once Floating City puts it on the market on the fifteenth, we will be helpless to stop its dissemination.'

'Either way, we're in trouble. We're running out of time. I'll go see Serman myself right away. I can make a morning flight.'

'You'll have to take the evening plane. I've had a message. It came in an hour before you arrived. You're to be at the 315 rendezvous point at noon tomorrow.'

'That's beside the Bird Lawn at Holland Park.' Vesper leaned forward, looking concerned. 'Three fifteen. You know the code as well as I do. He's going to want the update on Serman, and I'm not going to be able to give it to him.'

'He won't take kindly to bad news.'

'Not at this late date. He's never lost in his life.'

'But we've lost now,' Celeste said, 'haven't we?'

Ushiba met Tanaka Gin in the underground food courts at the Ginza branch of Mitsukoshi, Japan's most famous department store. Mitsukoshi's food courts were legendary, stretching in any direction for as far as the eye could see, or so it seemed. If it was edible, it could probably be found here. Everything was on display, from fresh-cut bamboo, vegetables, herbs, breads of all descriptions and varieties, to prepared foods in astonishing abundance.

Tanaka Gin liked to spend odd hours cruising the prepared-food stalls, gobbling down samples while his mind worked on a problem his chaotic office made it impossible to solve.

Ushiba had never seen Tanaka Gin sit down and have a proper meal. One could assume that at some point during the day or night he must do that, but that was a dangerous assumption to make about the Tokyo prosecutor. He was like a shark, always on the move, not so much restive as reluctant to allow inertia to catch up with him. Bodies at rest, Ushiba had often heard him say, were difficult to get into motion. He might have been speaking somewhat metaphorically about the bureaucratic red tape he daily battled against, but Ushiba did not think that was the sum of it. Upon contemplation, it seemed to Ushiba that Tanaka Gin had a horror of the world spinning on without him. Like a child who fights sleep while his parents' party is in progress, Ushiba suspected the prosecutor had an instinct that connected rest with death.

'How is your case against Yoshinori progressing?' Ushiba asked when he caught up with Tanaka Gin at a stall selling Thai spring rolls.

'Adequately.' Tanaka Gin took a spring roll, dipped it into a sticky orange sauce, devoured it in two bites. 'I think my biggest problem will be in keeping him alive until the trial.'

'Yoshinori wants to die?'

'His life is over.' Tanaka Gin took another spring roll as he headed to the next stall. The smell of frying peanut oil was as luscious as the sumptuous sweep of a woman's naked thigh. 'He knows it and we know he knows it. The matter has now passed beyond him to others. He is aware of this as well. It does not sit well with him that the life he has lived for so long now finds him all but superfluous.'

'I can only imagine the departmental questions if he dies prematurely,' Ushiba said in a neutral tone of voice. 'Would you like me to talk with him?'

Tanaka Gin paused with a sliver of grilled fish fin halfway to his mouth. He glanced at what he was about to eat, popped it in his mouth, wiped his fingers on a tiny square of waxed paper given to him by the woman who was offering the samples.

'You have thought this matter over completely.' Tanaka Gin's dark eyes lingered on Ushiba's beautiful face for some time. 'This is not a decision to be entered into lightly.'

'I do not want to end up as Yoshinori has, feeling superfluous.'

'I seriously doubt that was ever a possibility for you, Daijin.'

It wasn't often that Tanaka Gin called him by his title. That, along with the switch in tenses, told Ushiba that things had changed between them. He was on Tanaka Gin's team now, like it or not. He would have to play by the prosecutor's rules or suffer the immediate consequences. Ushiba nodded. He was prepared for whatever lay ahead. Akira Chosa's betrayal of their special friendship had sealed all their fates. Now, in a way, their karma had been intertwined with Tanaka Gin's. As improbable as that would have seemed to him even a month ago, it was now reality. But that was all right. He had become Daijin not merely because of his intelligence, ingenuity, contacts and good fortune. He had also proven himself adaptable to all kinds of situations and pressures. And he would adapt again, as the need arose.

They moved along the food courts, pausing here and there as Tanaka Gin saw fit. As for himself, Ushiba ate nothing. He rarely did these days, and when he managed to get something down, it came right up again an hour later. His body, racked by disease, was beginning to reject the staples of life. There was nothing to be done now but to play out the string. He was grateful that Tanaka Gin did not comment on his lack of appetite or on his increasingly gaunt countenance. He had long ago put away all mirrors in his house, refusing to watch himself waste away day after day. But perhaps that had been a mistake, because this morning when he had caught a glimpse of himself in the polished marble of his office lobby, he had started as if he had seen a ghost. In a very real way, he had, for he had been shocked to see how much like a cadaver he already looked, as if a good part of his physicality were already locked away beneath the ground, embalmed and entombed.

'I wonder if you would entertain a request,' Tanaka Gin said. 'Over the next weeks we will have much to discuss, and the long hours may prove inconvenient for me because you and I live on opposite sides of the city. I wonder if you would consent to be my guest for this time. I have a large house with a separate wing for guests. You could have absolute privacy, but I could have access to you when I need to take down your testimony or have you look over the depositions of others. How does this arrangement sound to you?'

Ushiba could not help closing his eyes for an instant. He was abruptly dizzy and, he hoped without the prosecutor's knowing, he moved closer to a stall dispensing *bento* boxes of sushi so he could grip its side to steady himself.

Of course he understood why Tanaka Gin was making this offer. It was to help Ushiba, not himself. He was well aware of how far along Ushiba was. He knew Ushiba lived alone, and that at the end he might not want to be. Tears welled behind Ushiba's eyes before he gathered the strength to clear them without a drop escaping. It was an odd thing to contemplate, but at the end of his life of power and influence it just might be that Tanaka Gin – a man who was an enemy of the Godaishu – might turn out to be his only true friend.

'I couldn't possibly inconvenience you to that extent,' Ushiba said, watching Tanaka Gin take up a pinch of gray baby eels and munch on them. 'My presence would throw your household into chaos.'

'Hardly, Daijin. Since I live alone, and have a cleaning woman in twice a week, your stay would be no inconvenience whatsoever. The woman has barely enough to keep her busy as it is. Besides, she's something of a show-off. She's always complaining I have no company she can cook for.'

Ushiba waited until they had moved to the next stall before bowing in acquiescence. 'In that case, I accept your generous offer. But only because it will make your job easier.'

Tanaka Gin smiled. 'Of course. It is gracious of you to accommodate me in this way.'

This rather formal dance of words was necessary to save face all the way around. Ushiba could not disclose his gratitude for a gesture that Tanaka Gin could not admit existed. If he did expose his true reason for making the offer, he would admit to Ushiba's humiliating weakness, and this was unthinkable.

'I've got a great deal of work ahead of me and, frankly, considering how overworked my staff is, I'm going to have to rely on you, Ushiba-san.' He wiped his hands, turned to face the Daijin. 'To be completely honest, now that the door has been breached, the skeletons are going to tumble out at an astonishing rate. The tentacles of Yoshinori's octopus are far-reaching. We are now not only compiling evidence implicating politicians and financial houses in illegal donations for favors rendered, but also in systematic bid-rigging with construction companies who paid Yoshinori to keep them working on the vast public-works contracts that the Americans have wanted in on for years. The Americans have accused us of running a closed shop, and they've been right. And it's becoming increasingly clear that this is just the beginning. We're very likely to find the same dirty situations in wholesale markets and retail franchises.'

Tanaka Gin glanced around the crowded food court with the kind of forced casualness that gave Ushiba the impression he was concerned about security. Perhaps his suggestion that they meet here was not such an arbitrary decision.

'In fact, Daijin, I admit to having a personal reason for enlisting your help. One of my lieutenants has uncovered a document in Yoshinori's home. I know it is just one document in a sea of paperwork, but this one is different. It is a personal letter from Yoshinori to one of his political party precinct bosses. It makes reference to an entity called the Godaishu. Does this name mean anything to you?'

'It doesn't, no,' Ushiba said with his heart beating so loudly he was terrified Tanaka Gin would hear it.

'I'm not surprised. It doesn't to me. The references were vague, but my lieutenant thinks he has overheard Yakuza using that word. If we can tie Yoshinori and his branch of the Liberal Democratic Party into the Yakuza, it would mean a major breakthrough in cracking the Yakuza's stranglehold on legitimate business.'

Ushiba said nothing for some time. They had left the food courts, and were riding the silent escalators up to street level. The Ginza was filled with sunlight, neon and a heady surge of shoppers, tourists and hurrying businessmen. None of this panoply seemed alive to Ushiba, who, increasingly, felt as if the world were closing down, his senses, if not his mind, diminishing to the point where someone would have to thrust a *tanto* into his chest in order for him to feel anything. For a long time now, the only taste he could recall was that of his own blood.

Tanaka Gin had a car waiting to take him back to his

office. 'Will you ride with me, Daijin? My driver will take you anywhere you want to go.'

'Thank you,' Ushiba said, ducking down to enter the car's interior. 'I need to return to my office for the rest of the afternoon.'

Tanaka Gin settled in beside him. 'I can have my driver be at your home any time you wish this evening to help you in packing.'

'Eight would be convenient.' Ushiba closed his eyes for a moment as the force of the vehicle's acceleration dizzied him. He was finding that sudden shifts in gravity, no matter how incremental, were affecting him substantially, causing him to feel as if he were falling into a great abyss. He now found elevators a menace, disorienting him for minutes at a time, but he had yet to figure out a way to avoid them at work.

The feeling of vertigo subsided slowly, and he came back to himself. He began to focus his mind on why he had asked for this meeting. Now was the time, he could feel it. If he was going to tread this new path, this was the moment to take the first step. Again, he felt the absence of Mikio Okami more acutely than he did his present surroundings. How present events would have been altered had the Kaisho been here now. Of all the decisions in his life, Ushiba regretted most his acquiescence to the plan to oust Okami. If he had known someone — Chosa or Akinaga — would take it one step further and try to assassinate the Kaisho, he would never have agreed. But he hadn't, and now, with Chosa and Akinaga, the two powerhouses of the inner council, apparently at each other's throats, he felt increasingly helpless to stem the rising tide of an internecine war. This feeling had been the prime motivating factor in his coming down on Akinaga's side when Chosa had overstepped his authority by enlisting the council's third *oyabun*, Tachi Shidare, to destroy Nicholas Linnear. The power-grabbing had to end. Mikio Okami had known that when he had set himself up as Kaisho, and now Ushiba knew as well. He just prayed he hadn't learned the lesson too late.

'Gin-san,' he said slowly, 'I have been thinking about what you have just told me. I have knowledge of a tangible connection between Yoshinori and the Yakuza.'

Tanaka Gin half-turned toward him on the seat. His face was very grave. 'Chief Minister, if this is the case, then I owe you a debt of gratitude I can never fully repay.'

'Repayment is not at issue.' Ushiba could feel his world sliding away from him. What would ensue from this moment he could not say, but certainly a new order was about to take hold. 'What I can tell you is that Yoshinori has had direct business dealings with Akira Chosa, *oyabun* of the Kokorogurushii clan.'

In the expression on Tanaka Gin's face, he could see it was done: their fates had now been set in stone, and they all trod upon a path strewn with unknown consequences.

'It's painfully simple,' Tachi said to Nicholas. 'Michael Leonforte killed my father.'

Niigata had gone out to the toilet on unsteady legs. The radiation had made his bones brittle as well as hollow.

'Three years after I left, I returned home from Kumamoto to make my peace, to show my father who I had become. To this day I don't know whether he understood what it is I do. Perhaps it is better that way; he lived his life in the way he had to. In any case, what was important to him was my one act of rebellion at school. He never looked at my arm, but I knew he was aware of the scars there and he was proud of how they had come to be there.'

Tachi kept an eye on the back door, watching, Nicholas supposed, for Niigata to return. 'My father had many business interests in Vietnam. He used to take me with him when he went. It would drive my mother to distraction because it was so dangerous. "Danger," my father always said, "is a beast best mastered at an early age." And he was right. I learned from him how to protect myself, how to lie low and how to retaliate. I learned to negotiate – which is retaliation's brother – and to compromise when the need arose. The best thing my father ever did for me was to put eyes in my back.'

The fire cracked and sparked, licking at the cast-iron pot in which the remains of dinner simmered happily away. The escaping steam sounded like a disapproving parent.

'My father was always expanding in Vietnam. He saw what others had not – that Southeast Asia was a shell in which pearls could be harvested at a fraction of the cost they could at home. He bought textile companies and electronics firms, fertilizer combines and interests in the old hotels of Saigon when everyone else considered them worthless. And he bought land. This was how he came in contact with Leonforte.

'Michael Leonforte was also buying up real estate, through a dummy corporation owned by him and Rock. What it came down to was they both wanted the same plot of dirt.

'For once, my father forgot his own rules. He would not back down and neither would Leonforte. Leonforte threatened him, but my father would not be baited. Then Leonforte came after me and my father went after Leonforte. He forgot to watch his back. I saw Leonforte shoot him down like a dog in the street. What's more, Leonforte liked it. He licked his lips and howled in glee, he did a little dance over my father's body before dragging it into the jungle.'

Nicholas watched Tachi as the painful memories worked their way through the muscles of his face like a paroxysm. In this, at least, Seiko had not lied. Tachi was indeed obsessed with infiltrating Floating City.

Nicholas leaned over, poured Tachi a cup of tea, pushing it across the tatami, into the *oyabun*'s hands. Briefly, he touched Tachi's fingers, which were very cold.

With the contact, Tachi's eyes refocused on Nicholas's face, then down at the cup of tea. He nodded in gratitude, took the cup in trembling hands, drank slowly. When he was finished, his fingers were steady again.

'Niigata hasn't forgotten how to make tea,' he said softly, and Nicholas gave him a small smile.

'Niigata escaped from Floating City, so it's logical to assume that he knows a way in.' Nicholas took the empty cup from Tachi. 'You'll get your chance now.'

Tachi nodded wordlessly as Niigata returned, and they began the last phase of the interview.

They left Niigata as they had found him, silhouetted in the open doorway, but to Nicholas he seemed more frail, as if the sickness were aging him at an impossibly rapid rate. He was not far wrong. Niigata estimated that he had outlived normal expectancy. 'Every morning when I open my eyes,' he told them, 'it is a surprise, and not always a pleasant one.' He did not have to go into the particulars of his somatic breakdown.

Outside, the cryptomeria swayed to the vagaries of the evening breeze. It had turned cold, and they hurried down the path toward the distant lights of the shrine compound, which glowed intermittently through the forest. At night, they were even more aware of the depth of the valley. The black hillsides loomed over them with a far different feeling from the one they had in the benign twilight.

Perhaps it was what they had learned from Niigata that chilled them so, but both were sober and uncommunicative as they reached the small clearing beyond which was the bridge to the shrine. The shrine itself was deserted, the corners of the red-lacquered wood structures burnished with light from hanging lanterns.

Still, the moonlight was strong, and as they moved forward it seemed to shimmer, rising up from the damp ground as if with a life of its own. It swirled in the night like mist, coalescing around a central point so that it seemed about to take on a specific shape before collapsing back on itself.

In the far distance, Nicholas heard a rhythm at once familiar and new. The heat of it fired his blood. He turned to see Tachi staring at him, and now he heard the beating at *kokoro*, the ancient magic of Tau-tau causing the transformation of thought into deed.

It was *koryoku*, the Illuminating Power, the sole path to Shuken.

'Open your mind, Nicholas,' Tachi whispered. 'Here is everything you've wanted. Here is *koryoku*.'

So close to his dream Nicholas hesitated. Could he trust Tachi this far? If he opened his mind, he would be vulnerable to a psychic attack by Tachi. But if he did not take the chance, then the threat of the Kshira teaching in his mind increased exponentially. He had no choice.

He drew his essence inward toward *kokoro*, the cosmic membrane, and he began the ancient rhythms of Tau-tau. The cryptomeria forest exploded into columns of smoke, obscuring the moonlight. The world canted over on its side as the present slipped out of focus, loosed from the yoke of time. Now he dwelled in the ether of magic where horizons were unknown and arbitrary man-made laws ceased to exist. Only the cosmos swelled and breathed all around him like a gigantic engine.

He became aware of another psychic presence on the opposite side of the glittering column of light. Tachi.

Koryoku stood between them like a charismatic lodestone toward which they both moved. The danger increased as both men approached the central column of light. Nicholas's mind was open wide. He could feel Tachi's essence and get a sense of its texture but not its substance. If Tachi was his secret enemy, this would be a perfect place to ambush Nicholas, now when he was engrossed in *koryoku*, dazzled by it, when his psychic defenses were folded away to allow the lesson of the Illuminating Power to flow through him.

He felt a ripple outside time, like a loop completing itself, and he once more experienced *shicho*, that peculiar and remarkable current of thought emanating from Tachi.

Now both men were so close to the coruscating column of light that Nicholas could see Tachi's face through it, illuminated by it, transfigured by it. He felt the other man's urging, and he reached out with his mind. Closer and closer he came to the glittering, mysterious column until he could sense the surge of ionized particles, feel the prickling sensation of their excitation on the surface of his mind.

Then something curious happened.

Nicholas heard Tachi in his mind.

I can't, Tachi said.

Can't what?

For an instant, the image of Tachi behind the column of light winked out and Nicholas sensed he was alone in Tau-tau. Then Tachi re-emerged into the light thrown off by *koryoku*.

Tachi, what is it?

401

Something . . . I don't know . . . There was an odd look on his face. *The Kshira is so strong . . .*

My Kshira? Nicholas thought. *Is my Kshira so strong it won't allow me to reach* koryoku? What else could Tachi mean?

Then Tachi's presence winked out again and Nicholas knew he was not coming back. He took one last lingering look at the column of light. Without Tachi's presence it was already beginning to break up, swirling ever more slowly like an engine without an energy source, and Nicholas pulled himself out of Tau-tau.

He found himself back near the shrine. He looked around.

Tachi was crossing over the bridge to the shrine, but he was not headed for the steep stairs that would take him back to the village. Nicholas was crossing the bridge after him when he heard a sharp sound coming from the nearest of the shrine buildings to their right.

He paused, peering into the lantern-lit gloom, but could see nothing.

Tachi had already entered the shrine.

'Tachi!'

'There's someone here.' Tachi's voice was breathless.

'It's just a priest or the caretaker.'

But Tachi shook his head. 'It's someone who does not belong here.'

He disappeared around a corner and Nicholas went over the bridge after him. The interior of the shrine was open, as was the custom. There were small covered areas, and a sacred fountain in the shape of the coiled serpent Noten O-kami. A small bamboo ladle lay along the stone basin, and it was this simple symbol of purity that Nicholas would remember long after that night was over.

'Tachi,' Nicholas said again. He caught sight of the *oyabun* in an open field facing the last building in which stood a series of stone statues of the venerable priests who founded this shrine centuries ago. They were set into the steep forested hillside into which the stone steps had been laboriously cut.

'Here!' Tachi said, pointing to a gap between two of the statues. He took a step up the slope, then abruptly spun around. What at first appeared to be a black rope arced out from him, his arms were flung wide, and he hit the ground.

Nicholas was already more than halfway to him. He saw, as he approached, the fletched end of the steel bolt that had pierced Tachi's heart. And along the sward, the black rope draped, a long, thick line of Tachi's blood.

'Tachi!'

He knelt beside the *oyabun*, put his hand to the side of his head. Tachi's eyes were open, an expression in them somewhere between surprise and outrage.

'What did you see?' Nicholas whispered, but Tachi was past hearing anything. *Shicho*, the current of thought that had run between them, had been severed, and he felt its absence like the loss of a hand.

Nicholas rose, leaping over the dead *oyabun* and, grasping the rough, lichen-studded surface of one of the statues, leapt upward into the first line of trees. He raced silently through the thickets of the forest, listening to the immediate environment as he went. A full moon rode in a sky rid at last of the mist of the day, and its light cast everything in an eerie chiaroscuro.

His ears detected a small sound, then a series, like leather struck against stone, and he changed direction, sprinting in an oblique direction to his left, toward the stone steps. His stride lengthened and his blood pumped. It felt good to rise to motion after the long hours inside Niigata's stupefying catafalque.

He could see the line of stone steps now, gleaming as

whitely as bones – Niigata's scantily covered bones – in the milky werelight.

Someone was on them, running upward, and he changed direction again, paralleling them, keeping to the shadows of the cryptomeria. It was difficult going; much of the hillside was scree, friable rock thickly carpeted with gnarled roots, lichen and moss, treacherous underfoot.

Where the stairs turned forty-five degrees and the massive bronze image of Yoshitsune's sword rose from its stone bed, he broke cover, coming obliquely toward the running figure. He could see that the lightweight titanium and boron hunting crossbow was loaded with another steel bolt. It was leveled at him, but as he approached, the figure dropped the weapon to its side. The next moment, it moved again, this time into a patch of moonlight, and Nicholas saw the face. He almost stumbled as he came up short on the steep, rocky slope of the hillside.

Seiko!

'Christ, what have you done?'

'He was poison,' she managed between teeth clenched in rage. Her eyes were darting this way and that. 'He would have destroyed everything.'

'You're wrong, he –'

'He would have taken you away!' she shouted, and lifted the crossbow.

Nicholas whirled and, with his muscles popping, wrenched the bronze sword from its stone. The sharp edges of the carved flames shone weirdly in the moonlight, making it seem as if they were real, flickering over the blade.

Seiko screamed and let fly the bolt.

Nicholas leapt, but she was not aiming at him. The bolt smashed into the thin layer of rock on which he was standing and, with the weight of the gigantic sword, he came down awkwardly on a mixture of stone shards and upturned earth that was already sliding down the steep slope.

He tried to grab onto a tree or an outcropping, but there was no immediate handhold, and he felt himself sliding down into the blackness of the valley as she, still striped in moonlight, dashed upward through the forest and away.

He kicked out, felt a gnarled root slam into his ankle, and immediately he bent his leg. The root held and he hung upside down, dizzy from momentum for a moment, before he plunged the tip of the sword into the side of the steep hill. He carefully unhooked his ankle. The sword held his weight. He swung up on it, reaching with his right foot for a sharp outcropping of rock. He gained purchase, balanced his weight, and let go of the sword.

Then he was scrambling back up the hill, scuttling on all fours to increase his speed and to keep himself in the shadows. He could feel her, knew the moment she paused, turning to look back down into the darkness of the forested valley, thinking of him.

That was enough for him to overtake her. He meant nothing more than to pin her to the ground, to question her, but he came out of the darkness with such appalling speed that she gasped. The crossbow came up, its metal bolt gleaming dully in the moonlight. 'Go ahead. Shoot me like you shot Tachi.'

She bit her lip, shook her head violently. 'You don't understand.'

'Why did you kill him?'

'He would have killed you,' she said softly.

'So you said, but I don't believe you. You were jealous of him because of the link he and I established. It left you out.'

'What does it matter what I say? You don't even have

to open your mouth; I can feel how your heart has turned to stone.'

What could he say when she knew the truth? Lying to her would be infinitely more cruel than his silence.

'Now I know I was fooling myself. Whatever we had came from me; whatever we had was an illusion.'

'Is that what you think?'

'It's what I *know*!' A tear leaked from her eye, then, gaining control of herself, she wiped it away.

'What do you care anyway? You're not interested in me.' She shook her head. 'That damn psychic link made you vulnerable. I could see you were suspicious, but then that link drew you to him.'

'You're wrong about Tachi. He was a friend –'

'Is that what you think?' She gave him a lopsided smile. 'I didn't send for Tachi, he came to me. He was sent by someone who wanted you dead.' She saw his expression. 'Don't believe me? Tachi was ambitious, but he was in a vulnerable position. He was appointed head of the Yamauchi clan as a kind of compromise. Because Tomoo Kozo had been a member of the Kaisho's inner council, the two remaining council *oyabun*, Akira Chosa and Tetsuo Akinaga, had to approve the third member. Tachi was the only one both would vote for.

'So you see Tachi had no real power base. His *oyabun* mentor was from a Yamauchi subfamily in Kumamoto, powerful there but without real consequence in Tokyo. I told you Tachi was ambitious, perhaps overly so. When an alliance with another, older *oyabun* was offered, he took it, no questions asked. He knew he might be signing away his clan's autonomy, but with his hubris he hoped to rectify that before it got out of hand. But first he had to destroy you.'

Nicholas looked at her for a long time. She had emerged like a downy duck from an evilly spotted egg. The layers of personality were peeling off her like slices of an onion, but with every revelation there seemed more about her he did not understand. In a sense, he seemed to be looking back through time's terrible telescope at his dead wife, Justine. They had fallen in love without ever coming to understand one another. He did not love Seiko in any traditional sense. But they had shared something so intimate and ephemeral that it eluded most lovers. He was determined not to make the same mistakes with this woman that he had made with Justine. Judging her too quickly or too narrowly was a start down a delusive and dangerous path he was not now willing to take.

'Assuming this is the truth,' he said slowly, 'why are you telling me now – instead of when we first met in Saigon?'

'Because at long last self-interest has murdered morality. I told you I owed Tachi an enormous debt. He saved me from myself. I was in danger of imploding – of falling into myself, of being lost in someone else's image of me.'

'Your father's?'

'Or my mother's or my boyfriends' . . .' Her gaze brushed his, bounced off as if burned. 'But why make a litany of it? There were so many. Tachi was the last, and there was some good in him. I could . . . sense it. But it was so deeply buried, so twisted in the mire of self-interest it was almost dead. I was good, then, at recognizing the almost dead.'

'So you were bound to Tachi.'

'Body and soul.' She was fighting not to cry. 'But not heart. At great personal cost I kept that free.' She looked up at him. 'For you.'

Her psychic aura, in the guise of heightened intuition, had made her vulnerable to suggestion and abuse. It had amplified her sense of her environment and those in it. *There was some good in him. I could sense it*, she had

407

said of Tachi. It was what had compelled her to seek an extreme non-traditional path, what had brought her to Nicholas.

He moved toward her, wanting to take the crossbow from her. 'Seiko –'

'Leave me alone!' she screamed, taking a stumbling step backward. 'I know you too well. You cannot forgive me for saving you from Tachi. You think my jealousy blinded me; you think that the precious gift you two shared would have been enough to change him. You're wrong. He was above all else a pragmatist. He was nothing without that deal. He would have found his chance and he would have murdered you.' She brandished the crossbow. 'I hate you for your righteousness, for not understanding that there are so many shades of gray between black and white.'

Nicholas leapt upward, knocking the weapon aside. It flew out of her hand, striking the ground butt first, and with a thick *twang!* the bolt was loosed.

It pierced Seiko at almost point-blank range, the force of its entry lifting her off her feet, pinning her to an enormous cryptomeria. Her eyes opened wide in pain, and her hands held the end of the bolt where it protruded from her stomach.

Nicholas, gaining the high ground of the path, could see the situation at once. He could not loose the bolt without her bleeding to death within seconds.

'Seiko.'

She shook her head mutely. Tears stood out in the corners of her eyes. Her chest was heaving and her mouth was filling with blood. He could not bear to see her suffering. Grasping the haft of the bolt, he jerked it free of the tree and of her. With a gasp, she collapsed.

He held her, and she did not try to push him away. He pressed his hand over the wound, but with his *tanjian* eye he could feel the life leaving her. With her psychic sensitivity she knew it too.

'Hold on. I'll get you to a hospital.'

'No. Don't lie to me. Not now. Not ever.'

'No lies.' He brushed a strand of hair from her damp cheek. Her eyes closed for a moment, and he bent down, kissed her gently on the lips. Her lids fluttered open.

She stared up at him and, at last, her eyes focused. What had she seen in that moment before she saw him?

'Nicholas,' she whispered. 'Go see my father. He'll tell you what you need to know.'

She was fighting to hold on. Her head lay on his shoulder as if they were simply lovers, sharing an intimate moment beneath the stars. Her eyes dulled over and she began to pant heavily. Her eyes closed and her lips parted.

'Remember me, that's all I ask.'

Down in the Dead Zone

Man must sit in chair
with mouth open for
very long time
before roast duck fly in.

Chinese Proverb

Tokyo

SUMMER 1947

'I think I've found our man,' Mikio Okami said.

'Really?' Colonel Denis Linnear looked up from his mass of paperwork from which, it seemed, he was as loath to part as Okami would be from a lover's arms. The Colonel rarely slept these days and only occasionally returned to his bed, as if home had become a vacation spot to visit now and again.

'Yes.' Okami nodded. 'He's perfect.'

'No one's perfect. Least of all a potential murderer.'

The Colonel sat back in his chair, loaded his pipe as he watched Okami move nervously around the small, stuffy room. It was early summer, but already stiflingly hot. If this heat kept up, he shuddered to think what Tokyo would be like in August.

'Let's take a walk,' the Colonel said, firing up his pipe.

Outside, Tokyo was a morass of destruction. Entire sections of the city would have to be rebuilt from the foundation up, and some felt the past had been incinerated along with lives and property. The economy was shaky, inflation was running rampant, and the Communists were on the rise – all destabilizing elements that made the country ripe for lawlessness.

The Colonel knew he and Okami were running out of time. Major General Charles Willoughby and his group were busy debriefing the cream of Japan's military generals, men whom they had saved from the war crimes tribunals in order to 'train' them as American spies and

413

to head up a new rearmed Japanese army that would become America's watchdog against the spread of Communism in the Pacific.

The Colonel was absolutely certain that this fascistic plan would bring ruin on a Japan struggling for economic survival and redefinition in the postwar world, and diplomatic and public relations nightmares to a United States already under the gun for unleashing two atomic bombs on its former enemy. A country that could hardly put rice on the table could ill afford the onerous expenditures rearmament would incur.

'All right,' he said at length, 'who's our pigeon?'

'Tokino Kaeda. He's a key man in the Yamauchi clan, an under-*oyabun* whose ruthlessness and ambition have of late made him Katsuodo Kozo's favorite.' Okami stopped, bought a bag of sweets from a street vendor. 'His ambition makes him both approachable and reliable.' Okami shrugged. 'Power over honor. This, I fear, is to be the nature of the new world you have brought us.'

'Yes, the world has changed irrevocably,' the Colonel said thoughtfully. 'It's too bad you lot came down on the wrong side of the war. Who is to blame for this wreckage?' They turned a corner, went down the street toward the Sumida River. 'But now is not the time for bitterness or recriminations. We must look to the future in order to make the present secure. I am convinced that the future of the world's commerce lies here in the Pacific. Between Japan and China, we have the collective will and the sheer population to create economic miracles. We've made it our mission, Okami-san, to ensure that Japan, at least, gets a chance. Life from the ashes of defeat, eh?'

They reached the bank of the river, which was slung like a boa around the shoulders of an insolent woman. Tokyo was that woman, maimed, violated and starving.

But at least she was still on her feet, and recovering from the worst of her wounds.

'Katsuodo is our first obstacle.' Okami leaned against the black iron railing, staring into the brown, sluggish water. 'He's dead set against any Yakuza involvement with the Americans. It's his belief that the Occupation command is using us as a shield to do the dirty work the American military prefer not to do themselves.'

'He's right, in a way. But it's myopic thinking. The Yakuza have as much to fear from Communist incursions into Japan as the Americans do. Why shouldn't they crack a few heads in public for the Americans? They're being paid handsomely for what they do so well anyway.'

Okami grunted. 'Dismiss what Katsuodo says. He's *oyabun* of the Yamauchi clan and he fears my power. Don't forget that I was the one who brought him to power. Now I see what a mistake that was. He's using this issue as a dye marker to test the waters. Which *oyabun* will side with me, which with him? This is why he's been so intractable in his position against us. And now, to further his cause of total isolationism, he's instigated incidents of violence between the clans. We can't afford this kind of divisive behavior. This is just the kind of situation Japan was in at the end of the sixteenth century when Iyeyasu Tokugawa came to power as shogun. If only we had a modern-day shogun to unite all the *oyabun* and keep them under control.'

The Colonel sucked on his pipe. 'An interesting idea, my friend. But, as yet, no one *oyabun* could command such allegiance.' He blew out a cloud of smoke, watched it dissipate along the riverbank. 'But as for the future . . .' He seemed intrigued by this notion. After a time, he said, 'You know, even the rumor of such a person would enhance the Yakuza status. That might be helpful to all of us.'

Once more Okami was dazzled by the Colonel's ability to take a simple idea and spin it out to its ultimate potential. In this way, he was truly able to make wheat into gold.

The Colonel reversed his pipe, knocked the dottle out of the bowl. 'Food for thought. But for now let's return to the problem at hand.'

'Katsuodo must be dissuaded, permanently,' Okami said. 'That's where Tokino Kaeda comes in. He's guaranteed me a foolproof method for Katsuodo's demise. It seems the *oyabun* can't swim. This is a closely guarded secret, but of course as Katsuodo's most trusted under-*oyabun*, Kaeda is privy to the information. A week from now Katsuodo's body will be found floating here in the Sumida, and we can get on with dealing with Willoughby and his cabal of war criminals.'

The Colonel nodded, reloading his pipe. Okami watched him from the corner of his eyes, wondering what was flashing through that magnificent brain. He had to admit, much as he tried, he could never quite keep up with the Colonel's mind. If he had chosen to play chess, Okami had no doubt he would have been champion grandmaster. His thoughts unspooled so many jumps ahead, they often made Okami dizzy. Okami had learned more from this one man than he had from all his teachers, tutors and *sensei*. The Colonel had an organic grasp of life in all its infinite varieties that bordered on the simple, ultimate truths of Shinto.

The man was stark, sometimes almost dour. There were bouts of levity, to be sure, but to Okami they seemed as carefully measured as the rationed food of a prisoner. It was as if the Colonel felt the entire weight of the new world upon his shoulders, a new world, Okami knew, it was his one burning desire to create. For, above all else, Colonel Linnear was an architect of dreams. His vision of what Japan would some day

416

become filled Okami's mind like the patterns of a kaleidoscope, and in those shifting designs Okami could see his empire expanding outward like waves in the Pacific, farther and farther until they encompassed the entire ocean.

Okami dipped into his paper bag, shoved a handful of soybean sweets into his mouth, letting them dissolve slowly. Better the sugar hit than the overindulgence of alcohol, which, the Colonel had pointed out, was slowly killing him. 'Shall I give Kaeda the word tonight?'

'Wait,' the Colonel said unexpectedly. 'I want to have a word with Katsuodo Kozo first.'

'What for?'

'I want to be certain that Kozo needs us and not merely a new tailor, that termination is our only viable option.'

Okami shoved more sweets into his mouth. 'Perhaps it's just as well. Katsuodo despises all Westerners. He'll be condemned by his own mouth.'

The Colonel presented himself at the home of Katsuodo Kozo the following afternoon. It was an impressive-looking walled compound on the outskirts of the city that sheltered four buildings, the main structure for Katsuodo and his family, the others for his bodyguards, advisers and the families of his two sisters.

The *oyabun* kept the Colonel waiting alone and without food or drink in a stark anteroom for almost an hour, an unforgivable breach of propriety. Except that the Colonel wasn't Japanese; as a barbarian he warranted none of the courtesies that were prerequisites for civilized men.

The Colonel did not mind; he was used to being treated this way by Japanese who did not know him or, perhaps, knew him too well. He used the time to peer out of the anteroom's windows at the compound,

417

taking the measure of it and, by extension, of Katsuodo and the clan he headed.

The Yamauchi had been a thorn in his side for some time. Like the industrial *zaibatsu* of Japan's prewar society, the Yamauchi had been on an expansionist course for almost all their history. Their *oyabun* seemed spun from the same cloth. They were arrogant men, confident in their course, secure in their power, and greedy for more of everything. They encouraged in their clan an extreme isolation that engendered in the already disenfranchised Yakuza a feeling of seeming invulnerability. If one did not belong to society, then its laws had no dominion.

'Searching for breaches in my defenses?'

The Colonel turned to contemplate Katsuodo Kozo. He had a face like a skull with the skin drawn tightly over occipital and malar ridges. His eyes were those of a man long in high fever, unnaturally bright with paranoid conjecture.

'Spoken like a true daimyo,' the Colonel said with a hint of amusement. It was clearly the wrong tack to take with Katsuodo, though he doubted there was a tack that would be right.

'I am no feudal samurai lord,' Katsuodo said with a ramrod-straight back maintained by smoldering indignation. 'I have none of the perquisites of caste that a samurai had by matter of birthright. Whatever status I possess I forged in the furnace of my own will.' He removed his slippers, shoved his feet into street shoes that had to be worn on the cool stone floor of the anteroom because it was not yet a true part of the house and, as such, was unclean. 'Not that my position means much of anything to the world at large. What prominence I may have stolen is like a unique work of art: I cannot display it beyond a small circle of like-minded individuals.'

'What did you expect? You're a criminal.'

A small smile crept across Katsuodo's skull-like visage. 'Correct me if I have it wrong, but aren't some of your closest acquaintances criminals?'

'My job requires me to liaise with every level of Japanese society.'

Katsuodo nodded. 'Still, it appears as if you've developed an undeniable fondness for what you have termed the criminal class.'

It was clear, at this point, that Katsuodo was not going to invite the Colonel into his house proper, but meant to keep him marooned in this no-man's-land room that served as a kind of bridge between the world outside and Katsuodo's private domain.

'You don't care for the work I do with Okami-san.'

Katsuodo laughed, baring yellow teeth. 'Is that what you call the vile mischief you and Okami are up to? It's a disgrace, Yakuza working with the Occupation forces. My stomach heaves just to have you this close to me. I ask you now to leave before violence occurs.'

'There will be no violence,' the Colonel said in as even a tone as he could muster.

'Good.' Katsuodo turned his back on him. 'Then we have nothing more to say to one another.'

'There is one more thing,' the Colonel said as Katsuodo was about to go through the sliding fusuma to the interior of his house. He waited until the *oyabun* turned around. There was no expression on his face; he might already have been dead.

'What Okami and I are doing is for the benefit of everyone – even you. That is why I have come here: to ask you to join us. We would both benefit from your insight and your wisdom.' Silence. His image had already faded from Katsuodo's eyes. 'You seek to stop us, but I assure you it is like trying to change the course of a mighty river by building a dam out of matchsticks.

It cannot be done. My work will outlive all of us; there is nothing you or anyone else can do to stop it.'

Katsuodo turned and, without a word, disappeared beyond the fusuma. The Colonel, left alone in the stone-floored anteroom, stared down at his shoes. He required some time to cool his boiling blood. The man was precisely as Okami had described him: infuriating in his adamantine resolve to dismantle the partnership that the Colonel had spent so much time in nurturing. The Colonel, looking into his reflection in his spit-polished shoes, could already read Katsuodo's fate as if he were a seer in a sacred trance. And, in a way, this was what he was.

At last he roused himself and, moving across the stone floor, sought to leave this place as quickly as he could. Already the scent of blood was in the air.

While the Colonel was trying to make peace, Okami was preparing to go to war. Major General Willoughby, who had earned the epithet 'the Little Fascist', was obsessed with the Communist threat in Japan. To that end, he had proposed to turn his Gang of Fifteen into the nucleus of an indigenous anti-Communist military. He was training Lieutenant General Arisue, former chief of military intelligence for the General Staff, to head up a contingent of his former officers within G-2, the American intelligence arm. Willoughby had buried his protégés in the historical section where, Okami had hard evidence, they were already reporting on Soviet troop movements in the area. In a mind-boggling display of putting the tiger in with the hens, Willoughby had placed another notorious war criminal, Colonel Hattori, in charge of local military demobilization. Hattori promptly returned the favor by saving his cronies from the war crimes ax. When and if Willoughby got his sorely wished for go-ahead for remobilizing the

Japanese military to act as an American puppet force, Hattori would oversee it.

Willoughby's actions were offensive to Okami on several counts. Besides not buying into Willoughby's Communist-under-every-doormat theory, he had no wish to see his country kept on America's short leash, which rearmament would surely accomplish. Also, as the Colonel correctly pointed out, the cost for startup and maintenance of a significant military force would undermine everything the Colonel had been working toward: a viable economy, free of high inflation, that would get Japan back on its feet.

But, if the truth be known, Okami had another compelling reason for wanting Willoughby's plan to fail. He held a grudge against a number of the Gang of Fifteen for their despicable orders during the last days of the war. Their treatment of the men under their command was abysmal, and a number of Okami's friends had suffered. Also, his brother had died.

Okami preferred not to think of his brother, who had died before he could experience the full flower of life. Some excused his death as being part of the caprice of war, but Okami was not fooled. He knew who was responsible for his brother's death and, though those people were currently under Willoughby's aegis, he had devised a plan to destroy them.

This he decided to do without the Colonel's help. For one thing, the Colonel had been inexplicably dragging his feet on the Gang of Fifteen situation. Despite daily reminders from Okami, he had yet to act. Lately, these reminders had degenerated into heated arguments that left Okami feeling frustrated, if not betrayed.

'Try being Japanese,' the Colonel had said heatedly. 'Be patient. There are many strands to this web. Let them play out in their own time.'

'I *have* no time,' Okami had said, matching heat for

heat. 'This is *my* country. Until you've walked in my shoes, you've no right to tell me how to act.'

Though he could understand the Colonel's need for caution – he was working within the confines of SCAP, where Willoughby currently wielded a great deal of power – Okami's burning desire for revenge required him to find his own path.

That he had done. With the Colonel's attention directed elsewhere Okami was left with only one source. He had spent many weeks examining the dire nature of the gamble he was being forced to take.

He would have to deal with the Communists.

If they were somehow to gain knowledge of the fifteen war criminals that Willoughby had saved from the tribunals, he knew exactly what would happen. The Russians were animals; they were big on primary responses, and on that level they were vicious. Diplomacy was a game they could only stumble through as ineptly as children.

He was aware that Soviet agents abounded in Tokyo, some of them in higher places than the Occupation command could imagine. If these people were to come into possession of the right intelligence, he had no doubt they could penetrate Willoughby's safeguards, especially if they were given a bit of clandestine help.

Yes, it would be fitting for the Communists to become the unwitting tool of my revenge, Okami had thought as he awoke on the morning the Colonel went to see Katsuodo Kozo. *Let them kill Willoughby's Gang of Fifteen and in the process avenge the deaths of my brother and my friends*.

But of course he had to sell it with the proper motivation. The Communists would know him so ideology was out. But money wasn't. Yakuza could be notoriously mercenary when the spirit or necessity moved them. To this end he began to spend his late-night hours in a sleazy bar where his informants had assured him

Communist agents hung out. He made a great show of getting drunk and then talking with a loose tongue, bragging to anyone who would listen that he knew about an American plot to harbor war criminals.

Eventually, a rat come sniffing around. Okami, who could be subtle when the need arose, had deliberately cut a wide swath through the bar. Subtlety was not the Soviets' strong suit.

One night a lithe, slight-shouldered Japanese man sat down next to him at the bar and said, 'I understand you and I have a similar point of view.'

'Is that so?'

'Maybe not. But it has come to my attention that you have information I could use.'

'I think I hear the rustle of money.'

'In that you may not be wrong. I have a grudge to settle with some wartime officers. I can use your help.'

Okami grunted. 'That depends on whether the rustle is far off or close at hand.'

'I assure you it's very close indeed. Tell me, friend, how did you come by this information about the Americans?'

Okami finished his Scotch, ordered another. 'It's none of your business.'

'It is. It's going to be my money.'

Okami regarded the man without seeming to try to size him up. 'I have my thumb squarely on the SCAP adjutant Jack Donnough,' he half-lied. 'What's it to you?'

'You're spraying this all over the place. Do you think that's wise?'

'Who cares?' Okami downed his Scotch and ordered another all in one motion.

'I do, for one.'

Okami cocked his head. 'And you are?'

'A friend of yours . . . maybe.'

Okami nodded. 'Okay, friend. Have a drink on me.' He gestured to the bartender, and when the other man had gotten his drink, they went to a vacant booth in the rear of the bar. Of course, it really didn't matter where they went, Okami's people were all around.

He knew the Communists' tactics. They would try to trap him. It wasn't enough for them simply to trade intelligence for money; they'd insist on their pound of flesh – a sword to hold over his head so that they would be able to control him forever afterward. It was sad as well as frightening, Okami thought as he slipped into the booth opposite the contact. This was how the Communists treated their own people, it was how their ideology had become as intractable as iron.

The man's name was Iwanushi. He was a factory worker, but more importantly he was a ranking member of Shin'ei Kinrō Taishūtō, the most virulent of the reactionary groups allying themselves with the nascent labor movement. Uncontrollable inflation, high unemployment, the Yoshida administration's unstemmed corruption and seeming inertia in trying to overcome Japan's postwar economic woes, the populace's general perception that SCAP's promises of a better life through democracy was a lie – all this was a highly flammable mix. It was tailor-made for Communist infiltration at the worker level, where frustration was at high tide. The Soviets were adept at using unionists and reactionary elements such as Iwanushi's organization as stalking horses to further their own ends. It was another example of how they used their obdurate ideology as a whip to exhort their disciples into what they so quaintly – and misleadingly – called 'revolutionary fervor'.

Iwanushi was typical of his kind: browbeaten, self-righteous, impatient, smug in the security that Socialism was the key to a new and better world, if only he were in power. But, as Okami knew, the Iwanushis of the world would never be allowed to gain power. Either the forces they sought to bring down would disperse them or the masters who controlled them now would continue to do so in a new world order. The simple fact was that people like Iwanushi had no clear idea of their own policy once the old guard was disposed of. And, of course, this was just how the Communists had planned it, because they were ready, willing and all too eager to impose the Communist way of life on Japan.

Okami did not hate Iwanushi; he pitied him. Someone had to. Neither the Communists nor the Yoshida government was in the least interested in the personal plight that had driven him into poverty and anger.

'You are Yakuza,' Iwanushi said when they had settled themselves. 'You are a collaborator working with SCAP. You are an enemy of the people so please do not expect me to be sympathetic. Information for money. I wish to engage in a simple business arrangement.'

Knowing this would be anything but simple, Okami said, 'I commend you for volunteering to get your hands dirty, comrade.'

Iwanushi gave him a hard look. 'I wish I had your ability at levity. You who live like a shogun cannot know our hard life. Try not to judge us.'

'It seems to me that a bit of levity would do you a world of good. It would help you step back and evaluate your situation.'

'Food is my situation or, rather, the lack of it. Also, a job. While you get rich and fat in the black market, my family and countless others like mine starve. This is how today looks from my perspective. Is it any wonder that I am fixated on making tomorrow better?'

'Better for whom? Your family or the Communists?'

'It's one and the same,' Iwanushi said with such conviction that Okami knew he had him.

*   *   *

425

The next evening Okami arrived unannounced at Iwanushi's house. He carried with him gifts of food and drink: fresh fruit, vegetables and fish that he knew were unavailable to the family. The place was tiny and ramshackle, a row house standing near enough the railroad tracks that the thin walls shook each time a train rushed past.

Iwanushi, glassy-eyed but polite, ushered him inside. It was just before the dinner hour and the entire family was home: Iwanushi's tiny graying wife and their three children. The place stank of boiled root vegetables.

Iwanushi bowed, accepting Okami's gifts mutely, but when he took them into the kitchen, Okami saw Iwanushi's wife throw them into the garbage. There was a brief argument. He heard her speaking in a hiss, could make out the word *shameful* and the awful epithet *futei*, which Prime Minister Yoshida had used to describe the unionists in a recently broadcast speech. The word meant 'subversive'.

When Iwanushi returned, he said, 'Perhaps we should go outside. The children must be fed and my wife cannot serve both us and them at the same time.'

'Yes, of course,' Okami said. 'It was thoughtless of me to come at this hour.'

'Not at all. We're used to inconvenience.'

Okami found himself unprepared for Iwanushi's implacable discourtesies, but he took them as object lessons. He felt it important that he understand what it was about these people that made them so vulnerable to the influence of a pipe dream like Socialism, which had no chance of survival in a world ruled by the human race. Humans were defined by the seven deadly sins. Only saints and ascetics could rise above those flaws, and some of those were themselves frauds. The territorial imperative was bred into humans as deeply as was their need for oxygen and water. The adjunct

426

to territory was the need for influence, status, power. Besides, there was always someone who was certain his way was better – or more righteous – than all the others, and though it had many faces, this was the sole seed of war.

'As you can see, we have nothing,' Iwanushi said. 'We need everything.'

Perhaps, Okami thought, this defined him as well as anything else. He was a have-not and, in a way, he reveled in his poverty, using it as both a club and a cloak to manufacture something out of nothing. In a strange way, Okami could relate to this, since as a Yakuza he had no status in the mainstream of society. Whatever prestige he maintained in his community was also formed out of nothing.

'Perhaps the government does not know this,' Okami said.

'I do not think that the government cares one way or another. They exist to feed one another and they are doing an admirable job of it. In times of prosperity their sins would go unnoticed because there would be enough to feed everyone, but now when starvation and unemployment squat like swordsmen of the Apocalypse astride Japan, they appear naked in their gluttony, greed and sloth.'

'You must be a Catholic to talk in such terms.'

'I have read my wife's texts, but what of it? There is no God in this world. Look around you. How could there be?'

Spoken like a true Communist, Okami thought. This was going to be a pleasure.

'Since it's clear we're not going to be the best of friends,' he said, 'I think it would be best if we consummated our transaction as quickly as possible.'

'That will suit me. What about tonight?'

'I don't know. I have a previous engagement.'

427

Iwanushi stared at him in that curiously defiant manner people who have nothing conjure up.

'All right. Tonight.' Okami wrote down an address on a slip of paper. 'Meet me here at midnight.'

Midnight came and Iwanushi arrived at the betting parlor. It was Yakuza-owned – in fact, Okami was the proprietor, but Iwanushi and his crowd wouldn't know that, no one did except the tightly knit Yakuza circle and the Colonel. Okami was playing *karuta* recklessly and losing. While Iwanushi looked on, rapt, Okami lost the equivalent of ten thousand dollars. He then proceeded to have a nasty altercation with the manager regarding his ability to pay the debt. When Iwanushi saw that Okami couldn't pay, his heart was warmed because he had been trained to look for just such vulnerabilities in his contacts. He now had his sword to hold over Okami's head.

'It looks like you need money more than I do,' Iwanushi said when Okami led him out into the street.

'I'll pay,' Okami said sourly. 'I always manage to find a way.'

'But you are Yakuza. You have power.'

'That man's *oyabun* has the power,' Okami lied, 'not me.'

'What a revelation! Even outlaws experience the inequities of the downtrodden.'

It took some effort for Okami not to laugh in the face of his naivety.

Iwanushi appeared to be sunk deep in thought for some time. At length, he said, 'What if I could guarantee you enough money to pay all your gambling debts and keep on going?'

Okami looked at him. 'That kind of sum would pay for a lot of food for you and your family.'

'Like power, money is an illusion. The future of mankind is more important,' Iwanushi said in the voice of

428

the true zealot. 'As a capitalist, you will be doomed with all the rest. My destiny is to help mankind on the proper path to a true classless society.'

'And paying me will do that?'

'In compensation, you will supply me with ongoing intelligence that Donnough provides to you as to the workings of the Gang of Fifteen and any other operation of significance the American SCAP forces are planning to put into action.'

Okami could see that Iwanushi had been a busy boy since the time they had first spoken in the bar. And his superiors had bitten. 'What kind of money are we talking about?'

'Ten thousand dollars a month,' Iwanushi said hopefully.

Okami laughed. 'You should go gambling with me more often. I go through that amount in a week.'

Iwanushi stood as firmly as he could. 'I would have to evaluate a sample of your intelligence. If it proved interesting enough, well, who knows? Ten thousand might be just the beginning.'

Okami was pleased. He now had confirmation that the Communists were directly handling Iwanushi. Only they would have deep enough pockets to provide this kind of monthly payout.

'Do you have the current intelligence on the Gang of Fifteen?' Iwanushi asked, his greed showing.

So much for utopia, Okami thought. 'I could gather it together tonight. I have it in memo form at home. A couple of days –'

'Do you think the man you owe will wait that long?'

'You're right. The sooner the better. Do you have the money?'

'I want to see the intelligence first.'

Okami took him to a small apartment in an affluent section of the city. Iwanushi goggled at how the other half lived, even in postwar Tokyo. Inside, Okami gathered the copies of the intelligence Donnough had provided, showed two of the juicier memos to Iwanushi, who devoured them, goggling some more.

'But this is infamous,' Iwanushi said, echoing Okami's own words to the Colonel. 'It is proof positive that all governments are the same. Saving these war criminals to use for their own ends while public war tribunals are making headlines is the height of hypocrisy. You see? This is what democracy has in store for us. More lies and deceit.'

Okami wished he had an adequate rebuttal to present, but the truth was in this instance he agreed with the Socialist. The world was awash in cynicism; only the Colonel's vision of the future provided Okami with any sense that what he did now would have some positive effect for all the tomorrows that stretched ahead of him. How eerily similar his yearnings were to those of Iwanushi. But he had no time to examine that particular phenomenon.

'Let me see more,' Iwanushi said.

'After I see the money.'

'I can't authorize payment until this has been evaluated and authenticated.'

'That wasn't our deal.'

Iwanushi shrugged. 'I may be poor, but I'm not stupid. If this material proves false, I'll have paid you for nothing.'

'All right. I'll give you half the material and you pay me half now. Then we can see if we can trust one another.'

Iwanushi nodded. 'That makes sense. I don't have to like you in order to trust you.'

Within forty-eight hours Iwanushi was back in touch with Okami. His handlers were elated with the material; they wanted to consummate the deal by exchanging money for the rest of the memos. This was what Okami had been waiting for. In among the remainder of the Donnough memos he had slipped one he had created that gave the location of the compound where the Gang of Fifteen was being housed. This was information Donnough would never have committed to paper, let alone delivered to a third party. The location came from another source entirely, and it had cost Okami plenty, not in cash or services but in the weight it had placed on his conscience.

He had discovered that Donnough's male secretary was a homosexual. He and his Japanese lover had shown up in one of Okami's late-night establishments that drew people from the soft underbelly of society like flypaper. Okami had only to show this man black-and-white photos of him and his lover entwined in several entertaining embraces for him to break down. Okami had seen numerous Japanese weeping in the throes of drinking bouts, but this was different. Looking at the naked back of this slender man, Okami saw in his mind the image of his mother, bent over his father, her hands literally filled with his blood as she tried to stanch the mephitic flow from multiple sword slashes.

This disturbing vision did not stop him from using the man to get what he wanted, but the incident did not pass from his memory as many more violent and traumatic events had done. Now it flashed again in his mind as if a spotlight had been cast upon a darkened stage. He could count the vertebrae, see the pale pink pigmentation, the mole on the left shoulder blade. He could smell blood.

'Was the man you owed content with half his money?' Iwanushi asked when they met.

'Content, no. But he's a realist. On the other hand, if I don't appear tonight with the remainder, I will be in big trouble.'

'Don't worry.' Iwanushi handed over a thick packet wrapped in rice paper. 'I am giving you your life back. Remember that if you ever think about selling your information elsewhere.'

Okami had no idea why but he felt compelled to follow Iwanushi back to his wood-and-plaster hovel beside the railroad tracks. He watched from the nighttime shadows as Iwanushi trudged to his front door and opened it. His tiny wife bowed to him and, though he came empty-handed into a house that had nothing, still she welcomed him with genuine respect and affection.

Okami stood in the darkness long after the door had closed and the lights had been extinguished. The stench of garbage and urine was very strong. A dog barked, presaging the passing of a train and, when it came, it rattled the row houses as if they were made of paper and wattle.

Ten days later, the headlines were splashed across the newspapers. A strong bomb blast had rocked a small residential section of the city that the SCAP forces had commandeered. Information was sketchy because the American military was involved but it seemed clear from preliminary reports that as many as twenty people had been killed, most of them Japanese nationals working for SCAP. Whether the explosion was an accident or had been the work of saboteurs was at the present time a matter for speculation.

Halfway through his breakfast of tofu and broiled fish Okami's phone rang. It was the Colonel.

'Have you heard the radio reports?' Colonel Linnear asked.

'No, but I'm reading the account in the paper now.'

'The Communists got to the Gang of Fifteen. It seems your problem's solved.'

Okami did not understand the tautness in the Colonel's

tone. 'If that is who was killed, you're right. It would make me happy.'

'How happy?'

'Excuse me, Linnear-san, but how do you know it was the Communists?'

'How do you know you've been bitten on the ass by a hornet?' the Colonel said tartly. 'Despite what you read in the papers, the blast was deliberately set beneath the buildings where the Gang of Fifteen lived. Our people are going through the rubble now, but they've already found enough to be certain of the signature. It was a Soviet-made bomb.'

'What is the problem with that?'

'Jesus Christ, are you dense this morning? Communists infiltrated a US government facility and murdered twenty people, five of them American guards. *That's* the fucking problem.'

Okami was silent.

In another tone entirely, the Colonel said, 'How did they know where the Gang of Fifteen was being housed?'

'Why are you asking me?'

'Was I? I was just thinking out loud.'

But Okami knew better. The Colonel had set a very clever trap for him and he had fallen into it.

'I want to see you tonight, Okami-san. My office. Midnight.'

The connection was abruptly severed. Okami did not care for the way in which the Colonel had spoken to him. On the other hand, he felt remorse for the five innocent guards who had been inadvertently killed. On further contemplation, knowing the Communists, perhaps it hadn't been inadvertent at all. Angry at himself, he shoved the remains of his breakfast away. Why hadn't he thought of this? He had been so smugly pleased with himself for having had the Communists

433

do his dirty work he hadn't considered the methods they would use. To be honest, it hadn't mattered to him. Vengeance was all that had been on his mind. Until now. He did not like having the deaths of five Americans on his conscience.

He went to see Iwanushi. Perhaps he wanted to protest, perhaps he meant to get the name of his Soviet handler. In retrospect, he was never sure.

He arrived at the row houses near dinnertime, when he was reasonably certain that Iwanushi would be home. He was less than a block away when he heard a low rumble on the street behind him. He turned, saw a convoy of US Army vehicles jouncing toward him. Pressed back into a darkened doorway, he was close enough to feel the martial stir of air as they passed.

They drew up in front of Iwanushi's house. Military police leapt out, their weapons at the ready. An officer rapped sharply on Iwanushi's door and, when he opened it, asked for his name. He gave it and the officer barked an order. Two of the MPs holstered their side-arms and smartly took possession of Iwanushi.

He shouted and squirmed as he was hustled toward one of the vehicles. A tiny figure appeared in the doorway. Seeing what was happening, Iwanushi's wife screamed and tried to rush to him. An MP restrained her.

She kept asking, 'Why are you taking him? Why? He's done nothing!'

'He's responsible for the deaths of twenty people, ma'am,' the officer said in abominable Japanese. 'Five of them were American soldiers. He's going to pay.'

'This can't be happening!' Iwanushi's wife wailed as tears streamed down her face. 'It's a nightmare!'

The officer did not answer. Perhaps he had not understood her. He climbed into the lead vehicle and the convoy pulled out, roaring over the dark streets, conducting Iwanushi to his destiny.

The office was filled with pipe smoke and agitation. Okami had felt it the moment he had entered. The Colonel, who had been pacing the floor like a caged tiger, had whirled as the door opened and he saw Okami.

'Well,' he said in the kind of strangled voice he used when he was busy stepping on his rage. Okami was not looking forward to the interview.

'Sit down, Okami-san.'

The Colonel spent some time knocking the dottle from his pipe, reaming it out and repacking it with tobacco. During this time he did not glance in Okami's direction. When he had it going, he took several deep breaths.

'This is the way it is,' he began. 'In three days' time Donnough was to deliver to MacArthur a packet of information that would incriminate Major General Willoughby, the führer of the Gang of Fifteen, so completely that MacArthur would have had no recourse but to move against Willoughby, and he would have done it willingly. He was beginning to see the mistake in hanging on to the Gang. Donnough and I were going to give him the ammunition to make Willoughby the scapegoat. Mac would have been out of it altogether, utterly blameless.'

'Can't you still go through with your plan?' In retrospect, the question was so thoughtless it was the second most serious mistake Okami made with the Colonel.

'You idiot!' Colonel Linnear thundered. 'This bombing has made Willoughby into something of a hero.' He towered over Okami like a god over a mortal. 'Of course Mac is relieved the potential public relations nightmare the Gang represented is a dead issue, but there's the

435

American servicemen to think of. Not to mention the fact that the Communists were so afraid of the Gang they decided to dispose of them. Don't you see, the Gang's violent death gives credence to Willoughby's raging paranoia about the Communist threat in Japan. His conservative position with Mac is stronger than ever. The movement to rearm Japan has got a shot in the arm, and you can be sure it will make our work that much more difficult.'

'But surely MacArthur hasn't bought into –'

'The fact is nobody knows how Mac feels about rearming Japan,' the Colonel said flatly. 'Especially now.'

Okami's heart was in his throat. Stupid, he thought. It had been just plain stupid to deal with the Communists himself. No. His stupidity was in losing faith with the Colonel. He vowed he would never do that again.

When he judged the dust had had time to settle, he said, 'The Americans have arrested a Japanese national for the murders.'

The Colonel's eyes blazed. 'So?'

'He didn't do it.'

'You mean he's innocent?'

How did this man know the right questions to ask every time? Okami wondered in awe. 'He's a Socialist. He works for the Communists, but believe me when I tell you he had nothing to do with the bombing.'

'Do you have proof I can bring to the provost marshal?'

'No, but . . .' Okami put his head down. 'No.'

The row houses were dark in the moonless night. It looked like death here, where nothing grew and even the trains did not stop. A mangy dog ran at Okami's heels as he stood, staring at the darkened windows of Iwanushi's house. It was a new feeling for him to be so

436

helpless. He listened to his heartbeat, the dog sniffing at his cuffs.

He crossed the street, knocked on the door, and a light came on almost immediately. He could imagine her, a tiny figure sitting in the dark, listening to the soft breathing of her children, wondering where her husband was.

The door was pulled open and she looked up at him with eyes wide with anxiety and terror. 'You! Have you news of my husband? Is he unhurt?'

'I have no news of Iwanushi-san.'

'Oh.' Her face collapsed.

'I've come to help.' He took a step toward her. 'I can –'

'Stay away! I want no part of you!' She spat at his feet. 'You are like an evil *kami*. You are a criminal, poison. You come into my husband's life and now the Americans have taken him. I warned him. I told him you would destroy us, but he said, "You are a woman, you know nothing of what I must do."' She glared at Okami like a demon out of a No play. Then her voice cracked and tears rolled down her cheeks. 'I know what I know. I will never see him again.' She slammed the door in Okami's face.

He stood in the darkness. The one light went out, a train rocketed by, shaking the walls of the row houses. He knocked on the door, but no one answered. In the ensuing silence he was sure he heard Iwanushi's wife sobbing. He looked around. Even the dog was gone.

After a very long time he turned and walked away.

BOOK IV: Dreams and Beasts

*Dreams and beasts are two
keys by which we find out
the keys to our own nature.*

Ralph Waldo Emerson

FOURTEEN

London/Tokyo/Saigon/Tien Giang

Morning mist clung to London's curbsides like the fingers of a mendicant. Croaker was at the 315 rendezvous site early. Holland Park stood at the western end of the city, not far from the larger Kensington Gardens. It was a relatively small park, but a beautifully planted space for all that.

Croaker had taken the tube to Holland Park station and, crossing Holland Park Avenue just west of Notting Hill Gate, had walked two short blocks, entering the park via the Rose Walk.

He spent some time in the Japanese garden, feeling nostalgic and wondering when he and Nicholas would meet up again. Four days until the ides; four days until Torch would be detonated. Not much time left. Nicholas had told him that he had corroboration that Torch was being manufactured in Floating City, that its target appeared to be Okami, and that he had been told by the dying Niigata that once it was in the target area, it would be impossible to trace. If Nicholas could not penetrate Floating City in time to prevent the delivery, a major disaster was imminent. It was imperative that they find out where Okami was and try to protect him; his enemies knew his approximate location, but Nicholas and Croaker did not.

From his present position Croaker could keep an eye on Bird Lawn where the rendezvous was to take place. It was now three minutes to noon.

Who had contacted Vesper? *He's going to want the update on Serman and I'm not going to be able to give it to him,* she had told Celeste. It must be someone very high up in the Nishiki network, perhaps even someone who had direct access to Okami. Also, Vesper had not been expecting it, so it was likely an emergency procedure. Crises always brought the big guns out of the woodwork. Perhaps, Croaker thought, luck is with me today. I'm close to the heart of Nishiki, I can sense it.

Nicholas was not the only person the Japanese garden reminded him of. He could not get Margarite out of his mind. Was everything he had believed about her false? He had known the dangers of falling for a woman who was, to all intents and purposes, on the other side of the law. But who could control love? Ever since he had followed her to Washington, Margarite had been set on a course for which he had been totally unprepared. How many lives did she lead? She was mother and wife in her family role with Tony D. and Francine; hidden within Tony D.'s shadow she was manipulating the reins of her late brother's underworld empire; she was Croaker's lover; and now she was involved with the Nishiki network, which had been compromised to its core by Vesper.

His mind filled with Margarite and Bad Clams' threat against her life, he saw Vesper striding toward Bird Lawn from the direction of the orangery. She was cloaked in a long, swingy coat rimmed in fur with a huge stand-up collar. She had on her head a fashionable take on the old Russian hat, which was also fur-trimmed. She walked with purpose and grace, her posture as erect as that of any graduate of a top finishing school. In her gait it was clear she held both power and femininity in the palm of her hand.

Her piercing cornflower-blue eyes quartered the area surrounding Bird Lawn with the precision of the seasoned professional, and this simple demonstration of tradecraft exposed a heretofore carefully hidden part of her: she was no amateur, no dilettante squandering her enormous intellect in playing vicious games to, say, subvert the traditional male-oriented playing field. She was deadly serious at everything to which she turned her hand, and he knew he must give careful consideration to her motives before he could devise a way of neutralizing her.

Then she turned her back to him, and he moved toward her, out of the Japanese garden, heading for Bird Lawn. Someone else was coming toward her, emerging from the direction of Holland House, just southeast of them.

Wrapped in a thick winter mackinaw, carrying an open umbrella, the figure was impossible to identify at this distance. He could see it was small – another woman, he surmised, until it came close enough for Vesper to break into a run, holding out her arms. She embraced the figure, wrapping her arms around it. The umbrella fell to the pavement, and Croaker, already very near Bird Lawn, could see the face.

He stood stock still, but a shot of adrenaline provided a massive jolt to his system. His mind was buzzing with the kind of terrifying electricity one experiences in the instant before elation or utter tragedy, because the person who had sent the unsigned message to Vesper, who was indeed high up in the Nishiki network, who was here now as undeniably alive as Croaker and Vesper, was the Kaisho, Mikio Okami.

'It's something of a miracle,' Dr Benwa said. 'Your cancer is in remission.'

Ushiba sat on the examining table, staring at the gaunt man with a white face and waxy skin in a green physician's smock. Dr Benwa represented something of a miracle himself. His withered right arm hung lifeless at his side. Benwa and his parents had been outside Hiroshima when the bomb was dropped. His parents had died and Benwa had been treated for radiation burns. The prognosis had been negative, but against all odds he had survived. It was as if his right arm had sacrificed itself so that the rest of the organism could live. Somehow, even as the radiation sickness had taken the flesh off his arm, he had walled it off from the rest of him. No doctor had an adequate theory as to how Benwa had survived, but here he was practicing oncological medicine.

'While this is undoubtedly good news, I don't want to give you false hope,' Dr Benwa said gravely. 'The human body is the world's greatest miracle. It is capable of surprising feats of heroism. But the fact is your condition could resume at any time. As I have told you, there has already been a great deal of organ damage that cannot be repaired. The malignant cells are still there, they haven't disappeared; right now for reasons we can't begin to understand, they're sleeping.'

As he dressed, Ushiba wondered whether the remission could in some way be related to his confession to Tanaka Gin. Had his vomiting up the litany of Akira Chosa's connections with Yoshinori provided a kind of catharsis that had flowed from his mind into his body? Ushiba was not a religious man, but he knew this was certainly possible. He had experienced the intimate mind-body alliance time and again through t'ai chi and meditation.

He went in to see Dr Benwa before he left the doctor's office. Benwa put aside a file in which he had been writing when Ushiba came in. He gestured.

'Sit down, Daijin.' He sat back, contemplating a spot on the wall over Ushiba's left shoulder. 'Tell me, how is it with you?'

Ushiba said nothing, waiting for the doctor to get to the point.

'As you know, we are doing everything medically possible.' He shrugged. 'But often that is not enough.' His eyes swung to Ushiba's face. 'Are you still alone, Ushiba-san? I am concerned, you see. There have been innumerable studies that prove that in serious illness as in old age loneliness can accelerate a terminal decline.'

'But I am in remission.'

'Yes. I am only offering you everything I can. I am incapable of doing less.'

'I can give no criticism of the care I have been receiving.'

Dr Benwa nodded his head. 'You are a great asset to this country, Daijin. Your death will make it the poorer. I have no wish —'

'Doctor . . .'

'Yes, yes, I know. I go beyond normal propriety.' He held up his withered arm. 'This, you see, has given me certain privileges. You cannot take offense; it would shame you.' He looked down at his cluttered desktop for a moment. 'Daijin, you are being treated by the most modern methods available. Forgive me, but what you need most now is love.'

'Well, Doctor, since we are being brutally frank with one another, I will confess that I am not sure that I would recognize it even if it was proposed.' Ushiba stood up. 'But to set your mind at ease I can report that I have been offered kindness. Much to my surprise I have accepted it.' He smiled thinly. 'Perhaps my disease is not such a terrible thing after all.'

It was twilight by the time he emerged from Dr Benwa's cave-like offices. The city rolled on around him, oblivious to his condition. He was all too aware of his increasing sense of isolation; the indifference of the world could be terrifying if he allowed himself to dwell upon it. In this sense, he knew the wisdom of Benwa's theory — his psychological state was important for his physical health.

Instead of climbing immediately into his car, he told his driver that he would walk for some time. He felt the need to be immersed in the river of humankind, to feel its press against his skin, to reduce the volume of empty space around him. It seemed to him as if he had been operating in a vacuum for months on end. His lofty position as chief minister of MITI was not the only factor in his daily isolation from life in the city; his position in the Godaishu removed him even further from society than did his official capacity.

This brief respite from having death's knife at his belly was proving surprising indeed. The clarity with which he saw his present position astonished him. He found himself wondering whether he and the rest of the Godaishu had any inkling of the world they so desperately wanted to control. What would they do once they achieved their goal of controlling international economic commerce? Would they gather in more money? More influence? More power? If so, what would it get them? How much money, influence and power was enough?

Walking the densely packed streets of his city, brushing against the people who daily pounded the pavement, took public transportation and struggled to pay their taxes, he became frightened. Not for them, but for himself and the other members of the Godaishu, because he sensed the answer to his question. Thinking of each individual in turn, he knew that no amount of money, influence or power would be enough to satisfy them. Was he included in their ranks? Surely, up until this moment, he had been. What did that make him? He closed his eyes, abruptly dizzy. He shuddered, invaded by his own private winter.

His eyes snapped open and he found himself staring into the curious face of a young woman holding her daughter's tiny hand.

'Are you ill, sir?'

'No. I'm entirely well, thank you.'

He left her behind, but he turned to watch her guide her daughter across the wide avenue. Her face was still in his mind. It was not an unusual face, but its very ordinariness moved him. He suddenly thought of Torch and of its implications. Torch would never have come to fruition without the Godaishu's assistance. And now the full horror of what they were perpetrating fell squarely upon his shoulders so that his stomach heaved and threatened to send whatever acids it contained rocketing into his throat.

We're mad, he thought. *All of us are quite insane.*

I've been foolish, Croaker thought. *How out of shape can I get? That sonuvabitch Bad Clams.* But it was his own fault. Bad Clams had warned him. *I got my eye on you*, he had said. *Just 'cause you're flying the pond don't mean I won't know where you go and what you do.*

Croaker had become aware of the man behind the newspaper just after Vesper and Mikio Okami had embraced. He would have spotted the tail sooner had he not been concentrating so on matching Okami with the images of the photos Nicholas had shown him before he had left Tokyo at the beginning of the year.

The tail had entered the Bird Lawn area from the direction of the Japanese garden, settling on a bench, opening a copy of *The Times*. Croaker could have kicked himself. Once he had ID'd Okami, he knew he had the last piece of the puzzle: Torch was going to be detonated in the heart of London.

Now Croaker was faced with a classic dilemma. He

447

had followed the Nishiki network back to its source; he had found Mikio Okami. But in the process he had led the opposition to its objective. His choice was to follow Okami back to his safe house and risk leading Bad Clams' man there or to deal with the tail now at the expense of losing Okami.

He had only one viable option.

As Okami and Vesper walked north out of Bird Lawn, Croaker strolled over to the bench where the man was sitting behind his newspaper.

'Howdy,' he said, sitting down next to the man.

The paper rustled, but there was no response. Croaker hooked a forefinger over the top of the paper, pulled it down. He found himself staring into the face of a sallow-skinned man with unnaturally black hair, thinning on top. He had quick, alert eyes that seemed to focus on nothing and everything all at once. He was wearing a cheap brown suit and had a mole on his chin. His nose had been broken several times and poorly set, and he was tough enough that the lines in his face might have been scars.

'I beg your pardon.'

'I'm sure you do.'

'Do I know you?'

'You do now,' Croaker said, slipping one hand into the man's jacket, extracting the gun from the shoulder holster. 'This is illegal here.'

'Not for me. I have a license.'

'We'll see.'

'Put it back.' The mole man bared his teeth. 'Or I'll take you apart with my bare hands.'

Croaker unloaded the gun, shaking the bullets out onto the ground. Then he returned the weapon to its holster. As he did so, he extruded the stainless-steel nails from their sheaths in the tips of his biomechanical fingertips, hooked them over the collar of the mole man's shirt. He jerked down, and the nails shredded shirt, tie, undershirt, flesh from neck to navel.

'Christ!'

Mole man tried to jerk away but Croaker held him fast with adamantine fingers. He exerted pressure on mole man's naked chest, jamming him back against the slats of the bench back.

'Don't threaten people you can't kill in a tenth of a second.'

Mole man was covered in gooseflesh, but his eyes burned so brightly Croaker could tell he was still more frightened of Bad Clams than he was of Croaker.

'I want you to give your boss a message.'

'Fuck you. Who cares what you want?'

Croaker exerted more pressure. 'You should.'

The mole man smirked. 'What're you gonna do? Kill me here among the birds and the kids in prams? Get real.'

Croaker hauled him to his feet. 'I've had about enough of you. Let's go over to New Scotland Yard. They have pits for people like you.'

The mole man began to struggle mightily. 'You've got nothing on me. You can't lock me up —' He broke free and, depressing the dial of his watch, opened his right hand as a small-caliber pistol appeared in it from a spring-loaded wrist-grip. He pulled the trigger just as Croaker lowered his shoulder and barreled into him.

Croaker closed his titanium and polycarbonate fingers over the weapon, wrenching its muzzle away from him. He took a pounding for it. The mole man was strong and he knew how to street-brawl. He got in two quick jabs to Croaker's ribs before he went for the groin.

Pain flared in Croaker's pelvis and he thought he heard the crack of a rib giving way. The mole man pressed his advantage, pummeling Croaker's right side, but this gave Croaker the opportunity he needed, and he exerted full force into his biomechanical hand. The mole man's wrist snapped back just as he landed a vicious blow into the flesh over Croaker's kidney.

Croaker saw stars, almost passed out, but managed to swing his left hand away from the fractured wrist. The extended stainless-steel nails slashed in a horizontal plane, flailing the skin and flesh from the mole man's cheek, the cartilage from the bottom of his nose. Croaker dug his nails in, catching them on bone and viscera, pulled down. The side of the mole man's head slammed into the pavement with a sickening sound. Then Croaker let go of consciousness.

He was roused by an urgent voice. He opened his eyes and found himself staring up into a bobby's face. He was young, almost boyish, and he appeared very frightened. Croaker was aware of a crowd and thought, *Christ, what a cock-up, as Major would say.*

'Don't move.' The bobby swallowed hard. 'You've been hurt and there's a lot of blood. An ambulance is on its way.'

Then, despite the bobby's warnings, he turned painfully over, saw the open eyes of the mole man staring blankly into his. He could hear the two-tone rise and fall of a siren, coming closer, but his ears were filled with Bad Clams' voice:

Don't try to cross me in London or wherever the fuck you wind up with this thing, because I'll come down on you with both my hobnailed boots strapped on and it won't be a pretty picture.

'Tachi's dead.'

Chief Inspector Van Kiet looked up at Nicholas. 'Shit. What happened?'

'Seiko happened. She put a crossbow bolt through his heart.'

Van Kiet slammed his palms down on his desk as he

jumped up. 'That bitch! I told Tachi not to trust her. Where is she? I want to interrogate her.'

'She's dead, too. Karma.' His words were far colder than he felt, but Van Kiet had held no love for Seiko, and Nicholas saw no point in expressing his feelings. Grieving had always been best left as a private affair, as far as he was concerned.

'One thing about this job,' Van Kiet said, apparently not hearing him, 'it's filled with roads not taken.'

'That's not a very oriental attitude. Don't you believe in karma?'

'Not anymore,' Van Kiet said wearily. 'I've been hanging out with too many Americans.' He looked at Nicholas. 'But Tachi must have proved his innocence. He knew the Yakuza who claimed Vincent Tinh's body.' Carefully monitoring the expression on Nicholas's face, he said, 'He did show you the copies of the photos I gave him?'

'He didn't,' Nicholas said with a feeling of cold dread.

Van Kiet's office was so cramped he would not have been able to close his door had he wanted to. Dossiers, leaflets, post-ups, wanted flyers, inter-office and inter-departmental memos floated everywhere like polka dots in a spotlight. The place smelled of stale food and staler sweat. A meat locker would have been preferable.

He rummaged around in a pile so high it seemed to be intact through sheer willpower. With all the elan of a magician he extracted a manila folder from the center without disturbing any of the other files, folders and circulars above and below it. He opened the folder, shoved three black-and-white surveillance shots into Nicholas's hands.

They showed a Yakuza in his mid-twenties. In one, he was seen entering a massage parlor. In the second, he was stripped to the waist. In the third, he was lying prone on a mat while a naked young woman with long hair bent over him.

'We're not as backward here as some might believe,' Van Kiet said dryly.

Staring hard at the Yakuza's *irizumi* – his tattoos – Nicholas said, 'This man belongs to Tachi's clan, the Yamauchi.' He pointed. 'The subject matter of Yakuza tattoos is as identifiable as signatures.'

Van Kiet seemed to brighten. 'But this happened last winter, before Tachi became *oyabun* of the Yamauchi.'

'True, but according to Seiko, Tachi was already in Tokyo, and had gained Tomoo Kozo's trust. By then, he was handling the Yamauchi's interests in Southeast Asia.'

'He could have been sent by Tachi, in other words.' Van Kiet seemed very sad indeed.

Nicholas nodded. 'At the very least, it's likely that Tachi knew about him,' he said as he put the photos back into their folder. This was evidence that Seiko had been telling the truth about Tachi. On the other hand, Nicholas still felt the Tau-tau pull of the Shuken. He suspected that given time Tachi would have confessed his involvement in the scheme to kill Nicholas. Nicholas preferred to believe that their friendship would have defeated Tachi's pragmatism. But perhaps that was just wishful thinking, and, in any event, time had run out for both of them.

Nicholas looked at Van Kiet. 'Are you prepared to tell me now who murdered Vincent Tinh?'

Van Kiet nodded. 'Sure. What do I have to lose now? I trust you not to open your mouth about it. It was Rock. Tinh thought he could weasel his way into Floating City, become a partner. Rock made an example of him; he needed to show very clearly what happened to people whose ambition gets out of control.'

Outside, downtown Saigon sizzled with the inexpert

giddiness only a massive infusion of capitalism and money could perpetrate. Music and horns blared in concert, and the sound of raised voices was, like diesel exhaust, always in the air.

'It's the same,' Nicholas said. 'Day or night, nothing's changed.'

'No,' Van Kiet said, 'it changes minute by minute. Every day there are more Japanese, Americans, Koreans and Thai. The entrepreneurs and their representatives – factors, agents and lawyers – flood Saigon, falling over themselves to set up shop.'

'You sound bitter.'

'Do I?' Van Kiet peered through the flyblown window glass, then turned back. 'I can't imagine why. In addition to having to struggle with encephalitis, yellow fever and meningitis, we now have AIDS and hepatitis epidemics on our hands. Little of our own culture has survived the wars and the superpowers, and our home is again invaded by those who swear they know what's best for us. The Party, which has led us, is dissolute, and the capitalists, who will lead us, are corrupt. There's not much to differentiate the two these days. But I apologize if I have offended you with my tone.'

'Come on. It's almost dinnertime. Let's go out and get drunk.'

Van Kiet took him to My Canh, one of several floating restaurants on the Saigon River. It was an unfortunate choice; Nicholas was reminded of his boat ride with Bay, leading to the ill-fated foray into the Cu Chi tunnels.

Lights from the city were cast across the muddy water like ghostly craft, only to be split apart by the wakes of their real counterparts. As he watched, the lights winked out in one *quan*, a common enough occurrence here. But in his current mood it was a melancholy sight. For all the capital flowing into Saigon it was still a miserable little third-world backwater. Its sweaty aspirations toward a low-cost free-market manufacturing hub were made wretched by its inability to master even the rudimentary services mandatory in any city.

Nicholas thought of Bay and the battered child prostitute who had propositioned him and Tachi at the Temple of the Whales. Somehow these two symbolized all the failed hopes of the populace here, dazed by historical betrayals and abrupt shifts in ideology and economy. Saigon was itself a floating city, cut adrift from both Vietnamese tradition and Communist cant, infected by foreign infusions of greed and lust that were poisoning its already unstable infrastructure. Business would survive – even prosper, of that he had no doubt. But what about the people? How would they survive?

Van Kiet, red-eyed and saturnine, said nothing before he had downed three shots of liquor. Then he spat over the side of the boat. 'I'm going to spend the night on the road, look for someone to shoot, and I won't care, seeing the poor bastard's face in the dust, covered with blood, because I won't be seeing him, I'll be seeing Tachi's back with a bolt right through it.'

Nicholas let him talk because that was what Van Kiet needed now. He was a violent man, given to wild swings of temperament, with an anger burning inside him that was expiated a little bit every time he pulled the trigger. He was barely civilized in a country that had never fully caught the concept of civilization. Vietnam was a warrior nation. Born in blood, it had feasted upon the indigenous Chams, the neighboring Cambodians and the Laotians. It was not a place where peace had been allowed to alight, let alone flourish.

Now Vietnam was reaping what it had sowed. If one believed in the concept of sin and punishment, this would be a perfect place to abide.

Nicholas waited patiently until Van Kiet's rambling homicidal diatribe had run its course. 'Seiko was convinced that Tachi would eventually have killed me.'

'What?' That startled Van Kiet out of his drunken torpor. 'She was a liar.'

'Maybe not.' Nicholas told him the story of Tachi's vulnerable position inside the Yakuza. 'She was right about one thing,' he concluded. 'With the continuing police crackdown on the Yakuza, if you're passed over for power, you're nothing. You might as well join a powerful clan as a street thug.'

'I guess it's impossible to know any man's heart,' Van Kiet said, staring bleakly out at his half-darkened city.

'I need to speak to her father. Do you know where he currently is?'

A bottle of liquor had been placed on their table. Van Kiet knocked back another shot, filled his glass.

'He has an apartment here but it's rarely occupied overnight,' Van Kiet said. 'He uses it almost exclusively for business meetings in the city. He lives on a large estate outside My Tho, the capital of Tien Giang Province. It's quite a magnificent residence, about fifty minutes by fast car south of here.'

'Will you drive me?'

Van Kiet nodded. 'First thing in the morning.'

Huynh Van Dich's estate overlooked the Tien River. It was surrounded by banana plantations straddling the river, which were owned by one of his many companies. He had leathery skin the color of mahogany, a handsome man even at the age of seventy-three, with silver hair and the eyes of a hawk. He had remained unaffected either by ideology or by politics. His cudgel was economics and he wielded it with ruthless authority. He made so much money for the country that no politician, military tactician or ideologue was prepared to cross him. Perhaps that was as much because of his self-imposed neutrality in all matters. He wouldn't threaten their maneuvering if they would keep their noses out of his business.

In its own way, the arrangement had worked; it had made him a wealthy man, though hardly influential in the succession of administrations that had come and gone in Hanoi and Saigon.

He was small and compact, leaning perpetually forward as if he were hard of hearing. In fact, he was in a hurry. When he walked, he ran, and when he ran, he sprinted like a deer. He seemed not at all to feel his seventy-three years.

He was not happy to see Van Kiet but was curious to meet his companion. He invited them in for a breakfast of fried bananas and rice with fish paste. They ate at a long wooden table that looked out on a terrace and, beyond, a stand of coconut palms on the slope down to the river. The sun, breaking through layers of blue-gray cloud, shimmered on the water like gold dust strewn in the shallows.

There was no sign of his new wife and family. All was still, save for the sounds of the birds and insects, the clatter of the wind through the palm fronds. Perhaps he liked to dine alone.

The three men said little through the meal. When the plates had been cleared and French-roast coffee had been served, Dich said, 'What brings you all the way out here, Chief Inspector?'

Van Kiet said nothing.

'*Chu* Dich,' Nicholas said slowly, 'I am sorry to have to tell you your daughter is dead.'

Dich looked at him inscrutably. 'The body?'

'I've arranged for it to be flown back to Saigon,' Van Kiet said.

'Do you wish to know the circumstances of her death?' Nicholas asked.

'I never knew the circumstances of her life, so I doubt

I could understand how or why she died,' Dich said with implacable logic.

Van Kiet stared out at the line of narrow dikes. A slender figure was crossing a pole bridge, its back bent beneath a heavy weight. He rose, excusing himself.

When they were alone, Nicholas said, 'If it's of any consolation, I was involved with your daughter; I cared for her.'

Now Dich swung his head in Nicholas's direction. 'So you say you cared for Seiko, *Chu* Linnear. Did you protect her?'

'In the end I think she protected me.'

Dich stood up. 'I need to go to make my rounds. Will you accompany me?'

They went through the open French doors out onto the terra-cotta terrace. The wet smell of the plantation was everywhere. Dich led Nicholas down brick steps and along a path that wound its way through a garden of colorful flowering plants.

At the end there was another set of steps that led down to an area of hard-packed earth. No foliage grew here and, despite the early hour, the sun beat down on them without mercy.

They came upon a series of wooden sheds within which were stacked bamboo cages of all sizes and shapes. Creatures writhed within them, coiling and uncoiling, though some slept like the dead.

'This snake farm is my hobby,' Dich said. 'I come here to unwind from the tensions of the day or night.'

Was he kidding? Nicholas recognized cobras, kraits, puff adders, but there were all manner of Viperidae that he could not identify. As they moved through the sheds, Nicholas saw huge aquariums filled with venomous marine snakes, appearing from behind rocks, undulating through thickets of translucent vegetation.

'We make all sorts of sera here,' Dich said. 'Cures for

457

ague, fever, anesthetics for surgery, and suppressants for coughing fits and hyperventilation. We extract not only the venom but the blood, gallbladder, brain gland and flesh, which we desiccate and grind into powder to increase and sustain sexual energy.' Dich went from cage to cage. 'In a way, these are like children. You feed them, house them, raise them in most instances, and if you are not painstakingly cautious, they will sink their fangs into your flesh.'

'Seiko asked me to come see you.'

Dich stared into the sun. 'So at last I understand something about my daughter.'

'Do you know she was involved with a Yakuza *oyabun* named Tachi Shidare?'

'I know something of Shidare,' he said noncommittally.

'She believed he had made a deal with another, more powerful *oyabun* in order to gain influence quickly in Tokyo.'

'Yes. Foolishly, Shidare had done just that.' Dich led him farther into the estate, where rows of magnificent orchids rose from the dark, rich earth.

Nicholas, surrounded by the almost unearthly beauty of the exotic flowers, felt a tightness in his belly. Now he had the confirmation he had been seeking that Seiko had told him the truth. *You cannot forgive me for saving you from Tachi.* He was filled with rage and frustration. He wanted her back, alive again and reunited with her father. He saw now that this would have been the only way to heal them both.

'Which *oyabun* was it?' he asked. 'Chosa?'

Dich, who was squatting beside a violet specimen speckled with gold, said, 'The older, more experienced, more devious of the two.' He checked the earth around the flower stem. 'Tetsuo Akinaga.'

When Nicholas heard the name, he knew in his heart

the enemy was Akinaga. The brother of his childhood friends, the son of the man who had been his second father, who had introduced him to Koei. Now Akinaga wanted him dead. And this simple truth lay at the core of his hatred for the Yakuza. It was what he could not tolerate and could never forgive – that those who were closest to you were often your most implacable foe.

'Tetsuo was always the brilliant tactician,' he said. 'The Shikei clan was perennially second-best when he ascended to *oyabun*, but he soon rectified that situation.'

Dich rose, dusted off his hands. 'Do you know why he would want you dead?'

'I loved his father, Tsunetomo. He was like a second father to me. I know that though Tetsuo outwardly revered his father, he was secretly contemptuous of his business acumen. He couldn't wait for Tsunetomo to die so he could assume control.'

'Could that be the entire explanation for why he's come after you now?'

Nicholas considered this. Perhaps it explained why the attack came in the devious and oblique fashion typical of Tetsuo, Nicholas thought, but it didn't answer the question of why. Was Tetsuo still jealous of his relationship with his father, or had there been some connection between Tsunetomo and the Colonel of which Nicholas was not aware? He knew there was a great deal about his father's life in postwar Tokyo he knew nothing about. He also realized this was because of deliberate actions on his father's part. Why? Too many questions he could not yet answer.

'I think this is a question of no little import,' Dich said, sensing Nicholas's confusion. He indicated they should walk along a path of flat stones that wound through the forest of orchids. 'It's all a matter of allegiance, you see.' Dich hurried along the path at his peculiar pace. 'Once, this was a simple affair. You joined forces with someone and then honor dictated that you upheld that alliance until the end. Now *honor* is a word that has been deleted from the current lexicon. It seems as if it's every man for himself and a knife in the back for whoever does not come in first. As a result, relationships slither away even before they can be formed. They have become, like Japan, superficial symbols, anachronisms that are manipulated like chess pieces to gain advantage. And like chessmen they are often expendable.'

Dich suggested they return to the veranda of the main house for drinks. They sat at a round bamboo table, drinking icy beers.

'It's a pity you're not here on business, *Chu* Linnear,' Dich said. 'After decades of intolerable strife Vietnam now has a legitimate chance to become a thriving business environment for companies of all nations. I have nothing but optimism for the future. It's just too bad that others here do not share my enthusiasm.'

'Do you think the Communists will try again to dominate the south?'

'Absolutely not,' Dich said flatly. 'They are in retreat, economically and morally. They no longer have a core, or a reason for being. The people have seen their lies put into practise.' He shook his head. 'No, Vietnam is safe from its old enemies. It is its new foes which worry me.'

As Dich continued to speak easily of his role in the new, open Vietnam, Nicholas could not shake the feeling that this mysterious man whom both Seiko and Tachi had been reluctant to talk about was the glue that held these particular dramatis personae together in a kind of magnetic frisson. How and why were the mysteries Nicholas suspected he'd be well advised to solve before he made his final assault on Floating City.

Dich extracted two more beers from an ice chest, opened them and slid one over.

'I cautioned Seiko not to become involved with the *oyabun* Tachi Shidare, but, as you no doubt gathered, she was a willful child and often did not know what was best for her.'

Dich drained his beer. 'I know who you are, *Chu* Linnear, and I have a message for you. It is from your friend Mikio Okami.'

'Okami-san is alive?'

Dich smiled thinly. 'Yes. But for now he must remain in hiding; the danger to him still exists. In fact, in some ways, it is greater,' Dich said softly. 'But, for now, that is beside the point. Listen to what I say. There are events that must occur before he can return. These events would not be happening had he stayed in place as the Kaisho.'

'I don't understand.'

Dich inclined his head. 'I think you understand quite a bit more than you're letting on. You know something of how Okami thinks. How could you not? He learned it from your father.'

Nicholas said nothing, and Dich was content – even determined – to press on while they were alone together.

'Like the Colonel, Okami thinks in great leaps – leaps of faith, some have called it. He is a strategist of the highest order. When he determined the strength of the plot against his life and that of his partner Dominic Goldoni, he developed a counterplan. He was too late to save Goldoni, which was a tragedy for all of us.'

Nicholas noted the 'us', and now – had Dich been right about this? – he began to see the skein forming, a widening web that overlapped cultures, national boundaries, even ideology. Something extraordinary was out there, spinning in the darkness, and he was acutely conscious that he was at last being given access to it.

'You're a third partner, aren't you? It was Okami, Goldoni and you against the Godaishu.'

Dich nodded, almost impatiently. 'Of course. My relationship with Okami goes back many years, but for now that is irrelevant. Okami saw the changes being wrought in the Godaishu. It was his creation, after all, so he could see the corruption beginning like veins of bacteria in tissue. The power of the Kaisho was being eroded from within the inner council, but there was no way of determining the enemy without bringing total civil war within the Godaishu and the Yakuza. This consequence was anathema to Okami, who had agreed to ascend to the level of Kaisho precisely to keep the peace among warring *oyabun*.

'So he disappeared. He knew the consequences of his absence, he could sense it through his ability with *koryoku*. But he also determined that he could more effectively pull the strings that needed to be pulled from the shadows of exile.

'His enemy will be revealed. The misshapen power politics that have infected the inner council will be purged, and the office of the Kaisho will be restored.'

'How can you be certain of all this?'

Dich pretended not to hear Nicholas. 'I know where you are headed and I want to do what I can to prepare you.'

'Prepare me? I don't understand.'

'You are going where no one has gone unbidden and survived. Before you make such an attempt you must be healed.'

Nicholas felt a kind of electric crackling along his arms and spine. Tiny hairs fluttered at the base of his neck. Why didn't he ask Dich what he was talking about? Was it because part of him already knew?

462

Dich glanced at his watch. 'I am required in another part of the estate for a little while. I could see you liked my children. Go to the snake farm, you know the way. You need to satisfy your curiosity.'

'You look like a regiment of the Green Howards trod on your face. I told you to be careful, old son.' Tom Major, in tweed overcoat and porkpie hat, stood in the hospital room, looking at Croaker like a nanny whose charge has been extremely disobedient. A combination of concern and relief was on his face.

'So you did, Dad.' Croaker threw the covers off his lower body. 'Why don't you make yourself useful and exert your influence to get me the hell out of here.' His body ached all over as if he had been thrown from a speeding semi, but his ribs had sustained no fracture and, all in all, he was in one piece.

'Already organized.' Major took Croaker's clothes from the closet, handed them to him. 'You'd bloody well better make it quick. The hospital has had several inquiries after your health by people you're not up to dealing with right now.'

Croaker, perched on the edge of the high bed, groaned as he lifted each leg to insert them into his trousers.

'Need any help, lad?' Major said jovially.

'Don't you dare.' Croaker gingerly put on his shirt, then buckled his belt. 'What kinds of inquiries are we speaking of?'

'The worst kind, I'm afraid.' Major shifted from one foot to another, either uncomfortable with the subject or anxious to be moving. 'Lewis, you aren't involved with someone in the American underworld, are you?'

'Why would you say that?'

'Because I know at least one of the blokes who's so concerned about your health.' Major held up Croaker's overcoat so he could get into it easily. 'He works for Caesare Leonforte, the same person who employed the man with whom you had your run-in in Holland Park.'

'Run-in?' That classic British understatement. 'I killed the bloody bastard.'

'That you did.' Major led the way to the door, held it open. 'But you must be getting old; in the process he almost did you in.'

They went down the quiet hallway, past open doors. You could smell the sickness along with the nauseatingly sweet scent of anesthetic. Major pressed the button for the elevator.

'What aren't you telling me, Lewis?'

'Everything that might compromise you,' Croaker said, stepping into the vast elevator. A man on a gurney was being handled by an orderly. He was hooked up to blood and saline. Just coming down from surgery, Croaker surmised. He didn't look in particularly great shape.

'Say no more,' Major said as the doors closed and they began to descend.

The elevator stopped at the recovery-room floor and the orderly rolled the gurney out. Two men stepped in. The doors closed.

Major stood with his back against the rear wall; the two men stood in front of the doors. Out of the corner of his eye Croaker saw Major's hand unobtrusively disappear into the pocket of his tweed overcoat, and he concentrated his attention on the two men. They were tall and broad-shouldered in tan winter Burberry storm coats with the cashmere linings showing around the collars. One had a bald spot much like a monk's tonsure. They didn't talk to one another, but stood silent, their hands jammed into their pockets.

Croaker was aware of an electrical charge in the air; he could feel the tension come into Major's torso, and he silently extruded the stainless-steel nails in his biomechanical fingers. Major gazed straight ahead at the backs of their necks, as if he could bore a hole in their flesh.

The door opened on the main floor and the men got out. They did not turn around but headed straight for the exit. Croaker and Major followed at a discreet distance.

'Anyone you know?' Croaker asked.

'Just playing it safe,' Major said, relaxing somewhat. He signaled to several plainclothesmen with electronic earbuds in place.

Outside, traffic whizzed by. A dirty wind was gusting, and Croaker could hear a siren wailing as it came closer, and he was back again lying in Holland Park while the white-faced bobby said to him, *An ambulance is on its way.*

Two police cars were bracketing a shiny black Daimler. A uniformed driver held open the rear door for Croaker and Major. Heavy condensation occluded the windows, and the windshield wipers were on. Croaker could hear the sound over the street noise.

'I want to get into Malory Enterprises,' he said.

Major gave him a rueful smile. 'Already been tried, old son. Afraid it's a dead end. I wasn't sitting idly by while you were in a faint. The offices house a legitimate import-export business. If anything funny's going on there, we haven't been able to find it.'

'I know there is. I have to –'

The siren was loud now as they climbed into the Daimler. Doors slammed and the driver went around and got in. He put the car in gear as the flanking police vehicles fired up their ignitions.

'You're in danger here, old son,' Major said, settling back against the plush seat. 'I don't know what you're really involved in and something tells me I don't want

465

to know. My advice to you is to take the first flight home.'

Again, Croaker was torn. He was so close to finding Okami; the Kaisho was here in London, and London was where Torch would be detonated on the ides unless Nicholas could stop it from leaving Floating City.

But Croaker had lost Okami and knew it was not enough to know he was somewhere in London. He had to find out where within the city the Kaisho was hiding. Only Vesper knew that. And again he tried to get inside her mind. She represented an enigma so profound he was drawn inexorably toward its center. She was like a train wreck – a mortal disaster, at once horrifying and fascinating. She was cruel, omnivorous, heartless – and yet it seemed as if she cared about Margarite and Celeste even as she sought to manipulate them. And over it all loomed her relationship to Okami. Was she working for him or against him, as Dedalus's mole inside Nishiki? Now that he knew she had direct access to the Kaisho, he had to get to her at all costs.

And yet at this moment she was on her way back to Washington to vet Serman at DARPA.

Major put a hand on his arm. 'Lewis, you've got some very bad blokes on your back. I haven't the time or the budget to babysit you while you're here.'

If only Major knew the threat Bad Clams had made against Margarite, Croaker thought. He debated telling Major about Torch, but what good would it do? Major could mobilize all his forces – assuming he could get his superiors to believe in the threat – and still be unable to stop its detonation. In the process, the news would inevitably be leaked to the media and a full-scale panic would ensue. Besides, anything he told Major would detain him here and he was now desperate to find Vesper. He resigned himself to keeping silent on the subject.

He concentrated on keeping his voice level. 'Perhaps you're right.'

'Good lad. Let's get you to Heathrow with all possible haste.'

The condensation had turned to a foggy drizzle. Through it, he could see the ambulance as it careened around a corner. It was heading for the emergency entrance and the police cars held back, waiting for it to pass. The Daimler's driver had already nosed out into the street, and now he stood on the brakes in order not to get clipped.

Perhaps it was the squeal of rubber on the slick tarmac that obscured the first burst of sound. Croaker saw the flashes as a hail of semiautomatic gunfire spewed out of the open rear of the ambulance.

Even as he threw himself sideways he saw the driver flung against the curbside door as clots of his blood shot against the inside of the Daimler's roof. Croaker jammed his elbow against the door handle, grabbed it, jerked it open. He tumbled to the ground, scraping his knees as he reached up to haul Major out after him.

The car shot forward as the dead driver's foot came off the brake pedal and Croaker's arm was almost wrenched out of its socket. But he had hold of Major's tweed lapels with his biomechanical hand, and he torqued it with the movement of the car, knowing that if it had been flesh and blood it would be fractured now. But the titanium and polycarbonate, both tough and flexible, did their job, and he managed to hold on to his friend as the Daimler shuddered, then with an almost human cry careened obliquely across the street, smashing into a pair of parked cars.

The ambulance was already gone, shooting around the far corner in a squeal of tires. One of the police cars was pulling out in pursuit; the other was blocked by the wreck the driverless Daimler had made of itself.

Croaker could hear the shouts of the policemen and the clatter of their running feet. The cold rain was soaking him, running down his collar and into his undershirt. He had turned Major over, saw the mess of blood right away.

'Ah, Christ,' he breathed. And then, lifting his head, shouted, 'A doctor! We need a doctor!'

A crimson swath had been stitched across Major's chest and right shoulder. Blood was seeping everywhere, flecks of it across his cheeks and in his hair.

Major's eyes focused on Croaker; his lips moved. 'I told you, old son.'

'Shut up!' Croaker said, holding him tight. 'You look like the entire Green Howards trod on you.'

Major tried to smile. 'Feels like it.' His chest was fluttering. 'You do as I say now, old son. Get out of England before something serious happens.'

'I told you to shut up!' Major was cold, and Croaker held him tighter. Where the hell was a doctor? They were only yards from the hospital.

Major began to shudder.

'Just you bloody well hang on or I'll –'

Major's eyelids closed. A deep rale came from inside his chest.

'Tom! Tom!'

The fog obscured the rooftops, rain dripped dolefully from the bare tree branches, the smell was of scorched rubber, cordite and death. Sirens sounded, the crackle of radios forming like lightning, the pounding of feet across the pavement.

'All right, it's all right,' someone said as hands began to gently pry Croaker away from his friend. 'Give him to us now.'

FIFTEEN

Tien Giang/Tokyo

The day was hot and still. Out on the river, boats plied the brown water. Workers were hunched over the banana plants, their capable fingers feeling for mature hands of fruit. Somewhere, high up, a monkey began to chatter, setting the serpents to slithering over one another. Perhaps they scented it.

Nicholas had come down from the veranda lost in thought. Now he turned. Someone had emerged from the depths of one of the sheds. Several kraits scented her and became excited, writhing up the side of their bamboo cage before dropping again to the floor.

You must be healed.

In a sense, he knew who was waiting for him here. Just as he had been waiting for her.

You must be healed. He suspected that Dich had said the same thing to her. But now, at the edge of the abyss, he hesitated, wondering if he was prepared for this confrontation. And, come to think of it, how in hell had Dich known he would eventually wind up here? Was this also part of the Kaisho's vast scheme, the consequence of, as Dich had said, pulling strings from the shadows of exile?

'Why do you hesitate?' said the voice from his past. 'Does seeing me again seem so frightening?'

And then he knew that the manner in which he had arrived here was irrelevant. Kaisho's scheming or mere happenstance, what did it matter so long as he was here? Her voice, so familiar to him, was like a strand of memory unaffected by time and circumstance. At once, he glimpsed again those cold autumn nights at the edge of a field where an owl hooted and they had shared an entire universe.

'Koei.'

She emerged from the shadows behind an aquarium of sea snakes. She seemed to have aged not at all, to have existed in another world for all the time they had been apart, and yet the girl had matured into the full flower of womanhood. The angles of her face were still unmistakable, though slightly softened. The luster of her huge eyes had only deepened.

A small, shy smile formed on the small bow of her lips. 'I see your face, your expression, and all the dread in my heart evaporates. You do not hate me.'

'I have hated you, and then later, I hated all that you represented – that world.' For a moment he was so overcome he could not continue. Knowing that, she was wisely silent. Patience was a virtue it had taken her so long to master it had become as precious to her as rubies or pearls.

'Let me look at you,' he whispered. 'I feel as if no time has passed.'

'But it has.' She took a step toward him, a look of concern on her face. 'I can see it in your eyes. Your wife . . .'

'Dead. A car accident while I was away trying to protect Okami-san.'

'And you haven't been able to forgive yourself.'

'Not for that so much as for not being able to see that the paths of our lives never ran parallel.'

'But life runs two ways, Nicholas. If our time together has taught me anything, it is this. The two of you chose something together. What was the crime in that?'

Of course she was right. It wasn't anything he hadn't

470

thought a dozen times since Justine's death, but hearing another person – and especially this person – articulate what he had been feeling was a source of the most profound relief.

He nodded wordlessly.

'And now you're here.' She reached out tentatively, touched his fingers with her own. With the contact, he felt a warmth wash over him, and it was as if the intervening years had turned transparent and, seeing the present through them, he could understand it all – everything that he had for so long buried deep in the dark recesses of his soul.

You must be healed, Dich had said. Now Nicholas began the process.

'For the longest time I turned my back on the world of the Yakuza,' he said, 'because of my rage, because of the death that was needlessly . . .' His voice, thick with emotion, was a whisper on the wind coming in from the open windows. 'But, in the end, I saw what had really happened. It was me I was angry with, not you, not the world of the Yakuza. The fact I could never face, until now, was that I had fallen in love not only with you but with that world. Just as my father had. I fought to bury it because it was inconsistent with my conception of honor and the rectitude of my martial arts.'

'You know, that was the one thing I could never understand. You – a ninja, who were society's outcasts in their day – had every reason to be drawn to the world of the Yakuza, who are outcasts in much the same way. It seemed so natural, and yet . . .'

'In *ninjutsu* there are only black or red, good or evil; there is nothing in between. I suppose that was how I saw everything. I never fully understood how my father could have been best friends with a Yakuza *oyabun*. Expediency was one thing. I knew he had been ordered

471

to work with Yakuza, but he was under no obligation to befriend one. And in a very real sense I was angry at him for that. It was the most difficult emotion to bear, and the one I buried the deepest. I revered my father, I loved him, but I also hated him for taking Mikio Okami as a friend.'

'Just as you took me for a girlfriend.'

Seiko was still in his mind. He knew he might never have reached this point of self-revelation without her. *I hate you for your righteousness, for not understanding that there are so many shades of gray between black and white*. She had known him better than he knew himself. He mourned for her. How was it, he wondered, that your own nature was the most opaque?

They stood very close, and he could feel time beginning to collapse, the years scattering like dead leaves in winter.

'Why?' Koei whispered.

That one word summed up everything in their lives that had wounded them and had not allowed that wound to heal.

'How alike we were,' she said. 'This should have made us closer. Instead, we wound up hurting each other.' She lifted her head. Her huge eyes peered up at him. 'I didn't want to lie to you, but how could I tell you what I myself could not face?'

'You couldn't. It was karma, and we all suffered in our own way.'

She extended her hands along his arms. 'I've been waiting such a long time for this moment. My whole life, it seems.'

His lips were very close to hers. In the periphery of his vision the vipers coiled and twined sinuously. He felt her thigh insinuate itself between his, felt the pink tip of her tongue along his lips.

A heat was rising and the serpents sensed it. Roused

from torpor, they raised their flat heads, tasted the musk on the air with the tips of their forked tongues.

The coiling kraits were in some way attuned to her vibrations. Their shiny bodies banged against the bamboo, making the cage shudder, and their hypodermic fangs, normally folded back against the roofs of their mouths, became erect.

He unbuttoned her gauze blouse, held her breasts in his hands. When his thumbs stroked her nipples, her head came down and, gasping, she bit the side of his neck. Their blood was boiling, strands of each other entwined in their minds. His *tanjian* eye was blazing, reflecting them both in its light.

Her nimble fingers unbuckled his belt, slid his trousers down. He gathered her skirt until it bunched around her hips. She was naked underneath. He pushed her back against a wall and she lifted one leg, hooking her heel against the small of his back. She guided the tip of him into her at the moment his lips came down over hers. Their mouths opened, and she opened fully.

She groaned into his mouth, made little sounds, vibrations that set the serpents to writhing. She arched up against him, canting her pelvis, fitting herself to his thrusts, climbing onto him, into him as deeply as he was into her.

She breathed like an engine, her mind empty of thought and of pain. Something inside her was freed, loosened in the well of the aura they created together, the intense pleasure that heated her groin and breasts and belly. Dazed, she recognized it as herself, a pure spirit that had survived the scars of bitter circumstance. *I exist*, she thought in dizzy wonder. *Oh, God, I am alive!*

She was intimate with the mechanism of sex, but this was a different kind of engine entirely. Consumed in the moment, she was outside time. The past no longer had the strength to shackle her in memory and habit; the present no longer imprisoned her in loneliness and resignation. It was as if she had awakened from a long, sorcerous slumber and now, empowered by that abiding spirit, was uncoiling toward a distant horizon.

She came in a rush, lurching drunkenly against him, sweat streaking her face and breasts, needing her own heat as well as his, thrusting against him as frantically as he thrust against her. And as she let go, she felt something rush into the space that had opened up, something mysterious, unique, her own, and she embraced it even as she clutched him to her, feeling him shudder powerfully, his thighs trembling, his aura expanding, washing over her like a tide at the edge of the shore.

'I was so wrong,' she whispered in the heat of the serpent shed, 'to do some of things I have done.'

Nicholas, still dazzled by what had just occurred, held her against him. She was still breathing fast, and he could feel the trip-hammer of her pulse as if it were a new source of energy.

All around them the vipers had come alive, the love-making scented on the tips of their tongues. The inside of the shed shifted and shook as the serpents expended themselves against their cages.

There was a silence for a time. Outside the shed, the clouds were building in the west, looking bruised now, heavily laden with rain.

'What are you doing here?' he asked.

'You know. Waiting for you.'

'What happened after I . . . after we separated?'

She looked beautiful and poignant, much as, Nicholas guessed, Shizuka had looked to Minamoto no Yoshit-sune during their brief exile together in thirteenth-century Yoshino.

'I had had enough of men.' She stared out at the

coming rain. 'The truth was after you left me I couldn't bear to have another man touch me. The thought of sex left me cold as a stone. I never laughed, and in my heart I wanted to die.'

'Koei —'

She turned around and her face was so full of feeling that he was struck dumb. 'No, don't,' she said. 'By that time I was already dead. And I knew I had only myself to blame. I knew how important honor was to you, so I suppose I must have understood the risk I took in lying to you.'

She watched him, rooted to the spot. 'For a time, I thought I would become a nun. That seemed safe and comfortable. How naive I was!' She gave an ironic laugh. 'All I lacked was faith, the essential ingredient. In the end, I went to Yoshino and trained as a *miko*, a sacred Shugendo shrine dancer.

'In fact, I did not dislike it. Shinto's naturalism caught me up, and, if I wasn't exactly happy, at least I wasn't constantly overwhelmed by memory.

'Then Tomoo Kozo came for me. He told me that, in my father's name, he had brokered a marriage. This marriage, he said, had grave significance for the future. It was my duty, he said, to my father, to him, to the Yamauchi clan.

'At first I thought, "Well, I am dead. What does it matter?" But after six months I knew that I had been wrong on both counts. I wasn't dead, after all, and it mattered a great deal. I couldn't marry this man, I couldn't go to my parents, and I couldn't return to Yoshino where Kozo had found me, so I did the only thing I could think of. I ran to the Kaisho.' She looked at Nicholas. 'It was Mikio Okami who sent me here.'

'Okami knew about us?'

'Oh, yes. I resolved to tell him everything. It was past

475

time. The burden of keeping those terrible memories pent up was crippling me. But, as it turned out, the Kaisho knew most of it anyway.'

'Why was that?'

She seemed surprised. 'I thought you'd know. Anything that affected you was of particular interest to him. Because of that he was willing to protect me.'

A distant boom of thunder along the horizon lent the air a sudden chill. The sun had disappeared. 'There's something else I need to tell you,' she said at last. 'The man Kozo wanted me to marry, who I was with for six months, is Michael Leonforte.'

Nicholas felt as if he had been delivered a blow to the stomach. 'The same Leonforte who is Rock's partner in Floating City?'

'Yes. He and Rock met in Laos. Michael was something of a lone wolf. He had been recruited by a group of American spies working inside the Pentagon to secure *the* major drug pipeline from the Shan States in the Burmese highlands. They picked the wrong man because instead of fulfilling his assignment, Leonforte went AWOL, commandeering the pipeline for his own use. In 1971, Rock was one of the people sent out by the spies under the guise of Special Forces to bring him back dead or alive. Instead, Rock and another man – a Vietnamese named Do Duc – went AWOL themselves and joined him.'

Do Duc, Rock and Mick Leonforte had been partners? *Good God*, Nicholas thought, *no wonder Rock wants me dead – I killed Do Duc*. Van Kiet thought Rock was after him because he had seen through the computer scheme – the second-generation neural-net chip Nicholas was supposed to have. Now he could see the outline of a conspiracy that was far wider, far more sinister than he could have imagined. One Leonforte was dealing drugs and arms illegally obtained from the US government from a hidden fortress in Vietnam, while another Leonforte had been the head of Looking-Glass, the most invisible spook outfit in America's history. Were these the same spooks who had been after the drug pipeline during the war in 'Nam? If so, they had it – which meant that an arm of the US government was trafficking in drugs.

'What was Kozo doing linking the Yamauchi with Mick Leonforte?'

'It wasn't the Yamauchi – it wasn't even the Yakuza, per se. It was the Godaishu. I didn't know it then – no one beyond two or three people did – but plans were already under way to oust Okami from the position of Kaisho. At first, the plotters – Chosa, Akinaga and MITI's Daijin, Naohiro Ushiba – meant only to oust him. But, somehow, the plan was changed and he was marked for assassination. Kozo, acting on Akinaga's orders, contracted with Do Duc to murder Okami and the people who had secretly joined him, Dominic Goldoni and *Chu* Dich. Because of you only Goldoni was killed.

'You see, Floating City became extremely important to the Godaishu – the new Godaishu, run without interference from Okami. In fact, the involvement with Rock and Michael was the breaking point between the two factions. Akinaga and the rest of the inner council wanted to forge a permanent partnership with Floating City; Okami bitterly opposed it. He knew Rock and Michael and he wanted no part of them. They were revolutionaries even among those beyond the law. They saw themselves as emperors. God-like, they presided over Floating City, reinventing business deals and justice alike.'

Rain began to beat against the corrugated tin roof of the shed, making the vipers slither and hiss. Fat drops rolled off the eaves, soaking into the hard-packed earth.

Then the sky turned black and the downpour began in earnest.

'Because of the reputations of these men, Akinaga and Kozo felt it imperative that a direct link be made with them. If I was married to Michael Leonforte, they believed, he would never renege on a deal with them.'

'So they were willing to sacrifice you.'

'You know they could never see it that way.'

'And Leonforte? How could they know whether he was even interested in marriage?'

'It was the barter they were all interested in – all the men. Love – or even sex – never entered into it. It was meant to be a straight business arrangement.'

Appalling as this sounded, brokered marriages of this sort had existed in Asia for centuries. 'I still don't see it from Mick's point of view.'

'No one could,' Koei said softly. 'It just goes to show you that no matter how smart you think you are you can't anticipate the skein of life. Against all odds, Michael fell in love with me.'

When Tanaka Gin appeared at Akira Chosa's door, he was trailed by three of Chosa's bodyguards, who clung to his vicinity like crabs to coral.

'Prosecutor,' Chosa said, opening the door to his apartment, 'is this a social call? It's an odd time for you to be working.'

Tanaka Gin showed Chosa his badge. 'Official business.'

Chosa, who was dressed in an informal silk kimono, said, 'It's almost midnight.'

'You have been at Ink Stick up until now. I did not want to interrupt your pleasure.'

Chosa shrugged and stood aside. 'There are two women in my bedroom who will be very disappointed if you stay long.'

'I won't be staying,' Tanaka Gin said, walking past the *oyabun*. 'But then neither will you.'

'I beg your pardon?'

Tanaka Gin, who had been contemplating the life-size wax replica of Marilyn Monroe, turned around because he did not want to deprive himself of the pleasure of seeing this Yakuza's face when he read off the charges against him and handed him the written indictment. He tried not to think of the two women, probably naked, waiting for the *oyabun* to return. He was not celibate by nature but rather by a supreme act of will. Youthful excess had taught him a sobering lesson about himself. It was far too easy for him to drown in a sybaritic life-style that, as a responsible adult in a job that demanded scrupulous morals, could only destroy him.

To his credit Chosa appeared stone-faced while Tanaka Gin rattled off the list of charges against him. But when Tanaka Gin handed him the next document to read, the color drained from his face.

'These are lies! Who would concoct such a litany of falsehoods?'

'Please, we have hard evidence connecting you to Yoshinori-san. We have eyewitnesses, direct and independent corroboration.' Tanaka Gin smiled, a glow of satisfaction expanding inside him. 'You are our doorway, Chosa-san, into the domain of the Yakuza upper echelons. We are going to root out all corruption like decay from a tooth.'

'If it's corruption you're after, look to your own department, Prosecutor,' Chosa spat out. 'I could name names, if I chose, and list criminal acts that would make your stomach turn.'

'Are you thinking of becoming my witness, of turning on your friends?' Tanaka Gin was curious at this response.

'I'm not stupid. I know where these charges come

from,' Chosa said, carefully folding the indictment. 'I assure you as of now I have no friends.'

'Then you should welcome the opportunity to work with me.' Tanaka Gin made a curt gesture. 'Come with me, please.'

Chosa made a show of looking toward the front door. 'Am I to deduce that you came alone on such a momentous occasion? Your career will be assured, Prosecutor, with my conviction.'

'I came alone,' Tanaka Gin said formally. 'Doing my duty is one thing; causing unnecessary loss of face is quite another.'

Chosa gave him a quick bow. 'It is time for the bell of the Shinto shrine across the street to sound. I would appreciate it, Prosecutor, if I could hear it one last time.'

'I have no objection.'

Chosa nodded. 'In that case, I'll get dressed.' He disappeared into the bedroom while Tanaka Gin took a longer look at the Marilyn Monroe replica in its Plexiglas case. He bent down, looking beneath the splayed-out skirt, which fluttered on its constant current of air.

The Shinto bell began to resound. One of the living room windows was partially open and Tanaka Gin went to it, looked down the twenty floors to the street below. He glanced at his watch, then strode to the closed bedroom door.

He was about to knock when he heard the sharp report of a pistol. He lifted his leg, kicked open the door. Two women, naked to the waist, were cowering on the bed. One was screaming; she had spots of blood on her cheek and shoulder.

Tanaka Gin stopped, staring at the form of Akira Chosa. He had obviously put the barrel of the gun in his mouth. The force of the large-caliber .357 bullet had torn the back of his head off as it had thrown him across

480

the corner of the bed. He was facing away from the prosecutor, toward the window, which was wide open. A blast of cold air brought the stench of death toward him. Chosa had dressed for the occasion. He was in a neat dark suit, white shirt and patterned tie.

Tanaka Gin could hear the sounds of running feet and, a moment later, Chosa's guards burst into the room. They stopped short, stood staring at their fallen *oyabun*.

Tanaka Gin, careful not to disturb anything, helped the two women off the bed and out of the room. He told them to wash up, get dressed and wait for him to take their statements. Then he went back inside the bedroom. He stared at Chosa, stretched out unnaturally across the corner of the bloody bed. Something was clutched in his left hand. Tanaka Gin squatted down, poked at the fingers with a pen. It was a photo, a glossy color publicity still from an American film called *The Misfits*. The photo was of Clark Gable and Marilyn Monroe. He was in blue jeans and a cowboy hat, a grin on his face. Perhaps he had just told a joke because Monroe, luminous as ever, was laughing behind one upraised hand.

The tolling of the Shinto bell echoed through the room, a mournful commentary on the Western-style suicide. Tanaka Gin rose and left. He thought himself a fool ever to have believed a man like Chosa would spill all the secrets of a lifetime of crime to anyone, let alone a Tokyo prosecutor. *Hubris*, Tanaka Gin thought, as he remembered Chosa slumped over on his side, *is a terrible thing*.

He did not return home until after three. A great deal of paperwork was involved in a death, even one so clear-cut as Chosa's.

Ushiba was still awake, reading by lamplight in an old overstuffed chair. He looked up as Tanaka Gin came

481

in, went into the kitchen and poured himself three fingers of neat Scotch. The prosecutor downed it in one gulp, poured himself another.

Putting aside his book of haiku, Ushiba walked silently into the kitchen.

'What has happened?'

'Chosa's dead,' Tanaka Gin said flatly. 'He put a gun in his mouth and pulled the trigger rather than be tried and convicted.'

'I can't say I blame him.' But Ushiba turned away, staring into the darkness of the strange apartment. Is this the ending he had envisioned when he committed himself to Ken's suggestion? How clever he had thought Kisoko's son was when he had proposed using Tanaka Gin as the means to punish Chosa. Of course Ushiba hadn't known this would happen. He wasn't so cruel and calculating as to have coldly signed the death warrant of a man who had once been his friend.

And yet how could he have not known? *I can't say I blame him*. His own words condemned him. He knew Chosa too well. The man was too deeply spiritual to allow himself to be paraded through the media, humiliated in court and confined in prison. Given the choice, Ushiba knew that he himself would have chosen seppuku – ritual suicide. To die in one's own way at one's own time had about it a dignity impossible in other circumstances. To be at the mercy of one's enemy, to have life reduced to the space of a barred cell, was unthinkable.

I've killed him. The thought was like a knife blade in his bowels. Chosa had betrayed their friendship, yes; he had betrayed the inner council and endangered the Godaishu, all in his pursuit of retribution against Nicholas Linnear. But was that enough to sentence a man to die? It had to be. Too late to believe anything else now. Too late . . .

'Ushiba-san?'

With an effort, the Daijin turned away from the darkness. He blinked in the light of the kitchen.

'It's very late and I am exhausted from a long day.'

Ushiba nodded, knowing that Tanaka Gin said this for his benefit. Tanaka Gin would never shame him by asking, Are you all right?

'I, too, am exhausted. But these days sleep escapes me. It is as if I've forgotten how.'

Tanaka Gin poured himself another drink. 'I go through periods where rest seems as remote as a vacation in Paris.' He shook his head. 'I am a poor host. Can I get you something?'

'I'm afraid nothing appeals.'

They went into the living room, Tanaka Gin lighting lamps as he went; he would permit no overhead lighting in the apartment because, he said, they provided no warmth. They sat facing each other in deep Western-style chairs.

Ushiba watched Tanaka Gin's face, which was gaunt and pale. 'You think you've failed. That you should have been more vigilant, but how can you know what is in a man's mind?'

'Yes, of course.' Tanaka Gin took some Scotch into his mouth, shuddered. 'Oblivion. When you witness another's death, you see reflected in it your own end.'

Ushiba, with sudden insight into this formidable man, said, 'It's only when you fear something too deeply that it can harm you.'

'Perhaps. But all too often it seems that one has no choice.'

Now he was convinced that Tanaka Gin had unwittingly disclosed his reason for becoming a prosecutor. It was the same reason that some men went to sea as a way of life: they feared it and, in seeking to master their dread, they contrived to control the circumstances

483

of it. The prosecutor's morbid fear of death was bridled by his daily proximity to it.

'Was it bad?' Ushiba asked after a small silence.

'Death is always bad. No matter the person or the circumstance.'

Ushiba thought that an interesting response from a Tokyo prosecutor, especially one such as Tanaka Gin, who had brought many a dangerous malefactor to justice.

'But perhaps this case proves the exception to your rule.'

Tanaka Gin looked up from his Scotch. 'How so?'

'I had always suspected that Chosa was being slowly corrupted by American ethics, American values. I've no doubt you saw the Marilyn Monroe replica in his apartment. That dress is the original. It was made for her. It cost Chosa more than your yearly salary. Chosa, I feared, was becoming cynical of the new Japan. The land of the empty symbol, he used to call it. I thought he'd lost faith in it.'

'I see. So the way he chose to die – his last gesture, in effect – affirmed his faith.'

'Yes. He chose to die like a modern-day warrior. Death before dishonor.'

'And that makes his death, what? More bearable or understandable?'

Ushiba could see Tanaka Gin struggling with the philosophical understanding of Chosa's death – and with that single ending a perception of death itself. Ushiba could see that his answer might be of profound import to this man. 'Neither,' he said simply. 'But it does give it form and substance. It wasn't just an empty symbol.'

484

SIXTEEN

Virginia/Tokyo/Vietnamese Highlands

The DARPA laboratory for experimental nucleonics in which Douglas Serman worked was in the wilds of rural Virginia. Fifty acres assured the government a minimum of nosy neighbors and, for those curiosity-seekers on the main road, the discreet sign for THE KNIFE RIVER RIDING ACADEMY, BY APPOINTMENT ONLY kept everyone else at bay. Of course a quarter of Washington knew a DARPA facility existed out here, but few asked questions about it.

In the seventies, at the height of the war in Vietnam, some arm of the federal government now long buried in a firestorm of red tape had conducted complex experiments in chemical warfare on animals here, mainly rats, but also, it was rumored, on a number of unwitting armed-services personnel. At that time, six separate lines of electrified barbed wire ringed the perimeter of the facility, which was patrolled by guard dogs and armed troops. In that department, at least, nothing much had changed, and it was a foolhardy individual who considered breaking into the place. In fact, no one had, not even during the worst moments of the now defunct Cold War, and the zealots involved in the hot war of global terrorism were, frankly, more concerned with the high-profile destruction of public buildings and priceless artwork than they were with top-secret installations where a total news blackout would negate their raison d'être.

Deplaning, Croaker had wanted nothing more than to sleep for a week, but there were only thirty-six hours to the fifteenth. Besides, he was too busy keeping an eye out for Bad Clams' people to be inclined to stay in one spot for very long.

A colleague of Major's had promised to radio the plane the moment Tom had emerged from surgery and was stable, and an hour before they had touched down in Washington, while those around him were lined up for the lavatory, a fresh-faced flight attendant had handed him a folded slip of paper with the news. It had been too soon for a long-range prognosis, however.

Croaker had phoned Margarite from the gigantic octopus of Dulles airport.

'Lew, what —'

'No time, honey,' he had said breathlessly. 'I want you to get Francie and get on the road.'

'But I —'

'Do as I say!' It had taken all his willpower not to shout it at her. His heart was hammering in his chest. If Bad Clams had made an attempt to hit him in London, could his threat to take Margarite's life be far behind? He didn't know but he could not take the chance. 'Take a couple of muscle boys with you.'

'Lew, you've got to tell me *something*.'

'Margarite —'

'For the love of God, Lew, are you all right?'

'For the moment, but let's just say your enemy has become my enemy.'

'Caesare?'

'Bingo. Please, Margarite, do as I ask.'

'Yes, of course, but, Lew —'

'Give my love to Francie,' he said hurriedly as he quartered the terminal again with his eyes. 'When you get to wherever it is you're going, call me and leave a message.' He gave her the Looking-Glass phone number. 'But *don't* leave an address. Find a phone booth and leave its number along with a time each day when you'll be there, okay?'

'Yes, yes, but Lew — God, don't hang up yet. Lew?'

He could hear her quick breathing. He had frightened her. Good. She'd take the necessary precautions now.

'I love you, whatever happens, whatever — '

'I love you.' He closed his eyes, imagining her, as if he could will her to be beside him. He wanted more than anything else to kiss her, hold her close, keep her safe from harm. Instead, he lowered the receiver into its chrome cradle.

He took a moment to compose himself, then he had phoned Senator Dedalus.

'I need access to the DARPA facility.'

'Where the hell have you been?'

'London,' Croaker said, knowing the senator was doing a tap dance while his computer-like brain worked on why Croaker would need access to DARPA.

'Did you find what you were looking for?'

'Yes and no.'

'What does that mean?'

'When you get me inside the facility, I'll be able to tell you.'

'Shit, man, DARPA has a dozen facilities. Which one do you want to get into?'

Right now, Dedalus was in the bull's-eye of suspects who had compromised a critical government security agency. Someone was feeding DARPA product — that is, prototype weaponry that was far beyond state-of-the-art — to Rock and Mick Leonforte in their Floating City outside Saigon. It couldn't be Mick's father, Johnny Leonforte, aka Leon Waxman, because he was dead. And though Croaker couldn't be certain until he vetted him, it was odds on that Serman wasn't running the program himself.

Vesper was involved and she worked for Dedalus; the late Dominic Goldoni had been involved and he had been friends with Dedalus; Margarite was involved and she had been introduced to Dedalus by her brother. There was only one name that kept reappearing.

He hadn't planned to tell the senator Serman's identity, but he could see now he had no other choice. He desperately needed to get his hands on Vesper and make her talk about where exactly Mikio Okami was in London.

Torch . . .

The horrifying specter of the impending disaster in London on the ides hung like a guillotine at the back of his neck. He could already hear the whisper of the thick blade as it hurtled down its prescribed track. Only thirty-six hours left until detonation.

'I heard a man named Serman mentioned in London in connection with the investigation. It may be nothing, Senator, but I can't afford to overlook any lead.'

'Are you sure it's Serman's name you heard? Dr Douglas Serman?'

'Quite sure.'

Dedalus grunted. 'All right. I'll send a detail of my men with you.'

'You do and I'll clear the area by the most direct route possible. You have feds blundering around in the bushes outside Serman's office and I guarantee you he'll be so scared he'll clam up tight.'

Dedalus seemed to think about this for some time. At last, he relented, giving Croaker specific directions to the DARPA lab for experimental nucleonics.

He knew he had taken an enormous risk going to the senator with the DARPA connection. On the other hand, what other choice had he had? He had neither the location of Serman nor access to him without Dedalus. Besides, if Dedalus was the mainspring of this particular timepiece, the information about Serman would make him nervous. It was Croaker's experience that, more often than not, nervous men made precipitous moves. It was usually all the edge he needed because it was all he got. For instance, Dedalus had not mentioned that DARPA was a top-secret national security program. Also, he hadn't brought up the meeting Croaker was supposed to have had with Vesper that never happened. Croaker wondered whether the senator knew that his operative had been in London at the same time as Croaker had been.

The ride out to Virginia calmed him down. He had slept fitfully during the transatlantic flight, and when he did, he dreamed of Major Tom's blood floating in the air like pink clouds. He had awakened, the muffled roar of the jet engines sounding like the frightening sounds of the medical machines to which his friend had been hooked up on the way to surgery.

At the Knife River registration office, he was handed his credentials by a flinty-eyed blonde in a well-worn suede riding outfit and, apparently, a steel shaft up her spine. He was also fingerprinted and given a retinal scan by two burly men who might have been brothers but were probably only graduates of the same military academy.

He asked the blonde if anyone else within the last two days had clocked in to see Dr Serman. No one had. He was then directed outside the academy building where a jeep with an iron-armed driver took him past corrals, riding rings with jumps and extensive stables and what looked like barracks buildings. A rutted lane led down an embankment, across a trestle bridge that spanned what he took to be Knife River. They stopped at the edge of deep woods, where a group of men with hunting dogs and shotguns slung casually across their arms appeared and studied Croaker's ID. They were waved on through, jouncing down the deeply rutted path carved into the woods.

At length, the trees gave way to scrub oak and brambles, and then they picked up speed across a meadow that would be beautiful in late spring and summer. Now it merely seemed barren and, wrapped in mist, melancholy.

The lab complex appeared, sitting on the east side of a succession of rolling wooded hills. Dogs barked, unseen, and Croaker wondered how much telemetry was homed in on them. The jeep let him off at the front entrance of a low, angular concrete structure with windows of black, reflective glass. It was no doubt meant to appear futuristic and forbidding. Instead, it merely looked governmental and dreary.

The recent history of the DARPA facility was clear in Croaker's mind as he introduced himself to Douglas Serman, who, more than anything else, reminded him of a rodent in his precise, repetitive movements, his bright eyes and his obviously anal retentive nature.

'Is there somewhere private we can speak?' Croaker said in his most neutral voice.

Serman, who seemed to make a habit of looking at everything out of the corner of his eye, said, 'Is this an official visit? Do I need my logs and such?'

'Not at the moment,' Croaker said. 'Doctor, is there a lounge or something?'

'Yes, of course.' Serman rubbed his hands together, ushered Croaker down a hallway that smelled of industrial-strength chemical cherry, as if it had just been converted from a mass urinal.

Serman pushed open a door that said PRIVATE with his shoulder. Croaker found himself in an unexpectedly homey suite of rooms that, with their frilly curtains and the chintz floral furniture fabric, seemed more appropriate for the public rooms at the riding academy.

Serman remained standing in the middle of the room as if he had had no experience with informality.

'You're one of the senator's people?'

'Yes, but I've just come from London.'

Serman peered at him politely, his hands dry-washing themselves with all the energy of Lady Macbeth. 'Never been there myself,' he said at last. Then he gave a small self-deprecating chuckle. 'Haven't been anywhere really. Not in some years. They won't let me outside the country, you see. Afraid I'll be abducted.' Another dry chuckle. 'As if I'm a national treasure.'

'In London I met a friend of yours. Vesper Arkham.'

Serman twitched like the subject of a Skinnerian psych project. Rat in a maze.

'Vesper who?' He was no good at this.

'Arkham, Doctor. Vesper Arkham.'

'I'm not sure I —'

'She's your normal contact,' Croaker snapped, abruptly dropping the facade of cordiality. Serman was like a lake in spring: he was covered with a sheet of very thin ice. 'And she's very concerned about the updates you've stopped giving her.'

Serman blinked. 'Updates?'

It was time, Croaker judged, to leave it to intuition and gamble everything. 'Yes, Doctor. From the project you and Abramanov have been working on. What is it called?' A sick look was coming to Serman's face, and Croaker felt a surge of triumph. 'Ah, yes. Torch.'

Serman's legs seemed to have turned to jelly. Croaker held him up by the elbows, directed him to one of the chintz-covered sofas.

'Are you all right, Doctor?'

Serman's bluish lips moved. 'Vesper promised me no one else would know about those reports,' he whispered.

Croaker was near the center, he could taste it on the

491

electrically charged air. 'What kind of deal did Vesper have going with you?'

Serman jumped up. 'It was Vesper who allowed the transmission between me and Abramanov to keep up. Without her, it would have eventually been picked up by the special subcarrier tracker used here as an anti-bugging security measure. In return, she insisted on being kept up-to-date on our high-flux neutron project.'

Serman jammed his hands in his pockets, went to one of the curtained windows and stared out. 'I want to make something clear. I'm not a traitor. I've worked for the government all my life. I've been a dedicated man. But dedication . . .' He turned around. 'Such dedication needs to be rewarded, dammit! Instead, I've been entombed here. I can't go anywhere, do anything, see anybody without forms to fill out, questions to be answered, suspicions raised. As far as the world at large is concerned I died five years ago. But, I'll tell you, this is worse than death.'

'Why don't you quit?'

Serman looked at him wide-eyed for a moment before bursting out into laughter that racked him so thoroughly tears spilled out of his eyes.

'Good God, man, look at where we are!' he gasped. 'You don't just walk away from a place like this. Your brain is too full of equations that impact national security.' He dabbed at the corners of his eyes with his sleeve. 'This is a lifetime job. The fact that they never tell you that when you sign on is another matter entirely.'

Croaker felt little sympathy for Serman. 'So staying had nothing to do with the high-flux neutron project.'

'Of course it did,' Serman said with the impenetrable logic of the scientist. 'He said with my help he'd had a breakthrough. He'd been able to create a transuranic isotope that was stable. Do you know what a transuranic isotope is?'

'Yes, it's a radioactive substance with an atomic number higher than uranium – that makes it potentially deadly to humans. And I also know that he's taken this isotope and has made a devastatingly dangerous weapon out of it.'

'Torch.' Serman abruptly sat down. 'Yes. I think I know what Abramanov did to create element 114m, but for some reason I haven't been able to duplicate his success.' He stopped, put his head into his hands. 'We had such hopes. An almost endless fuel, cheap to make, an end to the ongoing energy crisis. What a dream!' He looked up. 'But that's all it is, a dream. Abramanov has made the ultimate weapon out of it.' Serman looked bleakly at him. 'Because so little of it is needed for a powerful explosion, its potential use lies in hand-held nuclear devices. In today's world of terrorists and small ethnic wars it fits every criterion for the ultimate weapon: it's portable, devastating and clean.'

Croaker had an idea. 'Can you contact Abramanov now?'

'No. All communication abruptly ceased five days ago. I have had no reply to my repeated queries.'

'How are you involved with the weapons being stolen from DARPA?'

'What are you talking about?'

He could see that Serman knew nothing about Vesper's other activities inside DARPA. He had thought to bundle Serman off to the security office at the other end of the complex, but now he thought better of it. Somehow Croaker had to get Serman out of the DARPA facility and contact Nicholas. Now, more than ever, the Torch 315 detonation date must be stopped.

He had Serman fetch him one of the doctor's white

lab coats, then he pumped Serman in detail about the complex's layout and the doctor's daily route and routine.

Then he had Serman lead him back to his lab. He sat at the zinc countertop in the light of one lit Bunsen burner while Serman crouched beneath, hidden by shadows and the lab stool. It would have been easiest to change his plan and leave with Serman without waiting for Vesper to show up, but instinct told him that would be a mistake. He could not leave in place a mole planted so deeply inside the Nishiki network she had access to Okami himself. He had to take her down and do it now while he could have a degree of control over the killing ground. And yet something kept intruding, a tickle of intent at the periphery of his thoughts. Something Serman had said he had let slip through . . .

A shadowy figure crept silently through the doorway.

'So you *are* here.'

He recognized her voice, Dedalus's mole. He did not move, but he felt as if a laser beam was sighted between his eyes.

'Would you come with me. We have much to discuss.'

Croaker studied her face. She was taking it well, he thought. There was not a trace of surprise on her face. That capped it: Dedalus had told her he was here. She *was* his mole – and she had access to Okami. No wonder his adversaries had found Okami in London. She had betrayed him.

'You're a sight,' Croaker said, looking at this newest incarnation of Vesper Arkham. She wore black leggings and a quilted black jacket over a silk blouse. Her natural blonde hair was pulled tightly back from her face, which was set in a troubled scowl. She had never looked more beautiful – or more deadly. 'We do have much to discuss.' He smiled, raising his biomechanical hand, its stainless-steel nails fully extruded. 'But this time I'm ready for you.'

'You idiot,' she said, stunning him to immobility. 'Where the hell is Serman? I've got to get you both out of here before you're shot dead!'

'Tachi Shidare is dead,' Tetsuo Akinaga said. 'And now that Chosa has committed suicide, the inner council no longer exists.'

Ushiba said nothing. When he had received the message from Akinaga he had actually considered postponing the meeting. He was exhausted unto death. The guilt he felt over Chosa's death was only partially mitigated by the certain knowledge that it had been necessary. The security of the Godaishu had to be maintained at whatever cost. *You should get out before you make a fatal mistake and the force of your own politics runs you over*, Ken had told him. And he well understood the wisdom of his words, because he had answered, *When the game becomes a burden, the rules change and the hunter is most in danger of becoming the hunted*. He remembered his feeling of renewed power as he had said, *One is born smelling the blood*.

That statement, so filled with the arrogance of youth, was simply not true. The blood was what had made him so certain that Chosa's and Akinaga's vision of the Godaishu was sound, that their diatribes against the despotism of the Kaisho had to be acted upon. Only now could he see how the bloodlust for power had blinded all of them.

With Chosa and Shidare gone he could not help thinking that they would not have come to these dire straits had they not made the tacit decision to do away with the Kaisho. Mikio Okami's firm hand would have led them down an altogether different path. It was up

495

to him, now, to steer a clear path for the Godaishu and the council.

'What happened to the young *oyabun*?' he said now.

Akinaga shrugged. 'It was not of my doing. Shidare was struck down by an assassin in Yoshino.'

'Yoshino? What was he doing there?'

The two men were sitting in the sparely furnished main room of Tomi, the obelisk-like concrete structure Akinaga had built for himself as a retreat. It rose on a two-hundred-square-foot lot in the center of Tokyo. Tomi, which meant a kind of watchtower that could command a wide view, was one of the *oyabun*'s various secretive quarters. Like a commander during wartime, he had many avenues of escape from the pressures of his world. A set of steep stone stairs rose from street level beside a narrow parking space. Above was the room they were in, along with a tiny kitchen. A black iron spiral staircase in one corner led up to the bedrooms and bath. Ushiba had never found it a comfortable space, but it was efficient in the manner of a Spartan commander.

Blocks of beautiful kiaki – the only wood in the room – had been carved into a low table at which they knelt. Tea and cakes had been laid out when Ushiba arrived. Certainly, Akinaga had not prepared them; it was his subtle way of bringing to Ushiba's attention that there was someone else in the house, unseen but available if needed.

'Shidare was in Yoshino doing his job, one suspects,' Akinaga said. 'Tracking down Nicholas Linnear in order to kill him. It seems that, like Tomoo Kozo, Shidare was unsuccessful.'

'Now we're in for it,' Ushiba said. 'If Linnear knows Shidare was Yakuza and, further, a member of the inner council, he cannot fail to know where to come next.'

'Don't you find it interesting,' Akinaga said, shrewdly

496

changing the subject, 'that Linnear would be in Yoshino? Why? Perhaps that is where the Kaisho is in hiding.'

'Our first concern should be Linnear. Because of Chosa's foolhardy act Linnear is sure to come to Tokyo looking for you. I can help with –'

'I think you have done just about enough, Daijin.'

Ushiba looked in mute disbelief at Akinaga.

'With Chosa and Shidare gone, there is only me, Chief Minister.' The *oyabun* leaned over the kiaki table. 'Your position on the inner council was always of an advisory nature, but over the past year it has not been lost on me that your attendance, opinions and influence have been on the rise. It began even before we drove Okami from the Kaisho's position and ever since then you seem bent on gaining power exponentially.' Akinaga's face twisted. 'You see, that's what this little exercise has been in aid of.'

'What exercise?' A rime of ice was forming in Ushiba's lower belly.

'I gave you Chosa on a platter, and much to my satisfaction you ate him whole.' Akinaga gave a booming laugh. 'Imagine! I turned you against your friend! Amazing really.'

Ushiba was ashen-faced. 'You'd better explain yourself.' He could not quite manage to hold his voice steady.

'It was I who acted on the plot to assassinate the Kaisho. That weakling Chosa tried to steal my thunder.'

'But the plot failed.'

'It drove the Kaisho into hiding; it stripped him of all power and influence,' Akinaga spat. 'Okami might as well be dead; the result is the same.' He took out a cigarette, lit up leisurely. 'Then I suborned Shidare. I convinced him that he had no power unless he aligned himself with a member of the inner council. He was a

497

pragmatic young man and he agreed. So I sent him off to do away with Linnear.'

'You!'

'Of course! I knew that Shidare was *tanjian*. Only another *tanjian* had a chance to destroy Linnear, but I suppose I discounted Shidare's youth. He failed.'

'But Chosa –'

'Ah, Chosa!' Akinaga luxuriated in the smoke from his cigarette. 'Chosa and I were due to come to blows sooner or later. His ambition was to take over the Kaisho's position – and so is mine. The inner council wasn't big enough for the both of us.'

'But he had too much power for you to go after him yourself.'

'Precisely. I let you do it for me.'

'But Yoshinori told me –'

'Yoshinori told you what I wanted him to tell you. The old boy always does what I ask. We have an understanding that goes back decades. We could always count on one another.'

'And I believed him.'

'Why shouldn't you? I would have, in your place.' Now, to Ushiba's fury, Akinaga gave him a compassionate look. 'He was such a consummate actor. It was his hobby, you see, acting, a kind of grand passion. He loved it so!'

Akinaga rose, went to one of the small windows buried in the rough concrete wall. He stared down onto the narrow street where traffic whizzed by.

'Now I have what I want. With Chosa and Shidare gone there is nothing to stop me from succeeding Okami as Kaisho.'

'But Okami still lives.'

'Yes, he does.' Akinaga was truly terrifying in his calmness. 'But I know, more or less, where he's hiding. And when I take possession of Torch from Floating City,

498

Okami will be nothing more than a cinder floating above the rooftops, and Rock will have ringing validation of the power of Torch. Our partnership will be extremely fruitful.'

'So this is why you lobbied so hard for the Floating City partnership,' Ushiba said, stunned. 'You had made a private deal with Rock and Mick Leonforte for Torch.'

The ghost of a smile on Akinaga's face was positively eerie, and as Ushiba struggled to his feet, he could feel the chill of fear creeping through him. They were now in the situation that Okami had forestalled in becoming Kaisho: a despotic leader, one Japanese voice controlling the Godaishu. It was intolerable. 'This grasping for control won't succeed. I'll do everything in my power to stop you.'

Akinaga turned to look at Ushiba. 'Chief Minister, I fear you are overstepping yourself. You *have* no power.'

'By God, you've got nerve.'

'I've got more than that.' Akinaga's smile turned serpent-like. 'I feel sorry for you, Chief Minister, I really do. We're of the same generation, we enjoy many of the same sensibilities, but over the course of time I've sounded you out. You've changed since Okami was banished. Sometimes, I've been astonished when, talking to you, I've thought the Kaisho resurrected. I've come to the sad conclusion you're too much like him.'

'What if I am? There's nothing you can do about it.'

'Oh, but there is.' Akinaga stubbed out his butt in a green metal ashtray iridescent as the carapace of an insect. 'I'm holding all the cards.'

Akinaga walked to a black metal grid filled with books on architecture and history. From between them he pulled out a sheaf of rice paper. 'You know what these are,' he said, that deadly smile pinned to his face.

'*Torinawa*,' Ushiba said with a sick feeling in the pit of his stomach.

Akinaga brandished them over his head. 'Yes.' *Torinawa*, which was a special rope used by samurai for binding criminals, meant, in the perverse manner of the Yakuza, a pledge from a leaderless clan to follow the orders of another. 'Here I have the *torinawa* from the Kokorogurushii and the Yamauchi clans. They now follow me. I am, in effect, the inner council. And from this moment on I am the new Kaisho.'

Silence rolled like thunder through the ferroconcrete room. Ushiba wanted to run and hide, but like the good samurai he stood his ground and took his punishment. He should never have acquiesced to the inner council's plan to depose Okami. They had portrayed him as a power-hungry despot, while just the opposite was true. Kozo was planning to murder Nicholas Linnear, and Chosa and Akinaga were plotting against one another to become the next Kaisho. Even as all of them pledged that there would never be another Kaisho.

'So,' Akinaga said, 'now you understand the true nature of the present situation. I own you, Daijin, and believe me I plan to milk your influence and contacts for all they're worth. Within thirty hours Mikio Okami will be dead and my triumph will be complete. You will be my loyal right hand. I will give the orders and you will carry them out in the arena of international economics both at MITI and in the Godaishu.' Akinaga took two swift steps toward Ushiba. 'Is all this quite clear, Daijin?'

Ushiba took a deep breath, let it go. 'Yes.' That one word had a finality he could never have dreamed of before this moment.

'You're nuts if you think I'm going anywhere with you,' Croaker said. 'Every time I see you you're another person.'

'Another time, another place, another identity,'

Vesper said in the semi-darkness. 'For the love of God, come on!'

He did not budge. He could hear the quiet hiss of the Bunsen burner. By its eerie light he looked at Vesper, wondering which incarnation he was seeing. Watching her was like looking at someone reflected in a series of fun-house mirrors: each distorted image took you further away from the truth, the reality, until you felt as if the reflections themselves must be the reality.

Her head twisted. 'I hear him! He's coming!'

'Cut this out. I don't –'

'Dammit, you already gave Serman away to Dedalus! D'you want to sacrifice us both as well?'

In truth, he could hear sounds echoing down the hallway. Unmistakably, they were coming closer. Was she telling the truth? Was it Dedalus who was coming?

'Give it up,' he said. 'I know all about Torch. I know that Okami is in London and that he's targeted for the fifteenth. I know you've betrayed him to his enemies.'

'You've been talking to the wrong people. I'll explain everything to you if you'll just move out of here before we're both trapped.'

'You're a liar seven times over. I've proved to my satisfaction you're Dedalus's mole inside Okami's network. Which one of you am I to believe?'

He could hear the rising note of anxiety in her voice. 'Believe me if only for this one moment. We've got to get out of here. Now!'

Something wasn't computing. If she was the enemy, why didn't she just keep him here until Dedalus came? What was he to believe? And now that tickle at his consciousness took hold.

'Jesus,' he whispered, then, pulling Serman out of his hiding place, nodded to her. 'Okay. Let's go.'

He followed her as she rushed out into the hallway.

The sounds had coalesced into the click-clack of shoe soles. They seemed very close.

She ducked into the next room, which was a chemical storeroom. It was temperature- and humidity-controlled. She went to one of the freestanding refrigeration units, pulled it aside without any help from Croaker. Peering behind it, he could see an old screen leaning against the wall. Vesper removed this, revealing a panel that had been rough-cut into the wall.

She turned to him. 'We need that hand of yours.'

As he worked his stainless-steel nails into the narrow gap to pull the panel out, she said, 'Years ago, when this facility was being used for experiments on humans, some of the subjects found a way to escape.'

He edged the panel out and Vesper moved the refrigeration unit back as far as she could. Then she crawled into the opening, helped Serman through. Croaker followed her, then, turning, he used his biomechanical hand to pull the unit more or less back in place. There was a crude handle on the back of the panel, which allowed him to set it in place without difficulty.

He began to move off, but Vesper held him back.

'We stay right here,' she whispered. 'Those subjects never made it all the way out of here. Just sit tight.'

It was odd. He could hear her soft breathing, smell a faint scent coming off her, as from a peony, but he could not see her. Instead, he imagined her – as she had been when they had first met in the lobby of the Washington Holiday Inn; as he had seen her on Dedalus's estate as the gardener and, later, talking with Margarite; as he had seen her coming out of Heathrow and, later, with Celeste and Okami. In some alchemical way the darkness allowed these disparate images to merge, as if she were some film star who had stepped off the screen to sit beside him and speak.

'Who are you?' he whispered.

'What does it matter? All you need to know is that I work for Mikio Okami.'

He could believe her now – or, at least, begin the process – because Serman had made a deal with her, not Dedalus. Serman had been afraid that even Croaker knew that he was providing her with updates on the progress of Torch. If Vesper were working for Dedalus, Torch would not have had to be kept from him. Dedalus did not know about Torch, but Vesper did. Vesper had arranged for Serman and Abramanov to continue their clandestine dialogue. Vesper was bringing periodic updates on Torch's progress to Okami.

Still, Croaker felt compelled to say, 'I need to know more before I can be sure I can trust you.'

He could feel her staring at him.

'Margarite says I can trust you, but I'm not at all sure.' Then she seemed to acquiesce – to the situation if not to him. 'I think you're damned dangerous and I told her so. I think she should stay as far away from you as possible. Now, though, I'm not sure I was right.'

'Why should I believe you? As Domino you did nothing but lie to me; as Vesper you have as many personalities as an oracle. Besides, when I stole your ledger out of the safe at Moniker's, I broke your code. I saw the breakdown for Morgana, the arms merchant – the company you're running for Dedalus.'

'Dedalus owned Morgana, all right. But what you stole were photocopies I'd taken and was in the process of sending back to Okami.'

Croaker said nothing. What she said could very easily be the truth.

'You did your own share of lying,' Vesper said. 'And what's more, you scared the hell out of me. You were following Margarite – spying on her and me.'

'Yes, we both lied to one another. Also, you failed to mention that Senator Dedalus was in charge of DARPA.'

'And you failed to mention your afternoon in TriBeCa with Caesare Leonforte,' she said tartly.

In a flash, he could see how it would look to her and to Margarite. He and Bad Clams having lunch, thick as thieves. Good God, did Margarite think he had betrayed her? Why not? He had come perilously close to doing just that. How had he planned to elude Bad Clams when it came time for him to report to the don on the Nishiki network? He'd never quite worked that out, hoping for a flash of inspiration somewhere down the line.

'So you thought I might be working for Bad Clams. What changed your –'

He felt her hand over his mouth. He strained to listen to what was happening beyond their tiny cell, in the storeroom. He made out sounds, like the scraping of chair legs over a tile floor, and he knew they were looking for him. Deeper in the darkness, Serman huddled, shivering in mortal fear. His whole being was concentrated on listening to the sounds; he had forgotten Croaker and Vesper existed.

Dedalus's people.

In time, the sounds faded. Even then he could feel her waiting. At last, she took her hand away, said softly, 'The moment you attacked Caesare's man in Holland Park I knew I had made a mistake.'

'You knew I had followed you to London?'

'Before I left Washington I went back to Moniker's. It didn't take me long to realize someone had gone through my safe, and it didn't take a genius to figure out who.'

'If you knew I was on your tail, why didn't you stop me?'

'I tried. If you remember, I gave you false intelligence. You were too smart to fall for that. I should have known.'

'What do you mean?'

'What do you think I mean? Margarite's in love with you.'

His sense of relief was so profound he wanted to lean over and kiss her. 'It makes no sense.'

'When it comes to love, what does?'

'I mean it's utterly absurd, isn't it?'

'Only if you don't feel the same way.'

'But she and I are on opposite sides of the law.'

'Are you certain? Following your logic then, you and I are also on opposite sides. You know that's not true.'

She allowed him to ponder this for some time before saying, 'I'm taking an enormous risk in telling you all this. I would protect Margarite with my life.'

This was like a Chinese puzzle, he thought, where you figured out how to open a series of nested boxes one by one. 'I think I understand that.' He could feel her slowly unwinding, like a serpent whose coils and head had been in the strike position for a long time. 'How do we get out of here without Dedalus finding us?'

'There's only one way. We've got to follow the route the subjects took when they tried to escape.'

'But you said they never made it.'

'Right. We're about to find out why.'

I saw Leonforte shoot my father down like a dog in the street, Tachi had said. *What's more Leonforte liked it. He licked his lips and howled in glee, he did a little dance over my father's body before dragging it into the jungle.*

This was the man Koei had spent six months with, whom she had been meant to marry, the man who had fallen in love with her. Now, in all probability Nicholas would come face to face with Mick Leonforte. If he made it into Floating City.

The lure of his delirious reunion with Koei still exerted its magic on him, and it was almost too much

505

to bear to part with her again. His only solace was that she had promised that she would go to Tokyo. He had told her to go to his friend and partner, Tanzan Nangi, and stay with him until Nicholas returned.

'It's time I ended my exile here,' she had told him just before he had left with Van Kiet. 'The truth is I've been terrified of Michael ever since I left him. There was a look in his eye . . .' She had broken off, shuddering, and Nicholas had held her.

'Mick Leonforte can't touch you now,' he had said.

Koei had clung to him, not wanting him to go. 'You don't know him the way I do. He's relentless, and so very clever. He always gets what he wants, in the end.'

Nicholas had made her look into his eyes. 'Listen to me. When you get to Tokyo tell Nangi everything. He will know what precautions to take.' He had kissed her hard on the lips. 'You'll see me sooner than you think.'

Nicholas returned to the present. The jeep jounced along the rutted highway that stretched more or less straight north out of Saigon, which was already a half-day's travel behind them. Van Kiet was in a black mood. He had lost control the moment he had brought Nicholas to meet Huynh Van Dich, and he did not like that. Tachi was dead, and Nicholas knew the way into Floating City.

'When we get inside,' Van Kiet said, 'you'll leave Rock to me. I know how to handle his kind.'

Nicholas doubted that. Van Kiet was filled with rage, and that made for muddled thinking. Besides, he was hellbent on blowing away Rock and anyone else who got in his way. What Nicholas needed was answers. Why was Floating City so important to Akinaga and Chosa — and, he was beginning to suspect, to Mikio Okami as well? Rock and, for that matter, Mick Leonforte lying dead in the middle of their empire would do him no good at all.

'We need to consider our approach to Rock and Leonforte,' he said.

'*This* is the only approach that won't get us killed,' Van Kiet said, hefting a MAC-10 machine pistol.

'There's another way.'

Van Kiet, accelerating, shook his head. 'You don't know these bastards. Tachi and I have been hunting them for more than two years.' He maneuvered past a pair of lumbering, rattletrap trucks spewing diesel exhaust into the greenish early evening. 'There is only one way to deal with them. Talk is out of the question. Their ears are filled with the music of the spheres. What you or I say to them will mean as much as the wind through the trees. They – Buddha!'

The road opened up in front of them in a huge geyser of tarmac, stones and flying chunks of concrete. The explosion's shock wave tore the windshield off the jeep, and Van Kiet put his arms up, cried out as a fragment of metal struck him.

Scrambling over him, Nicholas stamped hard on the brakes, jerked the wheel hard over to the left. Fighting blowing ash and debris that pelted him like buckshot, he shoved Van Kiet out of the way. The jeep bucked heavily as it lurched toward the leading edge of the crater that had appeared through the violent windstorm explosion.

Nicholas, battling the headlong momentum of the jeep, saw they were going to go into the crater, and he stamped hard on the accelerator and, keeping the wheels straight, threw Van Kiet into the backseat behind him. Leaning hard over to his left, he felt the change in weight distribution in the jeep as it began to go over. The instant it lifted up onto two tires, he compensated with the wheel, keeping them at this angle.

The jeep rolled on, skirting the gaping hole in the

highway. He kept it skidding precariously on two wheels as he struggled to keep on the verge where the tires would have clear purchase.

He fanned the brakes as he drove the gears lower, until the jeep's speed was reduced enough for it to bounce down on all four wheels.

'Who the hell –'

A second explosion upended the jeep.

Nicholas allowed instinct and his *tanjian* eye to take over. He let go of the wheel and leapt clear, relaxing his muscles, rolling on his side and shoulder as he hit the slope by the side of the highway. But a third explosion ripped apart the slope near him and he tumbled backward, his head cracking against the bole of a tree. He lay dazed for a moment, trying to bring the world back into focus.

A hundred yards away, he saw Van Kiet, bloody and shaking, climbing from the jeep, which lay on its side, steaming, its entire back end crumpled where it hadn't been blown away altogether. Van Kiet had the MAC-10 out, and now Nicholas could see a giant of a man in jungle fatigues appearing over a heavily foliaged rise. Slung around one shoulder was a LAW-M72, a light antitank rocket launcher, an American weapon used extensively during the war. The man must be as strong as a quarter horse to carry it himself, Nicholas thought. He had a square, rugged face, tanned and fierce, dominated by oddly pale blue eyes. His blond hair was cropped short, in military style, but he bore no resemblance to any form of American military personnel Nicholas had ever seen. Rather, he moved like an Asian – that is, from the lower belly. He was centered, powerful mentally as well as physically. And his face was testimony that the war had exterminated from him any semblance of normal human emotion. As he aimed the weapon in Van Kiet's direction, Nicholas knew he was looking at Rock, the emperor of Floating City. He was up and running toward Van Kiet.

'Get away from here!' Van Kiet screamed. 'Are you insane? We have laws here.'

'You don't get it, do you, you fucking slant cop,' Rock said, advancing. 'You don't give the orders here. I do.'

Nicholas shouted a warning, but Van Kiet wasn't listening. His rage had gotten the better of him. He let go a burst from the machine pistol, but he had lost a lot of blood and, rocking on his feet, his aim was poor.

'Moron.' Rock kept advancing, and Nicholas changed course, heading obliquely toward him. 'Fucking cretin. I would have taken care of you if you'd come aboard.'

'I can't be bought,' Van Kiet shouted.

'But you can die.' Without any expression registering on his face, Rock pulled the trigger on the LAW, and Nicholas ducked down.

A great white-hot *Whoosh!* spun in a tight trajectory, exploding so close to Van Kiet it lifted him fifty feet in the air. Rock had picked him off as cleanly as if he had used a sharpshooter's rifle. Van Kiet, or what was left of him, came down in a shower of bits and pieces.

Rock was already striding through this viscous rain, sidestepping the mini-crater as he reloaded the deadly LAW, heading for Nicholas.

'I've been waiting a long time for this, fucker.'

Nicholas was using Tau-tau to clear his head and bring his reactions back to normal level. 'I was coming after you.'

Rock grunted. 'We'll see who's coming after who when you've spent a couple of days in Floating City.' He waggled the LAW. 'Come on. I'd like nothing better than for you to make a move.' He smirked. 'No? You'll probably regret it. It's the fucking cage for you.'

*   *   *

Ushiba was thinking of Akira Chosa. Sitting in the Daijin's grand office at MITI, he heard telephones ringing, the chatter of faxes coming through from all points on the globe, the hum of laser printers making hard copies of his policies for dissemination to other bureaus and the media. He had just finished a conference call with the prime minister and the minister of housing of which he had no memory. In twenty minutes he was due in the main hall to deliver his weekly press briefing with Tanaka Gin. He knew that, because he was staring at his electronic calendar, which his assistant updated three times daily. But, today, the words meant nothing to him.

All his life he had striven to do what was right for Japan. He had trained, given up most of his childhood and all of his adolescence to worship at the shrine of *kanryodo*, the cult of the samurai-bureaucrat. For this privileged career he had dispensed with any meaningful personal life. This was as it should be; all warriors led a life of self-discipline and austerity. He had not questioned its validity until this moment.

As if in a trance, he rose from behind his desk and, walking to a burl credenza, poured himself a glass of ice water. Drinking it down, he returned to his desk, where he sat staring out the window at the neon-and-glass spires of Tokyo. But his gaze was turned inward, his mind far away.

At the moment he had heard that Chosa died by his own hand, what had been his first thought?

To die in one's own way at one's own time had about it a dignity impossible in other circumstances. To be at the mercy of one's enemy, to have life reduced to the space of a barred cell, was unthinkable.

The continuing threat of the cancer he could live with; he had already resigned himself to carrying it around with him, sleeping or awake, for the rest of his days. In fact, he had come to think of it as a special friend, a visitor, perhaps, from another plane of existence. It served no purpose to rail against a condition one could not change.

But this was different. This was Tetsuo Akinaga. Akinaga, his enemy, who had bested him once and who now sought to lord it over him forever. It was unthinkable.

He blinked and his eyes focused on the contours of the city in which he had lived all his life. Tokyo was Japan – the soul of the new Japan, at least. He recognized rather belatedly that Chosa had been right about that, just as he had been right about the Americans. Like that of a parent with a frighteningly precocious child, the relationship between America and Japan had reached a new, unknowable stage. But like the ties that forever bind a child to its parent, the cord was severed only at the risk of jeopardizing the lives of both.

Chosa had been right to pursue his relationship with America. No matter what bad blood was stirred, resurrected and waved like a flag by those who would see the ties cut, the relationship would endure. The Japanese needed the American diplomatic methodology and inventive ideas, and the Americans needed the Japanese work ethic, sense of efficiency and its ability to refine and market new consumer products.

He had spent most of his adult life trying to keep the Americans out of Japan and it had all but killed him. Why had it taken Chosa's death to allow him to see the truth? This was only one of many questions without an answer. But that was the nature of human existence, to ask, whether or not answers were forthcoming.

He turned, flicked on his intercom, and asked for Yukio Haji, the protégé to whom he had given money when he had needed it. The young man appeared in his office sixty seconds later. He stood in the doorway, bowing deeply.

'Come in and close the door, Haji-san.'

'Hai.'

As Haji crossed the room and sat in the same steel-frame chair he had occupied when he had come to his mentor to solve his temporary fiscal problem, Ushiba opened a drawer in his desk. He stared down at the locked metal case built into it. On the day his cancer had been diagnosed he had filled the box with several items he deemed necessary. He might never use them, or even open the box, he had thought on that day, but somehow their presence had provided a measure of comfort.

'How has work been these last few weeks, Haji-san? I'm afraid my busy schedule has not permitted me to keep track.'

'Everything is being dealt with. There are no problems,' Haji said somewhat nervously. One wasn't called to a private audience with the Daijin every day. 'Of course, the land-trust issue has yet to be resolved, and I am awaiting confirmation of the microchip pact from the Electronics Policy Section of the Machinery and Information Industries Bureau. The International Trade Section is, of course, involved, so the matter is not a simple one to resolve.'

'Yes, yes. Quite.' Ushiba was sad. Once this kind of talk would have thrilled him, as it obviously did Haji. But now he had other matters on his mind, and they seemed far more pressing than the quotidian workings of MITI. 'As long as you are encountering no difficulties.'

'No, Daijin.'

'Excellent.' Ushiba lapsed into such a profound silence that it seemed he had ceased to breathe. At length, he reached down and, with a small brass key, opened the locked box. Inside was a neatly folded kimono of indigo and black. He removed this. Beneath it, was a *wakizashi* – a long ceremonial dagger lying in its rayskin sheath.

'Please excuse me for a moment, Haji-san,' Ushiba said, rising. When he returned from his private file-room, he was dressed in the kimono.

Haji jumped up, alarmed. 'Daijin, no!'

'Your duty is to help me,' Ushiba said simply. 'That is *kanryodo*.'

A terrible look of grief passed across Haji's face and was swiftly gone. He bowed his head. 'Yes, Daijin.'

On bare feet, Ushiba moved to the center of the room where he knelt, arranging the folds of his kimono in precise, concentric circles. From beneath the folds of the garment he produced the *wakizashi*. He gestured to Haji, said softly to him, 'Here is your last lesson. You must accept with your whole heart what must be done.'

'Yes, Daijin.' He knelt beside Ushiba.

'You must know it and you must believe it.'

'Yes, Daijin.'

Ushiba closed his eyes, preparing himself. It seemed vaguely ironic that he was about to take his life not to spare himself the indignity of the descent into the final stages of cancer, but to free himself from a cleverly designed man-made prison. The one he could accept far more readily than the other. He thought of Mikio Okami, and his heart was heavy that he had helped murder the one man who could have saved them all from the fiend Akinaga, hidden like a viper in their midst.

'Are you ready?'

'Yes, Daijin.'

The last person he thought of was Tanaka Gin, and he experienced a profound sorrow at their parting. They had been like two wayfarers on a desolate mountain

513

path far from home who come to one another's aid for the sake of simple human compassion. Then his mind was filled only with poetry, and the simple images of haiku focused him. Thus surrounded by beauty, he thrust the *wakizashi* into his lower belly. Strangely, except for a momentary pain he felt nothing. Then his hands began to tremble and, leaning forward, Haji put his hands over the Daijin's. Haji's lips were moving as if in a prayer. To whom was he praying? Ushiba wondered.

Then, together, as if they were joined in mind and purpose, they made the second, final cut.

Ushiba felt as if he were made of water. He heard a gentle lapping, and it reminded him of a haiku he had been reading last night at Tanaka Gin's house. The liquid changed to vapor; Ushiba felt himself rising from the floor of his office. He looked down and could see Haji, white-faced, half-supporting with his hands closed over the hilt of the *wakizashi* what appeared to be a dried-out husk of rice. Who was that? What was he doing?

Flooded with the poignancy of twilight, the brittle first day of autumn, the luminous last day of the cherry blossom's bloom, he wafted away.

SEVENTEEN

Floating City/Tokyo/Virginia

The cage was set up in one quarter of the packed-earth compound around which the main buildings of Floating City were arranged. On its right was the structure in which Rock and Mick Leonforte lived, on its left was the building housing the extensive high-flux neutron laboratories Rock had had constructed for Abramanov, including the hot cell, repository of every ounce that existed of element 114m, and now the place where Torch lay like a sleeping adder.

The cage smelled like a charnel house. Its hard-packed earth floor was stained by blood and feces, and in one corner, as if arranged by an interior decorator with a macabre sense of humor, was a human femur picked clean of flesh and sinew.

Rock picked up this bone as he accompanied Nicholas into the cage, slamming it repeatedly into one meaty palm. A half-dozen of his men armed with Russian-made AK-47 submachine guns ringed the cage. It was more than he needed, but there was a kind of show going on, Rock drawing a line in the sand, the demonstration of power. They had searched Nicholas roughly and thoroughly. On the other hand, Rock had come unarmed into the cage with Nicholas, and this manifestation of his courage was duly noted.

Nicholas had been given neither water nor food during the trip to Floating City. He had been blindfolded when he had been taken to Rock's vehicle and, just after, he had felt a sharp prick on the inside of his elbow. He had concentrated and, as he had done with the Russian, V. I. Pavlov, working in the furthest reaches of Tau-tau, he slowly raised his metabolism to prematurely break down the chemicals before they had a chance to tranquilize him.

'I see you've recovered from your tranked sleep,' Rock said in an amiable voice. 'We'll remedy that shortly.' He looked at Nicholas with the pragmatic interest of a plastic surgeon. 'In the meantime, it might interest you to know that many notable people have spent their last days here. Interestingly, their responses to the treatment imposed were all different. I suppose if I were a scientist, I could make a study of the human mind under extreme duress.' He slapped the femur into his palm. 'My partner Do Duc was such a man.'

'He was a killer.'

Rock smiled. 'We're all killers here, Linnear, you and I, just as Do Duc was. Don't think you can separate yourself from us.'

'But Do Duc *was* different. I know how the Nungs of Vietnam trained him; I know that he had taken the sacred white magpie as his talisman, how he was doomed by this messenger of God. But most of all I know that there was a woman who moved him, a woman he loved despite all the blood and pain he endured. I knew your friend Do Duc better than you think — and it makes me wonder about you.'

Rock said nothing; it was impossible to read the mind behind the mask of his face. 'Wonder all you want,' he said at last. 'Fuck your wondering.'

He stuck his hand through the bars of the cage, and one of the guards put a hypodermic into it. He walked over to Nicholas while the AK-47s were trained on him. 'Fuck thinking, fuck intellectualism, period.'

516

Staring into Nicholas's eyes, he jammed the needle home, depressed the plunger. 'And fuck you.'

He walked out of the cage, locking the door behind him. Picking up the LAW, he strapped it on, leveled it at Nicholas. There was a war going on inside him. Nicholas could feel it as viscerally as if time had folded upon itself and they were both back in the war. In a sense, that was what was happening. Rock was caught in a kind of time warp; he had never wanted the war to end. It had become his life as well as his livelihood. He had a number of compelling reasons for staying on here in Southeast Asia. Nicholas was willing to bet that the States was death for him – worse, perhaps, a living hell hamstrung by rules, regulations and laws.

That attitude of civilization had been burned out of him by exfoliant, carpet bombing and sniper fire at four in the morning. The stench of incinerated flesh clung to him like perfume on a doyenne. It was so much a part of him now it would never come off; he wouldn't want it to. He wouldn't know how to live without it. He had built his own world right here in the middle of Vietnam – his own Floating City – and the only thing that would destroy him was taking him forcibly from it.

Powerful narcotics again spread through Nicholas. Now he repeated the process he had used on his journey here to hypermetabolize the drugs. It was a strain on his system, but that couldn't be helped now. Night fell in a tropical rush. Insects buzzed busily, birds clattered in the trees, the occasional growl of a prowling predator punctuated the darkness flickering with torchlight and generator-powered lightbulbs. Cooking fires brought the scent of food, as no doubt Rock intended.

Lying on the noisome floor of the cage, Nicholas could see through slitted eyes four guards armed with AK-47s, and he began to calculate the odds, work out the vectors, while he summoned the inner strength he would need from *kokoro*, the heart of Tau-tau.

'Still here?' a voice said from close by. 'No, that's right, don't move. I believe you're supposed to be tranked into a stupor. At least, that's what Rock believes. But he has a bit more faith in himself than I do. Ever since Do Duc initiated him into the cult of the Messulethe, Rock thinks he's Superman. You and I know he isn't. He doesn't have Do Duc's extraordinary mental discipline. And, of course, you killed Do Duc. Extraordinary.'

Nicholas could hear the sounds of someone settling down just outside the cage.

'I have been curious to meet you. I'd heard so much about you. I know more about Tau-tau than Rock does, of course. But then he's quite a bit more monodirectional than I am. I knew that narcotic he injected you with wouldn't do any good. He could have made it cyanide and you'd still be here, breathing, wouldn't you? It's that hypermetabolizing thing you can do. Quite astonishing. It would rock a Western doctor to his foundations.' There was a little laugh. 'Oh, I'd like to see that.'

Silence for a time, interspersed with the chatter of the birds and the monkeys.

'Why don't you – ah, there we are. I was certain you'd want to take a look at me.'

Nicholas saw a man with a handsome face fronted by a prominent nose and clear gray eyes that were positively feral. His salt-and-pepper hair was long, and he wore a neatly cropped beard. It was a face born to give orders, the face of a man who harbored radical philosophies, whose personal worldview was iconoclastic and unshakable. Nicholas could already tell that he was a man who loved words and was therefore probably a disciplined and persuasive public speaker. His years in the Vietnamese highlands had changed him, perhaps, hardened his philosophies even as it had honed them. This could only be one man: Mick Leonforte.

'You're assessing the danger, aren't you? I think I can feel your Tau-tau at work, the projection of your *ki*, but that may only be something of self-hypnosis.'

Mick took out a cigar, bit off the end and lit up. He contemplated the blue smoke for some time before continuing. 'I know something of hypnosis. Mass hypnosis, actually. All philosophers learn the art in one way or another. And d'you know why? Because a philosopher is nothing without disciples, and as in religion, the more the better. And as in religion, philosophy is revolution. That's what I am. A revolutionary.' He blew out smoke. 'You should be familiar with revolutionaries; you were brought up by one.'

He smiled as benignly as an uncle tucking his young nephew in for the night. 'I have made an exhaustive study of your father. It hasn't been easy, stuck here in the back of beyond. And the Colonel was the most secretive man I have come across. More secretive, even, than my own father, who changed identities so often I wondered finally if he remembered who he really was.'

He shrugged. 'But, of course, secrecy was the beginning and the end of the similarities between Johnny Leonforte and Colonel Linnear. They were very different creatures.

'You may not want to believe this, but I admired your father deeply. I wish *I* were related to him. What a remarkable mind. He more or less single-handedly created MITI. You didn't know that, I see. Your father had a profound dislike for MCI, the old Ministry of Commerce and Industry, because it was a safe haven for so many war criminals. It had had almost absolute control over the wartime economy and the military. So your father got the bright idea of merging MCI with the

Board of Trade, which he knew intimately because its English-speaking personnel interfaced with SCAP. BOT was essentially an import-export ministry set up to handle trade with SCAP – meaning America. But your father realized that it had control over the Foreign Trade Fund, which funneled US aid with export receipts into one account.

'Your father the visionary, the revolutionary saw in 1948 that the way for Japan to survive was through international trade. So he and several Japanese created the Ministry of International Trade and Industry. He simultaneously began to put Japan on the right economic track while purging the enemies of the new Japan he had envisaged. With that one stroke of genius the Colonel set in motion countless events that continue their impact to this day.'

Mick inhaled, holding the smoke inside him for an unnaturally long time. 'And now the sons have met under what could only be considered unfortunate circumstances. However, that is irrelevant to me. I make it my business to ruthlessly deconstruct the past and re-create it in the image of the future. Do you understand? I doubt it. Rock doesn't and he's far from a stupid man. He came in here decades ago. Making him a partner was a smart move on my part.' He contemplated the glowing tip of the cigar. 'But all marriages fall apart, all empires crumble, and the future awaits. Rock is like most men, he lives in the present because he is comfortable with it, even when it is only a dream or a memory, a reflection of the golden past into which he has sunk.'

Mick stood up abruptly. 'Well, I for one have enjoyed this little chat. We must do it again sometime.' He flicked ash away and laughed, disappearing across the compound.

Nicholas watched him until he went through a door in one of the buildings. He lay on the ground, collecting his thoughts, working on several questions. Why had Mick come to see him? To gloat? Unlikely. He wasn't the type; Rock was. Perhaps he had been telling the truth – he was motivated by curiosity. But there was more. Amid his ramblings on philosophy, the deconstruction of the past, and the astonishing revelation of the Colonel's supposed role in the creation of MITI, he had revealed that he and Rock were no longer seeing eye to eye. Mick was ready to move on. *Empires crumble*.

Trucks rumbled through the compound, their headlights cutting swaths through the darkness. Nicholas carefully turned his head. Men had begun loading equipment in crates or covered in tarps.

Torch was ready to move. And so was Mick Leonforte. *With that one stroke of genius the Colonel set in motion countless events that continue their impact to this day*. What had Mick meant by that? He seemed to be hinting at some vast plan ticking away through time that was still on course. Was such a thing possible, or was Mick simply mad? Mick and Rock had amassed a fortune beyond imagining by working the arms and drug trade from the inside out. They had a proprietary edge over every competitor, many of whom had fallen by the wayside, as a result of either that edge or Rock's LAW. They were hooked into the US government via Dedalus and the Japanese government via the Godaishu. Now Mick said he was moving on. To what? What could be bigger than the deal they already had going? Before he left Floating City Nicholas knew he'd have to find out.

He checked the position of his guards. Then, closing his eyes, he sank down and touched *kokoro*. He began the tolling, the beating against the membrane of *kokoro* that would summon Tau-tau.

Now, for the first time, he could feel the split inside him. Akshara and Kshira flowed like two rivers – one light, the other dark and terrifying, twisting and turning upon one another.

The theory of integration is a myth, Tachi had said that night in Yoshino. *Do not be deluded. Shuken exists and* koryoku *is its only pathway, but what Shuken does is hold the two paths, light and dark, separate in one mind.*

Nicholas tried to separate them into parallel streams, but without *koryoku* he could only hold them apart for seconds at a time, and this took so much psychic energy he soon gave it up. But in that time, he had his first glimpse of Shuken from the inside and it showed him many truths. For one thing, it confirmed that he was still damaged – his *tanjian* training diabolically sabotaged. Having once been so close to Shuken with Tachi, he now knew it was imperative for him to separate the two paths of Tau-tau in his mind. Without Shuken, Kshira would eventually overwhelm Akshara, the darkness of evil consuming him as it had Kansatsu, his *tanjian* master.

Curled in a ball, he lay on the ground, picturing in his mind where each of his four guards was. The smell of Mick's cigar was still in his nostrils, cloyingly rich – too strong to be . . .

He carefully turned his head, saw the butt on the ground just outside the cage, its end glowing redly with promise.

. . . the true nature of the present situation. I own you, Daijin, and believe me I plan to milk your influence and contacts for all they're worth. Within thirty hours Mikio Okami will be dead and my triumph will be complete. You will be my loyal right hand. I will give the orders and you will carry them out in the arena of international economics both at MITI and in the Godaishu. Is all this quite clear, Daijin?

Yes.

Tanaka Gin watched the young man named Yukio

Haji as his finger depressed the stop button on the portable cassette recorder. For a long time, Tanaka Gin said nothing. His memory kept repeating the moment he had walked into Ushiba's corner office at MITI, responding to an urgent call. Outside, all work had come to a halt and everyone was standing at attention at their desks or in the hall as if frozen in time. It was as if he alone possessed the power of motion. He saw again the body of Ushiba crumpled on the floor. Yukio Haji had been standing over him, and Tanaka Gin's first word was 'Sit!' as if to an obedient dog. Then he had turned, closed the office door and called his office. Soon the police would be all over the place and Ushiba's final peace would be shattered.

'What happened here?' he had said softly.

He had listened to Haji's account. Then he had moved to the window and, staring out at the city, had said almost to himself, 'Why did he take his life?'

'I think I know,' Haji had said, and then began to play the tape.

'How did you come by this tape?' Tanaka Gin said. 'Did the Daijin ask you to give it to me after his death?'

'No. The Daijin had no knowledge of it. I —'

Holding up his hand, Tanaka Gin said in a moment of insight, 'What you say next might incriminate you. You might forfeit your job, your career, everything.'

But Haji was shaking his head. 'The Daijin was my mentor, Prosecutor. He taught me that *kanryodo* is all that matters.'

Peering at the young man in a different light, Tanaka Gin nodded curtly. 'Very well. Proceed.'

'Several months ago I was approached by one of Tetsuo Akinaga's people. You see, I have a gambling problem, Prosecutor. I play the stock market and, of late, I have had serious reversals. I have had to close out positions I have held on margin. You understand.'

'You needed more money than you made at MITI.'

Haji nodded. He sat very straight, his head held high. Tanaka Gin understood. In other circumstances such a confession would have brought him only shame, but now his pain had metamorphosed into sacrifice. Tanaka Gin admired this man's strict sense of honor.

'Somehow, Akinaga got wind of my circumstances and, in a foolish moment, I took his money. I settled my debts and began searching for a night job so that I could pay him back. That was when I understood how foolish I had been. Akinaga himself came to see me. He didn't want his money back. Instead, he wanted me to report on the Daijin's doings. He wanted me to spy for him.'

'You have told me that Ushiba was your mentor. You would not have been at MITI without him.'

'Yes.'

'Then Akinaga put you in a most unfortunate position.'

'That was what I at first thought. I tossed and turned all night in a frenzy of indecision. Then something odd hit me full force. What would Akinaga want with information on the Daijin unless there was some connection between them? And if there *was* a connection, what mischief was Akinaga up to, wanting me to spy on Ushiba-san? I made my pact with the demon. I accepted Akinaga's form of repayment.'

At that moment, there was a sharp knock on the door. Tanaka Gin barked a command and a pair of plain-clothes detectives entered the room. Tanaka Gin flashed his credentials, gave them a brief rundown of what had occurred, then hustled Haji out of there, claiming him as a material witness in his ongoing investigation of Yoshinori's activities. As they went out, he pocketed the cassette recorder with the tape Haji had made of the last conversation between Ushiba and Akinaga.

524

Outside, in the street, Tanaka Gin said, 'Have you any knowledge of Floating City or Torch?'

'None. I was mystified by that section of the conversation.'

'Akinaga spoke of killing Mikio Okami. You know nothing of this either?'

'No, sir.'

It was clear that the young man was telling the truth. 'Why did you throw in with Akinaga?'

'To help the Daijin, of course. I figured if I could find out what Akinaga was up to, I could warn the Daijin.'

Tanaka Gin snapped the tape out of the machine. 'Did Akinaga have you attend other meetings with Ushiba-san?'

'No. This was the first. He seemed to gain some perverse pleasure in it. I didn't understand why until I heard how he had gained control over the Daijin.'

Tanaka Gin knew this was why Ushiba had taken his life. It had not been the cancer; that had been in remission and, in any event, Ushiba had mentally mastered the disease. He knew from their talks that Ushiba would choose his own way to die. He could not bear being forced into a prison, which was what Akinaga had done.

'One other thing,' Tanaka Gin said now. 'Does the word *Godaishu* mean anything to you?'

'No.'

Tanaka Gin nodded. 'You've done well, Haji-san. Your Daijin would have been proud of you. But if I am to arrest and indict Akinaga, I can do nothing to shield you. Everything you have told me and perhaps more will come out. Your career at MITI is over.'

Haji gave a small bow. 'Thank you for your kind words, Prosecutor. In the days to come I shall not forget them.'

*   *   *

525

'You're Mikio Okami's mole buried deep inside Dedalus's machine,' Croaker said.

He could sense Vesper smiling at him. 'The detective at work.'

'I had it all worked out the other way around.'

'It's a good thing for you you were wrong. Dedalus sent me over here to the Knife River DARPA lab to find out what you were up to. But he neglected to inform me he was coming himself.'

'Then you've put yourself in extreme jeopardy. Once Dedalus figures out you've helped me your cover is blown.'

'We've got to get out of here first. But the truth is once you'd penetrated DARPA by asking him about Serman, all our fates were set. He decided to trap you here, and I knew I had to get you and Serman out of the facility. Once Dedalus got his hands on the doctor here, everything was going to blow up in my face anyway.'

They were still in their dark lair inside the experimental nucleonics complex. No sounds had come from the storeroom for some time. Serman had begun to shiver. This was not his metier, and he was clearly frightened, but he was doing his best to hold himself together.

Croaker moved a bit away from the scientist and, intuiting his intent, Vesper followed him. 'Okami's in the gravest danger,' he said. 'I think Caesare Leonforte knows he's in London. One of Bad Clams' thugs followed me while I was shadowing you. I took care of him, but later I was almost killed and I suspect Leonforte was behind the attempt.'

Vesper's voice seemed unsteady. 'Christ, if you're right I think now Okami will be killed along with countless Londoners unless your partner, Nicholas Linnear, is able to keep Torch from leaving Floating City.'

'We've got to get out of here and back to London as quickly as we can.'

'Dedalus will never allow that to happen.'

'Fuck Dedalus.' Croaker was worried about Serman. He did not like how nervous the scientist had become. 'We've got to back Nicholas up, whatever the cost. If he fails to stop Torch in Vietnam, it'll be up to us to do it inside London.'

'I agree, but we've got to be careful as we go along. Remember, the people who took this route before us never made it out.'

'What the hell are you two talking about? We'll never make it either.'

'Keep a stiff upper lip, Doctor,' Croaker whispered. To Vesper, he said, 'What did you mean before when you said Dedalus will never allow us to get to London?'

'Dedalus along with Caesare Leonforte and the Yakuza *oyabun* Tetsuo Akinaga want Okami dead, each for his own reasons. We now know that Akinaga lusts to be Kaisho; Caesare believes that killing Okami will stop the intelligence passed through the Nishiki network and cut off the Goldonis' main source of influence; and Dedalus, no doubt, has some nasty skeletons in his closet he doesn't want exposed.'

'You mean they're all involved with Floating City and Torch because they're all part of the Godaishu.'

Vesper nodded. 'That's the common denominator.'

'So this is what Okami has been maneuvering toward: flushing all his enemies out into the open.'

'Yes. He suspected that Floating City and its Torch weapon would provide too compelling a lodestone – their greed combined with their enmity to make them move precipitously against him. Now he's marked them all.'

Croaker could only marvel at the audacity and the

527

scope of the plan. 'But putting himself squarely in the crosshairs –'

'It was the only way to get them to come into the light.'

'But Goldoni lost his life because of it. This was a desperate gamble on the Kaisho's part.'

Vesper shook her head. 'I think *calculated* is a more accurate description; it was absolutely vital that we identify the person inside the inner council who was undermining the Kaisho's authority. The stakes are as high as they can get – Dominic Goldoni knew that when he and Okami formulated their plan together.'

On that point, Croaker could not argue. He scuttled over to where Serman huddled, spoke to him quietly for a moment before returning.

'Is he all right?' Vesper asked. 'He seems frightened out of his mind.'

'That's about the size of it. But he'll make it.' Croaker lowered his voice as he returned to their original subject. 'One thing still disturbs me. How would Okami, a Japanese, be privy to the secrets he passed on through the Nishiki network?'

'A good question. Someone is supplying him with the dirt.'

Croaker was stunned. 'Then Okami is not the source of the Nishiki intelligence.'

'Contrary to what Caesare and everyone else believes, no. But certainly it's his contacts who are providing him – and the Goldonis – with their leverage in Washington.'

They were heading down the dark shaft on all fours. Croaker kept one eye on Serman, who still appeared dazed by terror. He wondered what the scientist must be making of this conversation. Perhaps he was not even listening.

The air was clean, if not fresh, and they could hear

the whir of the exhaust turbines. Vesper was leading them toward the sound, and Croaker understood what she had in mind. The turbines vented air from the labs; they had to do that on the outside of the building. Had the tunnelers had the same thought? If so, what had stopped them from reaching the exhaust vents?

'What were you up to here?' he asked.

'By accident I stumbled on one of Abramanov's piggybacked transmissions to Serman. I followed up on it and discovered what the two scientists were working on. I reported to Okami. By that time, he knew that Abramanov was inside Floating City, and he became intensely interested in the transuranic isotope Abramanov had created. It was a terrible stroke of fate that it had fallen into the hands of Rock and Mick Leonforte, and Okami knew he had to do everything in his power to stop them from turning element 114m into a weapon. We were monitoring them every step of the way.

'Until the very end, when Serman here failed to deliver his final report.' She turned to the scientist. 'Why did you do that?'

'Once I discovered that I couldn't create element 114m, I saw the reprieve I had been given.' Serman looked at Vesper. 'I knew it couldn't be long before your people, who were reading my reports, would have asked me to re-create a similar isotope. If it wasn't to be 114m, then it would be 115 or 116 or 117 until I found a stable transuranic isotope that would provide as clean a fission event as 114m. I want no part of that because the destructive possibilities are too alluring for most men to ignore.'

Croaker saw Vesper's eyes glittering in the semi-darkness. Neither of them was in a position to contradict Serman. They continued along the shaft, the noise of the exhaust generators becoming ever louder. At length, the shaft split in two.

'Which way?' Croaker asked.

Vesper listened, then shook her head. 'I can't tell.'

'To the left,' Serman said.

'Are you sure, Doctor?' Vesper said.

'I know this lab better than you do, my dear.'

They took the left fork. It was becoming increasingly hot as the way narrowed. They were obliged to turn sideways in order to make any headway.

'If the shaft narrows any more,' Croaker said, 'we'll have to turn back.'

'We can't,' Serman replied, shivering. 'This is the only way.'

Vesper, who was leading, came up short. 'Look.'

Croaker peered over her shoulder. A rectangular beam of light glowed, emanating from what appeared to be a gap in the shaft, after which it continued into darkness.

'I think the gap's too wide for us to span,' Vesper said.

Croaker shook his head. 'I think I can stretch across it.'

'You won't have to try,' Serman said from behind them. 'We have to go down.'

'What?' Croaker turned around.

Vesper looked at Serman. 'But I can hear turbines from ahead of us.'

The doctor nodded. 'That's because there is a set of internal exhaust fans in that direction, but we daren't even get close to them. They vent the hot cells where we use plutonium and the transuranic isotopes. The fans direct the contaminated air into water chambers. Within minutes of inhaling the radioactive particles, we'd be so sick we'd be unable to go on. Within hours we'd be dead.'

Vesper and Croaker exchanged glances in the glow of the light rising up through the vertical shaft. Peering over the side of the abyss, she said, 'It's a helluva long way down. I can't see where it ends.' She turned to Serman. 'Are you sure about this?'

'I only know there's no other place for us to go but down,' Serman said, but, staring over the side, he looked dubious. 'Maybe this was why the test subjects never made it out of here.'

'It doesn't matter. We have no choice,' Croaker said, and Vesper nodded her mute agreement.

The problem was the humidity. He was in the tropics and, even in winter, the dampness had saturated his clothing.

It wouldn't burn, and that meant a major reassessment of the situation. He had figured to set his clothes on fire with the cigar butt Mick had dropped. That would have brought the guards, and they would have had to haul him out of the cage, and that was all he would need.

He knew what he had to do, of course, but part of him was rebelling. He was not at all happy with the prospects and had to force his reluctance down into a deep hole. He kept the reverberations at *kokoro* echoing in his mind. He hoped it would be enough. He had to direct his mind from the coming pain as well as the fright. He had the added distraction of Kshira, the dark side of Tau-tau, twining its tendrils deeper and deeper through his Akshara training.

At the corner of his cage, where the human bones were piled, were desiccated feces. He squatted down and, while he urinated, he scooped up the dried material and smeared it along his right arm, shoulder and that side of his chest. Then he rose and, pressing the smoldering cigar butt to his forearm, watched as the dried feces flared into flame and crackled and flickered up his arm.

He began to burn.

He dropped the butt and let out a piercing shout. But the guards, alerted by the initial flare-up, were on their way. One unlocked the cage while another stepped in to pull Nicholas out of there.

Sunk deep into Tau-tau, he felt the heat but not the pain. At first, it was only the feces burning, then his hair caught fire and, below, the flesh began to curl and crisp.

He smashed an elbow into the solar plexus of the guard who had stepped inside the cage, then shoved his flaming arm into the face of the guard who had unlocked the door.

The first guard made a lunge for him from behind. Nicholas swiveled and, grabbing the man's right wrist with his left hand, completed the circle, pulling the man's upper torso out and down. He bent his knee, following the man down in the direction of the attack, using the man's momentum against him, turning his wrist over in an *irimi*. The bone cracked and the guard collapsed.

The second guard, slapping at the sparks that had caught on his clothes, had pulled his handgun. Using the callused edge of his hand, Nicholas struck him at the point where the nerve bundle gathers at the side of the wrist. The guard dropped the gun, and Nicholas slammed the heel of his hand into the man's neck just beneath the chin, crushing the cricoid cartilage. The man went to his knees, unable to breathe.

All this happened in the space of a heartbeat. The remaining two guards were still heading toward the cage, but had not yet overcome the shock of their two fellow guards going down.

The third guard had his AK-47 leveled at Nicholas,

but he was unprepared for his target to launch himself directly at him. His finger froze on the trigger as, at that instant, Nicholas stepped inside his defense and, pivoting on his lead foot, broke the guard's ribs with a vicious kite.

The fourth guard, panicking, began to fire in rapid, irregular bursts. Nicholas grabbed the guard with the broken ribs and, using him as a shield, threw him into the line of fire while he ducked his head and shoulders and, rolling into a ball, made an oblique approach.

The firing continued until the fourth guard, realizing he was shooting his compatriot, abruptly pulled the muzzle of the AK-47 into the air. Nicholas's foot smashed into the side of his leg, fracturing the kneecap. He went down just as Nicholas struck his collarbone with a teeth-rattling blow.

Nicholas scooped up the AK-47 and sprinted across the compound, pulling the burning feces off his arm. His roll across the packed earth had already put out most of the fire, and he continued to damp down his pain receptors while he tried to keep from inhaling the stench of his burned flesh.

As he zigzagged across the compound, he tried to figure out what Mick Leonforte's motive might have been for leaving the lit cigar butt within his reach. He strongly doubted it could have been anything but deliberate. Had Mick wanted him to escape, and if so, why? He thought he had an inkling.

Up ahead, there was a storm of commotion. The AK-47 gunfire had not gone unnoticed, and what seemed an entire squad of men who had been loading the trucks were coming his way in double time. Nicholas ducked behind the corner of a thatched shed and, taking a bead on the last truck in line – the one nearest him – fired at the fuel tank.

The explosion rocked the compound, scattering the

men who weren't caught in the percussion. Nicholas darted from his hiding place and dashed for the doorway through which he had seen Mick disappear. He reached it while the echoes of the eruption were still thundering and plumes of black, oily smoke obscured the farthest buildings.

He had expected offices or sleeping quarters, but instead he found himself in a glass-walled anteroom overlooking what appeared to be series of climate-controlled laboratories. He took a rough concrete staircase down, then went through two metal doors. The atmosphere had changed radically. It was now noticeably cold; all the humidity had been sucked out and he knew he was breathing recycled air.

Still in Tau-tau he recalled word for word the defecting scientist Niigata's detailed description of the laboratory complex; he already had a complete image of this building's layout in his mind, and he headed straight for Abramanov's lab.

Two men armed with machine pistols raced around a corner. Nicholas, who had felt the vibrations of their psyches, headed into them. He kicked out, catching one in the groin. He slammed into the second. The machine pistol went off, showering them with shards of concrete and sparks. The lights in the corridor winked out. The man lifted his weapon high, intending to bring the butt down on Nicholas's head. Nicholas raised one arm, gripping the machine pistol, bringing it back down in the arc the man had intended. As Nicholas did so, and seeming not to move at all, he shifted his upper torso out of the way. When the machine pistol was waist high, he jammed the heel of his other hand under the man's left elbow, jerked it sharply upward. The man lost his balance and went over, and Nicholas used a kite against his windpipe.

He went inexorably on, knowing he was nearly at

Abramanov's lab. The steel door was just ahead of him, and he put his shoulder to it. It banged open and he raced inside.

There he found Abramanov. He was on his knees and Nicholas, projecting his psyche, knew he was too late. He knelt beside the stricken Russian. He had been shot through the stomach; Rock had picked a particularly painful way for him to die.

'Abramanov.' Nicholas wrapped the Russian in Tau-tau. If he could not save his life, then he could at least make his last moments more tolerable.

The Russian gasped, perhaps with the release from the blinding pain. His watery eyes looked up as Nicholas supported him.

'Who –'

'Where is Torch?'

'Rock . . . Rock took it . . .' The Russian's face was pale with the massive loss of blood. Nicholas could feel the life force fading, and he suppressed the pain receptors to their full limit. If he was not exactly inside Abramanov's mind, he was close enough to feel the encroachment of death. Even Tau-tau had its limits.

'Where is Rock?'

'Outside . . . the compound.' Tears leaked out of Abramanov's eyes and his nostrils flared. His lungs were filling with fluid. 'The danger . . . you don't know . . . There's more than . . .'

Nicholas could hear in his mind the beating, as of the wings of an angel. Then Abramanov pitched forward into his arms.

EIGHTEEN

Tokyo/Virginia/Floating City

Every Friday at precisely 6 p.m. Tetsuo Akinaga went to the *o-furo*, the public baths his father had erected decades ago. He took with him more than a dozen men, all of them armed, who swarmed through the *o-furo* with the thorough determination of carpenter ants before the *oyabun* set foot inside the bathhouse.

Akinaga was justifiably proud of the *o-furo* his father had built. Not that he himself was prone to such magnanimous gestures to the public weal; he did not have his father's disagreeable penchant for wanting to be loved and admired. Akinaga reveled in his outcast status; he wanted no opportunity to wade in among the masses. This weekly pilgrimage to the *o-furo* was a rite of respect for the memory of his father that the members of his clan spoke of endlessly.

As he disrobed in the steamy cedar locker room, Akinaga thought it ironic that in life Tsunetomo had fatuously mismanaged clan affairs but in death he had been elevated to a status close to that of the emperor. Deification was a natural concept to the Japanese, who were brought up to think of themselves as apart from the rest of the human race. Making a cult of Tsunetomo among the Shikei had been Akinaga's idea; it increased his influence while securing his position as *oyabun*. Like the Tokugawa shogunate, which lasted two hundred years, Akinaga was determined that his familial line would endure as *oyabun* of the Shikei for decades to come. He would not allow a replay of the clever coup Mikio Okami had engineered within the Yamauchi, ousting Seizo and Mitsuba Yamauchi, replacing them with Tomoo Kozo, a man outside the traditional lineal descendants.

He stepped into the tiled shower room, sat on a low wooden stool while one of his men poured hot water over him from a cedar bucket. He soaped up, then was rinsed off, the water sluicing away through the aromatic cedar slats. No one, other than his own men, shared the shower room with him.

Then he rose and, accompanied by six of his men, entered the *o-furo* proper. Steam rose from the six tiled pools sunk into the floor. Laced with herbs, each had a different medicinal property.

Akinaga, as was his habit, entered the birch pool, which had been cleared of other bathers. From the surrounding pools, men with cloths over their heads to keep the sweat from the clean water watched furtively as the *oyabun* settled himself in the deliciously hot water. He spread his legs out, leaned back against the tiles, and closed his eyes to slits. He thought of a haiku and, with its imagery, Ushiba. It seemed to him a shame that the Daijin had proved such a disappointment. He had planned to utilize Ushiba's influence inside MITI to solidify his economic position among the so-called reformers of the splintered Liberal Democratic Party. He recognized that Japan was changing, slowly, agonizingly becoming more Americanized, as Akira Chosa would have said.

In the purely pragmatic manner he missed Ushiba, he felt Chosa's absence as well. Chosa had known the Americans; he would have proved invaluable in this changing environment. But Chosa had been determined to oppose Akinaga and that had sealed his fate.

Perhaps it didn't matter. Money still spoke louder than rhetoric. Whatever lip service these so-called reformers were paying to ridding the political landscape of payoffs, mutual favors and closed shops, the underlying realities would change little. Bidding for jobs would become more commonplace as a sop to the public outcry and to the railing of the Americans, but already Akinaga was putting in place a system of rigging that would return the fundamentals more or less to the way they had always been. Japan was a master of surface symbology, of seeming to change while doing just what it had always done decade after decade.

Akinaga's head turned as he heard a disturbance. Two men dressed in suits had entered the *o-furo*. They began to sprint toward Akinaga's pool. One of his men drew a pistol, and a shot boomed through the large tiled room. Water sloshed over the sides of the pools as bathers jumped.

Akinaga's man fell across the top edge of the birch pool, his head in the fragrant water. His gun clattered on the tiles, skidding inches from where Akinaga's hand lay. The *o-furo* was suddenly full of men in suits. Blood began to stain the water, beginning as a bright crimson lily, then floating outward in beautiful tendrils. Akinaga's fingers twitched as his men held their positions.

'Go ahead,' Tanaka Gin said, striding toward the birch-scented pool. 'Pick it up.'

Akinaga glared at him with basilisk eyes. 'What is the meaning of this extreme discourtesy, Prosecutor?'

Tanaka Gin reached down and, with a handkerchief, retrieved the gun from the fallen Yakuza. Without looking back, he handed it to a plainclothes detective who stood almost at attention behind his right shoulder. The *o-furo* was filled with policemen, some of whom had been delegated the task of clearing the room of innocent bystanders.

Tanaka Gin stared down without expression at the *oyabun*. 'The media are outside, clamoring for an interview. It's up to you whether you meet them dressed or wrapped in towels. Either way, I'm going to parade you in the street; I'm going to make a spectacle of you.'

Now Akinaga allowed himself a crafty smile. 'Is this what you spend your time on, harassing citizens?'

'You're no citizen.'

Akinaga raised his eyebrows. 'That will come as news to my lawyers. I have harmed no one; I have broken no law. Ask your whipping boy, Yoshinori.'

'Yoshinori has said nothing of you or Chosa.'

'Then get out of here. You have already fouled my water.'

'Or Ushiba,' Tanaka Gin said implacably.

For the first time, Akinaga's sangfroid appeared to slip momentarily. 'The Daijin? I don't understand.'

Tanaka Gin said nothing. He looked around. Cops had Akinaga's men lined up against the tile wall, patting them down for weapons.

The blood was seeping through the water and Akinaga squirmed in the heat. He longed to get out of the bath, but he saw this as a loss of face, and he would not give the prosecutor the satisfaction.

'Is this why you have come here?' Akinaga said contemptuously. 'On a bluff?'

'It's no bluff,' Tanaka Gin gestured. 'Stand up.'

'You can't –'

'Do as I say!'

Tanaka Gin's voice was so thunderous that those Yakuza closest to him started. Akinaga rose, the pink water dripping down his naked flesh. He was aware of the cops and his men staring at him, and he vowed to make the prosecutor pay for this humiliation. Tanaka Gin was grandstanding. First, taking Yoshinori into

539

custody, and now this harassment. Akinaga knew there were measures he could take that . . .

All thought came to an abrupt halt as he stared at what Tanaka Gin had produced. A length of cord dangled against Akinaga's chest beaded with water and perspiration.

'I have here a *torinawa*,' Tanaka Gin said, taking the ceremonial cord and tying Akinaga's hands behind his back. 'I want all here to know you for the criminal you are.'

Akinaga stared bleakly into Tanaka Gin's face, his heart full of hate. 'What are you charging me with in this charade?'

'The extortion of the Daijin of MITI. You are also implicated in the deaths of Akira Chosa and Naohiro Ushiba.'

'Nonsense. They took their own lives.'

'Turn around and step out of the pool.'

Akinaga stood close to Tanaka Gin, his eyes boring into the prosecutor's. 'I don't know what you think you're up to, Gin, but I guarantee you my lawyers will have me home by midnight.'

'Not this time, I think.'

'Whatever evidence you've been given is trumped up. My lawyers will prove –'

'You'll be convicted by your own words. Now step out of the pool.'

For a tension-filled moment Akinaga did nothing. Then he said, in a voice so low only Tanaka Gin could hear, 'You have this one chance. I will accept the humiliation you have submitted me to in this room. But if this circus gets as far as the press, I cannot be responsible. I am warning you. There are mechanisms in place within your own department that will lead to your destruction. I give you this one last chance. Take the *torinawa* off me and leave with your people. Do it now and it will be as if this incident never occurred, I give you my word.'

With a shiver of recognition, Tanaka Gin recalled Chosa saying to him, *If it's corruption you're after, look to your own department, Prosecutor.* He thought of Ushiba, lying in a bloody pool in his office, released from the prison in which this man had incarcerated him, and he knew he could not waver from his purpose.

'Step out of the pool,' he said without another moment's hesitation. 'You are past due to meet your fate.'

There was no service ladder leading down from the horizontal shaft, and Croaker, Vesper and Serman were obliged to use their hands and knees to descend. It was difficult work, especially since the air was rapidly becoming superheated as they approached the exhaust complex.

Serman was having the most difficulty. Twice he slipped along the line of his sweat, his weight sending Croaker headlong into Vesper before Croaker's strength stopped their fall.

No one spoke; all their energy was going into movement. They had no way of knowing how far down they had come or how much farther they had to go. Serman was unsure how deep the exhaust shafts went before they ended at the vents.

Then, from just below him, Croaker heard Vesper breathe, 'I can see the bottom.'

At that moment, Serman slipped again. Croaker was ready for him. As he crashed down onto Croaker's shoulder, Croaker braced himself with both arms rigid. But at the same time Vesper was reaching up, trying to take some of the brunt of Serman's fall. Her fingers inadvertently closed around Croaker's left wrist, pulling it down.

He tumbled over, crashing into her, spilling a terrified Serman off his shoulder.

'Christ!' Croaker shouted as he made a grab for the scientist. But he had his own stability to think about, and Serman went through his grasp as his stainless-steel fingers drove into the metal of the shaft, holding him and Vesper aloft long enough for her to regain purchase with her knees.

'Serman?' he asked.

She was staring down and he saw her shake her head. 'It looks like his neck is broken,' she said.

They reached him and the floor of the lower horizontal shaft a moment later. Serman was dead all right.

They crouched over him for a moment. The whine of the turbines was very loud and, looking off to their right, they could see the huge exhaust vents. They had made it – they were at the end of the exhaust tunnel.

Croaker closed Serman's eyes. 'We only had a few hundred yards left.'

'Let's go,' Vesper said, and he nodded.

They crept down the shaft in cramped, uncomfortable fashion. Croaker was impatient to reach the exhaust grates, but Vesper appeared to be taking her time.

'Wait a minute,' she whispered. Ahead of him he could see her stretched prone on the floor. 'Take a look at this.'

He got down beside her. At first he could discern nothing in the gloom. Then, as he focused, he began to see tiny sparks in the air just above the level of the concrete shaft floor. They looked like nothing more than fireflies.

'What is it?' he asked, looking at the walls on either side. 'A DARPA surveillance device?'

'Worse, I think.' Vesper turned over on her back, staring upward through the field of sparks. 'Some kind of electrical field. I think it's meant to discourage unauthorized intrusion, but this – or something a bit less sophisticated – could be the reason those poor bastards never made it out of here years ago.'

Croaker looked at her. 'How the hell do you know all this?'

She pulled back from the verge of the field, turned over to face him.

When she made no reply, he said, 'You know, I have the distinct feeling I haven't the faintest idea who you are. If I'm right, neither do Margarite or Okami.'

She gave him an enigmatic smile. 'Do you know why actors act, Lew? It's because they love playing roles, yes, but it's also because inside they are no one – or they can't bear to let anyone see who they really are.'

'Is that how you are?'

She shrugged. 'I have become a product of the world in which I live. I could have been anything, anyone. Instead, I chose to become no one – everyone. Do you understand?'

'I'm trying – but you're chimerical.'

She seemed to come abruptly alive. 'Yes, yes, that's it precisely. And therein lies my power – the power that lies within all of us – men *and* women. It's frightening and it most often gets beaten down to the point of disappearing, but I was trained to recognize it and use it.'

'Trained? By whom?'

She gave him another enigmatic smile. 'We'd better find a way through this electrical field or we'll never get out of here.'

They turned their attention to the field, Croaker somewhat reluctantly. He felt she had been on the verge of divulging a pivotal facet of her makeup. He wanted to pursue the subject of her past but knew this was neither the time nor the place for it.

Vesper pointed to what appeared to be three dark parallel lines indented into the concrete of the wall on their left. 'Sensors. There's a thermal component to the field.'

'You mean the sensor picks up a person's body heat, a circuit is tripped and the field fries said human being.'

Vesper nodded. 'More or less that's it.'

'How do we disable the thing?'

She continued to stare at it. 'Once I got into it I know I could bypass the circuitry. Problem is getting close to it. Even the heat of my hand will set off the field.'

Croaker held up his biomechanical hand and grinned fiercely into the gloom. 'But mine won't.'

'Christ, you're right! No flesh, no blood, no heat.' She looked from his hand to the sensor array. 'Let's just hope we judge the distances right, otherwise while you're reaching for the sensor, your wrist will set it off.'

'Let's try it then.' Croaker rolled over until his left shoulder was against the wall. Then he reached out with his biomechanical hand. The titanium and polycarbonate fingers passed through the dancing sparks, then the hand itself.

'Watch it!' Vesper said sharply. 'Your wrist.' She shook her head. 'The sensor is too far into the field. You'll never –'

She stopped speaking as Croaker extruded the stainless-steel nails from the tips of his fingers until they passed across the array.

'Okay,' he said. 'Now what?'

Vesper nodded, talking him through the procedure. First, he pried open the protective clear Plexiglas cover, then he inserted one nail into a small slot in the center of the array. At her behest he turned his nail to the right, then the left. The front of the array popped off. It was attached to the guts of the unit by three color-coded wires.

'We're only going to have one chance,' Vesper said. 'There's a red, yellow and white wire. We've got to cut

544

the ground. That will short out the circuit into its fail-safe mode without tripping the field.'

Croaker could not even turn his head to look at her. 'Do you know which one's the ground?'

'Cut the red one.'

'Is that the ground?'

'Cut it!'

He did.

The field of dancing sparks disappeared and Croaker put his head down on his outstretched arm.

Vesper let out a small sigh. 'Thank God for the military mind. All the grounds at this base are red. I gambled –'

'You *gambled*!' Croaker raised his head, stared at her.

She got up. 'If you had a better gamble to take, you should have spoken up.'

He got to his feet. 'I trusted you.'

That enigmatic smile again. 'Good thing you did. We're through.'

Croaker led the way past the now quiescent electronic field toward the huge grilles at the far end of the shaft. But they were only halfway there when they saw the vents being lifted off.

'I think we've had our allotment of fun today, Mr Croaker.' Dedalus peered in at them. They could see his head and upper torso. He was holding a 9mm Beretta. 'Out,' he ordered. 'I'm quite the expert with this thing, you know.'

Vesper, crouched behind Croaker and hidden from the senator's view, whispered, 'It's like "The Lady and the Tiger", only this "lady" is toting a high-velocity weapon. Let's back up out of here.'

'And go where?' Croaker hissed. 'Back to the storeroom? Into the nuclear ventilation chamber? You heard what Serman told us about that.' He shook his head. 'Not good enough. Besides, I have a plan.' It was wild,

it was exceedingly dangerous, it meant gambling everything on one chance, but this box was too clever by
half; this was the only way out of it.

'Look, you don't know —'

'It's do or die now. I'm going to get Dedalus before
he gets us.'

'Impossible! The power he commands . . .'

'All his power is meaningless right now. Because I
know what he wants more than anything else, and I'm
going to give it to him.'

Vesper was abruptly wary. 'What are you thinking of
doing?' But she was a genius and she was already working it out. 'You can't.'

'I can and I will. Trust me, it's our only option. We've
got to give him the one thing we can't afford to: the
place where Mikio Okami is hiding.'

'If he thinks the two of us are up to something, he'll
eat us both for lunch.' She tossed her head. 'Forget it.
I know him, you don't.'

'I know as much about him as I need to; I know what
he wants most.'

He was right and she knew it. Perhaps it was a new
feeling for this genius creature to acknowledge intelligence on her level in another person. She must be so
used to dominating people easily, he was counting on
her being intrigued by someone else's manipulation of
a man who was her enemy.

She signaled him by putting her hand on his back. 'I
must be mad to listen to a madman.'

'Mr Croaker,' Dedalus called. 'I've shown you quite
enough of my patience for one day. Get down here and
tell me what you've done with my nuclear theorist.'

'I'm afraid Dr Serman is dead. He has met with
an unfortunate accident,' Croaker said as he leaned
back and, extruding his stainless-steel nails, slit open
Serman's wrist. 'Smear yourself with the blood,' he

546

whispered to Vesper. To Dedalus he said, 'He fell down the vertical shaft. I'm having trouble bringing him down to you.'

'Forget him,' Dedalus said impatiently. 'It's you I want.'

'I'm afraid it won't be as simple as that,' Croaker said and, turning, twisted Vesper's arm behind her back. She cried out at the force of it, which was the point. 'Your agent Vesper is here with me, Senator. You don't want her killed, do you?'

Dedalus, leaning farther into the shaft's end, aimed the Beretta at them both. 'Frankly, I don't give a rat's ass about her. All my agents are expendable. It's in their job description.'

'Nice old boy. I am dearly going to love this,' Croaker murmured under his breath. To Dedalus, he said, 'I was expecting something like that from you, so here's the deal –'

'No fucking deal, Mr Croaker. Slide out of there now, with or without Vesper, it's all the same to me.'

'The deal is you clear the area you're in and I'll come out –'

Dedalus barked a laugh.

'– and tell you where Mikio Okami is in hiding.'

Dedalus laughed louder. 'Oh, Mr Croaker, I already know Okami's in London. In a matter of twenty-four hours his brains will be blown all over the map. Come out now and stop playing at James Bond.'

Croaker took a deep breath. *Here goes*, he thought. 'Okami knows all about you and Leonforte and Akinaga, Senator. He's not in London anymore, but I know where he's gone.' It was a lie – a desperate one – and he could only hope that he was good enough to sell it to Dedalus, a born liar.

'My information –'

'Is out of date, Senator,' Croaker said. Timing was

everything, now. He must not allow Dedalus time to think. 'I met with Okami in Holland Park. Shall I tell you exactly where? Near Bird Lawn, right where –'

'I don't believe you.'

Jesus, he was sweating now. He was terrified it wouldn't work and terrified it would. What a plan. No wonder Vesper had called him mad. And yet she had gone along with him; this gave him a modicum of hope. But as Ben Franklin wrote, *He that lives upon hope will die fasting*.

'Why do you think I went to London? I was following a lead.'

'To Okami? You're supposed to be investigating Dominic Goldoni's murder.'

'Okay, Senator, let's call a spade a spade. We both know Do Duc killed Goldoni and we both know who hired him: Leon Waxman, your man running Looking-Glass. But Waxman was Johnny Leonforte, a major oversight in your vetting process. In the course of that investigation I discovered that Goldoni and Okami were partners in a global business network. Do Duc was hired to murder Okami as well, but, as we know, he failed and Okami disappeared. Are we beginning to speak the same language?'

'Perhaps.'

'You've been searching for Okami ever since, Senator. That's why you didn't throw me off the job the moment you met me. You figured since Goldoni's murderer had been killed and my investigation was still running I must be after Okami, just like you. And you were right. Only, unlike you, I didn't lose track of him. I know where he is now.'

'Where is he?'

'But you already knew that, didn't you?' Croaker said, ignoring him. 'Sure. Johnny Leonforte was working for you. If the father, why not the son? It was

548

Caesare's man who shadowed me in London. I took care of him, but until now it didn't occur to me there might be more than one who saw Okami in Holland Park. Caesare took the news of Okami's whereabouts right to you, didn't he, Senator?'

'Where is Okami, Mr Croaker?'

'Do we have a deal?'

'Jesus, Croaker,' Vesper whispered hoarsely. 'What the hell are you going to tell him when we get out there?'

'Shut up and follow my lead.'

'I ask you again, Mr Croaker –'

'Do we have a deal, Senator?'

Silence. Then Dedalus disappeared from the end of the shaft. Croaker took the opportunity to hustle them closer to the open vent aperture.

Dedalus reappeared and said, 'They're gone. Come out of your hole, Mr Croaker. Perhaps we do have something to discuss.'

'You'll pardon me if I don't believe you until I see for myself,' Croaker said, scuttling toward the senator. 'And, by the way, put down the Beretta. It does nothing at all for my sense of trust in this deal.'

Dedalus dropped the gun. Pushing Vesper out the vent, Croaker tumbled out after her. They stood in a small clearing along a densely wooded hillside. There was no one else visible, but Croaker did not for a moment trust Dedalus. The man dealt in lies the way others traded stocks or commodities. Croaker had known men like him and he knew their weakness: it was their lust for power. Here and now, tracking down Mikio Okami represented the ultimate power to Dedalus.

'Satisfied?' Dedalus asked in a neutral tone of voice.

'Hardly.' Croaker had regained his grip on Vesper and with her face and shoulder smeared with blood, she

549

looked just as he wanted her to. The senator seemed concerned at the sight of her. After all, he had sent her into the DARPA facility and he was facing the consequences of that act. It proved he was human, just like anybody else.

Dedalus peered at her. 'Such a beautiful face. Did he break your nose?'

'I think so,' she said in a peculiar nasal voice. 'I can't feel anything.'

'Shut up!' Croaker said.

'Let her go now,' Dedalus said, the stern father figure again.

'I need to be sure of our deal.'

'I've done everything you asked. What more do you want?'

'Reassurances, Senator. Once I tell you where Okami is, I'll need all your help. You know what happened to Do Duc.'

'You'll have my protection, provided the intelligence you give me is correct.'

'Don't worry about that, Senator.' Croaker was looking around. 'Do you have transportation near here? This place is starting to give me the creeps.'

'Just over that rise,' Dedalus said as he bent to retrieve the Beretta.

'Empty it, Senator.'

Dedalus did so without protest. Vesper was eyeing the trees. 'He's lying, Senator.'

Dedalus looked up. 'What?'

Croaker shook her hard. 'I told you to shut up!'

'Dr Serman is still alive. That's when Croaker hit me, when I was trying to minister to him. I think you'd better send some people in to get him.'

'But I've sent –'

'Senator, he'll die unless you do something.'

Dedalus nodded. He made a hand signal and a man

550

emerged from the underbrush. He was carrying a handgun, muzzle down, loosely and expertly at his side.

'So much for having your protection,' Croaker said.

'Do you think I'd leave myself completely vulnerable? We hardly know one another.' Dedalus gestured. 'Go into the shaft,' he directed his man. 'There's a scientist named Serman hurt in there. Bring him out.'

'Wait,' Vesper said as the man was about to climb into the vent. 'I'll have to go with him. There's an anti-intrusion device I'll have to get him around.'

'Do it,' the senator said, understanding immediately that she was using this chance to get away from Croaker.

'Forget it,' Croaker said, understanding dawning as well. This was the ultimate test of trust, but could he trust her? 'I'm not letting her go.'

'Why not?' Dedalus smiled. 'I've emptied my weapon, I've revealed my bodyguard. It's time for you to make a gesture of trust.'

'You bitch!' Croaker shouted at Vesper. 'If you hadn't told him –'

'But she did,' Dedalus said. 'It was her duty. Now, make the gesture, Mr Croaker.'

With a low growl, Croaker pushed Vesper away from him. She went stumbling over the ground, and the senator's bodyguard helped her back through the vent.

'Now that we're alone, Mr Croaker, I do expect you to tell me where Mikio Okami has gone to ground. I'll keep you in custody until we have him. Then you may go.'

'That's your idea of a deal? Forget it.'

'Unfortunately, I am in no position to forget it.' A small, silver-plated pistol appeared in the senator's fist. It was the kind of weapon instructors liked to start women on because the buck of the percussion was minimal. But at close quarters like these, it was as lethal as the Beretta. 'I need to get my hands on Okami and you're going to help me do just that. You're out of bargaining chips. Tell me where he's hiding or I'll put a bullet through your right kneecap. Five minutes later it will be your left knee, and so on and so on. You get the picture. You'll tell me what I want to know, I promise you.'

'Senator?' It was Vesper's voice.

'Yes, what is it?' Dedalus said in an annoyed tone. 'Have you gotten Serman out?'

'Serman's dead,' she said, poking her head and shoulders out of the vent. She was gripping the bodyguard's handgun.

'Where's Andrew?'

'I'm afraid he's —'

Dedalus had been taught to aim and shoot by an expert. He squeezed off a shot before Vesper did, but his small-caliber weapon was not accurate at that range. His shot spun off the inside of the shaft. He was about to fire again when Vesper shot him between the eyes. His arms flew out as he toppled over backward, an astonished expression on his face.

'You missed your calling; you should have been an actor.' Vesper looked at Croaker as she crawled out of the vent. 'You see,' she said, 'sometimes it pays to have a little trust.'

Out in the compound, Floating City was burning, or so it seemed to Nicholas as he emerged from the lab. The truck that had exploded was aflame, and the fire had spread to two other trucks in the convoy poised to roll out of the main gate.

The danger . . . you don't know . . . There's more than . . . There's more than *what?* What had Abramanov been trying to tell him? What was the danger?

552

As Nicholas ran, he was obliged to leap across the backs of men who had been caught in the initial blast. Then, out of the billowing black smoke, he saw the huge figure of Rock, striding toward the lead truck. The LAW was strapped across one shoulder, and he held a small Cobray M-11 with the telltale T-shape of its long magazine in one hand. He had re-designed and re-calibrated it into an exceptionally deadly and accurate weapon.

'Get out of there, you bastard! Fucking rat!' he screamed.

He was about to fire at the lead truck when he caught sight of Nicholas. He turned and grinned.

'So you got out. Mick warned me you would manage it by hook or by crook, but I didn't believe him. Now, of course, it doesn't matter.' He hefted his LAW. 'Same old weapon, you're thinking, right? Wrong. This is now loaded with the first Torch.'

Nicholas felt the tremor of Rock's intent a split second before he began firing the Cobray. Bullets flew at him as he dived against an unmoving corpse. Rock, firing the Cobray in short, accurate bursts, was moving steadily toward him. Blood, bone and gristle spattered Nicholas as the bullets began to eat up the corpse.

Rock came on, slamming home another long maga-zine into the machine pistol. In another few steps he would be within range to pick Nicholas apart. Nicholas looked around, saw an AK-47. He grabbed for it, but it was one of those Chinese-manufactured jobs and the firing mechanism was jammed.

Rock's grin was wider than ever. 'Come on, bad boy. You killed Do Duc. See if you can kill me.'

Nicholas broke down the AK-47, dismantling it as if for cleaning. Not good enough. He gripped it, one hand on the barrel, the other just above the magazine. Then he projected his psyche outward as he exerted all the pressure he could muster. The world pressed inward, light streamed past him as if he were on a speeding train, and sounds echoed in his ears as if he existed on a plane a long way off. The barrel abruptly snapped and he had his weapon.

Rock fired his first burst and Nicholas rolled along the ground, feeling the snapping of splintering stone at his ankles. But he had got the heft of the broken barrel now, and he rose from the ground. In the same motion, he leapt directly toward Rock, whose finger froze on the trigger as he swung the stubby muzzle of the Cobray toward Nicholas.

In that moment of suspended time Nicholas let fly the broken barrel of the AK-47. Deep in Tau-tau he projected a line of flight, like a shaft of invisible light, down which the missile flew. He was in a tunnel of strange dimension. He saw only the missile he had loosed. He felt its speed and the friction of the air against its steel edges; he felt the subtle drag of gravity exerting its influence, and he felt through a distance that had no meaning the synapses firing in Rock's body as he reacted to the threat.

He was far too slow. A strange whistling filled the air and then a sickening *thunk!* as the thin muzzle of the barrel struck Rock in the center of his chest with such force that he flew backward, twisting with the impact. Pierced just below the sternum, he lay staring up, blood fountaining from him.

Where was Mick?

The engine of the lead truck coughed to life, and without further conscious thought Nicholas sprinted toward it. As he came up to where Rock lay, eyes unmoving and glazed, he reached down, ejected Torch from the LAW, which was far too bulky for him to take wholesale; Torch was bad enough. He ran on, sprinting in zigzag fashion through the chaotic compound.

And now the sons have met under what could only be considered unfortunate circumstances, Mick had said.

Mick, at the wheel of the truck, threw it into first gear and it began to rumble toward the gate. Nicholas, picking up speed, closed the gap between them. Torch was heavy, but he was determined not to leave such a deadly weapon behind.

Perhaps Mick had spotted him in the side mirror because he risked stripping the transmission by crashing prematurely into second, then third gear. The truck protested, but lurched forward nonetheless, rolling ever more quickly toward the main gate.

Nicholas, his lungs burning, made a last desperate effort, leaning forward, straining toward the ropes that held the rear gate in vertical position. He wasn't going to make it. He could not maintain his maniac speed for much longer and, in a moment, the truck would begin pulling away from him. Then it lurched and seemed to pause as the right front wheel hit something, a guard perhaps. Nicholas's fingers felt for the rope, closed around it, and, as the truck righted itself and roared away, he swung aboard.

As he turned around, his chest heaving with the effort he had expended, Nicholas could see Rock. He was struggling to turn over. How could the man still be alive? He had six inches of blued steel in his chest. Nevertheless, he managed to roll over on his side. Then he reached under him, pulled the LAW into firing position.

Then the truck had gone around a bend and Nicholas lost sight of him. He sank into Tau-tau and the light turned aqueous. Time bent to his will, and even the hideous lurching of the truck seemed distant. In his mind, he could see Rock now, realizing that the LAW was empty.

The road bent again and, in the distance, the entrance

to Floating City was once more in view. Rock had collapsed again, or was he merely bending over? Something in his hand. Sunk deep in Tau-tau, Nicholas recognized it.

It was another Torch!

Rock slammed it home, and Nicholas again heard Abramanov's last fateful words: *The danger . . . you don't know . . . There's more than . . .*

There's more than one! That was what Abramanov was trying to tell him.

Buddha protect me, Nicholas thought, *he's going to fire Torch!*

Even at this distance he could feel Rock's murderous intent. With a superhuman effort, Rock swung the barrel of the LAW into firing position. Nicholas could see only a black hole.

Rock's finger tightened on the trigger, and Nicholas did the only thing he could do: he projected his psyche outward as if delivering a physical blow. He could not affect an inanimate object such as the LAW, but the bolt of psychic energy detonated in Rock's mind. Too late. Rock's finger jerked the trigger, and with an ominous *boom!* Torch was loosed.

But Nicholas had had some effect. Though they were already too far from the main gate of Floating City to discern Rock, Nicholas saw the missile streaking through the triple canopy of foliage in an almost perfect vertical trajectory. The projection of Tau-tau had been enough to make Rock jump, turning the LAW upward, deflecting his aim.

But now, as he left Floating City behind, Nicholas remembered that Niigata had said that two small bricks of element 114m could destroy four square city blocks. *Four*.

Mother of God.

Nicholas began to calculate, estimating the speed

556

of the truck, the height the LAW could shoot the Torch missile before gravity took over and it fell to earth.

Mick was in a hurry. The truck jounced and lurched over the rutted dirt road, heading down the mountain. In the manner of all mountain roads, it continued to wind through the terrain, and now they had lost all sight of Floating City. They were putting on distance very quickly, but Nicholas did not think it would be enough.

He looked around as the grade became more steep. One side was a virtual wall of rock and thick foliage, the other an abyss. The truck careened around a hairpin turn, and he could hear a sudden roaring. His blood froze. For an instant, he believed Torch had detonated. But then he saw the cataract spinning down from high on the mountainside, spilling into a swiftly rushing river far below.

The idea and the action were almost simultaneous. Surely, Torch was at this moment falling back to earth. When it detonated, he and Mick and everyone else in the area would be obliterated.

He let go his grip on the rope and, bending his knees, leapt outward over the steep mountain's edge. He grazed the edge of the waterfall and began to tumble. Tau-tau protected him as he flew down like an arrow loosed from a bow. He was fully extended when he hit the river and was instantly carried under. Torch was ripped from his grasp by the fierce current as it catapulted him downriver, faster than he could run, faster than the truck could travel, a projectile traveling in the deep.

A moment later, in a lurid flash of greenish gold that was almost beautiful, Torch came to earth no more than a hundred yards from where Rock had fired it. The detonation seemed almost soundless, but the percussion of the fission chain reaction shook the mountain to its core.

In the blink of an eye, Floating City was obliterated, excised as with a surgeon's scalpel. The shock wave caught the speeding truck, lifting it off the road, spilling it, end over end, down a rocky embankment that in the next instant had ceased to exist. It plummeted, its rear end torn away, only to break apart entirely on the teeth of rocks and trees far below.

Ides of March

On a night
when the moon
shines as brightly as this,
the unspoken thoughts
of even the most discreet heart might be seen.

Izumi Shikibu

Tokyo/Venice/Washington

SPRING PRESENT

Tau-tau and the deep waters had protected Nicholas. He had felt nothing, but he had been aware of the moment of detonation, and with a spasmodic contraction of his soul he had felt the instant withering of life. He had been far enough away from ground zero that when, miles away, he emerged exhausted from the river, he did not have to worry about fallout.

By the time he made his way back home to Tokyo, Croaker was there with Vesper. They spent all afternoon and part of the evening in his house filling each other in on the events of the last three days when they had been out of touch.

'Christ,' Croaker said, 'after what Serman told us I can't imagine the devastation Torch created when it went off.'

'Luckily, Floating City was in such a remote spot that only the people left in it were killed,' Nicholas said. 'Still, a team of nuclear experts will have to be brought in to assess the potential radiation spread. And they'll have to dredge the river for the second Torch.'

Vesper shuddered. 'It was a terrible lesson to learn about playing with nuclear weapons.' The two men sat while she stood, moving about the living room. Nicholas noticed her nervousness after dinner. He had gone to change the bandages on his right arm where the fire had seared his skin and had heard her on the phone.

They all went to bed early, but Nicholas was unable

561

to sleep. He kept seeing in his mind the fall to earth of Torch. He saw himself underwater and, far above him, Mick Leonforte in the careening truck, his foot pushing the accelerator to the floor. In an odd way he wanted to know Mick's end. It seemed clear now that he had saved Nicholas from the cage. Perhaps it was merely so Nicholas could finish the severing of the partnership with Rock, which, from Mick's perspective, had out-lived its usefulness. And, in an ironic way, Nicholas had done his best to save Mick's life when Rock had aimed Torch at them.

A shadow in the hall caused him to turn his head.

'Nicholas? May I come in?'

It was Vesper.

He rolled over on his futon, turned on a rice-paper and lacquered-wood lamp. She padded silently into his bedroom and knelt with her knees together. She pushed her hair back from her face.

'I know you want to spend some time with your friend.'

'To tell you the truth, for the moment that's all I want.'

She was silent for some time. 'I have orders to bring you to Venice.'

'Venice? What for?'

'I think you know.'

'Okami?'

She nodded. 'He needs to see you.'

He wanted to laugh. He wanted to tell her that he had spent these last months desperately trying to find the Kaisho, and now here he was being summoned into the presence. As easy as that. But he knew it couldn't be easy for Okami, still living under a death threat. Who wanted him dead? The inner council was no more; they had canceled one another out. Dedalus was dead. Who was left?

Staring into her cornflower-blue eyes he almost told her no. But he soon realized that was merely because in Venice he would see Celeste again, and, after his reunion with Koei, he didn't know whether he could face that.

'We can leave in the morning,' he said instead.

'I agreed to protect you, but that's all,' Nicholas said thirty hours later. 'Neither Lew Croaker nor I are required to condone what you're up to.'

Mikio Okami seemed unconcerned. He looked fit and not at all a man of some ninety-plus years. They were sitting two blocks from the Rialto in a wonderful restaurant that catered to fishermen and local families. Vesper had spent just enough time in Venice to deliver Nicholas to Okami personally before flying home to Washington via London.

Okami sipped his espresso. 'You are entitled to your opinion, of course, but I'm curious. How can you condemn what I'm doing without knowing what it is?'

'You're Yakuza. Your partner was Dominic Goldoni, one of the Mafia's top bosses. That's all I need to know.'

'Is it? Then try redefining the players in this game. You're attracted to two women. One is from a Yakuza family, the other is Dom's sister, who you know is involved with me. If that isn't enough try this: your father was my best friend — and partner.'

For a moment, the silence was so deafening that Nicholas thought he heard peals of thunder. But, outside, Venice lay in sun-drenched splendor. Then he realized he was hearing the pounding of his pulse.

'Did you say *partner*?' he said in a voice that had lost all timbre. Okami had told him he needed to redefine the players, but this revelation required more — it meant reinventing the game.

'Who do you think originally thought up the concept of the Godaishu? Colonel Denis Linnear.'

'Good God! What must he have been thinking of?'

'He was a genius, a true visionary. I became his disciple. When the Colonel died, I continued the vision – a global partnership that took advantage of that part of the world only criminals inhabited. He'd worked with the Yakuza – his job had required him to do so. But he saw in us what even we did not fully appreciate – our loyalty and bravery. He envisioned a partnership between business, government and the Yakuza – all the power players working in concert toward one goal.'

'But it could never work.'

'Of course it could. In fact, it did. The Japanese economic miracle is reality. In the space of three decades we rose from a broken nation, stripped of power and effective government, on the verge of collapse from inflation, unemployment and a sense of guilt to a modern-day economic colossus.'

Had Mick Leonforte told the truth? Nicholas asked himself. To Okami, he said, 'Was my father responsible for the merging of MCI with BOT to create the Ministry of International Trade and Industry?'

'Where did you hear this?'

'From Mick Leonforte. He said that he had made a study of my father.'

Okami grunted. 'Then it's a good thing he perished in the Torch detonation.' He took a sip of his espresso as he considered how to proceed. 'The mechanisms – the outward maneuverings – were necessarily done by Japanese, Yoshida and Shirasu. But the Colonel was behind them. In fact, when their last remaining foes in MCI sent a young man named Nagayama to spy for them, it was your father who brought him into the Yoshida camp. A year later, Nagayama became the first head of the MITI secretariat, and the Godaishu was on its way.'

'But how could all these forces work together? They'd be at each other's throats.'

'I told you the Colonel was a visionary. He saw in all of them the one common denominator that defined them: they were all rabid capitalists. Making money was their overriding dream, and he used that to forge an alliance: the Godaishu. Toward that end, he came up with the concept of the Liberal Democratic Party. He was a great student of history, your father, and he knew the danger of complete chaos was a very real one for us then. He intuited what Japan needed at that moment was a strong, firm hand on the tiller that would stay in place for decades to come. What he did, in effect, was propose we take a page from our own history.

'When Tokugawa Iyeyasu, the first and greatest of the Tokugawa shoguns, came to power at the beginning of the seventeenth century, he tamed a feudal, fractionalized country teetering on the verge of anarchy. He ruled with an iron hand, yes, and his law could be at times cruel, but he deemed it all necessary to stabilize the country, to focus it on one vision.

'This was how the Colonel counseled us – the core of politicians, bureaucratic ministers and Yakuza *oyabun*. He saw the LDP and the Godaishu as the modern-day equivalent of the two-hundred-year Tokugawa shogunate: a lens to focus the people on the job at hand – the building of a new Japan – while keeping them safe from the dangers of the very active Socialists and Communists.'

Okami wisely paused here, ordered another espresso while Nicholas sat stunned and utterly enthralled at the thought that his father had been, more or less, the architect of modern-day Japan. How had he done it, and what unforeseen ramifications had come of his visionary actions? Nicholas was in a frenzy to find out.

Knowing this, Okami continued, 'Over the decades, human nature had its way, as it inevitably will. Corruption set in. Your father was extraordinary in many ways, Nicholas, but never more so than in the elegant manner in which he was able to handle power.

'As I was obliged to expand the Godaishu's role and to bring in more *oyabun*, it, too, slowly became corrupted, until I knew that it had attained its own life – that I was no longer its guiding force. Its power had gone beyond even my abilities to handle. That is when I knew I needed to destroy it. Like a colossus out of control, it had begun to lurch into areas of terrible decay – Floating City, for one. Once Rock and Mick Leonforte became full partners, the Godaishu in its present form became a threat of catastrophic proportions. I knew they would carry Chosa, Kozo and Akinaga's perversion to its logical conclusion: a global economic network controlled by men who cared only about amassing more and more power. They would slowly corner legitimate markets as Floating City had already done with drugs and illegal arms. The ramifications were unthinkable.'

The lunch crowd had departed, leaving the white-jacketed waiters to clear tables and gossip among themselves. One of the chef's assistants replaced the shaved ice in the displays where the fresh fish were displayed. No one bothered the two men at their table.

'Imagine how I felt having to call upon you to help me,' Okami continued, 'knowing how you hated the Yakuza and the secret within me that your father had been my partner and my mentor. I knew you would honor your duty to your father. But I also knew something else. From Koei, I knew the love you had for one another, no matter how the relationship ended so long ago.'

You must be healed, Dich had said, and now Nicholas

566

understood the full nature of what he had meant.

'When you came to me here last year and I saw how full of hate you still were I could find no way to tell you the truth. In fact, I was convinced it would have been a disaster to do so. You would have called me a liar and reneged on your promise to your father. Because, in the end, I summoned you not to protect me – you have seen that I am well capable of doing that with my own resources. That was merely the pretext, the trigger to begin the process of understanding the truth that lay behind your father's carefully composed facade. And to accept that truth. It was time that you continue the work your father and I planned together.

'You see, you came to me poisoned – by your youthful love affair, by forces neither you nor Koei could then control or understand. But that first night when Celeste brought you to me in my *palazzo*, I saw immediately that you had been profoundly damaged in a way that your father could never have imagined. You were useless to me in that state – useless to yourself.

'I confess I must take some of the responsibility for that. I had to rectify the mistake I had made so many years ago in keeping away from you, in not protecting you from the terrible damage the world of the Yakuza can inflict. I had to find a way for you to see Koei again. To do that I had to withhold the truth from you – about me, Celeste and Margarite, Vesper. And especially about your father.

'Years ago, your father wanted me to meet you, spend time with you, but I kept fending him off. I was unhappy in those days, I drank a great deal – in fact, in that regard, I'm certain the Colonel saved my life. I could scarcely control myself, let alone the emotions of a teenager. For better or for worse, he chose Tsunetomo Akinaga. And so you met Koei. Karma, Nick-san.'

They paid the bill and left the restaurant. It was a fine

567

afternoon. The ochers, golds and burnt umbers of the *palazzi* shone as if freshly painted. The Grand Canal was filled with traffic, and the cafés along the *riva* were opening their quayside tables for spring. A gondolier sang a snippet of an aria.

There was so much Nicholas needed to know, so many questions that needed answering. But one thought overrode all his doubts and concerns. *With that one stroke of genius the Colonel set in motion countless events that continue their impact to this day*, Mick had said. Now Nicholas knew he was beginning to glimpse the nature of that genius. He breathed in the sweet air of Venice and was glad to be alive. He was even looking forward to his dinner tonight with Celeste.

Elation coursed through him. The Kaisho wanted him to continue the evolution of the Colonel's 'stroke of genius'. He was being given the chance to work with Mikio Okami, who, like Tachi, possessed *koryoku* and had promised to teach him the secret of the Illuminating Power; he was being given a unique opportunity to enter a whole new world. Not the world of the Yakuza, which he had shunned, but the secret life Denis Linnear had painstakingly created moment by moment. How could he refuse? Yes, he would have to get certain assurances from Okami, and he could not forget his duty to Tanzan Nangi and their company, Sato-Tomkin, but he would make certain he did not give that up. He had the distinct feeling that this was what his father had wanted for him all along; perhaps it was why he had made Nicholas promise to come to the Kaisho's aid should he ever ask for it.

Nicholas had already been given a precious gift. The past, he had been shown, was a living thing, affecting the present in ways most people could never imagine. As for the future, it would unfold in its own way. He was content now to allow that to happen.

*   *   *

The weeks after her return from Tokyo were busy ones for Vesper. For one thing, she was deeply involved in the Pentagon probe into Senator Dedalus's dealings with DARPA, as well as the internal investigation into Johnny Leonforte's hiring as head of Looking-Glass. For another, instead of sleeping she spent her off hours poring through the coded ledger she had scanned from Morgana's offices.

She had not had the time to decipher it, but Croaker had. He had given it to her in Tokyo just before she and Nicholas had left for Venice.

Along about the fortieth hour she determined there was something decidedly odd about some of the entries. It was a word that translated as 'Larva'. The first thing she did was check the ciphers to make certain she had decoded it correctly. It had no number attached to it, no price tag or shipment date, so it did not appear to be a weapon or a part of Morgana's inventory at all. But, further on, filling a page with only the heading 'LARVA' on it, were monetary amounts that seemed to go on and on and which, when she added them up, went into the billions. Whoever or whatever Larva was, Dedalus had been draining Morgana's accounts into it.

It was Celeste who provided Vesper with the first clue. They had rendezvoused as part of the Nishiki network, and Vesper had brought up the anomaly.

'It's odd,' Celeste said, 'because the Larva is one of the traditional Venetian masks. It's usually white, but very rarely one sees one in black. It's Latin for a specter or a ghost. The mask was also called a *volto*.'

The second clue was provided back in Washington.

'What was this three-hundred-thousand-dollar expenditure for?' Vesper asked the Pentagon investigator who was part of the team taking apart Dedalus's books for Looking-Glass.

'It seems Dedalus hired an outside firm to do the vetting of his staff for about eighteen months.'

'Isn't that odd?'

'Not really. Budget shortfalls mean periodic layoffs of non-essential personnel. During this period Dedalus let his vetting staff go along with some bean counters and secretaries.'

'What was the name of the firm Dedalus hired?'

'Let's see.' The investigator began leafing through pages of files. 'Here it is. A company called National Security Services.'

Vesper went to her computer, pulled up NSS from the data banks. Nothing seemed out of place until she noticed that NSS was a wholly owned subsidiary of some entity called VEU. She switched screens, did a global search for VEU.

When she found it, her heart skipped a beat. She sat staring at the screen for some time allowing the message to sink in. VEU stood for Volto Enterprises Unlimited. Volto. Larva. The ghost in white . . . or black.

Tumblers began clicking into place in her mind, but the implications were so terrifying that for a moment she sat, paralyzed, her fingers hovering over the keyboard. All she could think of was the immortal Hydra with its hundred heads. Lop off one or two and another would take its place. Could it be that they had all been wrong about Dedalus, that he wasn't the ultimate head of the Godaishu in America but was taking orders from someone else?

She found VEU's corporate address, which was in West Palm Beach, Florida, but she could not bring up the names of any of its officers. Her mind alight with fear, she switched screens again. Her fingers were like ice as they pressed keys faster and faster until . . . there it was, her worst fear confirmed, the address of the corporate headquarters of VEU was the same as that of an enormous white stucco mansion overlooking the ocean owned by a shell corporation. This corporation, based in the Bahamas, had no tangible business nor, at the end of each fiscal year, any profits to declare. And yet the FBI believed that millions of dollars flowed through its offshore bank accounts.

The man who used that mansion in winter months, who it was believed controlled the shell corporation, was Caesare Leonforte.

Vesper sat back, breathless. If she was right, Bad Clams' company had vetted Leon Waxman. No wonder they hadn't discovered that he was Bad Clams' father, Johnny. No wonder Johnny Leonforte had been welcomed as the new head of Looking-Glass. His son had masterminded it. And that meant Bad Clams had controlled Dedalus; he owned Morgana, Malory Enterprises and Avalon Ltd. He was Larva, the ghost, the black *volto* hiding his identity. All along they had been fighting the Hydra.

So it's not over, Vesper thought. *It's just beginning.*

The Ninja
Eric Lustbader

FOR 3000 YEARS LOVE HAS BEEN AN ART IN THE ORIENT. AND SO HAS DEATH.

Here is the origin of Nicholas Linnear, half English, half Oriental, who is about to enter a terrifying world of merciless assassins bound by the blackest codes of honour and skilled in the deadliest martial arts.

Caught between East and West, a past he can't escape and a destiny he can't avoid, he is trapped in a web of old lust and present passions that will converge in a terrifying moment of revelation and revenge.

A high-voltage novel of intrigue and sensuality, richly characterized, fuelled by relentless suspense, *The Ninja* is one of the great thrillers of our time.

'A striking performance . . . an East-West man-hunt of extraordinary tension and violence, by a man who understands both the Western and Oriental minds'

Robert Ludlum

ISBN 0 586 05153 8

Black Heart
Eric Lustbader

THE SUPREME NOVEL OF SUSPENSE
AND RETRIBUTION

When a US presidential contender is diabolically murdered, his best friend Tracy Richter begins a search for the mysterious assassin. Little does Richter know that he is about to embark on an epic journey of violence and passion into the heart of the Cambodian holocaust, into a deadly labyrinth of intrigue in which every action masks a sinister motive.

In the process, he becomes a target, for stalking him is a deadly killing machine. Born in the political maelstrom of the murderous Khmer Rouge, trained in the crucible of martial arts, the Black Heart has been unleashed.

Dazzling, intricate, sensual, suspenseful, *Black Heart* is one of the most powerful thrillers of recent years.

'A compelling read'   *Literary Review*

ISBN 0 586 05649 1

Black Blade
Eric Lustbader

The stunning novel from the bestselling author of *The Ninja* and *Angel Eyes*.

In New York City a chain of brutal murders begins. In Washington a high-level plot is hatched to bring the economic colossus of Japan to its knees. In Tokyo a deadly power struggle is under way within the shadowy Black Blade Society.

As Wolf Matheson, Chief of Special Homicide, begins his investigation into the chain of New York murders, he comes in contact with a mysterious force of unimaginable power. Blessed or cursed with the uncanny ability to track down killers, he is plunged into a terrifying spiral of betrayal, lust and evil.

Then Wolf meets Chika, the beautiful Japanese woman who will become either his saviour or his murderer. Together, as lovers and perhaps enemies, they join in a desperate search that will unleash mystical forces, madness and violence.

ISBN 0 586 21510 7

The Kaisho
Eric Lustbader

'A fast-moving thriller that combines the trademark Lustbader ingredients . . . a twisted web of intrigue, violence, double cross and his own brand of oriental esotericism. Here again he proves himself a master storyteller'

Publishers Weekly

Years ago, Nicholas Linnear promised that if ever Mikio Okami asked for help, he would give it. Now, with a summons to the beautiful, enigmatic city of Venice, the time has come. What Nicholas does not know is that Okami is the Kaisho, the boss of bosses of the Yakuza, the Japanese underworld.

In America, Mafia godfather Dominic Goldoni is killed in bizarre, ritualistic fashion. Lew Croaker, ex-cop and Linnear's best friend, is persuaded out of retirement to follow a mysterious trail into something altogether darker and deeper than a gang war . . .

The Kaisho is a brilliant excursion into adventure and romance, intrigue and sex, providing a feast of insights into the mysteries of the oriental mind.

'Lustbader returns stronger than ever . . . rich backgrounds . . . high-tension martial-arts battles'   *Kirkus Reviews*

ISBN 0 00 647596 5